BORROWED LIGHT

BORROWED LIGHT

Graham Hurley

WINDSOR
PARAGON

First published 2010
by Orion
This Large Print edition published 2012
by AudioGO Ltd
by arrangement with
The Orion Publishing Group

Hardcover ISBN: 978 1 445 89284 9
Softcover ISBN: 978 1 445 89285 6

All the characters in this book are fictitious, and any resemblance to actual persons, living or dead, is purely coincidental

British Library Cataloguing in Publication Data available

Printed and bound in Great Britain by the MPG Books Group

To memories of Kibbutz Shamir
1966–1968

But then? No then . . .

Description of a Struggle, Franz Kafka

Prelude

SINAI, EGYPT: MONDAY, 12 JANUARY 2009. *01.17*

Faraday was asleep when he went through the windscreen. He heard neither the warning klaxon from the oncoming truck, nor the shriek of the tyres as Hanif stamped on the brakes, nor the Arabic oath so abruptly smothered by the final collision with a roadside tree.

As the Peugeot settled in the dust, Gabrielle tried to reach forward from the back. Hanif, like Faraday, hadn't bothered with a seat belt. His chest crushed by the steering wheel, he was limp within seconds, expiring with a barely audible sigh which Gabrielle later chose to interpret as surprise. The blaze of the truck's headlights. The split-second swerve that avoided a head-on collision. The gnarled stump of the acacia briefly caught in the headlights. And then darkness again.

Fighting to make sense of what had just happened, Gabrielle was aware of the receding thunder of the truck. She could taste blood in her mouth. She felt herself beginning to shake. She called Faraday's name. Then she too lost consciousness.

*   *   *

The lost hours that followed took them to a hospital beside the Mediterranean at El Arish. Faraday's first clue, his eyes still closed, his breathing laboured, was the shouts of men running in the corridor outside the ward. For a moment he was back in the Bargemaster's House, unable to account for people yelling in Arabic on their way to his bathroom, then he drifted away again, awaking some time later to see a bearded face above a white jacket bending over him. English this time, lightly accented.

'Mr Faraday? You can hear me?'

Faraday nodded. More or less everything hurt. His head was bursting. For some reason he could barely swallow. He tried to speak, tried to struggle upright. Failed on both counts.

'You're in hospital, Mr Faraday. You understand me? Hospital?'

Faraday closed his eyes. Opened them again. Hanif. The driver. He'd borrowed Hanif's cap. It had been night, dark. He was tired. He'd tried to sleep, the cap pulled down over his face. It was a baseball cap. He remembered the taxi bumping along and the murmur of Gabrielle's voice as she chatted to Hanif and the smell of the cap, sweet with hair lotion, not unpleasant. So where was Hanif? And where, in God's name, was Gabrielle?

'You've been in an accident, Mr Faraday. Your lady too.'

The alarm in Faraday's face sparked a reassuring smile. He felt a hand cover his.

'Your lady is OK. Not so bad. Soon you will see her.'

Faraday withdrew his hand. He wanted to touch his own face, reacquaint himself with its familiar features, find out what had happened. He too wore a beard. So where had it gone?

'You're in a special unit, Mr Faraday. You understand?' The doctor tapped his own skull, pulled a face. 'We must do some tests, get you better. Rest now. Be still. Your lady is OK.'

Faraday's fingers were still exploring the heavy swathe of bandage around his head. Blood had dried and crusted on his temples. When he tried to answer, when he tried to do anything, he felt a stabbing pain in his chest.

The doctor told him once again to relax. Two of his ribs had been broken. There was a little damage to his shoulder. But on the whole he'd been very, very lucky.

Faraday was thinking of the baseball cap again. He shut his eyes, trying to visualise what it had looked like, trying to bridge the gap between the moment he must have drifted off to sleep and this bright place of pain with the splashes of sunshine on the wall.

'Should . . .?' He tried to shape a sentence, failed completely, but when he opened his eyes again the presence beside the bed had gone.

Then, from somewhere close by, came the cry of a child, plaintive, lost. He listened to it for a long moment, totally bewildered, then darkness swamped the sunshine and he drifted away.

*   *   *

Over the next couple of days he began to recover. Gabrielle, as promised, came to his bedside. Already walking, her arm in a sling, one eye blackened, a swelling around her mouth, she brought him fresh orange juice and crumbled biscuits on a paper plate. He was in a high-dependency unit on the hospital's top floor. They'd taken away the tube that helped him breathe and a second set of X-rays had confirmed that the skull fracture was less severe than they'd feared. His broken ribs were already on the mend and his shoulder, badly dislocated, had been reset. With luck, she said, he would soon be back on his feet again.

Faraday wanted to know more. Where exactly were they? And what had brought them here?

Gabrielle explained about the car crash, about Hanif losing concentration, about the truck that had so nearly wiped them out. Hanif was dead, she said. His chest crushed against the steering wheel.

Faraday stared at her. They'd been with Hanif for two days. He'd driven them to birding sites high in the mountains. With his quick intelligence, his grin and his wealth of local knowledge, he'd become a kind of friend.

'Dead?' he said blankly.

Gabrielle nodded. There'd be a session with the local police soon. They wanted a witness statement about travelling with Hanif. But in the meantime there was something else he needed to know.

'We're in a place called El Arish. It's very close to Gaza. You remember Gaza?'

Faraday nodded. They'd come to the Middle East on a midwinter break. The day after they'd landed in Amman the Israelis had begun to bombard the Gaza Strip. Jordan was full of exiled Palestinians. Wherever they went, it was impossible to avoid Al Jazeera TV in the cafés, newspapers in the hotels, huge demonstrations on the streets.

'And?' Gabrielle had his full attention.

'A lot of the people wounded come here. Terrible. Just terrible.'

The wards below, she said, were full of casualties from Gaza. Worst of all were the children. Kids. *En petits morceaux.* In bits.

'There's a child here . . .' she nodded towards the door '. . . in the next room. A girl. Maybe five, maybe six, nobody knows. They call her Leila. She has burns, chemical burns, here and here.' Her hands touched her chest, her wrist, her fingers. 'The poison makes her very sick. *Phosphore, n'est-ce pas?* The doctors think she may die. Maybe that would be for the best.'

Faraday was doing his best to follow these developments. He hadn't a clue about *phosphore.* He wanted to change the subject.

'How about you?' he said.

Gabrielle shrugged, said she was fine, a little bruised, a little shaken up. Then she checked her watch and glanced again at the door.

'They try and wake the little girl every morning.' She got to her feet. 'Maybe there's some way I can help.'

* * *

Faraday was nearly two weeks in the hospital at El Arish. Mobile again, waiting for the doctors to tell him he was fit to travel, he took to wandering the corridors, passing ward after ward, tableau after tableau. Gabrielle was right. The hospital was slowly filling with seriously wounded from the killing zone that had once been Gaza. Men with no legs, lying inert, their eyes dead, staring at the ceiling. A woman who'd lost part of her face to a mortar blast, her head turned away towards the wall. Sitting outside in the winter sunshine, Faraday could hear the roar from the city's airport as flights lifted more broken bodies to specialist facilities in

Cairo and Saudi Arabia. Back inside the hospital they were burning incense to mask the stench of rotting flesh.

This, to Faraday, was disturbing enough. Seeing the sheer physical damage inflicted on these people, it was difficult not to share Gabrielle's growing sense of outrage. They were defenceless civilians with no greater sin to their names than the urgent desire for peace and some kind of security. Instead, through no fault of their own, they'd lost everything.

Worse, though, were the moments Faraday paused outside the glassed-in rest room where the orderlies gathered between shifts to drink mint tea and gaze up at the big wall-mounted screen. The TV was permanently tuned to Al Jazeera and its non-stop torrent of live pictures from Gaza: wrecked schools, hysterical women, maimed kids sprawled in the dust, men filling ambulances with yet more bodies. From time to time among this grim carnage a camera would tilt skywards to reveal hanging white tendrils from an airburst artillery shell. This, according to Gabrielle, was white phosphorus, the evil wafers of burning gunk that had done the child Leila so much damage. She was still alive, just, and one of the reasons Faraday so rarely saw Gabrielle was the position she'd taken up on a chair beside the child's bed. This little girl has no one left in the world, she said. So it has to be me.

Faraday, in his heart, agreed. He'd glimpsed the tiny pile of bandages that was Leila and he was only too aware of the faces of the orderlies in the TV room when they noticed him out in the corridor. It was the tiny reproachful shake of the head that made him feel helpless and somehow complicit. It had been the same in cafés in Jordan and Egypt before the accident. The unvoiced accusation: you in the West did this, *you* with your American friends, *you* with your stake in Israel, *you* made all this possible.

At moments like these Faraday would beat a slow retreat to his room. His possessions had been returned from the wreckage of the taxi and he'd sit through the long afternoons sorting through his birding logs. There'd been a ring-necked parakeet glimpsed near the Old Fort on the seafront at Aqaba and a Barbary falcon a little further south along the coast. Earlier in the trip Gabrielle had been the first to spot a pair of Sinai rosefinches drinking at a spring near the Royal Tombs in Petra, and later that same day they'd spent nearly an hour watching a Bonelli's eagle riding the thermals above the deepest of the wadis. These were the kind of exotic sightings that he'd dreamed about in the depths of an English winter at the Bargemaster's House, but the excitement had gone now, swamped by the human wreckage that surrounded him.

On his last evening at the hospital he packed his rucksack and waited for Gabrielle to appear. She'd been in town, confirming the flights home, negotiating a decent price for a taxi to Cairo airport. Finally, when she turned up, she appeared to have no luggage. The flight left late the next day. Still exhausted, Faraday had little taste for sightseeing but wondered whether they might have time for a detour into downtown Cairo.

Gabrielle seemed surprised. There was something she clearly hadn't told him.

'I'm staying over, *chéri*,' she said. 'The taxi man

will look after you.'

'Staying over?'

'*Oui.* The child will need lots of care. I can help there. I know I can.'

Leila, it seemed, was at last out of danger. Gabrielle had been talking to the consultant looking after the little girl, who spoke French as well as English. He was a nice man, *sympa.* He knew London well, had friends there. He'd done a lot of his training in the UK and had good contacts at the Burns Unit in Salisbury. At Gabrielle's prompting he'd been on the phone, looking into the possibility of a surgical bed there for Leila, even taken a provisional booking on a medical evacuation by air. Around 30 per cent of her body had been burned. She'd need a series of skin grafts and lots of specialist nursing, but the care in the UK, according to the consultant, was world class. With luck, *inshallah,* Gabrielle's *pauvre petite* might have a half-decent future.

Gazing at her, Faraday realised just how cut off, how isolated, he'd become. The accident and its aftermath had locked him away in a bubble of his own making. How come all this was news to him? How come Gabrielle had never mentioned it before?

'But who pays for all this? How does it work?'

'*J'sais pas, chéri.*' Gabrielle offered him a tired smile. 'That's why I have to stay.'

* * *

Several hours later, more than a thousand miles to the south-east, Paul Winter was making a difficult phone call. Dubai time, it was three in the morning.

'It's over, Baz. Kaput. Finished. We have to take the hit, move on. It's the only sane thing to do.'

'Take the hit? Bollocks. The market'll turn. It'll come good. In this game you need patience, my friend. Thank Christ one of us hasn't bottled it.'

Winter tried to picture the scene in Craneswater. It would be late evening in the UK. Post-Christmas, Bazza was doubtless tucked up in his den, scrolling through the spreadsheets on his PC, patrolling the battlements of his commercial empire, doing his best to ignore the obvious. A glass or two of Black Label often helped.

Winter went through the numbers again, standing by the window, staring out at the long curve of the Corniche. Hotel after hotel after hotel, most of them unfinished, pools of darkness under the forest of cranes.

'The market's collapsed, Baz. The guys in the know out here are talking about a 40 per cent fall in property—and that's just the first quarter. Year end, we could be looking at 60 per cent off.'

Mackenzie grunted something that Winter didn't catch but he knew he was tuning in at last. You didn't get to a £20 million fortune without the ability to count.

'The hotels are dead, Baz. Most of the white guys I've met are on their way to the airport.'

He described conversations he'd had with bankers, lawyers, architects, consultant engineers. All of them had spent the last couple of years with their noses in the Dubai trough, feasting on near-vertical rates of growth. But those days were suddenly over.

'Half the construction projects are either on hold or cancelled. Take a stroll round the airport and you'll find parking lots full of dumped four-by-fours. These guys are totally maxed out. They leave the keys in the ignition and their credit cards in the glove box and leg it.'

'Why would they do that?'

'Because they've got brains in their heads. If you default here, everything stops. Bank accounts frozen. Assets frozen. Passport confiscated. House arrest. You end up in court and they're all speaking Arabic, and before you know it you're sharing a jail cell with some drugged-up zombie from fuck knows where. Probably for ever. You wouldn't know it to look at, but this place is medieval, Baz. I just hope they're not listening.'

Mackenzie wasn't giving up. He'd invested £750,000 in 10 per cent deposits, buying thirty apartments off-plan in a promising waterside development. Last year's spreadsheet told him he could sell on for a 20 per cent mark-up after just six months—£1.5 million for doing fuck all.

'Listen, mush. You're tired. You've been talking to the wrong guys. Take a break. Treat yourself to a couple of those nice Russian toms I keep hearing about. Then go and find Ahmed and get the thing properly sorted.'

Ahmed was Mackenzie's local agent, a smooth trilingual twenty-something with tailored white robes, wire-framed glasses and an Australian air hostess girlfriend.

'I can't, Baz.'

'Why not?'

'He's gone too.'

'Legged it?'

'Probably.'

'How come?'

'He went into liquidation last week. Like I said, it's not something you want to hang about for.'

'Shit.'

'Exactly.'

There was a long pause. In the background Winter could hear the opening music to *Match of the Day.* Saturday night, he thought grimly. And me stranded in fucking Do-Buy.

Mackenzie came back on the line, suddenly businesslike.

'You're right, mush, we have to liquidate. Find yourself an attorney, a real-estate agent, any fucking monkey. Get those apartments sold on. Whatever it takes, mush. Whatever you can screw out of these people. You got that?'

'Yeah. One problem. Did I mention the building itself?'

'No.'

'It doesn't exist, Baz. They never even started it.'

Chapter One

PORTSMOUTH: TUESDAY, 27 JANUARY 2009

Faraday went to his GP the morning after he arrived back in the UK and handed over his medical file from the hospital in El Arish. The GP studied the X-rays, took his blood pressure, shone a light in his eyes and asked a series of questions to establish that he could still add up, still tell the time, still function. Faraday passed each of these tests with flying colours and when the GP offered to refer him to a consultant for a further check-up he declined. He could do with a bit of time off, he said, to get his mental bearings, then he'd be back to work. The doctor returned to the file and muttered something about seat belts before typing an entry into his PC. A sick note would be in the post by close of play. In the meantime Faraday was to go easy on the booze and take painkillers if the shoulder or the ribs got troublesome. Ten days' rest, the doctor said, would do him the world of good.

And so Faraday retreated to the Bargemaster's House on the city's eastern shore, shutting the door against the world and putting another call through to Gabrielle. He'd already talked to her, after he'd got in from the airport yesterday. She'd been vague about the details but it seemed she'd made contact with some Palestinian charity in her home town of Chartres. They had links to Saudi Arabia. There was a definite possibility Gulf money could fund Leila's casevac flight and medical care in the UK. There might even be enough to pay for a translator to be with her full time. The fighting in Gaza had stopped now, she said, but the ambulances were still arriving from Rafah. More casualties, many of them kids.

'So how's Leila?'

'Still sick. But not so bad as before.'

'And the burns?'

'Horrible. Her back, her chest, most of all her hands.'

The doctors, Gabrielle explained, had been studying the few scraps of paperwork that had come with the child. The little girl, it seemed, had been living near the refugee camp at Jabaliya. Blast from an Israeli mortar shell had knocked her over, and after that it had rained white phosphorus. Bits of burning phosphorus had set her T-shirt alight. She'd tried to tear it off. Hence the damage to her torso and hands. This stuff burned and burned, deep, deep wounds. And it was poisonous too, damaging her liver and kidneys.

'Does she have a family, this little girl?'

'All killed. Every one.'

'*Every* one?' Faraday didn't believe it.

'*Personne ne le sait.* Gaza was on fire. Just like Leila.'

'And is that her real name?'

'*Ca personne ne le sait*.'

Nobody knows. The conversation had come to an end at this point, Gabrielle breaking off to take an important incoming call. She'd promised to phone back as soon as she could, but so far nothing. Now, nearly a day later, Faraday tried her number again.

No answer.

* * *

The following afternoon Winter arrived at Gatwick from Dubai. Bazza Mackenzie's son-in-law Stuart Norcliffe was in the arrivals hall to meet him. Norcliffe was a big man, prone to comfort eating, and lately the extra weight he carried was beginning to show.

His Mercedes S-Class was in the short-stay car park. Winter settled into the tan leather, adjusted the seat. The interior of the car, brand new, smelled of Dubai.

'Baz sends his apologies. He'd have come himself but he got nailed for another interview.'

'With?'

'Some freelance. Claims to be doing a piece for the *Guardian*.'

'What's he after?'

'She. The usual, I imagine. Baz thinks it's a laugh. Checked the woman out on Facebook. I gather he liked what he saw.'

Winter returned the smile. His employer's taste in newspapers seldom extended beyond the sports pages of the *Sun*, though lately Winter had noticed copies of the *Financial Times* lying on the kitchen table in Sandown Road.

'Shouldn't someone be holding his hand? Keeping him out of trouble? Some of these people are brighter than they look.'

'My thoughts entirely. Marie's worried sick. I don't think she's got over Christmas yet.'

'Yeah? You're telling me all that came as a *surprise*?'

'So she says.'

'She's playing games, Stu. She sussed him from the start. She knew he was serious all along. She told me so back in May.'

Winter remembered the conversation word for word, a lunchtime meal in a Southsea brasserie the day Pompey returned from Wembley with the FA Cup. The news that her husband had political ambitions came hand in hand with Marie's realisation that Ezzie, her daughter, was having an affair. The events that followed, in Stu's phrase, had stretched the family to breaking point, and even now the cracks still showed.

'So he's going ahead with this interview?' Winter wanted to know more.

'Big time. He's invited this woman down for lunch at the hotel. Full look-at-me treatment. You know how subtle he can be.'

Winter laughed. Bazza's pride and joy was a hotel on the seafront, the Royal Trafalgar. Its recent elevation to four-star status had prompted a celebratory knees-up that had lasted until dawn. For Baz, the fourth star was the clinching evidence that ten busy years in the cocaine trade could buy you anything—even the launch of a campaign to install himself as the city's first elected mayor, announced at a gleeful press conference two days before Christmas.

'The *Guardian* eat people like Baz for breakfast. Someone should have told him that.'

'I did.'

'And?'

'He says he can handle it, told me to fuck off. So . . .' Stu flashed the car ahead and accelerated onto the M23 '. . . here I am.'

Winter settled down for the journey south. When Stu wanted the full debrief on Dubai, he obliged. As far as he was concerned, the family business was three quarters of a million quid in the hole. As Stu, above all, would know.

Norcliffe winced. 'It gets worse,' he said. 'I've just done an audit on the rest of the portfolio. France is horrible, the UK's collapsing, those new places in Montenegro are still half built, and Spain's a basket case. Rely on the Arabs to make the thing come good, as Baz seems to have done, and you're looking at meltdown.'

Until recently Stu had been running a successful hedge fund. Premises in Mayfair, multi-billion-dollar turnover, black Porsche Carrera, the lot. The fact that he'd sold out for a decent price only weeks before Lehman went bust told Winter he knew a thing or two about the workings of big business. Putting your trust in the markets, like putting your trust in marriage, could take you to a very ugly place.

'So how bad is it?'

'You want the truth?'

'That's a silly fucking question.'

'OK, here's the way it is . . .'

At moments of stress, or high excitement, Stu affected an American accent. Winter had often wondered whether it was a defence mechanism, a form of temporary disguise, trying to kid himself he was someone else.

'Number one, most of the properties abroad are secured on loans of various kinds, mainly fixed-rate mortgages. As long as the earnings service the mortgages, *no problema.* When they don't, huge fucking *problema.*'

'And they don't?'

'No way. People are skint. They're not going on holiday. They can't stretch to a couple of grand a week for that nice hacienda by the beach. So the likes of my father-in-law have to start thinking long lets, semi-permanent tenancies, but that's no answer either because the hot money, the vacation premium, that's all gone. Rents just don't cut it, not the way Baz has structured the property holdings.'

This was news to Winter. He'd always assumed Bazza had simply swapped hookey cocaine dosh for all those bricks and mortar, part of the laundering process that had turned him into one of the city's top businessmen.

Stu shook his head. 'Not true. I thought exactly what you've been thinking, but it turns out the guy's way over-leveraged. The money he was making, he could have stayed virtually debt-free. Instead he decided to pile in. Why buy ten properties and make a decent return when you can borrow someone else's money and buy a hundred and score yourself a fortune? Works a treat. Until the bubble goes pop.'

Winter was thinking about the waterside plot of land in Dubai: 750K for thirty apartments that didn't even exist.

'So he's got to start selling? Is that what we're saying?'

'It's way worse than that. Start offloading now and you're talking fire-sale prices. That won't begin to repay the loans. You happen to know the Spanish for "negative equity"? Only it might be wise to learn.'

Winter lapsed into silence. These last few years, after binning the Job and turning his back on CID, he realised that he'd come to rely on the cocoon that Mackenzie's many businesses had spun around him. Club-class travel. Decent hotels. A three-week jaunt through Polynesia as a thank you for sorting out last year's marital crisis. Only now did he realise that most of these castles were built on sand.

'So what do we need?'

'Working capital.'

'How much?'

'A couple of million. And that's just for starters.'

'And Baz knows that?'

'Yes. Which I guess is the worst news of all.'

'Why?'

'Because he's still telling himself it's not a problem. And you know why?' He shot Winter a glance. 'Because the man has a plan.'

'You've asked?'

'Of course I've asked.'

'And?'

'Nothing. *Nada.* He won't tell me.'

* * *

At the Bargemaster's House, perched on the edge of the greyness that was Langstone Harbour, Faraday was becoming aware that his life was slowly slipping out of focus. He was developing an obsession with doors. He needed to close them quietly, deftly, measuring the exact effort that went into the push, savouring the soft kiss as the door seated into the frame. He tiptoed from room to room, longing for the coming of dusk, embracing the gathering darkness like a long-lost friend. On wet nights he cherished the whisper of rain against the French windows and lay for hours on the sofa, listening to the wind, his mind a total blank.

One morning, with a jolt of surprise, he realised that he was knotting and unknotting his hands in the most unlikely places—the bathroom, for instance, while he stared uncomprehendingly at the tiny array of waiting toothbrushes. He also started to talk to himself, recognising the low mumble that dogged him from room to room as his own voice. In his more rational moments he put most of this down to the accident, inevitable aftershocks from Sinai, but what was more unexpected was a growing sense of helplessness, of his mind playing tricks beyond his comprehension.

As the days and nights went by, he didn't seem to be able to rid himself of the same thought, the same memory. It came back time and time again: a man on a horse he'd glimpsed briefly, in the middle of the night, from the window of the hotel where he and Gabrielle had been staying in Aqaba, days before the accident. The horse and rider had appeared from nowhere, the clatter of hooves waking him up. He'd gone to the window and watched the man on the horse careering back and forth across the dusty parking lot, tugging hard on the reins. The man had looked angry. He'd carried a stick, slashing left and right at the empty night air. And then he'd disappeared. The breeze from the sea on Faraday's face had been warm, a kind of balm. But what remained was the sense of bewilderment. Why the horse? At that time of night? And what was the man doing there, riding from nowhere to nowhere? So violent? So manic?

This was bizarre enough, a tug on his wrist from which he couldn't shake himself free. But then, towards the end of his brief convalescence, he came across notes to himself that he must have left around the house, all of them recent. He couldn't remember writing them, nor work out what function they served, but the fact that they were there, that they existed at all, was frankly weird. They read like the jottings of a stranger passing by, a voice he couldn't recognise, and as his grip on reality slackened he sensed that he was becoming a spectator at the feast of his own undoing. Stuff was happening—puzzling stuff, troubling stuff—and he hadn't the first idea what to do about it. Should he return to the doctor and ask for medication, some magic pill that would bring his world back into focus? Or should he drive over to Major Crime, knock on DCI Parsons' door and plead insanity? He simply didn't know.

Then came the morning when he woke to find blood all over the pillow, Hanif's blood, still warm from the accident. Propped on one elbow, aghast, he tried to reach for Gabrielle to tell her what had happened, but Gabrielle wasn't there. Worse still, when his gaze returned to the pillow, the blood had gone.

'Mad,' he whispered to himself, slipping deeper under the duvet.

The dreams, if dreams they were, got worse. He was back in the hospital in El Arish, trying to explain to an old man with no head that everything would be OK. Then, inexplicably, he was crouched in a hide beside the Dead Sea, his binos steadied on the body of a child. A pair of crows stalked around, occasionally pecking at the child's eyes. Images like these awaited him night after night. And the best part of a bottle of Côtes-du-Rhône simply made them worse.

Finally, the morning he was due to return to work, his mobile rang. He was groggy, exhausted, wiped out by another night with his demons.

Gabrielle, he thought at once.

'Boss? Is that you?' It was D/S Jimmy Suttle. Something horrible had kicked off on the Isle of Wight.

Chapter Two

MONDAY, 9 FEBRUARY 2009. *07.53*

Faraday got himself to the Southsea Hovercraft Terminal in time to catch the 08.00 crossing to Ryde. He sat beside the window, readying himself for the brief trip, his hands tightly knitted in his lap, vaguely surprised to find the world around him so little changed. Here he was, listening to the pre-recorded safety announcement, his thumping head still full of families squatting among the wreckage of undone lives, the sky still plaited with shellbursts of white phosphorus. On the websites he'd consulted they sometimes called it Willy Pete. When surgeons cut deep into flesh to extract a fragment, it burst into flame again on contact with the air. Faraday shut his eyes. His lifejacket was under his seat. He ought to remember that.

Arriving at Ryde minutes later, he took a taxi to Newport, the island's biggest town. On the phone Jimmy Suttle had asked him to go straight to St Mary's Hospital, where the Home Office pathologist was due to start a series of post-mortems at half past nine. Suttle, obviously pressed for time, had been sparing with the details but made it clear that pre-autopsy X-rays would have a critical bearing on the course of the inquiry. Four bodies had been recovered from a major fire. There were already strong indications that they may have been killed beforehand. The presence of bullets or gunshot or other pre-existing wounds would be enough to trigger a Major Crime investigation.

Faraday sat in the back of the taxi, trapped in a long queue of traffic, gazing out at a bunch of schoolkids sheltering from the rain. Most of them were crouched over their mobiles, a blur of tiny fingers texting their mates. Four bodies, he told himself. House fire. Gunshot wounds. Must get the details right. Must retain them. Must—somehow—surface from this darkness that seemed to have engulfed him.

The mortuary was towards the back of St Mary's Hospital, beside one of the staff car parks. Faraday stood in the rain, waiting for a voice on the entryphone to buzz him in. He hadn't been to the island for a while and wondered whether there'd be anyone here that he'd know. In a way he hoped not. Just now there was safety in the company of strangers. They'd have nothing to measure him by, no reason to look twice at the vagueness in his eyes.

The door unlocked and he stepped inside. The first face he recognised belonged to the pathologist. He'd last seen Simon Pembury five years ago, here in this very same mortuary. He'd already changed into green scrubs and his handshake was wet and slightly soapy.

'Long time.' He grinned, gesturing at the rain still dripping from Faraday's tangle of grey curls. 'Same bloody weather, though.'

'Great, isn't it?' Faraday was trying to remember Pembury's daughter's name. He'd seen a photo once. Pretty girl. Durham University. 'How's the family?'

'Thriving, thank God. Susie's up in town now, registrar at Guy's, and the wife's badgering me to retire.' He grinned. 'You?'

Faraday was aware of giving the question more thought than it deserved. In the background, deep in conversation with the Scenes of Crime image specialist, was another face he knew.

'J-J's fine,' he managed at last. 'I think.'

Pembury stepped aside to find a pair of wellington boots that fit properly. Faraday, with a small jolt of pleasure, realised that he could put a name to the face across the anteroom.

'Darren . . .' he said. 'Darren Webster.'

Webster extended a hand. Five years ago, on the same job that had brought Pembury to the island, he'd been an eager young D/C keen to move to the mainland and test himself on Major Crime. Now there was a wariness in his nod of welcome, a definite sense that he had territory to defend.

'Boss.'

'Still hang-gliding?'

'Afraid not.' He managed a wry grin. 'Still chasing all those birds?'

The image specialist thought it was funny. Faraday too.

'Of course,' he said. 'Why would I ever stop?'

Faraday sorted himself a coffee, then headed for the loo at the back of the changing room. He'd often wondered what it might be like to be an alcoholic, having to cope with the real world in your face every morning, and now he was beginning to understand. Not because he was desperate for a drink—he wasn't—but because the sheer business of coping was suddenly so bloody difficult. House fire, he told himself again. Four bodies. X-rays. And maybe pellets of gunshot.

The X-rays were the first item on Pembury's agenda. A radiographer arrived with a portable machine and Faraday watched while each of the corpses was wheeled in from the fridge room. For some reason he hadn't anticipated the contents of the body bags. One of the mortuary technicians was double-checking the ID tag on the first bag against the file held by the Crime Scene Investigator. The CSI made a note of the time and stepped aside while the bag was unzipped and its contents transferred to the slab.

Faraday had seen what fires could do before, on dozens of occasions, and this blackened grotesque should have come as no surprise. Intense heat contracts the bigger muscles in the arms and legs, and the faceless figure in front of him seemed to have readied itself for a fight. The arms were raised, the fists clenched, the legs bent at the knees. There was something deeply primitive about the pose, Faraday thought, something that spoke of helplessness and anger as well as pain.

The radiographer retired while the machine took the first set of X-rays. Three more bodies followed. One, recognisably a woman, was more intact than the rest. When Faraday asked about what—exactly—they were dealing with, the CSI pulled a face. The farmhouse had been thatched, he said. The roof had collapsed inwards, leaving a bonfire contained by the outer cob walls, which even now, a day and a half later, were still warm to the touch.

Faraday could smell the smoke on the first of

the bodies to be examined. He watched Pembury carefully dissecting down through folds of cooked muscle, aware of an acrid aftertaste that seemed to reach deep inside his throat. The X-rays were available by now. All four indicated gunshot wounds and Faraday felt his spirits lift when Pembury's scalpel confirmed the presence of tiny pellets of lead. So far, the inquiry would have been handled locally. Now, under the iron grip of DCI Gail Parsons, everything would be folded into Major Crime. Not an accidental house fire at all, but multiple homicide probably followed by an act of arson.

The first of the pellets had appeared, a tiny sphere of lead, lightly coated in body fluids, glistening under the mortuary lights in the jaws of Pembury's tweezers. The image specialist stepped forward. First the stills camera. Then video. Faraday was looking at the head on the slab, at the smudge of blackened features, at the thin crust of liquid that had bubbled out of the skull under the intense heat. So far, to his relief, the sheer predictability of the post-mortem—the script that pathologist after pathologist was obliged to follow—had stilled the voices in his head. But then he caught the smell again, smoke laced with something sweeter, and his stomach churned as he remembered his first glimpse of the pathetic bundle of bandages that was Leila. This blackened gargoyle could have been her on the slab, he told himself. Easily.

The pathologist had found another pellet. The CSI stepped forward with an evidence bag and held it open. Faraday watched this tiny piece of theatre, his own hands knotting again, the squeeze and knead of thumbs against fingers, and knew he had to leave the room. He couldn't take this stuff any more. Not this.

He'd seen the shower earlier. It was in the changing room. He stood under the scalding water, as hot as he could bear it, his face tilted up, his eyes closed. The roar of heavy jets taking off from the airfield near the hospital. The morning one of the cleaners left a carefully folded newspaper on the table beside his bed. The paper was in Arabic. He hadn't a clue about the headline but it was the photo that had drawn the cleaner's attention and it was that same photo that came back to him now. After ten days of laying waste to Gaza, local newspaper editors no longer saw any merit in restraint. The child's body had no head. Dogs tore at the open throat.

Then, from miles away, came another noise that Faraday took a second or two to recognise. Opening his eyes, he found himself face to face with D/C Darren Webster. He'd pulled back the plastic curtain on the shower. He'd seen Faraday leave the post-mortem and wanted to know that he was OK.

'I'm fine.' Faraday wiped his face, thankful that the water masked his tears. 'Just fine.'

* * *

Winter happened to be at Mackenzie's house that morning. Between them, he and Stu Norcliffe had convinced Bazza that they must make a start on stemming the haemorrhage of funds that was edging Mackenzie's business empire towards the blackest of holes.

On the basis of the last quarter's figures, backed

up by a one-year overview, Stu had drawn up a list of enterprises that would survive the coming recession. These included Speedy Cabs, a brace of fast-food outlets much patronised by students, a martial arts gym, an upmarket seafood restaurant with a loyal clientele, a Fratton corner shop specialising in exotic reptiles, a jobs agency serving the call-centre sector, a security consultancy offering cut-price twenty-four-hour protection and the Royal Trafalgar. These businesses, said Stu, would thrive in hard times, and he was therefore proposing to float them off, ring-fenced from the dodgier areas of Mackenzie's empire. These, to Mackenzie's acute distress, included pretty much the rest of what he'd so carefully jigsawed together.

Bazza was sitting at the kitchen table in the big house in Sandown Road, pretending not to listen to Stu's thoughts about a retirement development on the Costa Esmeralda. In Stu's view, Playa Esmeralda was sucking the life out of the rest of the Spanish portfolio.

'So we bin it? Yeah?' Mackenzie was watching the big wall-mounted plasma screen. Fern Britton doing her best with a pink Pilates ball.

'Definitely. And *muy pronto*.'

'But half the fucking world are over sixty. They've got to live somewhere.'

'Yeah, but not in Spain any more. We've been through it, Baz. The poor sods down there are stuffed. Number one, they won't be getting interest on their savings any more. Number two, what's left is worth zilch.'

'Why?'

'Because of sterling. Because of the euro. The rest of the world has found us out, Baz. Have you tried buying a beer in Europe recently? The pound's fucked.'

'That's now, Stu. You're not telling me this is for ever. I say we wait, hold our nerve. Never did us any harm in the old days.'

Norcliffe shook his head. Talking to Bazza in this mood was a waste of time. He pushed his stool back from the breakfast bar and got to his feet.

'Where are you going?'

'Home.'

'Why?'

Norcliffe was stooping for his briefcase, Bazza's question ignored, when Winter heard the front door open. Seconds later, Marie stepped into the kitchen. The pinkness in her face and the brightness in her eyes told Winter she'd been swimming again.

'How many lengths?' he enquired.

'Fifty, since you're asking.'

'How far's that?'

'I haven't a clue.'

Winter watched her shake her towel out before bundling it into the washing machine. Since the troubles last year her life had been transformed. Eight months ago, after the trauma of little Guy's kidnap, she'd been resigned to her daughter and Stu and the kids all moving out to Spain. Instead they'd bought a huge old house in the next road and she saw her grandchildren pretty much every day. Life, she'd recently told Winter, couldn't be sweeter.

The retirement development on the Costa Esmeralda had always been Marie's baby. Bazza told her what her son-in-law had in mind.

Marie was at the sink now, rinsing out her Speedo.

‘Shame,’ she said, ‘but I’m sure Stuart knows best.’

‘And that’s it? That’s all you’ve got to say?’ Bazza shook his head in disbelief. ‘You’re off the planet, you lot. I work day and night putting all this together. I make it cushty for you—I make it legit, respectable—and now we just piss it all away? How does that work? Anyone care to tell me?’

No one offered him the satisfaction of an argument. Norcliffe left the room without a word while Marie asked whether Winter wanted a bite of lunch. After a solid hour in the water she was famished.

Winter said yes to prawn salad and fresh bread. He’d accompanied her and the kids to the pool on a number of occasions and had watched the impact she made on even the younger guys. A woman in her mid-forties, still blonde, still slender, she could still turn heads without a whisper of self-regard. In this respect, as in many others, Bazza didn’t know how lucky he was.

Bazza didn’t care a hoot about lunch. He had something else on his mind. ‘You talk to Stu about this new job of his?’ He was speaking to Winter.

‘No.’

‘Some new boutique bank? Whatever the fuck that might be?’

‘No.’

‘He says he’s giving it serious thought. It’d be Mayfair. Again.’

‘Is that right?’ Winter glanced at Marie. She’d hate having Stu back in London. She’d worry about Ezzie and the kids.

Marie appeared not to be listening. She’d got hold of the TV remote and had changed channels for the lunchtime news. After the weather forecast came the local round-up.

'That's Johnny's place . . .' she said quietly. 'I swear it is.'

Winter turned towards the screen. The remains of some kind of farmhouse were smouldering under a thin drizzle. It had no roof and the entire property was surrounded by police no entry tape. Through an open window, framed by the blackened wood, two Scenes of Crime guys were on their hands and knees, sifting through a pile of debris. The item cut to a different shot. A small army of officers was advancing inch by inch down a long meadow towards the hedge at the bottom. In the distance, behind the commentary, Winter could hear a dog barking.

'That's definitely their place.' It was Marie again. 'I recognise that tree.'

The reporter said that four bodies had been recovered. A police spokesman confirmed that enquiries were on-going.

Abruptly, the coverage cut to sport. A spokesman at Fratton Park had refused to confirm or deny rumours that Pompey were in deep financial trouble. Diarra sold to Real Madrid. Jermain Defoe up the road to Spurs. The club sinking like a stone. The cupboard, player-wise, dangerously bare.

Winter was watching Mackenzie. Since the item on the burned-out farmhouse, he hadn't moved.

'Baz?' he ventured.

'What?'

'Fratton Park? You believe all these gloom bags?'

Mackenzie's head came round. His face was the colour of chalk. He forced a smile.

'Never, mush.' His voice was a whisper. 'Never in a million fucking years.'

*　　*　　*

Faraday found D/S Jimmy Suttle in an upstairs office at Newport police station. He wanted to know about Gail Parsons. Brisk, he'd told himself in the taxi from the hospital. Keep it brisk.

'She's due any minute, boss. I got a call about an hour ago.'

'And she's SIO?'

'As far as I know. With you as deputy, assuming we hoist this thing in. Be gentle though, boss. She's not in a good place just now.'

Parsons, it turned out, had recently lost her dog. She had a boisterous black Labrador called Nelson and he'd come to grief under the wheels of a bus in Fareham High Street. Nelson was allegedly the closest Parsons came to any kind of private life and it seemed that photos of the animal still decorated her office at Fratton nick.

'She took a bit of leave, boss. Fun week in Madeira.'

Faraday smiled. DCI Gail Parsons had been his immediate boss for a couple of years now, a small combative woman with a carefully thought-through career plan and an impressive chest. The last time Faraday had seen her, a week before Christmas, she'd been spending every night reading up for her next set of promotion exams. That she'd make superintendent by the age of forty was in Faraday's view never in doubt. Whether she'd ever give herself time to enjoy the job was a wholly different question.

'So tell me . . .' Faraday settled in a chair and nodded at the pile of notes on Suttle's borrowed desk. 'Where are we?'

Suttle sat back, taking his time. Now twenty-nine, he'd been on Major Crime for a number of years, winning a reputation for intelligence, charm and the kind of dogged thoroughness that can prise open an otherwise difficult investigation and tease out a result. Tall, with a mop of red curly hair, he'd partnered Winter for a year or two, a relationship that had taught him a great deal about the blacker arts of crime detection. He was also brave, a quality that had nearly done for him when he'd tackled a drug dealer in Southsea and got himself knifed in the process. Lately, thanks to a long period of convalescence behind a desk, he'd become the must-have Intelligence Officer on Major Crime operations.

'Remember Johnny Holman?' he said at last.

The name sank like a stone through Faraday's memory. He frowned, shut his eyes, tried to conjure a face, an MO, the usual scatter of previous.

'Pompey boy?'

'Right.'

'Ran with the 6.57?'

'Spot on.' The 6.57 had been the hard core of Pompey's travelling away support, exporting serious violence wherever it was required.

'Off the scene now? Semi-retired?'

'Yeah. And as of yesterday probably dead.'

Faraday raised an eyebrow, wondering which of the body bags in the mortuary might have contained Johnny Holman. In truth he could remember very little about Holman, but that wasn't something he was about to share with Suttle.

'So what happened?'

'Hard to say, boss. Time-wise we're talking the small hours of Saturday night/Sunday morning. This is down the south of the island, out towards Freshwater. The place that caught fire is called Monkswell Farm. It's not a real farm, not a working farm, just the kind of pad you might retire to if you suddenly came into a whack of money and you fancied somewhere nice and peaceful.'

Holman, he explained, had always been a motorcycle nut. Most of his life he'd scraped a living from various jobs, mainly in the auto trade. What money came his way he'd invested in a big Suzuki, and his favourite gig was an annual visit to the Isle of Man to test his riding skills against the hairier corners on the TT circuit.

'This is something he seems to have taken pretty seriously, as you would. According to the people I've been talking to, he was a decent rider.'

'So what happened?'

'He used to stay for the best part of a week. This is several years ago. On the Thursday he was putting in another lap, nothing silly, and some old guy pulled out in front of him. Never looked, never checked, bang, *finito.*'

Holman, he said, was rushed to hospital in Douglas. They saved his life but it took the best part of three months to put him back together again.

From his hospital bed Holman hired a Manchester firm to chase an insurance settlement. They scored big time. A million plus. Enough, easily, to buy Monkswell Farm with enough left over for a few beers.

'But that's where it started going wrong.'

'The farm?'

'The beers. Holman had always been a drinker, famous for it. While most of the 6.57 were out of their heads on toot, Holman stuck to the Stella. After the accident it became a bit of a thing with him. Maybe he was still in pain. Maybe it was his way of coping. Fuck knows. All we know is it started getting the better of him. Too much time, too much money, pissed out of his head by lunchtime.'

'You've talked to people about this?'

'Yeah. He was a popular guy—at least he was once. He was a bit on the small side too. Women used to mother him.'

He had a son, Grant, Suttle said. The boy was twenty plus by now and had moved away somewhere.

'So we're putting Holman in the farmhouse? The night it burned down?'

'That's our assumption.'

'And who else?'

'There's a woman called Julie. Julie Crocker. She used to be a Pompey barmaid, well known around the town, bit of a looker in her day.'

'And she hooked up with Holman?'

'Yeah. Apparently she'd known him most of her life, had a scene or two with him, but after the accident she was the one who went over there to the island and sat by his bed and tried to make it all better again.'

After Holman's discharge, he said, she helped him find the kind of place he had in mind and ended up moving in with him.

'That's her and her two daughters, Kim and Jess. Kim was seventeen, very pretty, lippy with it, tons of attitude, bit of a nightmare. The other one,

Jess, was younger, fourteen, apparently Johnny's favourite.'

'Was?'

'We're assuming they were all in residence. All four of them were listed at that address. The local boys were running round all yesterday. They've recovered a vehicle from the property, a Land Rover. It's registered to Holman.'

Faraday nodded. As ever, Suttle was shaping the first tranche of intel into bite-sized chunks, easily digestible. Most of this stuff was open source, with a light sprinkling of background gossip from the more reliable informants. In the hunt for motive, assuming four homicides, he'd have to dig deeper.

'Timeline?'

'I've a feeling Holman may have been away at some point last week, but I've got to check it out. What we know for certain is that he's back by the Thursday because the postman delivers a parcel and he signs for it. Two days later, the Saturday, the youngest girl comes into Newport around lunchtime and hangs out with a couple of mates. They're all planning to crash some party or other and young Jessie has plans to kip over at a mate's place. I'm not sure why, but that plan never works out.'

'How do you know?'

'One of the guys here talked to Jessie's mate. Something kicked off at the party and got Jessie upset. She phoned her mum and said she was going to call a taxi and could she borrow the fare to pay the driver once she got home. But here's the interesting bit . . .'

'Yeah?' For the first time. Faraday had stopped thinking about the state of his head.

'Yeah.' Suttle nodded. 'According to Jessie's mate, the mother didn't want her home. She said to stay in Newport. Kip on a floor. Do whatever.'

'But don't come home?'

'Yeah.'

'Why?'

'No one knows, and in a way it's academic because our Jessie wasn't listening. She'd had enough of party night. She wanted out.'

'So she called the taxi?'

'Yeah. The guys here traced the driver. He stood everything up. The girl was in bits in the back. The driver said he thought it was boy trouble. Floods of tears. Couldn't wait to get home to Mum. As it turned out, thoroughly bad move.'

'If she's one of the bodies.'

'Indeed.'

Faraday sat back, staring out of the window. On the face of it, the locals had done very well indeed. No wonder Darren Webster was less than pleased to see him.

'So where next?'

'Difficult to say. As we speak, I'm still not sure it's our call.'

'You're kidding. Parsons? You really think she'd pass on something like this?'

'I'm sure you're right, boss.' Suttle checked his watch. 'Like I said, she's due any minute.'

The beginnings of a silence settled between them. Then Suttle asked about the accident.

'You know about that?'

'Of course I know about that. Everyone knows about it. Some kind of RTA? Am I wrong?' RTA. Road traffic accident.

Faraday didn't say a word. Returning from his

visit to the GP, he'd phoned Personnel to warn them that he wouldn't be back at work for at least ten days. Pressed for details, he'd muttered something about a car crash in Eygpt but had left a proper conversation for the moment his boss got in touch. The fact that the phone had never rung had been a bit of a mystery at the time, but now he realised that Parsons had been away in Madeira.

Suttle was still watching him.

'So how bad was it?'

'It was OK. Just a bit of a . . . you know . . .' He shrugged.

'Was Gabrielle in the car?'

'Yes.'

'And?'

'Took a knock or two. Bit like me.'

'So she's back?'

Faraday didn't answer. His partner was rapidly becoming a memory.

'She's not back?'

Faraday returned his gaze.

'No,' he said at last. 'She's not.'

Suttle nodded. The young D/S knew a great deal about the sharper bends in Faraday's relationship with Gabrielle, not least because he had a talent for interpreting moods and body language.

'It's none of my business, boss . . .' he began.

'You're right. So leave it.'

Suttle shrugged, his eyes still fixed on Faraday. Then came the sound of Parsons' voice from somewhere down the corridor. When she was revved up, she had a tendency to shout. Any minute now, Faraday thought.

Suttle was leaning forward across the desk, beckoning Faraday closer.

'Just get a grip, boss,' he muttered. 'Whatever it is, it shows.'

Faraday swallowed hard. He had no idea what to say. Then the door burst open and Parsons bustled in. She seemed to have got over the dog.

'Joe. Jimmy. Handover meet in half an hour. The D/I's office downstairs. Good news from the PM, eh Joe?'

Chapter Three

MONDAY, 9 FEBRUARY 2009. *14.34*

Bazza Mackenzie rarely came to Blake House these days. Which made his sudden appearance on Winter's video entryphone screen all the more surprising. A couple of hours ago Baz had abruptly disappeared into his den while Winter and Marie settled into the prawn salad. Now he was eyeing the CCTV camera over the apartment block's main door, visibly irritated.

'Press the fucking button, will you? It's pissing down out here.'

Minutes later he was in the flat, leaving a trail of wet footprints across the living-room carpet. Winter couldn't remember a visit from his boss that hadn't started with a check on his favourite view.

Winter joined him at the big French windows that opened onto a generous balcony. In the non-stop theatre of Pompey life, this was probably the best seat in the house. From here, on sunnier days, Winter could spend whole afternoons with his binos and a steady supply of coffees, keeping tabs on the busy stretch of water at his feet. Even today, the windows pebbled with rain, the racing pulse of Portsmouth Harbour seemed to reach into the room. The apartment in Gunwharf, Winter often told himself, had been the best investment he'd ever made.

Mackenzie seized the binos, tracking a figure on the harbourside walk that skirted the front of Blake House. Then his head went up and he swept the Gosport waterfront. The Camper & Nicholsons' marina, Winter thought. Old habits die hard.

'Look at that one, mush. The big bugger, the blue one. What do you reckon? Three hundred K? Four?'

Winter declined the binos. When it came to pricing yachts, he hadn't a clue. This was a game Bazza liked to play, largely with himself. If you'd once had big money, he thought, it must be strange to realise that you could have laid hands on pretty much anything.

'Maybe you should have bought one, Baz—' he headed for the kitchen to put the kettle on '—while the going was good.'

'You think I couldn't't? Even now?'

'I know you couldn't.'

'Then you're fucking wrong, mush.' He'd appeared at the kitchen door, his face still shiny with rain. 'There are dozens of businessmen in this town who must be crapping themselves just now. Happens I'm not one of them. You OK with that?'

It was a direct challenge. Stay on board or fuck off. Winter asked whether he'd prefer tea or coffee.

'Stolly, since you're asking. Easy on the ice.'

Winter kept a bottle of vodka in the fridge. Misty had finally tired of Bacardi and Coke. He splashed a generous measure into a glass, threw a look at Bazza, then doubled it.

'You having one, mush?'

'No.'

'Why the fuck not?'

For the first time Winter realised that Mackenzie was pissed. There was a madness in his eyes that Winter hadn't seen for a while.

'You want to talk about it, Baz? Or do we just stand here and shout at each other?'

Mackenzie eyed him for a moment. In these moods, as Winter knew only too well, his boss could lose it completely. In his glory days with the 6.57 he'd been a legendary warrior on football terraces throughout the country. Even the police spotters, the plain-clothes guys with a memory for a face or two, had paid tribute to the Little Un's appetite for raw violence. Weekend after weekend he did Pompey proud, and Winter had once seen a police video compilation of his fiercest rucks. Towards the end of the sequence, up in Leeds, he'd taken on three guys at once, huge bastards twice his size, and still come out on his toes.

'Sometimes it's good to listen, Baz.' He was steering his boss into the living room again. 'Stu knows how money works. Sometimes I think he invented the stuff.'

'And you think I don't? You think all this—' he waved a vague hand around Winter's living room '—happened by fucking *accident*?'

'It's mine, Baz. I paid for it. Or most of it.'

'And the rest, mush? Where did that come from?'

'Maddox.'

'Who?'

'Maddox. The tom you fancied—you know, my

friend from a while back.'

'The arty one?'

'That's her.'

'Not me, then?'

'No, Baz. Not you. You pay me well. We have some nice times. No complaints. But this place, since you ask, is mine.'

Mackenzie was looking confused now, and just a little lost. He enjoyed owning people, bunging people, sprinkling them with a quid or two when the fancy took him. The fact that his first lieutenant, his favoured ex-cop, had a life of his own had always been a niggle.

He studied his glass for a second or two, then tipped his head back and emptied it.

'Any more, mush?'

Winter got to his feet and returned with the bottle. Something's happened, he thought. The death spiral of the last couple of months has just got deeper.

Mackenzie uncapped the bottle and helped himself. To Winter's surprise, he poured no more than a dribble. Then he looked up.

'Tide Turn, mush?'

'What about it?'

'You think that should go too? Only it's costing us a fortune.'

'Stu, Baz. It's costing Stu a fortune.'

'Sure. But get rid of Tide Turn and we could use Stu's dosh somewhere handier.'

Winter gave the suggestion some thought. The Tide Turn Trust was Mackenzie's investment in good works, a charity pledged to get alongside the harder elements among the city's wayward youth and haul them out of the jungle of a Pompey adolescence. Lately, it had been prospering under the leadership of a genius Dutch social worker. It had cost a fortune to tempt the guy over from the slums of Rotterdam, where he'd made his considerable reputation, but Stu had been happy to foot the bills. Henrik van Oosten had made some startling moves, not least in the area of youth offending, and the media applause was getting louder and louder. Just one of the reasons why the *Guardian* appeared to be taking Bazza Mackenzie's bid for the mayorship so seriously.

'You think you can afford that?'

'I'm not with you, mush.'

'This mayor thing. If you really want it, then binning Tide Turn would be the kiss of death. Half the city still thinks you're a gangster. The rest have got you down as some Copnor hard case who's seen the light. From where I'm sitting, that's probably very good news. Assuming you get the referendum through.'

A city-wide referendum was the key to Mackenzie's political ambitions. If it ever took place, and if enough people said yes, then the mayor would henceforth be elected by popular vote.

'Gangster?' Mackenzie looked hurt.

'Sure. This is Pompey, Baz, not fucking Islington. Gangster plays well. It buys hotels. Café-bars. It creates jobs. It still goes to Fratton Park. It even sorts out dodgy kids. It's real, Baz. People know who you are. Local boy.'

'Made good?' He was grinning now.

'Definitely. Big time.'

'So Tide Turn?'

'Hang on to it. That's my advice.'

The bottle again. More vodka. Bit of a celebration.

'Cheers.' Bazza got to his feet, swayed a little, checked his watch. 'Off, now. Need to sort one or two things out.'

'No, Baz. Sit down. Tell me what's happened.'

Winter guided him back to the sofa. He could feel Bazza's muscles bunching under the thin leather jacket. Mackenzie hated being touched. His eyes were glassy. He stared at Winter.

'What's this about, mush?'

'My question exactly. Something's happened. So maybe you should tell me what . . .' he smiled and patted the sofa '. . . for all our sakes.'

* * *

Suttle drove Faraday to Monkswell Farm. It was raining even harder now, the country lanes towards the south of the island sluicing water from the surrounding fields. Suttle peered ahead, the wipers on double speed, checking the route against a scribbled map on his lap. He'd borrowed the Fiesta from the local CID boys. They didn't stretch to satnavs.

'Punchy, wasn't she? A result on this job will set her up nicely.'

'What for?' Faraday's eyes were closed. Half an hour of Parsons at full throttle had robbed him of everything.

'The Superintendent's job. She'll get the exams sorted, no problem. What she needs after that is the next vacancy. There's a queue. Like always.'

'You think she does queueing? You think she *ever* did queueing?'

The thought of Parsons meekly waiting her turn brought a smile to Faraday's face. At the end of the meeting, oblivious to Faraday's lack of input, she announced that Operation *Gosling* would be transferring to the satellite Major Incident Room at Ryde police station. Given her ever-increasing workload on the mainland, she'd be bossing the investigation from her office in the Major Crime suite at Fratton. Which put Faraday, as Deputy SIO, in charge of a sizeable team of detectives on the spot.

A tight corner threw him sideways against the passenger door. For a second or two he thought he was in Eygpt again, at the mercy of another set of doctors, but then the car came to a halt and Suttle was winding down the window to offer his warrant card to the uniform beside the flapping blue and white tape.

'Over there, sir. Beside the white van.'

Suttle parked the Fiesta and killed the engine. For a long moment Faraday could hear nothing but the steady drumming of rain on the car roof and the sigh of the wind in the trees overhead. A thick hedge hid the farmhouse and outbuildings and it was tempting to wind the clock back half a generation and imagine that he was Suttle's age, out by himself at the start of a long weekend, preparing to tramp deep into the countryside in pursuit of chiffchaffs or siskins. In those days he'd have had his deaf-mute son for company—a whirl of fingers and thumbs, oblivious like his dad to the weather. By the age of eight, J-J could describe a dozen birds in fluent sign, an achievement which, even now, brought a smile to Faraday's face.

'OK, boss? You up for this?' Suttle gave

Faraday's arm a squeeze.

Faraday looked him in the eye. 'Yes,' he said. 'Bring it on.'

Suttle grinned at him, another squeeze, then he was out in the rain, wrestling with an umbrella he'd found in the back of the car, stepping round the bonnet to open the passenger door and offer shelter. Faraday, grateful, walked beside him down the track towards the farmhouse. The path had been churned up by the fire engines and all the other vehicles that had attended since, and there were deep tyre gouges on the verge, exposing slicks of glistening clay beneath the sodden grass.

Beside the open gate they paused. The remains of Monkswell Farm lay before them. The property occupied a hollow, slightly below the level of the surrounding fields. It was a long, squat, narrow building, all four walls still standing, the white cob walls blackened with smoke. Two brick chimney stacks had also survived the fire, standing proud among the black tangle of assorted debris, somehow adding to the sense of ruin. Not just a building, Faraday thought, but a family too.

Despite the rain, a couple of Crime Scene Investigators were sieving debris onto a layer of clear polythene beside what must have been the front door. One of them spotted Faraday and offered a nod of welcome. Inside, among the wreckage, Faraday glimpsed another figure—tall, a fireman in a helmet and a red tabard, stooping from one pile of wreckage to another. As Faraday watched, he produced a camera, took a few shots, then scribbled himself a note. This has to be the Fire Investigator, Faraday thought, the guy who'd try and tease some kind of conversation from the sour breath of the sodden embers. How the fire had started. How it had spread. And who may have helped it have its way.

The Scenes of Crime caravan was parked next to the barn. Suttle had already briefed Faraday about the Crime Scene Coordinator in charge of the forensic team. Her name was Meg Stanley. She was new to Hantspol, not bad-looking, and had apparently scored a university degree in theology before joining the men in blue.

She was waiting for them in the caravan, a small neat woman in her mid-thirties with a generous mouth and a flawless complexion. She was wearing a two-piece grey suit that lent her an air of slight severity, and at once Faraday could imagine her behind a lectern in a pulpit, or robed beside an open grave. This was someone, he thought, you'd be wise to take seriously.

She offered tea or coffee from a nest of Thermos flasks. The fact that the pathologist had found shotgun pellets in all four bodies had given the forensic search an extra edge. Unless she could demonstrate otherwise, the fire had been deliberately set.

Faraday was looking at the pile of paperwork beside the laptop on the tiny desk. Incidents this challenging were mercifully rare. If you wanted to muddy a multiple homicide, a thatch fire was a near-perfect way of reducing everything to sludge. From the forensic point of view, the hours and days to come would be critical. Any tiny clue spared by the fire. Any evidence that might begin to chart the final hours of the four blackened corpses in the hospital mortuary.

'So what have we got?'

Stanley talked them through her progress to date. As the on-call CSC, she'd been alerted twenty-four hours ago after the discovery of the first body. She'd taken the hovercraft to Ryde, met the Crime Scene Manager on site and framed the Forensic Strategy that would flag the various pathways forwards. Inside the house itself, once the building surveyor had declared the remaining structure safe, they'd be working inwards from the areas of least damage. A fire dog trained to hunt for accelerants had been shipped in from the mainland, and the CSM had led a flash search of the immediate area in case something obvious was staring them in the face. In the absence of a dropped wallet or a signed confession, alas, she'd briefed the Police Search Adviser to map out coordinates for a more thorough trawl of the surrounding fields and hedgerows.

Faraday was keeping a mental log, ticking off each action. In his experience no one got to the giddy heights of Crime Scene Coordinator without seizing a situation like this by the throat. You had to get structure and process into these first busy hours. You had to fold the forensic priorities into the firefighting operation and make absolutely sure that the cracks didn't show. Above all, once the investigative machine was cranked up, you had to make certain that nothing was lost as gaps started to widen between an army of marauding detectives, the guys in the Incident Room and the painstaking recovery of evidence out here in the field. On paper or in the classroom it always looked simple. In reality it could easily become a nightmare.

Stanley had already confirmed a blank on the accelerants—the dog had found nothing. Now

Faraday wanted to know about the state of the place when the fire brigade arrived.

'Was the front door locked?'

'Yes. But not bolted.'

'Key on the inside?'

'No.'

'No key in the property? On a hook? Under a window sill?'

'Not so far. It's still early days.'

'What about the phone landline?'

'It came out of the house just under the thatch. None of that survived the fire so we don't know whether there was any interference.'

'Was the place alarmed?'

'Yes. It was an oldish system. No cameras. The suppliers are coming over this afternoon to take a look at the control box.'

'It's still intact?'

'More or less. Scorch marks. Nothing serious.'

Faraday nodded. He wanted to know about the POLSA search. According to Stanley, it was still in progress.

'Anything so far?'

'Not much. A couple of cans of Stella out in the fields. The remains of a kite. It's still early days though, like I say. We live in hope.' She flicked through the paperwork on the desk and extracted a sheet of paper. 'You might want to take a look at this. The estate agency that sold them the house faxed it over this morning.'

Faraday found himself looking at a layout plan of the property. Upstairs there were five bedrooms and a bathroom. Downstairs there'd been a kitchen/diner, a long sitting area that served as a lounge, a lavatory and a largish room at the other end of the building that the previous owners had used as a kind of workshop. Scattered across the ground floor were four pencilled question marks, two in the lounge and two in the kitchen.

Faraday raised an eyebrow. Stanley was beside him. She had beautiful hands, very pale. No rings.

'This is our best guess as far as the bodies are concerned.' A perfectly manicured nail tracked from pencil mark to pencil mark. 'The upstairs floor collapsed under the weight of the fire and the bodies were buried beneath the debris. It's just possible that the bodies fell vertically but none of them were in or beside the beds. We can't prove it but this is where they appear to have been ante-mortem.'

Before death. Faraday nodded. It was a logical supposition, carefully hedged.

'So the balance of probability . . .?'

'Would put them downstairs.'

'Where they were killed?'

'Impossible to say. They may have been killed downstairs, like you're suggesting. We might be looking for one perpetrator—two, three, who knows? They may even have been killed off site and brought to the farm for disposal.'

Disposal. Yet another line of enquiry.

Suttle asked her about two shotguns registered to the premises. Yesterday's house-to-house enquiries had turned up a neighbour who used to go rabbiting with Holman. The licence demanded that the shotguns be kept in a locked steel container.

Stanley shook her head. So far, on site, no one had found any kind of safe. She was looking at Suttle. She wanted to know what kind of lives the victims had led.

Suttle produced notes he'd made earlier, the intel harvest from the local enquiry teams.

'I'm getting the impression these were party people,' he said. 'We know Holman was a drinker, big style. Apparently they had a thing about candles.' He looked up. 'Candles?'

'Night lights.' Stanley nodded. 'A fire like this, all you get left are the little metal discs in the middle.'

'And?'

'Lots of them. Lots and lots.'

'What about mobiles? Laptops? PCs?' It was Faraday this time.

'One mobile so far. It survived pretty much intact. It's pink. We think it may have belonged to the older daughter.' She consulted her notes. 'We sent it over to Newport this morning. It's bagged and tagged. You haven't seen it?'

Suttle shook his head. With the investigation still in local CID hands, the mobe had probably found its way to their own intel cell. He made himself another note, checked his watch. He had to get Faraday to Ryde within the hour for yet another meeting. He folded his pad and stored it away. By tonight, he said, he might have another couple of blokes to help him pull the intelligence together.

Faraday said he'd make it happen. The more he looked out of the window at the remains of the farmhouse, the more he sensed that Operation *Gosling*'s best lines of enquiry probably lay elsewhere.

'So what's the intelligence telling you?' Meg Stanley was talking to Suttle.

'Holman's Pompey through and through,' he said. 'A lot of his mates go way back and some of them are persons of interest. I'm not sure how much you know about Pompey, but the place is tribal. Blood ties, often literally. We've got a lot of ground to cover and not a lot of bodies to do it with. Same old, same old. I'll bet it was the same where you came from, eh?'

'West Mids?' At last a smile. 'They could be quite generous sometimes. Depended really.'

'On what?'

'On the state of the overtime budget. On whether or not the enquiry rang the right bells at headquarters. On racial implications.' The smile again, warmer. 'Same old, same old.'

Suttle got to his feet. He knew that Faraday had already fixed the first squad meet for six o'clock. By then Parsons would have shipped a dozen Major Crime D/Cs across from the mainland, together with the civvy inputters who would staff the Major Incident Room and bring the HOLMES system to life. By early evening, with a fair wind, the Major Crime machine would have hit top gear, with outside enquiry D/Cs dispatched on action after action. At the heart of this operation lay the core management team, of which Meg Stanley was very definitely part. Faraday was about to brief her about this evening's meet over at the MIR but Stanley got in first.

'One thing I forgot to mention.' She nodded towards the farmhouse. 'We found an area of of excavation round the back.'

'A what?' It was Suttle.

'A hole. Someone had been digging. We've no idea when or why but it's not a small hole. If we're looking for motive . . .' She shrugged, then reached for an umbrella, still dripping into an empty catering tin of coffee beside the desk.

Faraday and Suttle followed her out of the caravan. The rain had eased a little by now. At the rear of the property, out of sight of the farmyard, was a small garden. Beyond the garden, beside a wooden hut, was the hole.

It was about two metres across, maybe a metre and a half deep, with an inch or two of muddy water at the bottom. Beside it, mixed with soil from the excavation, were sodden scabs of something that looked like dung. Faraday could smell it. A sweetness that spoke of horse manure.

'You've had a dog in here?' It was Suttle.

'Yes. Not the fire dog. We shipped in an Alsatian from the DHU.'

Dog Handling Unit. These were animals trained to hunt for drugs.

'You're thinking narcotics?'

'I'm guessing it's a possibility. Along with a million other things.' She shrugged. 'Money. Weapons. Whatever.'

'What about a septic tank?' Faraday was still looking down at the hole.

'We checked that out, talked to the water people. You need all kinds of permissions.'

'And?'

'They'd heard nothing.'

'What about the dog?'

'Zilch, I'm afraid.' She offered Faraday a brief smile. 'Shame, eh?'

* * *

It was Mackenzie's idea to go for a late-afternoon Chinese. He'd reached the point where no more alcohol could touch him and announced that nothing in the world would be sweeter than a plate of king prawns in black pepper sauce. Winter, assigned escort duties, had noticed this with Bazza before. Against every reasonable expectation, after half a bottle of vodka and whatever else he'd necked, the man had the ability to suddenly sober up.

They walked across Gunwharf to a restaurant called the Water Margin: Winter's choice. He came here often, with Misty in tow, and the staff knew him well. One of them, a Hong Kong Chinese called Charlie, led them to a table at the back.

'Nice to see you, Mr Winter.' He flashed a smile at Mackenzie. 'And you too, sir.'

Courtesy always made Bazza suspicious. He sat back in his chair, watching Charlie retreat to the bar.

'What's he want, mush?'

'Nothing, Baz. It's just a Chinese thing.'

'What?'

'Being polite.'

They ate from the à la carte menu. After an afternoon of abuse from Bazza for sticking to coffee, Winter treated himself to a bottle of Tsingtao. After the waiter had gone, Bazza beckoned Winter closer.

'Listen, mush, you want to know what *really* upset me?'

'You mean apart from the ten squillion quid we've lost?'

'Don't be an arsehole. I'm serious, son. Just sometimes life gets on top of you, know what I mean?'

Winter nodded, waited, said nothing.

'Well?'

‘Well what, Baz?’

‘Fucking ask me. Ask me why I got pissed. Ask me what made me shut the door and pour malt down my throat. Ask me what I was doing in Blake fucking House looking for more. You were a detective, weren’t you? Or has that bit of your brain seized up?’

Winter let the storm subside. Charlie turned up again. Fizzy water for Mr W’s guest.

‘Well?’ Mackenzie didn’t bother with a glass.

‘It has to be Johnny Holman.’

‘Brilliant. You’ve still got it. It’s still in there. I didn’t spend all that moolah for nothing. Little Johnny Holman.’ He shook his head, looked away. ‘Gone.’

For the next half-hour, all Winter had to do was listen. How Holman had been one of the earliest faces to sign up with the 6.57. How game he’d been, how up for everything, how crazy, how totally off his head. The day the 6.57 shipped over to France and laid waste to the Café Southampton in Le Havre, it had been Johnny H with a beret on his head prancing up and down, pelting the locals with their own fucking onions. Later that afternoon, at some poxy stadium up the road, it was Johnny again, giving it plenty, wading in, doing his rape and pillage number. On the boat home he’d done his best to empty the last barrel of Stella, and when there was obvious grief waiting at Customs at the Pompey end, it was Johnny who was one of the first to hurl himself overboard into the harbour. Jumping from a height like that took serious bottle, and the thing was Johnny only remembered he couldn’t swim when he was halfway down. Daft cunt, the *daftest* of cunts, sorely fucking missed.

'So what happened, Baz?'

'He died. Died in that fire. They said so on the news. Four bodies.'

'I meant in the harbour.'

'They fished him out. Dried him off. Stuffed him in a taxi. He was always lucky that way.'

'Yeah?'

'Yeah. Until his fucking luck ran out, eh?'

Winter wanted to know more. He'd come across Johnny Holman on a couple of occasions in his CID days, but by that time the booze had turned him into a Southsea character, tucked into the corner of one bar or another, telling war stories from his 6.57 days. Winter had tapped him up on one occasion, hoping for a whisper on this or that. Holman took a few drinks off him then told him to fuck off.

'Had some kind of accident, didn't he?'

'Yeah. Big time.'

Bazza explained about the crash on the Isle of Man. Insurance money had bought him the spread on the Isle of Wight. Lovely place. Great views. Enough land to hire out to off-road trials bikers. Used to drive the locals mad. Johnny, he said, had been lucky in his choice of company too. Julie Crocker, bless her, was salt of the earth, real Pompey, do anything for you, even an old toerag like Johnny. Them two girls of hers too. Lookers, just like their mum.

'You're telling me you know this place?'

'Yeah. Johnny invited me over a couple of times. I took Mist once. Midsummer, it was. She spent all night shagging me senseless in one of them barns he had. Always loved the smell of horse shit, Mist. Must explain a thing or two.' He looked darkly at Winter but got no response.

Winter was picking at his sweet and sour pork. Half past four was a bit early for dinner.

'So what did he do for money, Holman?'

'Nothing. That was the problem. Johnny was never work-shy but he lost the plot a bit after the accident. In the end, the way I hear it, Julie had to find herself a job to make ends meet. Care home? Teaching fucking assistant? Fuck knows.'

'What about the insurance money?'

'Down his throat.' Bazza waggled one hand under his chin. 'You know what I hope? You know what I *really* hope?'

'What do you hope, Baz?'

'I hope the other night, whenever it fucking was, I hope he was totally out of it, slaughtered, bladdered, rinsed. I hope he never woke up. I hope he turned over in bed and thought this is nice and warm and—ping—his lights go out.' He looked up at Winter. 'You think it might have happened that way?'

'I doubt it.'

Mackenzie fell silent. The restaurant was empty. A lone waiter patrolled the spaces by the door, a black silhouette against the last of the daylight.

Winter gave up on his food. Bazza's plate of king prawns was untouched. He wouldn't look Winter in the eye.

'Sad old fucking life, eh?'

'Yeah, for Holman.'

'And what about Julie? Them kids?'

'Sure. No one enjoys getting burned to death.'

'There'll be a funeral, mush.'

'I'd say so.'

'You want to come over with me? Pay our respects?'

Winter didn't answer. Things were slowly getting clearer in his head. He knew Mackenzie well by now. Well enough to understand that Bazza's every conversation had a subtext, not immediately obvious, not even perhaps to himself.

Charlie was approaching. Winter waved him away.

'What do you really want, Baz?'

'I just told you, mush. I want you to sort out your best suit, put a few quid in your pocket, come over with me, buy some flowers, make a night of it afterwards.'

'Sure. And what else?'

At last Mackenzie's head came round. His eyes were dry now.

'The Filth'll be all over that place, am I right?'

'Yeah. Any fire these days is automatically suspicious. And you know what? My lot are usually right.'

'*I'm* your lot, mush.'

'You are, Baz. You asked me my opinion. As an ex-copper I'm telling you they'll have the place squared away. You saw it on the telly, the guys in the funny suits. Scenes of Crime. Fire dogs. Arson experts. The works.'

Mackenzie ducked his head and reached for his chopsticks. He stabbed at a prawn and then had second thoughts.

'So what will they do?'

'They'll take a nose around. You know all this, Baz. It's what they do on the movies. Real life's no different.'

'Right.'

'And something else . . .'

'What's that, mush?'

'People just don't die in fires. Not the way they seemed to have died. People wake up. They *get* up. They yell. They escape. They do anything they can not to end up dead.'

'Smoke?'

'The place was probably alarmed.'

'Something else, then?'

'Yeah. Which brings us back to my original question.'

Mackenzie nodded, picked up the chopsticks again, changed his mind, emptied his second bottle of fizzy water, shouted for the waiter, demanded the bill.

Charlie gone, they were cocooned in total silence again. Darkness on the harbour by now, the lights of a ferry slipping past the window.

Winter leaned forward.

'So?' he said. 'What do you want me to do?'

Chapter Four

MONDAY, 9 FEBRUARY 2009. *18.05*

Faraday was on automatic pilot by now. A muttered excuse to duck into the hotel down the road from Ryde police station, block-booked for squad overnights. Another long moment in front of the mirror in the tiny bathroom, staring at a face he'd once recognised. Another shower. Another fruitless attempt to raise Gabrielle, wherever she might be. Should he declare his partner a Misper? Or should he simply consign the relationship, along with pretty much everything else in his life, to the lost property office?

Back at the Major Incident Room, his hair still wet, he found Suttle in the SIO's office. There was a hint of impatience in his voice.

'Time's getting on, boss. Everyone's waiting for you.'

Faraday followed him into the MIR. The room was cramped compared to the facilities at Fratton and there was barely space for the dozen or so detectives who'd made their way across to the island.

The D/S in charge of Outside Enquiries stilled the buzz of conversation. Faces turned towards Faraday. He found a perch on the edge of a desk, glad of the small comfort of physical support.

With a briskness that surprised him, he summarised developments to date. As everyone pretty much knew, four bodies had been recovered from a major fire. One male, three females. All four bodies had gunshot wounds and the post-mortem confirmed that they'd all been dead before the fire started. Dental records would confirm all four IDs but in the meantime *Gosling* was working on the assumption that the bodies belonged to Johnny Holman, his partner Julie Crocker, and her two daughters, Kim and Jess.

Timeline? He turned to Jimmy Suttle.

'The fire was phoned in at 03.25 on Sunday morning. We're talking quite a remote rural area and this couple lived in a bungalow half a mile downwind. The old guy smelled smoke and got up to check. He could see flames coming from the farmhouse roof and knew the place was thatched.'

Appliances, he said, arrived within half an hour, by which time the property was well alight.

There were two vehicles in the farmyard. On the assumption that there were people inside, the Watch Commander declared 'Persons Reported' and radioed for back-up. An area car was on site by just gone four and the uniformed sergeant at Newport deployed two P/Cs to start hot enquiries locally. QuickAddress had confirmed four persons in residence and a Records Management System search in the name of Holman raised a report of a recent domestic between him and the elder girl. This RMS report included phone numbers: a landline and two mobiles. None of the numbers answered.

A hand went up. One of the older D/Cs wanted to know more about the domestic. A nod from Faraday told Suttle to explain.

'I'm having a bit of trouble on this one,' he said, 'but it seems that our lot got there after the girl's boyfriend. If anyone knows what happened, my guess is that he does. He lives with his mum in Newport. Mum's away at the moment and we can't raise anyone at the house.'

'Name?' It was Faraday.

'Robbie Difford. According to the DVLA, he's twenty-two.'

Faraday told Suttle to carry on. Local house-to-house, he said, had produced intelligence on Holman's shotguns, plus some gossip on the kind of people they seemed to be.

'And?' The question came from the Outside Enquiries D/S.

'Party people, definitely. Lots of music, lots of young kids roaring up and down the lane. There was trouble over off-road bikes too, though that seems to have gone away. Julie was well-liked. She seems to have made a bit of an effort.'

'All this aggro. Anything serious?' Still the Outside Enquiries D/S.

'Nothing flagged. Nothing that would justify something like this. The way I read it, there are loads of incomers around, mostly retired. It's a bit of a lottery, really, who you get as a neighbour. Like I say, Holman was definitely a pain.'

Local CID, he said, had blitzed the enquiry next day. Seized CCTV at local garages and the ferry terminals, automatic number plate recognition camera checks, plus an ever-widening trawl of local addresses. To date, no one had reported vehicle movements in the small hours of Sunday morning. Neither was there much regret at what had happened. The latter produced a small ripple of laughter around the room. One of the three female D/Cs asked about the girls. They'd have mates at school. What was their take on life at Monkswell Farm?

Suttle said he didn't think this line of enquiry had yet been actioned. So far the intel operation had concentrated on Johnny Holman. This was a guy with interesting Pompey connections. He'd never been arrested or convicted for any serious offences, but his name featured in a number of informant reports. He'd long been mates with some of the bigger figures in the Pompey underworld, and if you were looking for motive then his address book would be a great place to start. At this point in the inquiry Suttle wasn't prepared to tie Holman to anyone in particular, but person or persons unknown would need a very good reason to justify a multiple homicide like this.

'So what are we thinking, skipper?' It was the

female D/C again. 'Someone gains entry to the house? Ties them up? Kills them? Sets a fire?'

'That's a possibility, sure.'

'Why? What for?'

'We don't know. Not for certain,' said Suttle.

'But?'

'There's been some digging round the back of the property. A fair-sized hole. It may be recent, it may not. We don't know why it's there but there's obviously a possibility that Holman may have been sitting on something valuable.'

'And someone took it off him?'

'Maybe. Maybe not. At this stage it's speculation. If you fancied a punt, I'd put my money on toot.'

Suttle acknowledged the nods and smiles around the room. As far as motive was concerned, he was still keeping an open mind, but speaking personally he viewed intel enquiries around Holman as an obvious way forward. Over the years the guy had put himself around. In short, the key to *Gosling*'s door might lie in Pompey rather than on the island.

Faraday agreed. Picking up on the work of the local CID, he'd already given the Outside Enquiry D/S a list of actions for tomorrow. He wanted more work done on the CCTV. He wanted careful briefings for the local media. He wanted the female D/Cs out among the dead girls' associates, developing whatever lifestyle intelligence they could acquire. Everyone would be traumatised by the prospect of the forthcoming funeral—the perfect opportunity, in other words, to get these people onside.

'And the young lad? Robbie whatever?' The question came from Meg Stanley.

'An absolute priority.' He shot her a nod of

gratitude. 'We have to find the boy.'

Minutes later the meeting broke up. Returning to his office, Faraday settled behind the desk and scrolled through the calls and messages that had stacked up on his mobile over the last half-hour. Most of them were *Gosling*-related. One, a text, wasn't.

Gabrielle.

* * *

It was nearly eight o'clock by the time Winter got to Eastfield Road. Jimmy Suttle lived in the bottom half of a red-brick Victorian terrace. This was where Southsea dribbled into an area called Milton, much favoured by estate agents desperate to breathe some life into the market. They talked of the 'village atmosphere' and the 'vibrant social scene', code for street after street of bedsits, many of them occupied by partying students.

Winter waited on the doorstep, then rang the bell again. He hadn't been here for nearly a year. Finally the door opened. Lizzie Hodson was Suttle's partner, a small vivid woman with a bright smile. She seemed to have put on a bit of weight.

'Paul.' She stood on tiptoe and gave him a kiss. 'He's not here.'

'Inviting me in or what?'

She looked at him a moment, uncertain. She had nothing on her feet and her toes were curling on the cold tiles.

'OK,' she said. 'Why not?'

Winter followed her into the flat. The kitchen was at the back. Whatever she was frying included a hefty whack of garlic.

Winter helped himself to a seat at the breakfast bar.

'How's tricks? Still working you to death?'

Lizzie was a reporter on the local daily paper, the Pompey *News.* Winter, who was a bit of a fan, made a point of keeping up with her career. Lately, she'd been doing a series of features on the prospects for the local economy: how the credit crunch was affecting Pompey families, how people were coping with lost jobs.

'Work's fine. You want a beer or something?'

Winter settled for a bottle of Stella. The mountain of rice in the frying pan reminded him how hungry he was. Maybe he should have eaten earlier, while he had the chance.

'You fancy some of this?' Lizzie was ahead of the game. 'I was expecting Jimmy back but it's not going to happen.'

'Away, is he?'

'Yeah.'

'Might I ask where?'

'Haven't a clue.'

Winter grinned at her. This was a game and they both knew it. As a veteran D/C, Winter had taught Suttle every trick in the investigative book. Rule one: don't admit anything unless you absolutely have to. Rule two: if in doubt, change the subject.

'That boss of yours . . .' Lizzie was ladling rice onto a couple of plates. 'Whose idea was it to tap up the *Guardian*?'

Winter blinked. As far as he knew, the interview with Baz had yet to make it into print.

'You know about that?'

'Yeah. It's in tomorrow's paper. It's a feature piece so it's on the *Guardian* website already. You want a look?'

She gave him a plate and disappeared into the lounge at the front of the house. Winter got off his stool and peered at a number scribbled on a pad beside the phone. By the time Lizzie returned, he was tackling the fried rice.

'Delicious,' he said. 'The boy doesn't know what he's missing.'

'That's what I tell him. Here.'

She put the laptop on the breakfast bar and angled the screen towards Winter. The photo of Mackenzie must have been taken in the restaurant at the Royal Trafalgar. Winter recognised the stretch of Southsea Common through the window and the grey lick of the Solent beyond. Bazza had adopted his statesman pose for the benefit of the snapper. He was even wearing a tie.

'You've read it?' Winter glanced at Lizzie.

'Of course.'

'And?'

'He sounds quite plausible. A referendum for an elected mayor? Giving Citizen Joe a proper shout? Blowing the cobwebs off local government? Returning power to the grass roots? I don't know who's been feeding him all this stuff but he's certainly ticking the right boxes.'

'And you think it might happen?'

'Depends. There's a general election next year and Labour are going to lose. That probably puts the Tories in. Have you read their proposals for local government?'

'Of course I haven't.'

'Then maybe you should. They're going to offer referendums just like this one to the ten biggest cities in the country. For exactly the reasons your boss is talking about here. So …' she shrugged '… if it works in Birmingham or Leeds, why not Pompey?'

Winter was impressed. To date, if he was completely honest, he'd regarded Bazza's political ambitions as an ego trip, or maybe some kind of wind-up. Lizzie Hodson, it seemed, was telling him he was wrong.

'So you think it's doable?' Winter wanted to know.

'I think there might one day be a referendum, yes.'

'And you think Baz might be the man for the job?'

'I think this is exactly the kind of city that might take a step like that, yes.'

'You're serious? Bazza? Lord Mayor? Big car? All that bling they wear?'

'Sure, Paul, but power too. Real power. That's what turns him on, isn't it? Or are you telling me that Tide Turn is just window dressing?'

Winter steadied himself. This conversation was fast turning into an interview.

'Bazza loves this city,' he said carefully. 'Always has done, always will. He wants to do the best by it. He wants to get it sorted.'

'Are we still talking Tide Turn?'

'Yeah. And one or two other things.'

They looked at each other, amused, an unspoken acknowledgement of what Bazza's toot money, carefully washed, had done for the likes of Southsea. The quietly tasteful café-bars, largely Marie's doing. The Royal Trafalgar with its fourth star. A whole raft of jobs for kids from Portsea and Somerstown who'd otherwise be up to all kinds of wickedness. And now Tide Turn.

'So . . .' Lizzie gestured towards the laptop again '. . . no wonder the *Guardian* are impressed.'

'They gave him an easy ride?'

'It's much worse than that. They seemed to believe him.'

'No mention of—' Winter frowned '—the 6.57?'

Lizzie peered at the screen a moment. '"A passion for football and a talent for mixing with all kinds of people took Mackenzie to every corner of the kingdom. The skills he picked up on the terraces should stand him in good stead in the cut and thrust of political debate."' She looked across, grinning. 'How's that sound?'

'They're taking the piss. Either that, or Baz is.'

'On the contrary, they're telling him he's passed the test. Believe me, you don't get profile like this by accident.'

Winter nodded, returned briefly to the remains of the rice. There was a name he wanted to run past her. Someone who Bazza was keeping under wraps.

'Leo Kinder?'

'What about him?'

'You know this guy?'

'I've met him a couple of times, yes. Lawyer? Young? Good-looking? Political ambitions? Right wing? Fell out with the Tories, big time? What are you telling me, Paul?'

'Nothing, love. Just curious.'

'Curious, bollocks. Is Kinder thick with Mackenzie? Is that it?'

'Might be.'

'Has to be. That's where all this comes from.' Her eyes returned to the laptop. 'Kinder knows the Tory manifesto by heart. He probably helped write the thing. In the end his face didn't fit, and for my money he's gone looking for a new political home.' She laughed. 'They're made for each other, those two. Beauty and the Beast. Shit . . .'

Winter was studying his hands. He hadn't been so effortlessly kippered for years. Lizzie was a class act.

'So who's the Beauty?' he enquired

'Kinder, of course.'

'I'll tell him that.'

'Who?'

'The Beast.' Winter pushed his stool back and stepped away from the breakfast bar. 'So where's young Jimmy?'

'You asked me that before.'

'I know I did. I'm asking you again.'

'Same answer. No comment.'

'Shame.' He stooped to give her a kiss. 'But thanks for the hospitality.'

She saw him to the door, said goodnight, promised to remember him to Jimmy when he got back. Only when Winter was back in his car did he scribble down the number he'd clocked beside her phone.

01983 prefix. The Isle of Wight.

* * *

Je suis à Salisbury, chéri. Avec la petite. Gros bisous. G. Faraday was back in his room, rechecking Gabrielle's text. She was evidently in Salisbury. *La petite*, the little one, had to be Leila. Somehow she'd secured the funding and flown the broken little doll he'd glimpsed at El Arish to the UK. He knew nothing about the Burns Unit—what it entailed, where he might find it—but for the time being that didn't matter. More important was the fact that Gabrielle was still intact, still in touch. The word *bisous* flooded him with a deep sense of relief. *Gros bisous* meant 'Lots of kisses.'

Twice he'd tried to phone her back but both times she was on divert. Now, almost light-headed, he checked his watch. It was gone nine and he hadn't eaten since a snatched sandwich in the police station at Newport. He knew that Suttle had joined a bunch of detectives at a pasta place on Ryde High Street. He'd been nice enough to leave directions in case Faraday fancied it, but the thought of an evening of Job-talk filled him with gloom. Thanks to Gabrielle, he seemed to have regained a little of the ground he'd lost since the accident. He didn't know how much faith to place in this welcome moment of sanity but he knew he didn't want to squander it. On the point of wandering out on his own to find somewhere quiet, he had another thought. He'd stored Meg Stanley's mobile number. No, she hadn't eaten yet. And yes, she'd like to join him for a curry.

They found a restaurant in Union Street, the Ryde Tandoori. Midwinter, with flurries of rain still blowing in off the Solent, the place was empty. They chose a table beside the Calor gas heater and ordered drinks. Cobra for Faraday. Orange juice for Meg.

'Strange being here . . .' She was gazing out at the street.

'Why's that?'

'I went to school up the road. Five of the worst years of my life.'

It had been a boarding school, she said. Her

father worked in the oil business, a geologist prospecting all over the world, and most of the time he took his wife with him. As a result, Meg had been dumped in a series of boarding schools. Yuk.

'How bad was it?'

'On a scale of ten? Probably four or five, but that doesn't count at the time because all you've got to go on are the people around you. I was an only child. I never had a problem with that. Not until I was chucked in with hundreds of others.'

The experience, she said, had been the steepest of learning curves, and the known limit of the real world had been here in Ryde.

'We used to get leave out once a month, always a Sunday. There was a bus you could catch to get down to Ryde. I used to stand on the end of the pier and watch those huge oil tankers sail past. Oil was something I knew about. It paid the fees, for one thing, so I blamed it for banging me up. I hated the place, loathed it.'

'You said learning curve.'

'Yeah.'

'What did you learn?'

'Serious question?'

'Serious question.'

'I learned how to be alone. To be properly alone. Back home it was easy. Just little me. In a school with a couple of hundred other gals, it's trickier. Still . . .' she ducked her head '. . . like I say, you learn.'

'And now?'

'Still alone.'

'And happy?'

'Very.'

'Excellent.' Faraday raised his glass. 'Here's to

solitude.'

They talked about the Job for a while but without much passion. She'd never dreamed of ending up in the police, but a postgraduate degree in forensic science had given her a taste for putting all her knowledge to the test and in the end she'd won herself a post as a Crime Scene Investigator in the Devon and Cornwall force.

'Exeter,' she said. 'Lovely city.'

From there, she'd won promotion to the West Midlands as a Crime Scene Manager, before heading south to her current desk with Scientific Services at the Training HQ at Netley.

'So how does all this stuff sit with a BA in theology?'

'Rather well, since you ask. I've always regarded God as the biggest mystery, totally unsolvable. Forensic science gives a girl like me a bit of hope.'

Faraday laughed. 'Do you use that line at parties?'

'I don't go to parties.'

'Never?'

'Not if I can avoid them.'

'So, where are you living?'

'Lock's Heath. I bought a horrible little newbuild. It's a tent. It'll meet my needs for a while. Then I'll move on.' She smiled at him. 'How about you?'

The question took Faraday by surprise. He was glad not to be talking about charred bodies but there was a directness about Meg Stanley that left him nowhere to go.

'Me?' He frowned. 'What do you want to know?'

'Are you married? Kids?'

'Partnered. One child.'

'Yours? Plural?'

'Mine. His name's J-J. Joe Junior. He's in his thirties now.'

'And his mum?'

'She died way back. Her name was Janna. Cancer.' He touched his chest.

'How old was J-J?'

'When she died? Two months.'

'So who brought him up?'

'I did.'

She registered neither surprise nor admiration. She wanted to know more.

Faraday studied her a moment, then shrugged. If he wanted solid ground under his feet after weeks of near-drowning then here it was.

'We were lucky. Janna was American. Her parents had a bit of money and that paid for a house in Pompey. I still live there. It's down by the water beside Langstone Harbour. It gave me a base for everything.'

He warmed to the memories, bending into the conversation, totally at ease now. How he'd begun to notice how odd, how out of touch, his infant son could be. How he'd taken the child for tests. And what had happened when the specialist announced the diagnosis. J-J was deaf. In a clamorous world he couldn't hear a thing.

'Christ.' At last, a reaction. 'So what did you do?'

'I had to find a way of talking to him, a way of getting through. You try all kinds of stuff. Sign's important, of course it is, but I knew I had to build a stronger bridge. In the end I met someone in exactly the same situation and I did what they'd done.'

'Which was?'

'Go birdwatching.'

'Birdwatching?'

'Yeah. Think about it. It's a visual thing. They catch the eye. It gets you out. They come in all shapes and sizes. You learn about the weather, about migration patterns, about the tides, about feeding habits, about the pecking order, about family life in the wild.' He smiled at her. 'And that's just me. J-J loved it. He was a gawky kid. He'd flap around, pretend to be a stork, a heron, an egret, whatever. We were the Odd Couple. No question about it.'

'And you were a copper by now?'

'Yeah. I joined to pay the bills. The money from Janna's parents stretched to an au pair but the rest was down to me. Pretty soon I crossed to CID and . . .' he shrugged '. . . here I am.'

'Impressive.'

'D/I at fifty-two? I don't think so.'

'I meant the child. The lad. J-J.'

'Yeah?'

Faraday sat back. If he was honest with himself, those early days with J-J had been the best. These last few years, by contrast, had been difficult. His boy got on with Gabrielle, no problem, but father and son rarely saw eye to eye. Like his mother, J-J had made a bit of a name for himself in the world of art photography. He'd also got involved with a series of women who'd frequently taken advantage. One of them, a French social worker, had nearly broken his heart. Another, a rich Russian, much older, had used him for recreational weekends. On every occasion Faraday had done his best to mark his card, but at thirty-two, even with word-perfect signing, J-J didn't want to listen.

'The boy's like his father,' Faraday heard himself

murmur. 'He piles all his money on one card and trusts the roll of the dice.'

'And that works?'

'For him? I guess it must do.'

'And for you?'

Faraday smiled at her, reached for the menu.

'We should eat,' he said. 'Before they throw us out.'

Chapter Five

TUESDAY, 10 FEBRUARY 2009. *07.03*

Faraday finally got through to Gabrielle early the next morning.

'Where are you?' he asked.

'Joe?'

'Where are you?' he repeated.

'*Dans une chambre d'hôte à Salisbury.*'

A bed and breakfast in Salisbury. She sounded flustered, defensive, and Faraday was aware of a steeliness in his own voice that he normally reserved for the interview suite. He couldn't help it though. He had to know what was happening.

'I'm having my breakfast, *chéri.* What's the matter?'

What's the matter? Faraday wondered where to start. Ten days without a whisper of contact? A dozen or so calls unanswered? Nearly a fortnight without a shred of interest in what might be going on back home? In his own life? *What's the matter?*

Faraday fought to still the clamour in his head. One thing at a time.

'How's Leila?'

'Still bad. She's in hospital here. The Burns Unit. I go to be with her every day.'

'So what are they doing for her?'

'To begin with, they take skin and make . . .' she hesitated '. . . *des greffes*?'

Grafts. He tried to picture the little bundle of bandages he'd last glimpsed in the high-dependency ward at El Arish. Was she still critical? Were they still fighting to save her life?

Gabrielle was doing her best to explain. The doctors in Egypt had done a good job. They'd made her well enough to fly. Just. Now, here in Salisbury, they'd taken off all her old dressings and put new grafts on the burns. Some of the burns were infected. This morning they'd have to change the bandages again. That would be bad, very bad. They'd take the child to the operating theatre and put her under *anesthésie* because of the pain. Gabrielle had bought her new toys yesterday, and some colouring books.

'But how is she?'

'I told you, *chéri*. Bad. Sick. *Malade*.'

'I mean in herself?'

'*Comment ca?*'

'Is she . . .' Faraday found himself hunting for the right word'. . . talking?'

'She talks only Arabic.'

'Then how do you communicate?'

'We have a translator. Riham. She speaks French, English.'

'And she comes in every day?'

'She stays with the child. She sleeps with her. She has a bed in the room.'

Faraday scribbled the name on the pad next to

the phone. Dimly, in a conversation way back, he remembered mention about flying a translator over from Egypt.

'Riham?' he repeated.

'She's Palestinian, like Leila. She lives in El Arish.'

'Is she some kind of relative?'

'Leila has no relatives. She's here alone. That's the whole point, *chéri.* My little girl has no one. *Tu ne comprends pas ca?*'

The line went dead. Faraday stared at the mobile, at the grey rectangle of screen. *Tu ne comprends pas ca?* Don't you understand? He hit redial. The number rang a few times, then he was listening to the Orange messaging service. His eyes closed. He took a deep breath. He could leave a *billet doux* for Gabrielle if the mood took him. He could tell her what a relief it had been to hear her voice, to know that she was in one piece, that the child was in good hands, that all would be well. God knows how, but he could offer to find time to get back to the mainland and drive up to Salisbury and give her a hug and a kiss and a bit of support. He knew that's what he should be doing. He knew he should be bigger than the sum of all his troubles. But he knew as well that it was utterly beyond him.

He sat on the edge of the bed, still clutching the mobile, trying to ignore the hot waves of anger flooding through his body. He'd spent most of the night in the sweet anticipation of making contact again, real contact, but for some reason it had led to this. He didn't understand why, and worse still he hadn't the faintest idea what to do next. No wonder she stayed out of reach. No wonder she didn't answer his calls. No wonder she'd hit the red button and slipped the mobile back into her bag. In her situation he'd probably do exactly the same.

He got to his feet and went across to the window. A glimpse of the Solent would have been nice; instead he found himself looking at the back of a tenement. A woman was standing in the kitchen on the second floor. She was wearing a black T-shirt. She was filling a kettle at the sink. The moment she saw Faraday she reached forward, a brisk decisive movement. Faintly, he heard the clatter of the venetian blind. For a moment or two longer he stared at the pale slatted oblong of light. Then came a knock at his door.

It was Jimmy Suttle. He apologised for the early hour but he'd just taken a call.

'Who was it?'

'Winter, boss. He's after a meet.'

* * *

It was barely eight o'clock when Winter rapped on Colin Leyman's door. The tiny house was in Eastney, a stone's throw from Jimmy Suttle's place. There was no front garden for the brimming wheelie bin, and when Winter took a peek inside he could see nothing but pizza home delivery boxes and grease-stained bags from McD's.

Finally, the door opened. Leyman was a dumpling of a man. He was way over six feet and his sheer bulk spilled over the camouflage army surplus bottoms he must just have dragged on. His hair was a mess and he'd obviously given up on shaving. For a man in his late forties, thought Winter, he could do with a week or two off the burgers.

'Bloody hell, you.' Leyman's lopsided grin told

Winter he was welcome. He pumped the offered hand and waited for Leyman to shuffle inside before joining him in the narrow hall. For a moment he thought Leyman might get stuck. Then, seconds later, they were in the kitchen together.

'Long fucking time, no fucking see. Yeah?'

Winter was looking round. The kitchen was tiny, everything within reach. There was a powerful smell of cat piss.

'How's your mum?'

'Died last year, Mr W. Miss her like you wouldn't believe. Still—' he gestured round '—she left me the house.'

He retrieved a soiled T-shirt from a pile of laundry by the oven and dragged it over the huge wobble of his belly. Then, to Winter's amusement, he had second thoughts and swapped it for a Pompey top in the same pile. The last time they'd met, three years ago, Leyman had been pondering Winter's invitation to become an informant. In the end it had never happened, not least because Winter's days in CID had come to an end, but that, in a way, was irrelevant. Leyman's MO was written all over his big moon face. He could never make his mind up.

'So how's tricks? What's keeping you out of mischief?'

At first Winter thought Leyman must have gone deaf. He didn't seem to have heard the question. Then his big meaty paw seized Winter by the hand and led him towards the door. He'd always been childlike this way, the gentle giant who couldn't wait to be your friend.

'You wanna see something, Mr W? Come with me.'

They were back in the hall. The living room was off to the left. It was bigger than Winter had expected, but there wasn't a stick of furniture in the room. Instead, spread across the floor, was a carefully painted model landscape, complete with rising hillocks, tiny clumps of trees and a scatter of buildings. There were primitive roads too, criss-crossing this beautifully reconstructed stretch of countryside. Winter stood in the open door, shaking his head in admiration. Papier mâché, had to be. Days of work. Weeks. Months.

'You did this, Col?'

'Yeah.' The grin again. Simple pride.

'Where's it supposed to be?'

'Guess, Mr W. You're an educated bloke.'

Winter took another look. For the first time, in the shadows beneath the window, he saw the lines of tiny painted soldiers. Officers on horseback. Infantry carrying muskets. A troop of cavalry frozen in mid-canter beside the skirting board.

'Abroad,' Winter said.

'Spot on.'

'France?'

'Close.'

'Spain?'

'Try the other way.'

'Germany?'

'Didn't exist.'

'Fuck.' Winter's grip on history was woeful. 'I give up.'

'Flanders, Mr W. What we call Belgium today. You know what you're looking at? You've got it. The Battle of Waterloo. See here?' He reached for a billiard cue propped against the wall and pointed at a tiny collection of buildings, every detail perfect.

'That's Hougoumont. That's where we held the French. Come back tonight and I'll show you how.'

'That's kind of you, Col. I'm impressed. Is there somewhere we can talk?'

They returned to the kitchen. Winter found himself a space on the two-seat sofa beside a pile of war-game magazines, remembering vaguely that Leyman's earlier passion had been for the Royal Flying Corps. Go upstairs to the loo, and you had to make your way through squadrons of immaculately painted biplanes suspended from the Artex ceiling.

Leyman wanted to know whether Winter was still doing the biz with Mr M.

'Young Bazza?'

'Yeah.'

'You know about him and me? Still keep your ear to the ground?'

'Yeah, too right. Best time of my life, back then. You'd be amazed who I still run into.' He tallied a list of names, counting them on his fingers, frowning with the effort the way a child might.

Winter smiled. The cast list was perfect. This was going to work out, he knew it.

'Seen Bazza yourself at all?'

'Not for years, Mr W. He was stuck at the traffic lights the other day, them lights in Albert Road. He was in the Bentley with that Marie of his.'

'And?'

'I just walks past. Bentleys? Posh crumpet?' He wiped his nose on the back of his hand and then inspected the results. 'He's got a big place in Craneswater, ain't he? Fair play to him. He was always the one with the brains.'

Winter leaned forward, gave Leyman's knee a pat. His flirtation with the 6.57 had lasted less than a season. The kind of faces Mackenzie ran with didn't have much time for simpletons, but they tolerated Leyman because of his sheer size, and for a while, in the depths of winter, he became a kind of mascot. Once, for an away fixture at West Brom, they dressed him up in a bear suit and got him to dance in front of the rival crew as an aperitif to the usual ruck. The local A & E department weren't used to eighteen-stone grizzlies with blood all over their fur, but Leyman seemed to regard his injuries as a badge of honour. Shortly afterwards, according to Baz, he hung up his bear suit and called it a day.

'Baz'd love to see you. Maybe up at the hotel. Want me to sort something out?'

A look of alarm darkened Leyman's face. He shook his head.

'Like I say, I gets to see some of the old faces, but no thanks, mush.'

'You're sure?'

'Yeah. All that stuff, it ain't me—know what I mean?'

'All what stuff, Col?'

'Fancy places. Big cars. I does all right. Don't get me wrong. But no—' he shook his head again '—thanks all the same.'

Winter waited for the huge head to come up. Leyman radiated enormous heat. You could feel it.

'Skint are you, Col?'

'Me?'

'Yeah. Only I could maybe help there.'

'Why? How?'

'By giving you a little job. By asking a favour, if you like.'

'Does this come from him? Baz? Is this him talking?'

‘Not at all. In fact I’d prefer you kept shtum about this conversation.’

‘Right.’ He seemed relieved. ‘Right. So what would you want me to do?’

Winter took his time. He wanted to frame this as a joint effort. That way Leyman might view it as friendship rather than a simple bung.

‘You remember Johnny Holman?’

‘Yeah. Who fucking wouldn’t?’

‘He’s dead, Col.’

‘I know. That place of his on the island, the one that burned down. It was in the paper.’ The big face was like a concertina when he frowned. ‘So what’s that got to do with anything?’

‘I’m not sure, Col. What we need to do is talk to friends of Johnny’s. You know them better than me. Maybe you could have a conversation or two.’

‘What about?’

‘Well . . .’ Winter tried to hold his gaze ‘. . . we need to know what Johnny’s been up to this last year or so. Who he’s been seeing. Who’s gone across to the island. What might explain a fire that killed four people.’

‘You mean—’

‘I mean some tosser might have killed them all. Fires like that don’t happen by accident, right, Col?’

‘Right, Mr W.’ Leyman appeared to agree. ‘And this is urgent, yeah?’

‘Very.’

‘Like tonight?’

‘Today, Col.’

‘*Today?*’ Not alarm this time. Something closer to panic. ‘I’ve got a mate coming round. We’re going to fight the whole of the first day. June the eighteenth. Right up to sunset.'

'I'm not with you, Col.'

'Waterloo, Mr W. It's tricky, that first day.'

'So Johnny Holman ...?' Winter sat back, his hands spread wide, a gesture of matey disappointment. I understand, he was saying. Better some poxy long-ago battle than helping out a mate.

Leyman wavered. He wanted to look anywhere but at Winter. Winter inched a bit closer, got his wallet out, laid five twenty-pound notes in Leyman's lap.

'This is drinking money, Col.'

'Bazza's?' Leyman was staring at the notes.

'Mine.'

'A hundred quid?'

'Yeah. With more to come if you fancy it.'

'Fancy what, Mr W?'

'Helping Johnny out.' He gave Leyman's thigh a little squeeze, then got to his feet. 'By tonight, eh? I'll give you a ring.'

Chapter Six

TUESDAY, 10 FEBRUARY 2009. *11.04*

Nadine Lorrimer was one of Kim Crocker's best friends. The Communications Intelligence Unit had extracted her contact details from the mobile recovered from Monkswell Farm. She lived with her mother on an estate on the edges of Newport. On compassionate grounds she'd been excused college for a couple of days.

Suttle drove across with one of *Gosling*'s D/Cs,

Patsy Lowe. Lowe, in her early forties, had a great deal of experience as a Family Liaison Officer. She was small and overweight, with a quick smile and slightly punky hair. She'd grown up on one of Pompey's rougher council estates and had the knack of making most people quickly forget she was a police officer. It had been Faraday's idea to put her alongside Lorrimer.

Nadine turned out to be a goth. She sat in the darkened front room with the remains of a roll-up, dressed in black, stroking a tabby cat called Ron. Suttle, wary about the tea Nadine had just made, was glad to be spared tears. Mum was out at work.

'So how well did you know her, Nadine?' This from Lowe.

'Kim? Really well. Really, *really* well. Not just mates, more sisters. Know what I mean?'

'And what was she like?'

'Sound. And beautiful. A beautiful person. And a laugh too. I could tell you all kinds of stuff but I'm not going there.'

'What kinds of stuff?'

'The kind of stuff we used to get up to, girlie stuff . . . You don't want to know.' She turned her head away, fumbled with a lighter, sucked at the roll-up. A thin grey light through a crack in the curtains washed over the room. 'She used to stay over a lot, Kim. Like I say, she was a laugh.'

'Did she talk about her home life at all?'

'All the time.'

'What was it like?'

'Mad. Her dad was off the planet most of the time, total headcase. Actually he wasn't her dad at all but he used to . . . you know . . .'

'Used to what, Nadine?'

'Used to get really heavy.'

'Physically, you mean?'

'Not really. He never hurt her or anything, not that she ever said. It was more the way he was out of it all the time, just falling around, shouting at everyone, really irritating stuff. Kim would defend him sometimes, say it was the drink talking, say it wasn't his fault. She was silly like that, Kim. She knew how to look after herself, stand up for herself, but she always gave people the benefit of the doubt, even Rat Face.'

'That's what you called him? Rat Face?'

'Yeah. He must have had this really bad acne, you know, horrible pitted scars. And his face had gone a kind of funny colour, a yellowy colour, maybe with all the booze.'

'What about Julie? Kim's mum?'

'She was lovely, really nice.' For the first time there was a tiny catch in Nadine's voice. 'She's the one that held everything together. Rat Face was hopeless that way. Couldn't hold a job down. Couldn't bring the money in. Total waste of space. To be honest, I don't know how Kim's mum put up with him. If it was me . . .' She bent to the roll-up again.

'So you're saying, between her mum and her dad . . .?'

'Nothing. They had nothing. Just rows all the time. That's why Kim spent so much time here. She couldn't stand it at home . . .' Her voice trailed away.

It was dustbin day. Suttle could hear the truck grinding up the street and the hollow *thud-thud* as the dustmen returned the empty bins.

'Kim had a boyfriend,' he said. 'Robbie Difford.'

'You know Robbie?' She seemed surprised.

'No. We're trying to find him. Do you know where he might be?'

Nadine gave the question some thought.

'It's Tuesday, yeah? He'll be at work. That exhaust place on the industrial estate.'

'They haven't seen him since Saturday.'

'Maybe he's off sick then. He lives with his mum. Like all of us do.'

'No. He's not there either. We checked.'

'His mum's away. She went to Tenerife for a week. Maybe he's asleep. Maybe you should knock harder.'

Suttle exchanged glances with Patsy Lowe. If they couldn't find Difford by lunchtime, Faraday had authorised a forced entry to the house. These days grief could do the strangest things to kids.

Lowe wanted to know more about Kim and Difford. How long had they been together?

'Not long. Couple of months? I dunno.'

'So what's he like? Difford?'

'He's good, really cool. He sings in a band, pub stuff mainly. The music's crap but he's got an OK voice. He really looked out for her, Kim. She liked him a lot.'

'And Robbie?'

'He was mad about her. Couldn't get enough of her. We used to laugh about it sometimes, me and my mates. They were always at it.'

'Where?'

'*Where?*'

'Yeah. Here? Other friends' houses?' Lowe paused. 'Or Kim's place? Out at the farm?'

'I dunno. Wherever, I guess. Definitely here a few times, when my mum was out. Why? Is this kind of stuff supposed to matter?'

Lowe didn't answer. Suttle leaned forward, his elbows on his knees.

'Did you ever get the impression that Robbie could be jealous?'

'About Kim?'

'Yes.'

'I'm sure he could . . . you know . . . if anything ever kicked off.'

'And *did* anything ever kick off? That you can remember?'

Nadine looked at them both, then reached for her Rizlas. Neither Lowe nor Suttle said a word.

'You're talking about that stuff that happened last week, aren't you?' she said at last. 'You must know about that. It must be on all those records you keep.'

'You mean some kind of incident?'

'Yeah. The Old Bill were involved, your lot. Kim told me.'

Suttle nodded. 'So what happened?'

'I dunno. Not the details.'

'But you do know something happened?'

'Yeah.'

'Like what, Nadine?'

Her head went back. A tiny shred of tobacco on her lower lip.

'Kim said her stepdad came on to her.'

'Came on to her?'

'He wanted to have sex with her.'

'And was that the first time it had happened?'

'No.'

'It happened a lot?'

'I don't know. She never liked talking about it. But more than once. Definitely.'

'So what happened last week?'

'He did it again. It was in the evening. There was no one else in the house. He came in pissed and tried to . . . you know . . . grab her.'

'So what did she do?'

'She hit him. She yelled at him. She told him he was an animal. She was really upset.'

'And he stopped?'

'Yeah. And Kim says he apologised too. Said he hadn't really meant it. Just a joke, yeah?'

'So what did Kim do?'

'She went outside and phoned 999. Then she had second thoughts and phoned Robbie as well.'

'And?'

'He drove straight up there. Confronted the bloke.'

'They had a fight?'

'Not really. Robbie's a cool guy. He's fit too. I think he just told Rat Face to sort himself out.'

'And what else?'

Nadine let the question hang in the air. She was wary now. Suttle could see it in her face. She'd said too much. She wanted this conversation to end.

'Well?' It was Lowe again.

'I dunno.'

'Yes, you do, Nadine. Because Kim told you.'

'Yeah? You're sure about that?'

'Yes.' Lowe nodded. 'And if Kim still matters to you, which I'm sure she does, then maybe you ought to tell us.'

Nadine gave the suggestion some thought. She lit the roll-up, took a deep lungful, then exhaled. The thin plume of smoke hung in the chilly air.

'We're talking about Robbie, right?'

'Yes.'

'He's really wound up. It's the heat of the moment. All that stuff.'

'And?'

'You still want to know what he said?'

'Yes, please.' Lowe nodded. 'Then we'll leave you alone.'

'Really?' She frowned, then ducked her head.

'Well?'

There was a long silence. Finally, Nadine stifled a cough before looking up.

'Robbie said that if Rat Face ever touched Kim again . . .' she shrugged '. . . he'd kill him.'

Lowe bent her head and scribbled herself a note. Nadine watched her, aghast.

'There's no way—'

'No way what?'

'No way Robbie had anything to do with what happened. Rat Face was the crazy one. Not Robbie.' She looked from one to the other. 'Yeah?'

Suttle shrugged, said he didn't know. Police had responded to the 999 call. An area car had driven out to Monkswell Farm to find Kim, Robbie and her stepfather in the house. On the phone, hysterical, Kim had talked about some kind of assault. By the time she was offered the chance to make a full statement she seemed to have had second thoughts. The boyfriend's recent arrival may have had something to do with this, and on the RMS entry the attending officer had noted the details and suggested a possible referral to Social Services. At seventeen, Kim Crocker was still a minor. Better safe than sorry.

Suttle asked Nadine about Saturday night, the night of the fire. What had Kim been up to?

'I dunno. I saw her at college on Friday and she

said she'd phone Friday night in case anything was going down over the weekend. But . . .' she shrugged again '. . . it never happened.'

'So what do you think she *might* have done?'

'I haven't a clue. She worked at WH Smith's on Saturdays. Saturday night she was probably with Robbie. They were getting to be like an old married couple. Cosy cosy.'

'Her place? His? Out somewhere?'

'Dunno. There's a girl called Rachel works with her on Saturdays. She might know.'

Lowe made a note of the name. Nadine couldn't supply a number.

Suttle was curious about access to Robbie Difford's place. Might a neighbour be holding a key? Or maybe a close friend?

Again Nadine shook her head. She'd had enough by now. Her roll-up had gone out. She had a headache. She wasn't sleeping too well. There was stuff she had to do before the funeral. She gave them a few more names, other mates of Kim's, then walked them to the door. On the point of saying goodbye, she asked what had happened to Kim.

The question stopped Lowe in her tracks.

'I'm not with you, Nadine.'

'Like where is she?'

'Now? Still in the mortuary, I imagine.'

'You've done one of those post-mortems? Cut her up? All that stuff?'

'I'm afraid so.'

'Horrible. Yuk.' She gave herself a hug, shivering in the chill wind, her face the colour of chalk. Then she brightened. 'Tell Robbie to give me a ring, yeah?'

Suttle phoned Faraday from the Fiesta. He was

in conference with Gail Parsons and couldn't spare time for more than the briefest conversation. Suttle said they'd talked to the girl Nadine. In his view they needed to take a good look at Robbie Difford's place. Like now.

Faraday smothered a yawn.

'Do it,' he said.

* * *

Winter was at the Royal Trafalgar by half ten. A couple of calls on other mates of Johnny Holman had been fruitless—no one at home at either address—and in the end he'd decided to wait and see what Leyman might come up with.

At the hotel he was supposed to share an office in the basement with Stu Norcliffe. Neither man had much liking for Bazza's take on working space—two second-hand desks from a government surplus store in Highland Road, plus an enormous filing cabinet Baz had acquired from a repo company he was in the process of buying—but Norcliffe, for once, was sitting behind his battered desk.

One look at his face told Winter all was far from well.

'You won't fucking believe this . . .' Stu said.

'Tide Turn?'

'Too right. You know that new minibus of ours? The one I bought a couple of months ago? It went missing last night. Henrik thought someone had nicked it and he was right. Three guesses.'

'Kieron O'Dwyer?'

'Spot on.'

Winter hid a smile. He'd spent the best part of a miserable year in charge of Tide Turn, trying to pretend that the likes of Kieron O'Dwyer were human beings. Thankfully that job had come to an end, but nothing he'd learned at the helm of Bazza's favourite charity had changed his mind about the hard core of Pompey youth. These were the kids, he told himself, whose forebears had scared the French shitless at Trafalgar, and nothing had changed since. Afloat or on dry land, they were programmed to get in your face.

O'Dwyer, it seemed, had nicked the keys from the Tide Turn office in Albert Road, picked up a bunch of mates in Somerstown, made another couple of stops in Portsea and Buckland, and headed north. By the time the minibus demolished a garden wall in a pretty village on the West Sussex border, O'Dwyer and his crew had emptied the first litre bottle of vodka and were starting on the rest of the stash. When the police arrived, they were partying in a nearby graveyard, out of their heads on White Lightning and handfuls of assorted tabs.

'The vehicle?'

'I haven't seen it. According to the police it's a write-off.'

'Baz'll be pleased.'

'I've told him already.'

'And?'

'He told me to leave it to him. I gather he's got some ideas on the subject.'

'You mean O'Dwyer?'

'Yeah. He was after the boy's address.'

Winter nodded. O'Dwyer had form. At fifteen, he'd forgotten what it was like to go to a normal school, to get up at a respectable hour, to lift a finger in anyone's interest but his own. After endless skirmishes with the criminal justice system, and now Tide Turn, he'd realised that most of what he wanted in life was there for the taking, a conclusion that no adult had yet to contradict. Maybe Bazza would come up with something novel, he thought. Before O'Dwyer was old enough to become a proper criminal.

'So where is he?'

'Still banged up at Central. Still waiting to shout at his social worker.'

'I meant Baz.'

'No idea, Paul. According to Marie, he's got a lot on his mind just now.' He pushed his empty mug towards Winter and nodded at the coffee pot on top of the filing cabinet. 'Surprise, surprise, eh?'

* * *

Meg Stanley was bent over her laptop in the Scenes of Crime caravan when one of the Crime Scene Investigators appeared at the door. He had a sheet of paper in his gloved hand. Part of the barn across the farmyard had been converted into a couple of rooms. One seemed to have served as a kind of bedroom while the other had been used as an office, chiefly by Holman. Before giving both spaces the full SOC treatment, the CSI had done a flash intel search, looking for anything that might, in his phrase, give *Gosling* a kick up the arse.

'And?' Stanley was enjoying the thin sunshine through the open door.

'I found this.'

He passed it over. Stanley found herself looking at a photocopied advert for a private clinic offering a variety of sexual goodies from penis enlargement to wholesale deals on vaginal lubricants. Consultations were available for most forms of dysfunction, confidentiality guaranteed. The address put the clinic in north London, and someone had scribbled a series of notes down the edge of the page.

'That's Holman's handwriting. We found a couple of chequebooks in the same drawer.'

'You're sure?'

'Ninety per cent.'

Stanley returned to the advert. The handwriting was indecipherable but a date and a time caught her eye: 4 February, 14.45. She made a note of the contact details and then reached for the phone.

* * *

Suttle and Lowe drew a blank at Robbie Gifford's address.

Local uniforms secured entry with a commendable absence of drama, and Suttle went through the property room by room. It was hard to be certain, but the general state of the place told him that Difford had been living here alone for at least a couple of days. The kitchen sink was piled high with unwashed plates and a cardboard box on the floor was full of discarded fast-food wraps. Half a pint of milk in the otherwise empty fridge was starting to go off and the pile of laundry at the foot of the stairs had yet to see the inside of the washing machine.

Upstairs were two bedrooms. The one with a double bed appeared to belong to his mum: frocks in the wardrobe and photos of a much younger son neatly arranged on the dressing table. Next door had to be Difford's room. The bed was unmade and he hadn't got round to pulling the curtains. There was an ankle-deep scatter of clothing on the carpet and a pile of men's mags beside the single bed. The PC was on, with an offering from YouTube still hanging on the pause button.

Next to the PC was a wallet. Suttle flicked quickly through the contents. Credit cards, cash-machine stubs, a receipt for twenty quid's worth of petrol and a sheaf of passport-size photos. The cards were in Difford's name and the shots showed a couple snapped together in the intimacy of a photo booth. He was dark, fashionably unshaven, grade-one haircut, black hoodie. She was blonde, striking, a curl of mischief in the smile. In three photos they had their heads together, gurning for the camera. In the last one they were necking. Gifford and Kim Crocker. Had to be.

Suttle checked the bathroom, just in case, then rejoined Lowe downstairs. One of the local uniforms was on the phone, making arrangements for repairs to the lock and the door frame.

Lowe lifted an enquiring eyebrow. Suttle shook his head.

'No one here,' he said. 'But he's definitely not done a runner.'

* * *

Faraday wanted a management catch-up meeting for two o'clock and it was already lunchtime. Suttle dropped Lowe at Newport police station to continue enquiries among Kim's college mates and then drove over to Ryde.

Faraday was in his office with Parsons, toying with a half-eaten ham and tomato sandwich from the

Spar shop round the corner. Parsons was finishing a call on her mobile.

'Ma'am. Boss.'

Faraday waved Suttle into the spare chair. He wanted to know what Nadine had said. Suttle gave him the headlines. To no one's surprise, life at Monkswell Farm had been a bit of a nightmare. Holman was pissed most of the time and had made a couple of passes at his elder stepdaughter.

'We can prove that?' It was Parsons.

Suttle explained that Patsy Lowe would be returning this afternoon to press Lorrimer for a statement.

'And we believe her?' Faraday this time.

'Yes, boss. I can't see why she'd lie about something like that. She and Kim were close. She's also got a bit of a thing about Difford, the way I read it.'

'No sign of him yet?'

'None.'

'Car?' Difford drove an ancient red Corsa. Local CID had accessed the details a day and a half ago.

'It's not at the house, boss.'

Faraday nodded, reached for the remains of his sandwich. Suttle thought he looked exhausted. Parsons, as ever, wanted to build what little evidence they had into the beginnings of a timeline.

'So what do we know, Joe? What can we stand up in court? Apart from the four bodies in the house?'

Faraday finished his sandwich, brushed the crumbs from his lap, then went through the list from memory.

'We know that Holman has been tied in with faces in Portsmouth. How current that might be we can't be sure about, not yet at least. We know that the relationship at home wasn't working. We know, or we think we know, that he's coming on to his stepdaughter, who's a pretty girl, and from what Jimmy's saying we think that the boyfriend might have a thing or two to say about that.'

'So you think he might have motive?'

'To burn the house down? With his girlfriend inside?' He shook his head. 'No way.'

'I agree. So where next?'

'Scenes of Crime have come up with an interesting lead that relates to the previous Wednesday. It seems Holman had been in touch with a clinic in London. Sexual dysfunction.'

Suttle blinked. This was new to him. Faraday explained about the advert the CSI had retrieved from the office in the barn.

'Has anyone actioned this?'

Faraday nodded. A D/C in Suttle's intel cell had been in touch with the clinic. They weren't prepared to go into details but confirmed that Holman had attended for an afternoon session on the Wednesday.

'And then he came home again?'

'They couldn't say. Our next sighting is the Thursday morning. Local CID talked to the postman first thing Monday. He says he delivered a parcel on the Thursday and Holman signed for it.'

Suttle nodded. He'd read the statement only last night. 'He also said that Holman stank of horse shit,' he said, ' which made a change because he normally stank of booze. Plus he'd obviously been doing something pretty physical because he told the postie he was knackered.'

'And the inference is?' Parsons was lost.

'There's a big hole at the back of the property,'

Faraday explained. 'Someone had been digging and we think they may have had to shift a load of horse manure first.'

'Why?'

'Good question.' Suttle again. 'We're going to re-interview the postman. See if he remembers any strange vehicle. It's a punt, but you never know.'

'And you'll ask him about the Friday too? If he delivered there that day?'

'Obviously.'

Parsons wanted to know more about the hole. How big it was. What it might have contained. Suttle paced it out on the office floor. Parsons was impressed.

'Fair size.' She frowned. 'So Holman goes to London on the Wednesday to this clinic. Something's not working for him, something's wrong with his willy. Is that a fair assumption?'

'I'd say so.' Faraday was smiling at last.

'He then comes home and starts moving this pile of horse shit. Big pile? Small pile?'

Faraday was trying to visualise the scabs of sodden manure. They'd been scattered everywhere, exactly the way you'd do it if you were in a hurry.

'There was a lot,' he said. 'Certainly enough to cover what may have been underneath.'

Suttle nodded. 'And cover the scent too.'

'Scent. Ah . . .' Parsons was beaming now. 'Are we all on the same page here? Horse manure? Something stashed underneath? Big hole? House burns down a day or two later? Four bodies inside? Are we getting warm?'

'Warm', under the circumstances, was unfortunate. Suttle and Faraday exchanged glances. In some past life Parsons must have been a bloodhound or a Labrador. Once she got a sniff, nothing put her off. A stash of something valuable. Valuable enough to justify four homicides.

Suttle was still looking at Faraday, who seemed to be perking up.

'Have you mentioned Winter, boss?'

'*Winter?*' Parsons' eyes were gleaming now. 'Where does he come into this?'

'We're not sure.' Faraday was checking his watch. 'He contacted Suttle first thing this morning. He wants to come across for some reason. He wants a little chat.'

'Does he know about the fire? About us?'

'I imagine he must. It's been all over the media.'

'So what's his interest?'

'Difficult to say unless we meet him.'

'We?'

'Jimmy. It's Jimmy he wants to talk to.'

'I see.' Parsons was appraising this new development, studying it from every angle.

At her command level, thought Faraday, life was one long risk assessment. 'Anything to do with that man is a problem,' she said at last. 'Just ask Mr Willard.'

Detective Chief Superintendent Willard, like Faraday himself, had been badly burned by Winter on a number of occasions. Since the D/C's defection to the Dark Side he'd avoided trap after trap, much to the Head of CID's disgust. The temptation to nail him was still there, though. Not least because Winter offered a key to putting Mackenzie away.

Parsons was still weighing the odds.

'You both know him, yes?'

'We do.' Faraday nodded. 'Jimmy trained under

him. I used to be his boss.'

'But I take it you don't meet socially?'

'No.' Suttle shook his head.

'Never?'

'Never. I like the man.' It was Faraday. 'I've always liked the man. But you're right. He has an agenda. And it isn't ours.'

'Well put.' Parsons turned to him. 'So what do you suggest we do, Joe?'

'About Winter?'

'Yes.'

Faraday gazed at her. For the last hour or so he'd had *Gosling* under control. Things were progressing at a reasonable pace. One action was folding neatly into another. They had the beginnings of a timeline. And now, with the speculation about the hole, they had some clue as to motive. Drugs? A decent stash of cocaine? Holman maybe liquidating a pension he'd been hoarding for a while, or even babysitting a consignment for someone else?

'What do we do about Winter?' Parsons was getting impatient.

'I think we run with him. See what he's got to say. He's fronting for Mackenzie. He has to be.'

'Exactly. And might that not play to our advantage?'

Faraday nodded.

There was a knock at the door. It was the Outside Enquiries D/S. He'd just taken a call from the pathologist. Simon Pembury had some news that might be of interest.

'And?' It was Parsons, her face upturned.

'They've finished checking the bodies against dental records.' He was still looking at Faraday. 'It turns out none of them are Johnny Holman.'

Chapter Seven

TUESDAY, 10 FEBRUARY 2009. *18.46*

Kieron O'Dwyer lived with his Auntie Karen, a spinster in her fifties who was a keen spiritualist. On Tuesday evenings she attended a meeting at her local Temple. Kieron, newly released from the custody suite at Central police station, was playing Grand Theft Auto 3 on a games console he'd lifted from a kid down the road.

At first he ignored the knock on the front door. His auntie had some weird friends, skinny old blokes her own age who banged on about messages from outer space and talking to their dead mums. Then he remembered some mates who'd texted him earlier. Maybe they'd scored some dosh from somewhere. Maybe they could all pick up where they'd left off.

He parked Grand Theft on hold and went through to the bedroom at the front. He peered down but the angle was tight and he couldn't see anyone at the front door. Then came the knock again. The alarm clock beside the single bed said ten to seven. Had to be Connor and Riley. Had to be.

Kieron clattered downstairs and opened the front door. For a split second he glimpsed a face above the Adidas track top. Then the face disappeared inside a khaki balaclava. There was someone else on the doorstep too, much bigger, the face already hidden. He felt a hand grab his throat as he fell sideways. The back of his head smashed against the wall. The hand was squeezing tighter and tighter. Flailing with his arms and legs, he began to choke.

Moments later, pinned against the wall in the front room, Kieron watched the smaller of the two men pull the curtains tight. He was trying to yell but nothing seemed to work. The big guy still had him by the throat. He stank of aftershave. Calvin Klein.

The smaller one turned on the table light beside the telly. He dumped an Asda bag on the floor and then came across. The chokehold slackened. Kieron waited until the little guy was in range and then kicked him as hard as he could, just under the knee. Big mistake.

The little guy paused. The hand around his throat was squeezing and squeezing and the room was going a funny grey colour. The big guy's weight was pressed against his body and he could hear him breathing hard. Semi-conscious, he felt himself being pulled away from the wall. Then, with a deft twist, the big guy was behind him. Both his arms were bent double behind his back, his fists pinned between his shoulder blades. Colour was flooding back into the room. It felt like his arms were popping out of their sockets. He screamed with the pain.

The little guy had found some gloves from somewhere. They looked like boxing gloves, only smaller, lighter. He stopped rubbing his leg and pulled the gloves on. Then he came very close, the balaclava inches from his face. His voice was low, barely a whisper.

'I'm gonna say this once, my friend. You've got to stop twatting about. You understand me?'

Kieron tried to muster some kind of reply. Couldn't. The guy had the scariest eyes he'd ever seen. Cold. Blue. Unblinking. He was testing the gloves, flexing the fingers, making himself comfortable.

'What I'm gonna do now is break your jaw. It's gonna hurt like fuck for a couple of weeks, and just in case you don't get the message I'm gonna do the other side as well. Best to keep your mouth closed, son. Otherwise you might bite your tongue off. You hear me?'

Kieron nodded. It was all he could do. Keep your mouth closed. Shit.

The little guy took a step back. The tiny nod of warning must have been meant for the bloke behind him. He felt the grip on his arms tighten. He couldn't take his eyes off the man in the balaclava. The way he positioned his body. How light he was on his feet. How perfectly balanced.

Then, as if from nowhere, came an explosion of pain, a blinding white light that reached into every corner of his brain. His face wasn't a face any more, just a big fat crater full of scalding water. He felt his body sag. He could taste his own blood. The guy behind him propped him up, got him ready again. He lifted his head, tried to plead for mercy, tried to say sorry, tried to do any fucking thing to stop the pain. Then came the second blow, the other side of his face, another meteor hit, another explosion, more lights in the darkness.

The floor came up to meet him. He felt himself fighting for air, the way you might if you were underwater, his grasp of time and distance gone. His stomach was heaving. He was trying to throw up through the wreckage of his mouth. Very close, a voice in his ear, the warmth of someone's breath.

'Don't even think of going to the Filth. Otherwise

we'll do it again. Yeah?'

He tried to nod but it hurt too much. Far away he heard the front door open and then close. Everything was a blur. He tried to focus. The Asda bag was inches from his face. On top, some kind of leaving present.

He shut his eyes, started to cry. Some time later, he didn't know when, he managed to move, managed to reach for the bag, managed to make sense of whatever it was they'd left. A can of mushroom soup. With a single straw.

* * *

Faraday rode the hovercraft back to Southsea, bumping and bucking across the darkness of the Solent. A taxi on the Southsea side took him home, where he showered and changed. By half past seven he was heading west on the motorway. Salisbury, at this time in the evening, was less than an hour away.

He'd found time during the day to put a couple of calls through to Gabrielle. On the first occasion she'd been on divert. When he tried again, mid-afternoon, they'd had a brief, strained conversation. She was at the hospital with Leila. The little girl was asleep. She'd had to step outside to take Faraday's call. She needed to be back beside the bed in case Leila woke up. Faraday said he understood. He was planning to drive up this evening to see her. Where might she be?

This news seemed to take Gabrielle by surprise. At first she said she'd be at the hospital. Then she changed her mind and gave him the name of the bed and breakfast where she was staying. It was called the Avon View. Finally, when Faraday said he'd try and be there by half eight, she told him to come to the hospital. There was a big car park at the back, she said. Then just follow the signs to the Burns Unit.

The turn off the motorway was a few miles beyond Southampton. From here the road headed due north. Too late Faraday spotted the traffic queue ahead. The A36 was notorious for high-speed accidents. Already trapped by a stream of vehicles behind, he knew he could be here for some time.

He pulled the Mondeo to a halt. Since leaving the island he'd done his best to forget the million decisions he'd left on his desk in the Major Incident Room. Parsons had returned to the mainland in mid-afternoon, due at a cold-case review at headquarters in Winchester. The news about Holman had tied *Gosling* in knots. If he hadn't died in the fire, then where was he? And just who was the fourth unidentified body?

In Faraday's view the latter question was the key to everything, and he'd instructed Suttle to re-interview the taxi driver who'd driven the younger daughter home on the Saturday night. This was a priority action and Suttle himself had driven across to Newport to knock the guy up. He worked regular night shifts throughout the week and spent most of the day in bed.

Suttle had checked in an hour or so later. The taxi driver remembered another vehicle parked beside Holman's Land Rover when he'd dropped the girl off. He couldn't be absolutely certain but he thought it might have been a Corsa. Robbie Gifford, Kim's boyfriend, drove a Corsa. Odds on, he'd been at Monkswell Farm that night, protecting his beloved against her predatory stepfather.

Faraday had put a call through to the pathologist. Pembury's phone had been on divert so he'd left a message with Difford's details and asked him to access the boy's dental records. Pembury had yet to come back, but Faraday sensed already that the fourth body had to be Robbie Difford.

Quite where that would leave *Gosling* was anyone's guess. There was still plenty of room for some kind of narco involvement but the real question mark hung over Johnny Holman. Intel enquiries generated by Jimmy Suttle were now reaching deep into the Pompey underworld and word had come back that seemed to tie him to a woman called Lou Sadler.

According to Suttle, Sadler ran an escort agency called Two's Company from premises in Cowes, servicing the classier end of the market. She imported girls from the Baltic states, chiefly Estonia and Latvia, paid them well and kept her clientele extremely happy. Suttle had talked to a fellow D/S in the Southampton Vice Squad. He said that Sadler peddled her wares to visiting businessmen on the mainland, a handful of regulars on the island and minted yachtie types during Cowes Week. When Suttle mentioned Holman, the Vice Squad D/S had laughed. She gives him a little treat from time to time, he'd said. He's a lucky boy, that Johnny Holman.

The traffic jam was inching forward. Ahead, in the far distance, Faraday could see a flashing blue light. His mobile lay on the passenger seat beside him. Should he phone Gabrielle again? Warn her he wouldn't make it by half eight? He decided against it. Maybe he could make up the lost time once he was free of the jam. Maybe she'd hang on at the hospital, give him a hug, tell him how much she'd missed him. Maybe.

He sank a little deeper into the worn seat, all too aware he'd lost control of this relationship he'd treasured. They'd been together for more than three years now, ever since that first meeting. He'd sat beside her on a local bus deep in the back country near the Burmese border. Faraday had been in Thailand for a couple of weeks, entranced by the smells and sounds of the jungle. It lay like a thick green pelt over the mountains flanking the valley of the River Kwai, and he remembered telling her about the treks he'd made, camping rough, and the deafening chorus of birdsong that greeted each new dawn. He remembered the way she'd listened to his description of a white-throated kingfisher he'd spotted looking for frogs in a paddy field, and he remembered as well the quick grace of her smile when he'd showed her some shots of the bird on his camera. The way she shaded her eyes against the glare of the sun. The way her fingers had rested so briefly on his peeling arm.

Gabrielle had been on a solo journey of her own, a chance to duck back into real life after six months cooped up in her apartment in Chartres, desperately trying to finish a book. She was an anthropologist by trade, scouting remote areas of the planet, happy in her own company, and Faraday knew within minutes that he'd fallen in love. She was a good deal younger than he was, but they shared the same sense of curiosity, the same hunger to open new doors in their lives. They'd swapped phone numbers on the bus and later that week they'd met again. Back home he'd half-drowned her in a torrent of emails. With them he'd sent trophy photos from his jungle treks.

Later, at her invitation, he'd gone over to France. She had an old VW camper van, and from Chartres they'd motored south, criss-crossing the remoter corners of the Massif Central, Faraday trying to figure out exactly what he'd done to deserve such happiness. One night, camping *au sauvage* beside the headwaters of the Dordogne, he'd asked her whether she felt the same. She'd reached up for him, kissed him, nodded.

'*Oui*,' she'd murmured. '*Pourquoi pas?*'

Why not? At the time he'd put the phrase down to a perfect sunset and too much wine, but now—years later—he was beginning to wonder. They'd made a decent life for themselves at the Bargemaster's House, excitement and novelty hardening into something more permanent. To Faraday, the relationship had felt closer and more real than anything he'd ever experienced, yet he knew that parts of this extraordinary woman would always remain beyond reach. With Gabrielle, he realised, you took nothing for granted, and when the invitation arrived from Montreal for a two-semester attachment at McGill University, he knew with absolute certainty that she'd say yes.

Alone once again, bound hand and foot by a job he increasingly viewed with near-despair, he'd missed her desperately. Night after night, week after week, he'd asked himself whether any relationship was worth this kind of torment. And then, with Faraday on the point of locking the door and shutting her out of his life, Gabrielle had returned. She said she'd missed him. She said she was glad to be home with her grumpy old *flic.* She had plans for another book. Faraday, sick of his own company, told himself he was the luckiest man on the planet. As autumn gave way to winter, and rafts of brent geese came and went on the harbour beyond the big picture windows, he made plans for a Christmas like no other. Hence the trip to the Middle East.

Faraday consulted his watch. Nearly quarter past eight. He picked up his phone and hit one of the presets. Suttle answered within seconds. Winter had been in touch barely minutes ago. He'd be on the next hovercraft. They were going to meet at a pub on the seafront. Was Faraday having second thoughts?

'Not at all. Just a couple of things, though.'

'Yeah?'

'Don't tell him about the excavation. All we've got is four bodies and the scene from hell. No hole round the back. No evidence of digging. None of that stuff.'

'And Holman?'

'Tell him we're still assuming Holman's dead. If Winter's after early thoughts, which he will be, we're starting to wonder about a bunch of intruders wanting to settle some debt or other.'

'But no hole?'

'No hole.'

* * *

Winter stepped out of the hovercraft. The taint of fuel hung in thechill night air and propeller wash blew curls of seaweed across the tarmac. It had been raining again and he avoided the larger puddles, following a fat woman towing a huge case towards the terminal building.

The pub was a couple of minutes away, a big Victorian alehouse advertising a curry and a pint for £5.99. Winter pushed inside. Suttle was in a booth towards the back. To Winter's delight, a pint of Stella was waiting for him.

'Cheers, son.' Winter unzipped his leather jacket and hung it carefully on the back of the chair. 'Present from Marie, if you're wondering.'

'I'm not. How are you?'

'Starving. They do food here or do we eat later?'

'Whatever.' Suttle shrugged. 'I'm on the meter.'

They sparred for a minute or two. Suttle had never hidden his disgust about the journey Winter had made. He agreed that the Job got harder by the day, but that was no reason to rat on your mates. Mackenzie was an evil little scrote, and nothing would ever change that. Not a million-quid house in Craneswater. Not a Bentley in the garage. Not the likes of the *Guardian* getting suckered by Tide Turn Trust.

'You finished, son?'

'Just thought I'd mention it.'

'And you saw the piece in the *Guardian*?'

'Lizzie read me the best bits on the phone. She's like me, Lizzie. Loves a good fairy tale.'

'Son . . .' Winter reached for his drink. 'Like it or not, you're looking at the next Mr Pompey. Bazza wants it. And what Bazza wants he normally gets. Cheers. Here's to crime.'

Winter went to the bar and ordered cod and chips. When he got back, Suttle was looking at his watch.

'How long have we got, son?'

'Twenty minutes. Tops. I'm due back at the ranch

for a meeting at nine.' He reached for his own drink. 'Happy days.'

Winter wanted to know about Johnny Holman.

'The guy's dead, am I right?'

'As far as we know.'

'Is that confirmed?'

'Pretty much.'

'What does that mean, son?'

'It means that we've done the PM, looked for non-existent fingerprints, sent off a DNA swab for analysis, applied for his dental records. He's the right sex, right shape. Plus he lived there.'

'Means nothing.'

'We can put him in the property at one in the morning.'

'Who says?'

'A taxi driver. Delivered one of the daughters back home. Holman was the one who ponied up the fare.'

'Right.' Winter nodded, thoughtful. 'So who'd want to kill him?'

'Good question. And since you're here—' Suttle smiled '—what do *you* think?'

'I don't know, son. What's the scene telling you? All those guys you've got on site?'

Suttle didn't answer. Since Faraday's phone call he'd been thinking hard about Winter. There had to be a reason he was here. Nail down the exact nature of his interest and *Gosling* might take a giant step forward.

'The scene's telling us fuck all,' he said at last. 'Whoever torched the place knew exactly what they were doing. If you want to talk evidence, we're looking at about a ton and a half of sludge. These people even got the weather right. First the fire brigade dump a thousand gallons of water on the place. Then it never stops raining. To be honest, I think we're stuffed.'

'People?' Winter didn't miss a trick.

'Person or persons unknown. You know all about Holman. This is a guy who's spent half his life in dodgy company. I haven't a clue who he's been upsetting lately but it might have been wise to wind his neck in.'

'You think this is some kind of slapping?'

'No, it's got be more than that.'

'Like what then? Why would anyone set fire to four people?'

'No idea.'

'You're lying, son. Do me a favour, eh? Just pretend I've got a brain in my head. You're right about Holman. In the day he had his fingers in all kinds of pies. But that's history. Since the accident he's done nothing but piss his life away. He might have run up a decent bill at Thresher's. They might be after a cheque or two. But they ain't gonna burn his fucking house down.'

'Thresher's, eh?' Suttle was grinning now. 'We ought to give you your job back. Busy tomorrow, are you?'

'Fuck off, son. Treat me like a grown-up. I'm telling you what you know already.'

'And what's that?'

'Holman crossed someone. And that someone was upset enough to kill him. The question is why?'

'Maybe you should ask that boss of yours.'

'Why should I do that?'

'Because they've been talking recently.'

'How do you know?'

'How do you think I fucking know?'

Winter nodded. Suttle was right. There were a million ways the guys on Major Crime could help themselves to bits of Holman's life. Phone records. Bank statements. Even intercepts if he'd qualified for sneaky-beaky.

Suttle was watching him carefully.

'You didn't know about Mackenzie and Holman?'

'You're winding me up.'

'You think so?'

'I know it.'

'How?'

'Because Mackenzie pays me to know. And if I knew, I wouldn't be sitting here talking to you.'

'Fishing expedition, is it?'

'Fuck off.'

'It *is* a fishing expedition. You know something . . .' He beckoned Winter closer. 'If I were you I'd go home to that nice Mr M and ask him why he never told you about Holman.'

'Told me what?'

'Just ask him. Just put the question. And then ask him why he pays you all that money and *still* keeps you out of the loop.' His hand closed over Winter's. He gave it a little squeeze. 'You get that for free, mate. One for the old days, yeah?'

Winter stared at him. For once in his life the uncertainty was showing in his face and he knew it. He stood up, slipped on the leather jacket, ignored the girl from the kitchen approaching with a plate of cod and chips.

'Been a pleasure, son,' he muttered. 'As always.'

Chapter Eight

TUESDAY, 10 FEBRUARY 2009. *21.27*

It was nearly half past nine by the time Faraday got to Salisbury. He followed directions to the district hospital and came to a halt in the huge car park at the back of the complex. At this time of night the building was nearly empty, the last dribble of visitors queuing to pay their tickets at the machine.

The hospital looked brand new. Faraday found his way inside and took the stairs to Level 4. A long broad corridor stretched ahead, not a person in sight. He had no idea if he could get into the Burns Unit at this time of night but he was determined to try.

The entrance to the unit lay to the right. The two swing doors were locked. Through the window Faraday could see another corridor disappearing into the ward. There was no sign of anyone. Beside the door was an entryphone. He buzzed twice. Nothing. He waited a full minute for someone to answer then buzzed again. At length a nurse appeared. She studied him through the glass, then opened the door an inch or two.

Faraday introduced himself, apologised for the lateness of the hour, asked whether a woman called Gabrielle was still inside.

'The French lady?'

'Yes.'

'I'm afraid not. She went about half an hour ago.'

'I see.' Faraday checked his watch. 'Was she going back to theB & B?'

'I don't know. She didn't say.'

'Did she leave a message at all?'

'Not to my knowledge.'

'OK.' He was looking beyond her. There was another figure in the corridor, an older man, checking everything was OK. 'The little girl, Leila. How is she?'

'I'm afraid I can't give you information like that. You'd have to ask the sister in charge.'

'Is she here?'

'She is but she's busy just now.'

'OK.' Faraday toyed with pushing the conversation a little further, offering to wait until the sister was free, but decided against it. He'd come to see Gabrielle, not start a ruck with the National Health Service. He gave the nurse a nod and turned on his heel, hearing the sigh of the door as it closed behind him.

In the Mondeo he fired up his satnav. The Avon View was down the road. Minutes later, spotting the name, he parked at the kerbside and killed the engine. A bus whined past, empty except for a single passenger. Faraday looked up at the house. It was a decent size. Once it might have served as a family home. Now, upstairs, a single light. He pulled his coat around him. He felt cold and uncertain. This was a long way from the Burmese border.

He phoned Gabrielle from the crescent of gravel in front of the house. He explained he was outside and looked up at the window, half-expecting her shadow to appear against the curtain. Her room was at the back, she said. She'd be down *tout de suite*.

Faraday waited. The wind tasted of rain again.

Far away, the hoot of an owl.

The front door opened. Gabrielle was wearing a dressing gown he didn't recognise. She must have been in Salisbury since getting back from El Arish, he thought.

'Mind if I come in?'

He stepped inside without waiting for an answer. She closed the door behind him. No kiss. No hug of welcome.

'This way, *chéri*.'

He followed her up the stairs. There was a smell of furniture polish and cheap air freshener. Cold.

Her room was tucked away in a kind of annexe. She'd left the door open. The single bed was unmade, light from the corridor throwing soft shadows over the rumpled sheets. Gabrielle's rucksack lay abandoned on the chair beneath the window. Various bits of clothing were draped over the back of the chair. On the shelf beside the bed, a copy of *The Seven Pillars of Wisdom.* Faraday had found it in a bookshop in Aqaba. She'd nearly got to the end.

Gabrielle turned the light on and gestured round. She was camping here, she said. She was always apologising to the cleaner for the mess but she hadn't had time to do anything about it. Most nights, like now, she just wanted to go to bed. Faraday nodded. The message was clear: he was an intruder.

He sat down on the bed, looked up at her. He wanted to cry. Knew he mustn't.

'I've missed you,' he said.

'I know. I'm sorry.'

'You *know*?' He blinked. None of this made sense. The not phoning. The not being there. The not sharing this secret life she'd suddenly decided to make her own.

She sat down beside him. He felt her hand over his. It was the touch of a mother or a nurse, a small obligatory gesture of comfort. He took his hand away. Anything but this, he thought.

He looked sideways at her, two passengers on a train going nowhere, robbed of conversation, robbed of everything.

'So what's happening?' he said. 'What's going on?'

'You know what it is, *chéri.*'

'I don't. I should but I don't. So why don't you tell me?'

He felt a small hard pebble of anger deep in his belly. He tried to ignore it. Failed completely.

Gabrielle had pulled the dressing gown more tightly around her. She looked pale and thin but the bruising from the accident had gone. Leila, she explained, had been back to the operating theatre for another change of dressings. The staff were lovely to her, the doctors too, but they didn't hide how serious her condition was. Burns were horrible, especially these kinds of burns, and the *phosphore* had made things worse. The Israelis, she said, were *des salopards.* They'd killed without mercy, without even thinking about it, and the worst of it all was kids like Leila, hundreds of them, marked for life, inside and out.

'*Des salopards*,' she repeated. Nasty bastards.

Faraday felt himself nodding. He'd never seen her like this, so angry, so intense. Maybe this explained a little about the last month or so. What had happened in Gaza had swamped her little boat. She was oblivious to everything else.

'So what's going to happen?' he said again. 'As far as Leila is concerned?'

'*J'sais pas, chéri.*' She was staring at her hands. 'She has a translator with her, Riham. She talks to Riham a little. Riham says she wants to go home.'

'Of course. She would.'

'But to what? *Gaza est complètement détruit.* Wrecked. Her family too. *Morte.*' Dead. Gone.

'All of them?'

'I think so.'

'Do you *know* that?'

Her head came up and she looked at him.

'You talk to me like a *flic.*'

'I am a *flic.*'

'*Alors.*' She shrugged. 'So maybe she has an aunt, an uncle, I don't know. If she gets better . . .' She shrugged again. '*J'sais pas.*'

Faraday knew how important it was to keep talking. On the floor, half hidden by a Médecins Sans Frontières T-shirt, he'd spotted another book. *Arabic for Beginners.*

'So what are the options?' he said quietly. 'If she doesn't go home?'

Gabrielle shook her head. She didn't want to answer, didn't want to think about it. She went to the hospital every day. She was there first thing in the morning to be with Leila when she woke up. In the afternoon, when she slept, she'd take the bus down into Salisbury. She'd found a little delicatessen where she could buy halloumi cheese and baklava and figs, tastes the little girl would recognise, little treats that might help build a bridge between them. The staff had a special fridge to keep stuff like this. Leila liked stories too.

'Who reads to her?' Faraday's gaze had returned

to the book on the floor.

'Riham. You know what Riham means in Arabic, *chéri*? It means a fine rain that lasts for ever. Isn't that beautiful?' For the first time she was smiling. Faraday wanted to kiss her. Instead, he took her hand. It was cold, stiff, unresponsive.

Faraday asked her how long Leila would spend in the unit. Gabrielle frowned. The doctors were saying a month at least, probably longer. It depended on the antibiotics they were giving her. The burns were badly infected. She was already weak.

'And afterwards? When she comes out of hospital?'

Another silence. Then another shake of the head.

'I don't know, *chéri*. You tell me.'

'Me? *Me* tell you?'

'*Oui*.' She nodded and then summoned a small brave smile. 'She could be ours, *chéri*. This little girl.'

* * *

Winter took a cab to Craneswater. Sandown Road was one of a handful of leafy avenues off the quieter end of Southsea seafront. Ownership of one of these big Edwardian villas conferred a certain status in what passed for the upper reaches of Portsmouth society. It meant you were successful, probably white and almost certainly wealthy. Bazza Mackenzie, to his immense satisfaction, ticked all three boxes.

Winter, still angry, settled his cab fare and turned to look at the house. Unusually for this time of night the big metal security gates were still open. Beyond, beside Mackenzie's Bentley, were two other cars he hadn't seen before. One was a Mercedes coupé, the other an Audi. He gave the nearest of Mackenzie's CCTV cameras a curt nod and walked to the front door.

Marie let him in. She knew at once that Winter had something to get off his chest.

'We're still having dinner.' She looked him in the eye and then gave him a kiss. 'Come and join us.'

Winter followed her into the dining room. Faces turned briefly towards the door before the buzz of conversation resumed again. Mackenzie was deep in conversation with a sleek thirty-something across the table. Designer jeans, crisp white collarless shirt, winter tan, a hint of stubble. Leo Kinder.

Winter found himself a chair and sat down. Mackenzie pushed the bottle of Remy Martin in his direction.

'Leo here thinks we're sitting on a gold mine. And he thinks we're about to cash in big time. Isn't that right, Leo?'

'Politically . . .' Kinder nodded. 'Yes.'

Kinder favoured Winter with his soft brown smile. Winter hadn't trusted him from the off. Too smooth. Almost feline.

'How does that work then?' he heard himself say.

'Politics is all about catching the tide, Paul. Just now I get the sense that the tide's running in our favour. You know something's happening when papers like the *Guardian* come knocking on your door. This stuff's viral. If they take us seriously then word spreads.'

Winter loved the way he said 'us'. A couple of months ago no one in this house had ever heard of Leo Kinder.

'*GQ*, mush.' Mackenzie was grinning fit to bust. 'Leo says they're up for a big piece for some spring special they're planning. And it doesn't stop there, eh, Leo?'

'By no means.' The smile again. 'Since the *Guardian*, the phone's been ringing non-stop. Everyone wants a piece of what Baz has to say. I'm telling them to form an orderly queue at the door. This stuff's free. It doesn't cost us a cent. Plus editorial is the best kicker of all. You can't buy this kind of coverage, no way. It's the old story, Paul. The right time and the right place. Like I say, all we have to do is ride the tide.'

'You're a sweetie, Leo, you really are. I love your optimism. I love your *faith.* No wonder the Tories kicked you out. But where's all this stuff going to take you?'

The question came from a woman at the end of the table. She was Kinder's age, maybe a year or two older. She had a lean gym-honed face and the scoop-neck T-shirt beneath the linen jacket would have kept Mackenzie happy all evening. The Mercedes, thought Winter. Fashionably black.

'Selina,' Marie did the introductions, 'meet Paul. Paul Winter.'

Winter noted the flash of recognition in her eyes. There wasn't a particle of warmth in her smile. She was still waiting for an answer from Kinder. Tarting around with the likes of the *Guardian* was fine, and well done for blagging the interview, but politics was part of the retail business these days, so what exactly did Mr Pompey have to sell?

'There's a hole in the market, Selina, a niche we can fill. The old Labour core vote has given up on this lot. They're white, lots of them are skint, jobs are hard to find. They've been around a while and they quite liked Mr Blair in the early days, but he turned out to be a Tory so that pissed them off. Brown's let them down even more. He's Blair without the charm. These people are lost. They're in the fucking wilderness. So where do they go?'

'The BNP, if they've got any sense.'

'They hate the BNP. It's in their DNA. And you know something else? They hate politicians too. That's New Labour's great achievement, *numero uno*. They've debauched the currency. And I'm not talking money. We need a new kind of politician, someone recognisably human, someone in touch, someone with a bit of guile, a bit of experience. Someone who's been out there and made a quid or two and knows the way things work. We used to call them Tories, but these days even the Conservatives are New Labour clones. So there you are. You've had it up to here with politicians, you think they're all a waste of space, but the country still has to muddle through. So where do you spend your vote? Who gets to catch your eye?'

His hand extended across the table towards Mackenzie, an almost courtly gesture of introduction. Bazza, unusually gracious, offered a nod in acknowledgement. Very papal.

Selina wasn't convinced. 'So it doesn't end with Pompey? Is that what you're saying?'

'I'm saying the time is right to start thinking laterally. For my sins I keep my ear to the ground. Like I say, politicians are damaged goods already, but the way I hear it, things in that department may well get a whole lot worse.'

The credit crunch, he said, had pushed the bankers against the wall. The government had bailed them out with oodles of public money and they knew they were in for a caning. No more fat year-end bonuses. Loads of regulation. Their greedy hands tied firmly behind their backs.

'And there's something wrong with all that?'

'Not at all.' He smiled at her. 'Unless you're a banker.'

To his certain knowledge, he said, a CD had been acquired from a back office in the House of Commons which contained details of MPs' expenses. The bankers had footed the bill for the CD and were now trying to figure out the best way of making this stuff public.

'Getting your revenge in first?' It was Bazza.

'Exactly. These guys are bright. They didn't get rich by accident. They eat politicians for breakfast.'

Selina wanted to know what was on the CD. Kinder shrugged. He'd seen some extracts, bait to tempt the major broadsheets, and by bankers' standards the sums were pathetic. But that wasn't the point. The Brits loved being outraged. Few people ever bothered with the small print, and it would be child's play to tar every MP with the same brush. Evil grasping bastards. Every last one of them.

Selina was intrigued. She, like everyone else in the room, had never heard of this impending media storm.

'So when is this going to happen?'

'Give it a couple of months or so. Whichever paper does the deal will need to be lawyered up. And believe me, lawyers take their time.'

There was laughter around the table. Kinder himself was a lawyer. Lizzie Hodson had said so.

'OK.' There was a hint of admiration in Selina's

grin. 'So all politicians are doomed. And about bloody time. But where does that leave our candidate? What do you stand for, Baz? Where are you going to take us all?'

It was a big question, and Winter knew it was far too late in the evening for Mackenzie to tussle with the mighty issues of the day. Whatever thoughts he had about Afghanistan, global credit flows, the EU, climate change or even—God help him—local government remained a total mystery. But that wasn't the point. What mattered, he said, was this town of theirs.

Pompey was in danger of becoming a disgrace. There were people out there, he said, I wouldn't even wipe my arse on. People with no sense of history, of civic pride, of what it really meant to be living in one of the UK's greatest cities. These were people who did fuck all except keep their heads down and their noses clean, and feather their own nests. To them Fratton Park was a bit of grass and a bunch of tulips, somewhere to walk their fucking dog. They'd given up on armies of students running riot, and litter all over the fucking street, and the council spending squillions of quid on poncy art installations. The place needed a shake, he said, and he'd be only to happy to oblige. Then would come a dose or two of the old medicine, pick-me-ups that his own mum and dad would recognise. Proper care for the old folk. An open-doors programme for Pompey's heritage. Lots of money into sport. New stadium for the football club. And a bit of serious discipline in the classroom.

Selina appeared spellbound. When Mackenzie came to a halt she mimed a silent round of applause. At first Winter assumed this was ironic, that she was taking the piss, but watching her he decided that she probably meant it. This is someone, he thought, who loves grabbing the inside track. She's heard about Bazza. She knows exactly where the money's come from. She gets a little jolt of excitement from an evening with Pompey's favourite gangster. And now it occurs to her that Bad Bazza might be serious and that—far more importantly—this crazy thing might just work.

The evening broke up shortly afterwards. These were busy people. After tomorrow's 6 a.m. session at the gym there'd doubtless be more meetings, more flesh to press, more networking. Marie saw them both to the door. Bazza told them to look out for themselves. Then he grabbed the bottle of Remy and towed Winter into the den.

'Face like thunder, mush. What's the problem?'

Winter didn't answer. The poster on the wall was new: Tony Adams and the first team posing in front of the Fratton End. Adams was Pompey's ex-manager. Someone, presumably Bazza, had obliterated his face with a red Pentel.

'What does SB mean?'

'Sad bastard. A squillion straight games without a win. A rock round our necks would have been cheaper.' He offered the Remy. 'You gonna give me grief or what?'

Winter declined more brandy. 'Who's Selina?' he said.

'Selina Price. Finger in every fucking pie you can name. Nothing moves in this city without the nod from her. Awesome woman. So what's the problem, mush? You're not talking to me.'

'I went to the island, did some poking around, just

like you wanted.'

'Yeah?' Mackenzie looked genuinely surprised. Maybe he's forgotten, Winter thought. Maybe all these political fantasies have gone to his head.

'Johnny Holman?' Winter said. 'That farm of his?'

'Yeah, yeah . . . and?'

'I was right. The Old Bill are crawling all over it. MCT are involved as well.'

'MCT?'

'Major Crime Team.'

'So what have they found?'

'I don't know, Baz. What do you think they've found?'

The balloon of Remy was halfway to Mackenzie's mouth. It stopped. At last Winter sensed he had the man's full attention.

'What sort of fucking question is that, mush?'

'I don't know, Baz. You tell me to get my arse over there. You tell me to knock up the odd contact or two. But like always you don't tell me why.'

'Why?' Mackenzie put the glass down. '*Why?* Johnny Holman was a mate of mine in case I never mentioned it. Mates in this town are important. In fact this town *is* fucking mates. The guy's been all over the place these last few years. Made a fucking spectacle of himself, poor bastard. In those situations you help out. Who do you think kept them going when the money ran out? Who bunged Julie a grand or two from time to time so she could keep Johnny in beers? Who got them all out to Spain for a fortnight in one of the apartments? Me, mush. And why? Because the guy was a mate. And now he'sgone.'

'So you've been in touch with him recently? Is

that what you're telling me?'

'Yeah. Absolutely. You want a date? I haven't a clue. But where I come from, getting in touch is what you do. You have a problem with that?'

Winter shook his head. He was thinking of Jimmy Suttle. Not a wind-up after all.

'So what did you sort out over there?' Bazza still hadn't touched the Remy.

'Not a great deal. I talked to the lad Suttle.' Bazza knew Suttle from way back.

'And?'

'He's driving the intelligence cell.'

'What does that mean in English?'

'It means it's his job to try and work out why anyone would want to burn Holman's house down.'

'And?'

'They're thinking intruders. Someone after something. Or maybe someone settling a debt. Either way Suttle gets to start looking hard at Holman's associates.'

'I bet.'

'That includes you, Baz.'

'Us, mush.'

'So . . .' Winter shrugged '. . . are we clean on this one? Nothing to hide? Only now's the time, Baz.'

'Yeah?' He tipped his head back. 'You know something, mush? There are cunts in this city, straight cunts, who just love people like us. Them two clowns tonight couldn't wait to come round here for dinner. And you know why? Because we're bad. Because we broke the rules. Because we made lots and lots of moolah and didn't do what Johnny did, didn't piss it up against the wall. That makes us a bit special, a bit exciting. Weird, isn't it?'

Winter nodded. He'd been right about Selina

Price.

'You're not answering the question, Baz. Just tell me you didn't do anything silly with Johnny Holman.'

'What does Suttle think?'

'I don't know. He wouldn't tell me.'

'And what do you think?'

'I think what I always think. I think what I thought this morning. I think it's time to go out and talk to a few people.'

'Like Suttle?'

'Yeah. And one or two others.'

'Like who?'

'Like Colin Leyman, for starters.'

'Fattie Leyman? The guy's mental. He never got out of nappies. What the fuck are you doing talking to Leyman?'

'Because he's still in touch with the odd face or two.'

'But what's the point? The bloke's a dimlo. He should be in a home.'

'Sure, Baz. And that's why they'll tell him things. Because they think he'll never understand. Because they'd think it'll never go any further.'

'And are they right?'

'Of course they're not. Leyman's a lot brighter than you lot ever gave him credit for. You think I'd waste my time otherwise?'

'No, mush, I'm sure you wouldn't.' Baz was frowning now. 'So what did you ask him? What's he out there looking for?'

'Anything that could explain why someone burned Johnny Holman's house down. We used to call it motive in the Job.'

'And?'

'He left me a message. Says he's got something for me.' Winter consulted his watch, then got to his feet. 'Wish me luck, Baz. I'm round there first thing.'

Chapter Nine

WEDNESDAY, 11 FEBRUARY 2009. *07.24*

Faraday was back at the Ryde hotel in time to join Jimmy Suttle for breakfast. After four hours' sleep, the world was slipping out of focus.

'How was Winter?' He smothered a yawn.

'Strange. Off the pace. To tell you the truth, boss, I expected better.' Suttle offered Faraday the bones of their brief encounter. Winter, he said, had wanted chapter and verse on *Gosling* and had been all too easy to rebuff.

'You think he's getting old?' Faraday ducked his head, gave his eyes a squeeze. 'You think he's losing it?'

'Dunno, boss. You're about his age. I expect it can get a bit tricky sometimes.' He sawed through a rasher of fatty bacon. 'Do you have a view on that?'

Faraday knew exactly what he was saying. They were up to their necks in an inquiry that demanded total concentration and there were plainly limits to the slack he was prepared to cut his boss. Faraday shot Suttle a look. Back off.

'I had Parsons on just now,' Faraday said. 'She wants to put Winter under obs.'

'That has to be Willard.'

'Exactly my feeling.'

‘Is she going to action it?’

‘As far as I know. She’s still excited about the hole behind Holman’s place. On the assumption that something is missing, she thinks that same something might belong to Mackenzie.’

‘So he burned the house down? Is that how it goes?’

‘I don’t think she’s got that far yet. But now Winter’s in the equation, she seems to think it changes everything.’

Faraday helped himself to a slice of cold toast. Both Parsons and Willard dearly wanted to put Mackenzie away. For years he’d been flaunting his wealth, trailing his matador’s cape across the bullring that was Pompey, and putting Winter on the payroll had for Willard been the last straw. Mackenzie had always been careful to protect himself and his interests. In this sense, Winter was simply another layer of body armour, making Mackenzie even less vulnerable. Unless. Unless.

‘So what do you really think?’ Faraday had abandoned the toast.

‘About Winter?’

‘Yes.’

‘I think he’s starting to get tired of the game.’

‘You’re serious?’

‘Yes.’ Suttle nodded. ‘I never thought I’d hear myself saying this, but I think he’s starting to ask himself whether Bazza Mackenzie was such a great idea.’

* * *

Winter was back at Colin Leyman’s before the milkman called. This early-morning stuff is becoming a habit, he thought. He rang again, then a third time. It was freezing cold, an icy wind blowing in from the sea, and he could hear a radio on inside. At length, stepping away from the house, he caught sight of Leyman peering down at him from an upstairs window. Winter tapped his watch and raised an eyebrow. Time's moving on. Let me fucking in.

Leyman, when he finally made it to the front door, wouldn't look him in the eye. He said he wasn't very well. It might be infectious. His mum was due any minute. Best to call round some other time.

'Your mum's dead, Col. Don't be a twat.'

Winter stepped into the house, trying to encourage Leyman's bulk towards the kitchen. It wasn't in the man to resist. Never had been.

'Tea please, son. And toast would be nice.'

Leyman had the sulks now. Bazza had been right: the man was a child. Winter waited to see whether he'd put the kettle on, then did it himself. Leyman was farting fit to bust. Nervous. Good sign.

'So what have you got for me, Col?'

'No way.' He shook his huge head. 'I can't, Mr W.'

'*Can't?* How does that work? Last time I checked my mobile you'd sent me a text: *Got something for you, Mr W.* So . . .' Winter shot him a matey grin '. . . what is it?'

'I was wrong.'

'Wrong how?'

'To send the text. I never meant it. It never happened. Oh fuck.' He had his head in his hands. His shoulders were heaving. 'Why don't you just leave me alone?'

Winter made the tea. He found half a loaf of Hovis and some other bits and pieces in the fridge. The toaster was on the windowsill.

'Jam or Marmite, old son?'

Leyman was still crying. Marmite, Winter thought. Finally, the head came up.

'That won't help at all, you being nice. You were always nice, Mr W. I liked you for that.'

'And now?'

'Now's no different. It's just that I . . . you know . . . just can't.'

Winter held the plate out, told him to take it, spooned four sugars into a mug of tea. Guessing what had happened here wasn't difficult.

'Someone's been onto you, haven't they?'

'Who?' His eyes were wide. He looked terrified. He sucked gratefully at the tea.

Winter let him take a mouthful or two before leaning forward, intimate, confidential, keen to help.

'Who do you think, Col?'

'I . . . dunno, Mr W.'

'Think, son.'

'I can't. I . . . Shit, I hate this.' He started to cry again.

'It was Mr Mackenzie, wasn't it? It was my boss. He's given you a ring, probably last night, and told you to keep your mouth shut.' He reached for his own tea. 'Am I right, Col?'

Leyman blew his nose on a dishcloth. He didn't want to hear any of this. He wanted Winter out of his house, out of his life. He wanted to be back in the front room doing something safe. Like organising the slaughter of umpteen thousand Frenchmen.

‘I can’t say, Mr W.’

‘You don’t have to, Col. Because it’s all changed again. And that means it’s all going to be OK.’

‘Changed how?’

‘I saw Mr Mackenzie this morning. He said not to worry.’

‘Not to worry how?’

‘He meant it was OK to tell me. Something’s happened. Things have changed.’

‘Really?’ Relief flooded into his face. For a moment Winter thought he was going to get a kiss.

‘No problem, son.’ Winter patted his knee. ‘Just tell me what you were going to tell me. Then you get to keep the hundred quid and I’ll fuck off. How’s that?’

‘It’s not the money, Mr W.’

‘Of course it’s not.’

‘I’d have done it without the money. For you, I mean.’

‘Fine, so what happened?’

Leyman turned his head aside, his brow furrowed, his eyes closed again.

‘First I went to the place you and me used to go.’ He named a pub in Albert Road. ‘Frankie was there. Frankie’s always there. He wanted to know where I got the money but I never told him. We had a couple of drinks then went round to Kev’s place.’

‘Kev Sangster?’

‘Yeah.’

Winter nodded. Frankie Drew and Kev Sangster had been hard-core members of the 6.57, both mates of Mackenzie. Winter hadn’t seen them for years.

‘And?’

‘We phoned for a takeout. A Chinky.’

'And?'

'I told them about Waterloo. The charge of the Household Brigade. Said they were welcome any time, you know, like you do.'

'And?'

'Then I asked about Johnny. Like you wanted.'

At first, he said, they hadn't given much away, but Frankie had made him stop at the offie in Albert Road for a couple of bottles of vodka and some lagers, and pretty soon they were talking about Johnny again.

'And what did they tell you? About Johnny?'

'They said Mr M had been good to him, looked after him, given him money.'

'And what else?'

'They said Mr M never did anything for nothing.'

'Meaning?'

'Johnny did something in return, looked after something.' Leyman's eyes were wide. He desperately wanted Winter to be pleased. 'Two million quid's worth of cocaine? Tucked away for a rainy day?' He blinked. 'Does that sound about right?'

* * *

Confirmation on the ID of the fourth body got to Faraday shortly before ten o'clock. Pembury was on the phone with a perfect match against Robbie Difford's dental records. Unless a fifth body was to be found in the remains of Monkswell Farm—increasingly unlikely—then Johnny Holman was still alive.

'We obviously need to find him, Joe.' Faraday had contacted Parsons with the news. 'Will you talk to the media or shall I?'

Faraday assigned the task to a D/C in the incident room. An old passport of Holman's had been recovered from the office in the barn, and although the photo showed a younger man, Faraday was prepared to run with it. Calls to local press and TV outlets secured a promise to broadcast the mugshot, which was scanned and emailed within minutes.

Faraday summoned Suttle to his office and told him about the positive ID.

'Difford's car,' Suttle said at once. 'Holman must have taken it.'

Faraday nodded. He was numb with fatigue. He should have thought of this already. Why did it take Suttle to prompt him towards something so obvious?

'Circulate the details,' he muttered. 'Flag the bugger up.' Within the hour, force-wide, uniforms and CID would find themselves looking at the latest twist in *Gosling*'s brief history. Breaking news for busy coppers.

Suttle made for the door but then turned back.

'I hate to say this, boss . . .' he began.

'I know, I know.' Faraday held his hands up, an involuntary gesture of surrender.

'You want to talk about it?'

Faraday stared at him for a long moment. Then he nodded. 'Yes,' he said. 'I do.'

'Wait here. Give me five.'

Faraday had no memory of waiting. For once the phone didn't ring. Then Suttle was back again. He'd organised the heads-up on the Corsa. He looked, if anything, stern.

'We have to box this off, boss.'

'What?'

'You. Whatever it is. People are talking already. Even Parsons'll notice in the end.'

'What are they saying—as a matter of interest?'

'Most of them know you had an accident. The guys with half a brain think you maybe came back too soon.'

'And the others?'

'You don't want to know.'

Faraday nodded. He'd never bothered much with canteen gossip but knew that certain things never changed. If you reached the giddy heights of D/I then you were always in line for a kicking.

'So?' Suttle had sat down.

Faraday shook his head. This was the timeline from hell. He literally didn't know where to start.

'I went through the windscreen,' he said.

'You *what*?'

'Had a crash. Hit a tree. I was asleep at the time.'

'And everyone else?'

'The driver died. Guy called Hanif. Sweetest man—' Faraday broke off, stared at the wall.

'So why . . .?' Suttle brought him back, touching his own face.

'Why no scars? I had a baseball cap pulled down over my face to help me sleep. It must have . . .' He shrugged, lost for words.

'So you remember nothing?'

'Nothing.'

'And Gabrielle? She was there too?'

'In the back.'

'And?'

'You tell me.'

'But she's OK?'

'She's back.'

'In one piece?'

Faraday stared at him, realising that he didn't know the answer. Then he shut his eyes, hearing a voice telling Suttle exactly the way it had been: coming round in hospital, trying to piece his life back together, trying to let his body heal itself, aware all the time that something profound seemed to have happened. Not simply a roadside tree. Not simply the body of the driver slumped beside his. But another bend in the road—sharper, altogether more alarming.

'I've lost track, Jimmy. I've lost faith, focus, whatever else you need to get through. I wish I could make a better job of describing it but I can't. Nothing seems to matter. This . . . me . . . whatever. I wake up in the morning and there's just nothing. I've still got the directions somewhere but I don't give a shit any more. And you know what happened last night?'

'You went to bed early. Sane man.'

'I drove to Salisbury. Gabrielle's living in some godforsaken B & B. She's brought a little girl back from Gaza.'

He explained about Leila in the Burns Unit, about the white phosphorus, and about Gabrielle, incandescent with anger.

'It's changed her, Jimmy. Me? It's probably the accident. Gabrielle? It's the little girl. This is pretty tricky stuff, but you know what? It gets worse.'

'How? Why?'

'She wants to adopt. And to make that easier she thinks we ought to get married.'

'Right . . .' Suttle nodded. 'And is that a bad thing?'

The question appeared to take Faraday by

surprise. He stared at Suttle for a long moment, began to voice a thought, frame an answer, had second thoughts.

'No,' he said at last. 'No, it's not.'

'So what's the problem?'

'I don't know. Maybe that's the problem. That I don't know.'

'Do you still love her?'

'I love us. I love what we were.'

'And now?'

He shook his head, his lips shaping the same unvoiced thought, the man trapped underwater, his last lungful of air slowly leaking away.

I don't know.

They studied each other for a long moment. Then came a knock at the door. It was D/C Patsy Lowe. Suttle had asked her earlier to accompany him to Cowes. They had to take a look at Lou Sadler, the madam who ran the escort agency. Was Suttle still up for it?

Suttle glanced at Faraday. Faraday was staring into space. He waved a hand in dismissal.

'Off you go,' he muttered vaguely.

* * *

Winter was back at his apartment in Gunwharf by midday. He made himself a coffee and settled on the sofa, aware of the rain blowing in from the harbour. He'd been to see both Frankie Drew and Kevin Sangster. At both addresses he'd had to wait for ever to get them out of bed.

Drew occupied a squalid basement flat in one of the streets to the north of Albert Road. Semi-naked, he'd picked his way through the litter of empty bottles strewn over his living-room carpet, complaining bitterly about the students upstairs. They get pissed all the time, he said, and play shit music. When Winter asked him about Johnny Holman, he said he couldn't remember a thing. When Winter pushed him harder, he told him to fuck off.

Kevin Sangster, if anything, was in a worse state. He shared a flat with a Filipina of uncertain age. Either he or his lady friend had a gastric problem because the place stank of vomit. This time Winter wanted to know about the money. According to Leyman, Sangster had nicked the rest of the hundred quid. He'd said it without any rancour, as if the money had really been Sangster's all along, but Winter wasn't having it. He'd calculated the Chinky and the booze at around fifty quid, and when he spotted two twenty-pound notes tucked beneath an ashtray, he'd helped himself. Sangster saw him do it, demanded the money back. It was Winter this time who told him to fuck off, an invitation which sparked the information he was after.

'That's fucking mine,' Sangster yelled. 'I was the one who told him.'

'Told him what?'

'Told him about Bazza's little fucking nest egg.'

Now, draining the last of the coffee, Winter was still brooding on this latest development. The last couple of years had taught him never to expect the whole story from Bazza. The key to his world was power, keeping the upper hand, and the currency he dealt in was information. He gave it to you in tiny parcels, carefully weighed, forever keeping the tally in his head. Who knew what. Who'd said what to whom. Who owed him. Who didn't. Winter, who'd always had a very similar MO, had been amused at first. It had felt like a game, and there'd been days when he'd definitely stolen an advantage or two. But lately, this last year especially, he'd begun to tire of watching his back, of interpreting and reinterpreting the most casual asides, of studying the man's body language for clues to the real story. Wearing a blindfold, as he'd once told Bazza, does nothing for your sense of humour nor for your self-respect. And so here he was, stumbling around in the dark again while his boss laid plans to take over the whole fucking city.

Was it really worth it? Sweeping up after a bloke who simply refused to establish any sensible ground rules? Who vested so much faith in his own judgement? Who appeared to believe that no Pompey door could resist the weight of his shoulder?

In truth, he didn't know. He'd got used to the money and the lifestyle, and in the shape of Marie and maybe even Stu Norcliffe he'd found real friendship. But all of us, he told himself, are tiny whirling fragments in the teeming chaos of Bazza's busy little brain, and there was something slightly Roman in the realisation that he might face the downturned thumb at any moment. The prospect of that kind of endgame, the pitted brick wall at the end of the cul-de-sac, was beginning to haunt him. If not Bazza, he thought, then someone else might be in charge of the firing squad. Maybe Willard. Maybe Faraday. Maybe, God help him, Jimmy Suttle.

He glanced at his watch, then fumbled for the remote. At moments like these, bleakly introspective, he always sought comfort in the TV news. He switched on the set, waiting through the final moments of *Bargain Hunt.* Then came the bulletin. Lloyds Bank was trying to fight off seizure by the government. Business leaders were warning about a surge in unemployment. Winter emptied his cup, wondering whether anything remotely interesting had made the local segment at the end. Then, without warning, he was staring at a photograph of Johnny Holman. He looked years younger, exactly the way Winter remembered him from his CID days. The newscaster was reminding viewers about the recent tragedy on the Isle of Wight. Four bodies had been recovered from a burned-out farmhouse and police were keen to trace the grinning pockmarked owner, who appeared to have gone inexplicably missing.

Winter hit the mute button. Johnny Holman. Alive and kicking. He tasted betrayal. He felt physically sick. Suttle, he told himself, must have known all along.

Chapter Ten

WEDNESDAY, 11 FEBRUARY 2009. *13.03*

Lou Sadler had a fourth-floor apartment on the seafront in Cowes. The curtains were drawn across the biggest of the windows at the front and on the entryphone beside the communal front door there was no name listed beside Flat 8.

Suttle buzzed for a third time, enjoying the thin sunshine after all the rain. According to the D/S on the Vice Squad, Sadler drove a scarlet Renault Megane convertible with leopardskin covers on the seats. Suttle had already checked the parking lot to the rear of the building. The Megane was occupying a space in the corner. Unusually for a cabriolet, it had been fitted with a tow bar.

'Yeah?' A woman's voice, drowsy.

Suttle introduced himself. He was a police officer. He and his colleague would appreciate a conversation in relation to a recent incident on the island.

'What kind of incident?'

Suttle wasn't prepared to go into details. The door buzzed open. There was no lift.

Concrete steps led up, two flights per floor. The carpet had seen better days but there were some nicely framed photos on the walls. Heeling yachts under full sail during Cowes Week. A dramatic sunset flooding the Solent in gauzy yellows and golds. Sadler was waiting for them at the top, barefoot on the landing, her arms folded over the front of the navy-blue dressing gown. She was a big woman with a strong face and a tumble of auburn curls. She wore a thick gold bangle on one wrist and sported a huge ruby ring on her other hand. Her fingernails were the same colour as the Megane.

She looked at Suttle's warrant card, then nodded at the open door and followed them into the apartment. Patsy Lowe was still catching her breath. Suttle paused outside the kitchen. Among the clutter in the sink was an upturned bottle of Moët. In the hall a thin blue plume of scent curled up from a fresh joss stick stuck in a flowerpot. The flowerpot was home to an extravagant fern, and the blaze of sunshine from the living room at the end of the hall threw frond shadows across the parquet floor. Sadler must have pulled the curtains while they were making their way up, Suttle thought, wondering who else might be in the apartment.

Sadler led them through to the living room. It was bigger than Suttle had somehow expected, the decor spare, almost Japanese. Carefully plastered white walls. Occasional rugs on the polished maplewood floor. From the big picture window, the curve of the promenade framed a view he recognised from one of the photos in the stairwell. A line of dinghies bobbing on the tide at their moorings. The low swell of the mainland beyond.

Suttle and Lowe took a seat on the black leather sofa. Sadler, still standing, wanted to know exactly what they were after.

Suttle briefly explained about the fire at Monkswell Farm. It was his understanding that Sadler knew Johnny Holman.

'That's right.' She nodded. 'I did.'

'Did?'

'He's dead—isn't that what I heard? The fire you just mentioned?'

'No.' Suttle explained about the post-mortem findings. Johnny Holman, as far as they knew, was very much alive.

'So you guys need to find him, is that it?'

'Of course.'

She nodded. The news that Holman had survived the fire didn't appear to spark any reaction.

'You were friends with Holman?'

'I knew him.'

'Well?'

'We did business.'

'What kind of business?'

Sadler looked from one face to the other. She seemed irritated. She'd obviously been in bed. She carried a strong smell of recent sex.

'Should I phone for a lawyer? I mean, is this official or what?'

'It's a conversation,' Suttle said. 'Four people died in that fire. We need to know more about Holman. We need to talk to his associates, to people who knew him. You can call it background if you like. Anything you know about Mr Holman would be helpful.'

'But you know what I do for a living, right?'

'We know that you run an escort agency. Is that relevant?'

'Of course it is.'

'Why?'

'Because that's what I did for Johnny. He wanted company from time to time. I made that happen.'

'Company?'

'Girls. Women.'

'He bought them?'

'He paid my fees. It's all legal, invoiced, receipted. I'm a businesswoman, not whatever else you're thinking.'

Suttle scribbled himself a note, aware of Sadler watching him. The Vice Squad D/S had been sure that Holman was on a freebie. Not, it seemed, true.

'Was it always the same woman? The same girl?'

'Yes.'

'Why?'

'*Why?*' The laugh was derisive. 'Because he fancied her, I imagine. Because they got on. Don't ask me what they did because I don't know. All I ever care about is that my girls get treated nicely and everyone has a fun time. Whatever else happens is their affair. Does that sound illegal?'

'Not in the least. Did I suggest it was?'

'No, but— Forget it.' She checked a watch she'd produced from the pocket of the dressing gown. It was a man's watch, heavy, a Rolex. 'Is that it? Only I have to be on the road by half one.'

Suttle shook his head. He wanted a name and contact details for the girl Holman had been seeing.

'I'm afraid that won't be possible.' The girl, she explained, had gone home to Estonia. Her name was Kaija. It was unlikely she'd be back.

'Why?'

'I've no idea. Maybe she's made enough money. Maybe there's someone else in her life. A girl does what she has to do. That's fine by me.'

Suttle asked about the spelling of the name and wrote it down. Kaija.

'Surname?'

'Luik. It means swan.'

She helped with the spelling again.

'And is that her real name?'

'As far as I know—' she shrugged '—yes.'

'But you'd have seen her passport, surely?'

'I don't know. I can't remember.'

'What about an address?'

'In Estonia?'

'Yes.'

'I don't have one.'

'So how did you contact her in the first place?'

'She came to me. I run a successful business. It's called word of mouth.'

'Do you run the business from here? Or do you have premises somewhere else?'

'Here.'

'And you really don't have a home address for the

girl?'

She looked down at Suttle for a long moment, then shook her head.

'You guys kill me. Have you any idea what it's like to make a living? Try and keep your head above water? OK, so here's a little secret. These days business has never been tougher. Never. And all this stuff isn't making it any easier.'

'Four people died,' Suttle said again. 'In my business that's not insignificant.'

'I'm sure.' The watch again. 'But if you'll excuse me . . .'

She waited for Suttle to get up. He didn't move.

'We need you to account for your movements on Saturday night,' he said.

'Now?'

'Yes, please. Unless you've forgotten.'

'Can I say no?'

'Of course.'

'And then what?'

'I arrest you and we continue the conversation at the police station.'

'Arrest me for what?'

'Obstructing the course of justice.'

'You're kidding.'

'Try me.'

'OK.' She frowned. 'Saturday night I was over at a get-together in Southampton. It was a fund-raising thing. For a Down's syndrome charity. I got the late hydrofoil back and then I went to bed.'

She gave Suttle the details of the function. A hotel on the outskirts of Southampton. The name of the woman who'd organised the whole thing. She hadn't got a number but she knew the woman's address.

'She's in the book. Give her a ring. Send a copper round. She loves men in uniform.'

Suttle ignored the dig. He wanted to know where Kaija Luik had been living on the Isle of Wight.

'Why?'

'Because we need to make enquiries.'

'About Johnny?'

'Yes.'

Sadler shrugged, then left the room. Suttle heard a door open down the hall and there came the low murmur of conversation. A man's voice, indistinct. Minutes later Sadler was back beside the sofa. She'd scribbled down an address. It was in Cowes.

'You've got a phone number for Kaija? Email?'

'No.'

'No mobile number?'

'No.'

'I find that hard to believe.'

'That's your choice.' She shrugged.

'So when did she go? Kaija?'

'The weekend, I think. Sunday maybe.'

'Which airline?'

'No idea. She might have gone by coach. She made her own arrangements.'

Suttle turned to the Cowes address. 13a Darcy Road.

'What was the set-up there?'

'It's a flat.'

'Was she sharing it? Was there someone else there?'

'I've no idea. I'm not her keeper.'

'Really?'

Suttle held her gaze for a second or two.

'These girls advertise on the Web, am I right?'

'Yes.'

'You'll have a photo then. Bound to.'
'Of course.'
'May we have a copy?'
'Of course.' She shrugged. 'I'll have to talk to the bloke who does the website. He took her entry down, but he'll still have the file. He's away just now but should be back any day. Is that OK?'
'Sure. Sooner the better though, eh?'
Suttle got to his feet. He thanked Sadler for her time and gave her a card with contact details. She could send Kaija's photo by email.
Sadler barely glanced at the card. Suttle stepped towards the front door. On the right was a bathroom. The door next to the bathroom was shut. Suttle paused outside it. Then turned back to Sadler.
'One last question . . .'
'Go on.'
'Why did you bother answering the entryphone?'
'I thought you were someone else.' She smiled at last. 'Got that wrong, didn't I?'

* * *

According to Marie, Bazza was planning to spend the afternoon at the house. He had a speech he needed to sort out for a function in the evening. The local Rotarians, intrigued by what they'd read in the *Guardian*, had invited him at short notice after their scheduled speaker had gone down with flu.
Winter drove across to the house. Mackenzie had yet to return from the hotel but Stu Norcliffe was in the kitchen, talking to Marie. Winter had a key. When he appeared at the kitchen door, Marie told Stu to go through the story again.

'Remember Kieron O'Dwyer?' Winter nodded. How could he forget? 'I just got a call from Henrik. The boy's in hospital. Double fracture of the jaw. Here and here.' Stu tapped both sides of his face. 'Apparently the lad's in a bit of a state. He's had one operation already to wire the jaw up. He's due another one this afternoon.'

'No point asking how it happened, I suppose?'

'None. He's not saying a word.'

'I'm not surprised, in that state. How about a bit of paper and a pencil? Nothing complicated. Just the easy words.'

Marie wasn't amused. According to Stu, it would be weeks before the lad could even eat properly.

'So, are we sorry for young Kieron?' Winter was frowning. 'He's aggression on a stick, that boy. Sooner or later someone was bound to give him a slapping. Eh, Stu?'

'I don't think it's as simple as that.'

'You don't?'

'Kieron lives with his auntie. She came back last night to find him semi-conscious on the living-room floor. According to the guy who did the first operation, there were no other facial injuries. Just the two blows to the jaw. Bang bang. He thinks that's unusual.'

Winter nodded. Stu was right. Most fights serious enough to put a bloke in hospital were hopelessly messy, one drunk flailing at another, blood everywhere. This one sounded very different. The application of carefully measured violence. Precise, almost clinical.

'So what are we saying? You think Baz had anything to do with it?'

'Baz?' Stu looked shocked.

'You told me he was after the boy's address. I don't suppose he sent him a letter.'

'You're telling me . . .?'

'No, Stu, I'm just asking, that's all.' He turned to put the same question to Marie but she'd left the room.

Mackenzie returned shortly afterwards. A call from Leo Kinder had put him on standby for a *Newsnight* interview. They had a TV crew in the area and might have time to pay a visit before returning to London. According to Kinder, this could be the breakthrough.

'Again?' Winter followed him into the den. He hadn't prepared a speech, he wasn't even angry. All he wanted to know was where he stood.

'I'm not with you, mush.'

Mackenzie was scrolling through his emails. One caught his eye.

'Listen to this,' he said gleefully. *'Couldn't believe all that bollox about discipline and respect and cleaning up Pompey. Is this the same Bazza gave me a toeing back of Waterloo? That day we pissed all over you lot at the Den?'* He looked up. 'Remember Fergal?'

'No, Baz.'

'Millwall face. Hard as you like. Really good bloke. What the fuck's he doing reading the *Guardian*?'

'I don't know, Baz. Mail him back. Ask him.'

Too late. Bazza's fingers were already moving over the keyboard. Then he stopped, peering at the screen again.

'Here,' he said, gesturing Winter closer. 'Look at this.'

'Look at what, Baz?'

'This—here. *Cleaning up Pompey.* C-U-P. Geddit?'

Winter was lost. He had no idea where Mackenzie was going next and in truth he wasn't very interested.

Bazza was already reaching for the phone. For Winter's benefit, he hit the hands-free button. The call answered on the second ring.

'Baz?' Kinder, Winter thought. Responding like a puppy to his master's voice.

Mackenzie was telling him about the email, and about the phrase buried in the middle. C-U-P. Cleaning up Pompey.

'That's it, Leo. That's the one. That's what we've been looking for. A badge, a moniker, a handle. *Are you up for the Cup?* Maybe a poster like those famous ones in the First World War. The guy with the mustache. The guy that wanted you to sign up.'

'Kitchener,' Winter said drily.

'That's it, that's him, Kitchener. Paulie here thinks it's a blinding idea, don't you, mush? Me on the poster. Me pointing. *Are you up for the Cup?* We print hundreds of the fuckers, thousands of them, stick 'em up all over town. *Clean up Pompey.* Has to work, doesn't it? A line like that?'

'Brilliant, Baz. I'll get back to you.' If Kinder was underwhelmed it didn't show.

'When, mush?'

'Soon as. I'm in a meeting.'

'Yeah? Fuck off then.' He barked with laughter and ended the call, returning to the rest of his emails. Winter noticed one from *billy.angel* marked *High Priority*. Mackenzie skipped over it. Finally, after another chortle over a cleverly Photoshopped image that showed Ronaldo as a transvestite, he settled back in his chair.

'Rotary fucking Club, mush?' He reached for a pad and a pen. 'Any ideas?'

'I went to see Leyman this morning.'

'Yeah? And what did he have to say for himself?'

Bazza's grin widened. Winter had been waiting for this moment for most of the day.

'He said you stashed two million quid's worth of toot over on the island just in case. He said you'd parked it for a rainy day. He also told me who was looking after it. Johnny Holman.'

Mackenzie's grin had frozen. If there was one thing he hated in life, it was being taken by surprise. He'd put a call through to Leyman last night, warned him off, shut the fat fucker up. Now this.

'He's lying.'

'No, he's not. Leyman doesn't do lying. That's his charm.'

'You believe him?'

'Every word. And you know why? Because it's not just him.'

'So who else is peddling this shit?'

Winter shook his head. No more clues. No more names. Just a word or two about what might happen next.

'I've worked my bollocks off for you, Baz. I've got no complaints. You pay me OK, it's been a lot of fun.'

'Been?'

'Been.' Winter nodded. 'I'm looking at this from your point of view, Baz. Why waste your money on someone like me when you could get some other monkey for half the price? There are blokes in this town that would do anything to get on your payroll. They wouldn't mind in the least if you dicked them around, pulled their strings, kept them out of the loop half the time. In fact they'd probably think it went with the territory. Work for Bazza Mackenzie. Sit in the fucking dark and get yourself shat on. It's not clever, Baz. It's not even funny. To tell you the truth, I'm disappointed. I thought you were better than this.'

He got up. He'd said it. He was off. The last time he'd felt this good was the day he'd said something very similar to Detective Chief Superintendent Willard. Stuff your job.

Mackenzie stared at him.

'You're joking.' He leaned forward and patted the empty chair. 'Sit down, mush. You're upset. I've been working you too hard. You've got this stuff all out of proportion.'

'No, Baz. That's what you said before. And the time before that. It happens I believed you. But hey—' he shot Mackenzie a smile'— sometimes in life you get these things wrong.'

Mackenzie wasn't having it. He was at the door before Winter, his back pressed against it, no way out. Winter looked down at him.

'Are you going to open that door?'

'No, mush, I'm not. Not before you let me have my little say.'

'But why should I do that? Given what you never tell me?'

'Because you should. Because you must. Because this stuff's about you too.'

'What stuff?'

'The toot. Johnny. Everything. If you don't give me a hearing, you'll regret it, mush. I'm telling you now.'

Mackenzie took a tiny step forward, testing

Winter. Then another. Then a third before he moved sideways, gesturing at the door. His confidence had returned. Help yourself. Be my guest.

Winter studied him for a while, then shook his head.

'I've had enough, Baz.' He reached for the door handle. 'Say goodbye to Marie for me, eh?'

Chapter Eleven

WEDNESDAY, 11 FEBRUARY 2009. *18.45*

Faraday was doing his best to concentrate on Lou Sadler. Patsy Lowe sat in his office beside Suttle. The door was closed.

'Tell me again, Jimmy.'

Suttle described their encounter with Sadler. Faraday wasn't impressed.

'So she's on the game, you catch her at it—or nearly at it—and in a polite kind of way she tells you to fuck off. That's standard MO, isn't it? Someone like her? You don't have to be a criminal to hate the likes of us.'

'That's not the point, boss. She lied. I've checked again with the D/S I mentioned.'

'The one on the Vice Squad?'

'Yeah. He's certain Holman used to blag shags off her. Not her personally but one of the girls she runs. He says Holman used to boast about it.'

'Maybe Holman lives in a dreamworld. A fantasist.'

'Fine. That's possible. I admit it. But Sadler's telling us that Holman was a regular punter. He saw lots of the girl. Sadler says he paid his way, but maybe there's more to it. Maybe he copped freebies as well, like the Vice D/S says. So maybe there's some kind of relationship.'

'When?'

'Now.'

Faraday was trying to keep up. Suttle's impatience, he thought, was beginning to show.

'You're suggesting Holman's with this tom of his? What's her name again?'

'Kaija Luik.'

'So where is she?'

'Sadler says she's gone home. She's Estonian.'

'We've got an address?'

'No. Only a name.' Suttle had typed it out. He slid it across the desk. Faraday glanced at it.

'Luik? You think it's a common name?'

'Dunno, boss.'

'Have you got a photo?'

'Not yet. Sadler says she'll ping one over.'

'You need to action this. Talk to Interplod.'

'Done, boss.' Giving Interpol nothing more than a name, with the promise of a photo to follow, was a big ask. They'd take at least a week to come up with any kind of result. Assuming, of course, that Luik had really gone home.

'What about here? Where was she living?'

Suttle gave him the address in Cowes. He and Lowe had called in on the way back to Ryde. The address was the lower half of an end-of-terrace property near the chain ferry across to East Cowes. There'd been no response to their knocks at the front door and a glance through the front window suggested the place was empty.

'Upstairs?'

'No one in. I'll check the Land Registry next. See who owns it.'

'Neighbours?'

'One old couple next door. Pretty clueless, to be frank. Keep themselves to themselves. We need to check at some more addresses once we've got a photo.'

Faraday nodded, then his eyes returned to the slip of paper Suttle had given him. Kaija Luik. Someone else no one could find.

'Chase the photo,' he said.

Suttle took this as a gesture of dismissal. He and Lowe left the office. Faraday reached for the Policy Book and glanced up at the clock on the wall. In a quarter of an hour he was due to conference with Meg Stanley. She'd sent her apologies earlier, pleading to be excused from the 6 p.m. squad meeting on the grounds that the SOC operation was nearly at an end. With luck she would present their preliminary findings before close of play.

Faraday had emailed her back, saying no problem. In the event, he thought, she'd missed nothing. With the possible exception of Kaija Luik, *Gosling* appeared to have hit a brick wall. No Johnny Holman. No shotguns. No sign of Robbie Gifford's car. Nothing definite from the Pompey underworld beyond vague rumours of a buried stash of cocaine. These mutterings, almost inevitably, had been linked to Mackenzie, partly because he had the means to bankroll a consignment of that size and partly because it was a handy fit for the colourful urban legend that was Pompey's favourite gangster.

From Faraday's point of view the latter was especially troubling, not least because Parsons and Willard seemed all too eager to hitch their horses to the get-Mackenzie bandwagon. In the end of course they might well be proved right, but in the meantime it was Faraday's job to keep an open mind on every line of enquiry until the evidence told him otherwise.

He opened the Policy Book and began to transcribe the scribbled notes he'd made during the day. In this way he could keep a real-time check on the investigation as it developed, noting the decisions he'd made and the reasoning that lay behind them. Months or even years down the line, if *Gosling* ever made it to court, the Policy Book would protect him against marauding defence barristers in court, eager to exploit the tiniest chink in *Gosling*'s armour. A tiny procedural slip here, a wrongly attested statement there, and the entire case could fall apart. Years ago, as a D/C and then a D/S, he'd seen it happen on countless occasions. You spent months closing the investigative net around the prime suspects. You spent week after week trying to make the file lawyer-proof. And then, for the silliest reason, you fucked up.

He bent to the Policy Book. At Suttle's instigation detectives were rechecking ANPR cameras in the hunt for sightings of Difford's Corsa early on the Sunday morning. House-to-house enquiries had widened around Monkswell Farm, yielding little more than confirmation that the Holman ménage had been a bit of a pain. There'd been more interviews with school and college friends of the two dead girls, again with little result. The only absolute certainty was the abrupt return from holiday of Robbie Difford's mother. A Family Liaison officer had been dispatched to Gatwick to meet her and drive her back to the island. It was conceivable, just, that she might throw fresh light on her son's relationship with the volatile Johnny Holman.

There was a knock on the door. It was Meg Stanley. She apologised for being early, hoped it wasn't a problem. Faraday, to his slight surprise, was pleased to see her. It seemed an age since they'd shared a curry.

She unpacked her briefcase and slipped a typed report across the desk. It looked predictably neat.

Faraday picked it up, flicked quickly through the dozen or so pages, put it carefully to one side.

'Give me the headlines,' he said. 'Start with the fire itself.'

Stanley nodded. She'd shared the draft preliminary report with the Fire Investigator and he'd agreed that at this stage their conclusions were largely speculative. The fire appeared to have been started in the roof space beneath the thatch. Apart from an empty bottle of vodka beside Difford's body, there was no evidence of accelerants. A multi-seat fire—setting the thatch alight at several separate locations—would have been all too possible. Bundles of newsprint would have done it, or anything else that could have served as kindling.

Once the thatch was burning, she said, all you had to do was leave the trapdoor into the roof space—plus a couple of windows down below—open. The updraught would fuel the blaze, and each of the tiny reeds that composed the thatch itself would suck the superheated air still further inwards until the whole of the roof was acting like one huge bellows. This process, said Stanley, had put her off thatched roofs for ever. Thank God her rabbit hutch in Lock's Heath was tiled.

'Would the fire be visible by now?'

'Not for an hour or so. The old people in the bungalow across the fields reported it at 03.25. By that time, if you'd started the fire, you could be long gone.'

'And once it had taken hold?'

'The place has pretty much had it. The fire brigade ended up with every appliance they could lay their hands on. Even with all that resource, all they could do was wait until it burned itself out. You're looking at one huge bonfire. Whoever did this got it spot on.'

Faraday scribbled himself a note. This was no more than he'd expected.

'So what did you recover?'

'The four bodies, obviously, plus everyday stuff that would survive any fire. Basically we're talking metal: bed frames, the springs from armchairs, cutlery, bits and pieces of circuitry from the electronic stuff.'

'P/Cs?'

'Yep. Two of those plus a laptop. Nothing useful, though. We shipped the hard drives to Scientific Services but they were fried.'

'Mobiles?'

'Same situation. We recovered three mobiles in all. Given where we found them we think we've linked them to three of the bodies. That's Julie and the two girls. Kim's SIM card was intact. The other two were useless.'

'And Difford? Any sign of a mobile?'

'No.' She shook her head. 'Nothing.'
'You're sure?'
'Positive.'

Faraday scribbled another note. Difford's car, he thought. Maybe he'd left his mobile in the Corsa. Tomorrow he'd ask Suttle to sort out billing. Difford's mother would have her son's number, and if Holman had used the Corsa to get away from the farm, and if Difford's mobile was on the dashboard, then there might just be a chance he'd been making a call or two since.

He looked up. Stanley had her hands held wide. That, she said, was pretty much it. From the start she'd assessed the job as a nightmare, and nothing that had happened since had changed her mind.

'I feel like I owe you an apology', she said. 'I'm used to being more productive than this.'

'When do you release the scene?'

'We're thinking tomorrow. Around noon. You'll obviously get the full report as soon as I can manage it.'

'Sure.' Faraday didn't bother to hide his disappointment. Monkswell Farm had just swallowed a sizeable chunk of the SOC budget. With very little to show for it. 'So what's your take on what might have happened?'

The word 'might' was key. Like Faraday himself, Meg Stanley had little time for conjecture, though in this case there was hardly an alternative.

'I would have thought that Holman has to be the prime suspect. Through the taxi driver we can put him at the farm in the early hours. Holman's a big drinker. His relationship with Julie is rocky. He's coming on to her eldest daughter. He's fallen out with the daughter's boyfriend. Plus he has access to two shotguns.'

'You found shells from the gun?'

'Yeah, the metal bits on the end. I should have mentioned them.'

'How many?'

'Four. The PM found lead shot in each of the bodies. Again, location is important. We're pretty sure now that they were all killed downstairs, two in the lounge and two in the kitchen. Robbie and Kim were in the kitchen. Mum and Jessie were in the lounge. It's all in the report, page 9.'

Faraday nodded, trying to picture the scene. Killing four people wasn't a simple proposition.

'So how did he do it?'

'Good question. The way we see it, he must have used both shotguns. My guess is that they were pre-loaded and ready to hand.'

'So he'd figured it all out? Planned it?'

'Definitely. Waiting until Robbie and Kim were in the kitchen would have made it possible. Two guns to hand. First one couple, then the other.'

'An execution.'

'Exactly.'

'An angry man.'

'Off the planet. Totally insane. Just like everyone says.'

'And the guns themselves? No trace?'

'None. You'd have been the first to know.'

'But he did *have* the guns?'

'Must have done. As well as the shells, we ended up finding the metal box he used for storage.'

'Empty?'

'Yes.'

Faraday nodded. Through the fog that had once been his brain another thought had emerged.

‘What about the alarm system?’

‘The guy from the installing company came out to have a look. There’s a chip you can interrogate. It tells you when or whether the alarms have been turned off.’

‘And?’

‘It wasn’t there. Someone had removed it.’

‘Holman?’

‘I would have thought it’s more than possible.’

‘But why would he do that?’

‘It gives him breathing space. Or maybe it tells us this is an intruder, someone professional, someone who knows how to cover their tracks.’

‘Or muddy the trail.’

‘Exactly. Which would take us back to Holman.’

Faraday nodded. He reminded Stanley about Holman’s visit to the London clinic, the suspicion—not evidenced—that he’d reported some form of sexual dysfunction.

‘That would make sense. We found a pile of pornography in that office of his, video and print, plus a load of condoms.’

‘Still no sign of an address book?’

‘No. He must have taken it with him.’

‘Phone numbers he might have scribbled down? Little notes he might have written himself?’

‘A couple of bits and pieces. I sent them all over to D/S Suttle.’

Faraday sat back, trying to clear his mind, trying to assign each of these tiny fragments some kind of priority. Maybe Parsons was right, he thought. Maybe, in the end, it’s all about the hole they’d found at the back of Monkswell House.

He asked whether there’d been any kind of re-investigation around the digging.

'We had another go, yes. We sieved every particle of the excavated soil, plus the manure that must have been on top.'

'And?'

'Nothing you wouldn't expect. I did some sums though, if you're interested.'

'Always.'

'I gather we might be talking cocaine, yes?'

'It's more than possible.'

'Right. Cocaine comes in one-kilo blocks. Normally, they're double-wrapped in industrial clear polythene and secured with brown tape. Each block is roughly the size of a flattish house brick. I did some measurements in the hole, tried to calculate what kind of consignment there'd have been space for.'

'And?'

'We could be talking fifty blocks. Easily. That's a rough calculation, a finger in the wind. But fifty is a conservative figure. I'd be amazed if it was anything less.'

Faraday was looking for a calculator in the desk drawer. Stanley beat him to it.

'Use mine.'

Faraday did the sums. The street price of cocaine, as far as he knew, had been sinking recently. At £5 for a wrap, you were looking at £25 per gram, or £25,000 per kilo. On the basis of Stanley's guesstimate, therefore, Holman could have been sitting on one and a quarter million quid's worth of toot.

He showed his workings to Stanley. She shook her head.

'At source we have to assume this stuff's reasonably pure. We also have to assume this is a wholesale consignment. Whoever buys it down the line will step on it.' She nodded at the calculator. 'You should double that.'

Faraday nodded, put a line through his arithmetic, told her she was right. Sleep, he told himself. I need sleep. Two and a half million quid's worth of cocaine. Easily the price of four bodies.

'So you think that rules out Holman killing all four of them? You think we might be back to someone taking the cocaine off his hands?'

'Not at all. God knows what happened on the night. I certainly don't.'

Faraday smiled. For an ex-student of theology, it was a neat conclusion. He wondered about the possibility of another curry, decided against it. Meg Stanley would be less than impressed if he dozed off on her.

Stanley had reached for her briefcase, balancing it on her knees. Faraday had noticed her legs in the restaurant—slender, beautifully muscled.

'Do you mind if I ask something personal?' She inched her skirt a little lower.

'Not at all.'

'Is there something the matter?'

'In what sense?'

'I don't know. I was thinking about what you said in the restaurant the other night. Or strictly speaking what you *didn't* say.'

'I'm not with you.'

'OK.' She looked at him for a moment, her face pinking with embarrassment. 'I'm sorry. That was out of order.'

She got up, muttered something Faraday didn't catch and left the office. Faraday gazed at the door as she gently closed it behind her.

Out of order? He shook his head, reached for her report, slipped it into his briefcase. Bedtime reading, he thought. Can't wait.

He got to his feet, then had second thoughts and put through a precautionary call to Parsons. She was still at her office in Kingston Crescent. He ran through the afternoon's developments and updated her on Stanley's preliminary report. He was about to outline the actions he'd authorised for tomorrow when she cut him short.

'Winter's been at home since half past two. Odd, don't you think?'

'You got obs on him?'

'Yes. We've been waiting to get into that apartment of his most of the afternoon. He doesn't make it easy for us, does he?' She laughed, then put the phone down.

Chapter Twelve

WEDNESDAY, 11 FEBRUARY 2009. *20.43*

Winter, with half an eye on his favourite wildlife programme, was brooding. In the space of a single day circumstances had seized him by the throat and given him a thorough shaking. First the realisation that Jimmy Suttle had played him for a fool. And now the abrupt end of his stake in Mackenzie's business empire.

The latter, in a sense, had come as no surprise. There were limits to the kind of circles he was able to square on Bazza's behalf, and he knew that two million quid's worth of toot—if Leyman had this thing right—could easily put them both inside. Old habits, he thought, die hard, and the more he thought about it the more he realised that Bazza's peasant cunning was to blame for this latest development.

Bottom line, Mackenzie had always trusted the white powder to make him rich, and on reflection Winter knew he should have anticipated this little rainy-day stash. In a way its exact whereabouts was irrelevant. The Major Crime lot would probably find it, and if that happened then they'd work day and night to link it back to Sandown Road. By that point it was conceivable that his ex-boss might be running for Lord Mayor, an escapade that was already giving Bazza exactly the kind of profile he'd always craved: the buccaneering local boy with his own robust take on the city. Thus far, it hadn't occurred to Mackenzie that there might be limits to his ambition, but the weeks and months to come were bound to be ugly. Up like a rocket, thought Winter. Down like a stick.

The near-certainty that he and Bazza were heading for disaster filled Winter with gloom. But far worse, in a way, was his latest encounter with Jimmy Suttle. There'd been moments in Winter's life, especially during his long tussle with a brain tumour, when the boy had felt like the son he'd never had. He'd been there for him. He'd helped him through the darkest times. When Winter had been close to chucking it in, Jimmy Suttle had first kept the monsters at bay and then chased them away. In some ways he owed his life to Suttle, and ever since then there'd been a warmth, an unspoken kinship that he treasured. Until now.

Earlier, as dusk gathered over the harbour,

he'd fired off a text. *I never thought the day would come*, he'd written. *Thanks a fucking bunch.* Now, watching a python swallowing an entire antelope, he wondered whether Suttle would spare the text even a second glance. The world moved on. The boy had plates to juggle, crimes to solve. Winter, all too literally, was history.

The phone rang twenty minutes later. It was Suttle.

'I don't get it,' he said. 'There are rules here, consequences. You made a decision. That's fine. That's your call, your privilege, but don't blame me when it all turns to fucking rat shit.'

Winter knew at once that he'd been drinking.

'Forget it,' he said.

'What?'

'Bin it, ignore it. At my age, son, you're allowed a mistake or two.'

'What do you mean? You're talking about the text you sent, right?'

'Yeah . . . and the rest.'

'What rest?'

'You know what rest. Baz. The business. All that shit.'

'What are you telling me?'

'I'm telling you it's over. Finito. I've had enough, mush.' He laughed. He never said 'mush'. It felt like the final derisive wave of farewell, the departing *adieu.*

'Don't fuck about, Paul. This is for real?'

'Yeah. And before you try and fit me up for anything sneaky, the answer's no. I've had enough, son. I think I'll call it retirement. A little job on the beach maybe in the summer. I might find myself an allotment for the rest of the year.'

'Sneaky', as they both knew, was code for going u/c. Working undercover, staying alongside Mackenzie but reporting back to the likes of Jimmy Suttle, had absolutely no appeal. Winter had tried it once, before throwing in his lot with Bazza, and it had nearly got him killed. Just now he fancied something gentler.

He bent to the phone again. 'So why the call, son?'

Suttle took his time. The news that Winter had parted company with Pompey's cocaine king seemed to have sobered him up. Finally he said he wanted to mark Winter's card. This was something private, personal, just the two of them.

'Yeah? How does that work?'

'Don't ask.'

'I am asking, son. This is Faraday, isn't it? And Willard? And that other clown? The woman? Parsons?'

'No, mate. It's little me.'

'I don't believe you.'

'Suit yourself.' Suttle paused. 'There's a woman in Cowes. She runs a bunch of high-end toms. It's an Internet-based thing, Two's Company. Her name's Lou Sadler. Johnny Holman knows her. Maybe Mackenzie too.'

'And?'

'You ought to have a poke around.'

'Why?'

'Because there's lots she's not telling us.'

'About?'

'Johnny Holman.'

'You've tried?'

'Of course I've fucking tried. She good as blanked me. We've got nothing on her. Not yet.'

'So what makes you think she'll talk to me?'
'She probably won't.'
'So what the fuck am I supposed to do? I'm lost, son. You're talking in riddles. Plus I just told you, I don't do this stuff any more.'
Suttle ignored him. He told Winter to find a pen and a bit of paper.
'I've got a name for you. Kaija Luik. She's one of the toms. And she's Johnny Holman's special girl.'
'Meaning what?'
'Meaning she'll probably know where he is.'
'Holman?'
'Yeah.'
'So why don't you pick her up?'
'We're trying. You get that for free.'
Winter stared at the phone. This, he knew, was a fork in the road. Seconds ago he'd been making a difficult peace with one of the bigger decisions in his life. Now this. His copy of the *Daily Telegraph* was still on his knee. He reached for a pen.
'Spell it,' he said.

*   *   *

Fifteen minutes later, busy in the kitchen, Winter heard the *buzz-buzz* of his video entryphone. He padded through to the hall and checked the upturned face on the tiny screen. Misty Gallagher.
'You're early, Mist. I thought we shagged on Fridays?'
She blew him a kiss, told him to let her in. She was freezing. She wanted a drink.
Winter buzzed her in. By the time she made it to the third floor, he was waiting by the door. Weekdays Mist drank vodka and Coke, easy on the

ice.

'You having one too?' She gave him a hug. Winter caught the faintest breath of cigars.

He returned to the kitchen, sorted out a Stella and joined her on the sofa in the big living room. Misty Gallagher had been Mackenzie's long-term mistress. Like countless other men in the city, he'd fallen for her guile, and her frankness, and her gypsy good looks. Winter had always enjoyed her company, but the last couple of years, with Bazza increasingly occupied elsewhere, he and Mist had got way beyond conversation. Winter knew how territorial Mackenzie could be, but so far, fingers crossed, he and Mist were still intact.

Winter wanted to know why she wasn't at home tucked up in front of the telly. Wednesdays was *Relocation, Relocation*, her favourite show.

'I was. Then I got a call from Baz.'

'And?'

'He's really upset. Really sorry.' She sipped at the drink. 'You two had a ruck, am I right?'

'I told him to stuff the job. There's a difference, Mist. No ruck. Just me out the door.'

'And you meant it?'

'Yes.'

'That's what he thinks.'

'Then he's right for once. Thank fuck he bothered to listen.'

She smiled at him, dipped a finger in the vodka, moistened his lips. Winter loved the way she painted her nails. She always used the same colour, a deep, deep scarlet, and it never failed to stir him. She found his hand, gave it a little squeeze. Winter wanted to know why Bazza had phoned her.

'He wants to say sorry. He wants to make amends.

He wants you two to be mates again.'

'Kiss and make up?' It was Winter's turn to smile. 'Quaint.'

'He means it, Paul. He's serious. I haven't seen him like this since . . . you know . . . that business with the nipper . . .'

Winter raised an eyebrow. Last year Bazza's grandson had been kidnapped. For days Mackenzie had barely known how to cope.

'I'm flattered,' he said. 'Did he tell you why I walked out?'

'No.'

'I'm not surprised. The man can be a complete twat sometimes, his own worst enemy. It's happened before, Mist. This time he's pushed it too far.'

'I bet.'

'What does that mean?'

'It means I sympathise. I spent years with the man. I know him better than he knows himself.'

It was true. Before the move to nearby Hayling Island, Mist had lived in a Gunwharf apartment similar to his own. Just her and a million stuffed animals for the nights when Baz chose not to turn up.

'You need another one of those.' She nodded at his glass. To Winter's surprise, it was nearly empty. He watched her through the open kitchen door as she raided the fridge for another Stella. Mist never did anything by accident. So just why had she paid him this visit?

'Baz said something else too, on the phone.' She was back on the sofa beside him.

'About what?'

'Us, Paul.'

'*Us?* How does that work?'

'He says he won't mind any more. He says he thinks he can wear it.'

'Wear what? You and me shagging?'

'Yeah. And—you know—being together.'

'Really?' Winter was astonished. 'So how would that work?'

'He'd just . . .' she shrugged '. . . put up with it.'

'Fuck.'

'Exactly.'

'He *must* be desperate.'

'Thanks.'

Winter felt her stiffen beside him. He patted her knee, said he was sorry.

'No offence, Mist. You mean we'd be . . .' He struggled to find the right word. 'Legit?'

'Yeah.' Mist nodded. 'Exactly.'

Winter looked at her, trying to work it out. Life with Misty Gallagher had always been exciting, not least because of the consequences of being caught.

'You think it would be the same, Mist? No Bazza in the wings? No chance of getting my bollocks ripped off?'

'You're telling me you'd miss that?' Her hand had settled on his crotch. Another little squeeze.

'Not at all,' he said, 'if you're offering.'

'My pleasure.' She kissed him lightly on the cheek. 'But we have to do something about Baz.'

'Why?'

'Because he's outside in the car. And he wants to have a chat.'

* * *

Winter phoned Mackenzie a few minutes later and

told him to come up. Mist had disappeared into the bathroom. She'd switched on the little radio he kept in there and over the fall of the water in the shower Winter could hear her singing along to Radio Two. Carly Simon. 'You're So Vain'.

Mackenzie had rain on his coat when he appeared in the hall outside. He said he'd been out on the Millennium Walk, getting some fresh air, having a think. Winter took his coat, offered him a drink. Mackenzie never did contrition, couldn't quite make it work.

'Listen, mush.' He'd downed the first Scotch, wanted another. 'If sorry makes any difference, I'm really fucking sorry. That's an apology, by the way.'

'Yeah?' Winter was sitting across from the sofa, the remains of his Stella untouched.

'Yeah. You and me, mush, we made a team. Maybe I forgot that. Maybe there were some little things I should have attended to. Like I say, I'm sorry.'

'That's good to hear.'

'Is it, mush?' There was a tiny spark of hope in the question.

'Yeah. Like I just said to Mist, it means you must have been listening.'

'I was, mush, I was. Don't think I haven't been taking you for granted, I fucking have. I know it. I'm like that. I take everyone for granted. You, Marie, Ezzie, Stu, Mist, the whole fucking world. It's what I do. It's what I am. Fucking deaf, mush. That's me.'

This had the makings of a speech. Winter wondered how well it might play in front of an audience of Pompey Rotarians.

'Something else too. About Mist. She's told you

what I said on the phone? I fucking mean it, mush. I know you've been knobbing her for years. Fuck, I told you to help yourself a couple of times. But that's different. What I'm saying now is . . . you know . . . get it on properly, if that's what you both want. I know Mist does. Fuck knows why.' He risked a grin before stripping the cellophane from a small cigar.

Winter didn't respond. When Mackenzie asked for a light, Winter said he didn't have one.

'You're telling me not to smoke?'

'Yes.'

'OK.' He left the cigar, unlit, on the table.

'So why are you here, Baz?'

'You want the truth? We're in the shit.'

'I don't understand *we*.'

'You and me, mush.'

'How does that work? I've been looking after your best interests. I've spent most of the last couple of years keeping you *out* of the shit. So what else haven't you told me?'

Mackenzie was nursing the last of his drink now, head down, shoulders hunched. Mist was right, Winter thought. He'd never seen him so forlorn, so physically diminished.

'You remember Tommy Peters, mush?'

'Yes.'

'He's been pushing me for money, serious moolah. Like every other cunt these days, he's finding it hard to make a living. He thinks I owe him, big time. He's been talking silly figures. He's totally lost it.'

'How much?'

Mackenzie wouldn't answer, not at first. Winter just looked at him, waiting. Finally the head came up.

'He's after 250K.'

'That's hush money. Blackmail.'

'I know.'

'So what did you say? What did you tell him?'

'I told him to fuck off. I said I'd paid him the rate for the job, twenty K, cash on the nail, notes on the fucking table, and that was that. In fact it was you, mush, that gave it to him.'

Winter nodded. A couple of years ago Mackenzie had taken out a contract on a man called Brett West. West had a distinguished record as Bazza's favourite enforcer but had gone seriously off-piste. Tommy Peters had blown his face off in an unfinished bar north of Malaga, and killed his girlfriend as well. Winter, as bagman, had been a metre away from them both. The memory of that hot afternoon had never left him.

'So what's Peters saying now?'

'He still wants the money. We're talking stand-off, big style.'

'Any threats?'

'Yeah. Plenty.'

'Like what?'

'Like he might grass us both. Unless.'

'And you said?'

'I said he'd never do that.'

'But he might.'

'I know, mush.' His head went down again. 'But there's something else I think he's done already . . .'

He let the silence between them stretch and stretch. Mist was still under the shower. Carole King. 'It Might As Well Rain Until September'.

Mackenzie was evidently finding the next bit hard. Winter saved him the trouble.

'You think he's helped himself to all that toot at Johnny Holman's.'

'I know he has.'

'How?'

'Because he's that kind of bloke. Just wades in.'

'But how did he know about it in the first place?'

'Because I told him.'

'You did *what*?'

'I told him, mush. Biggest mistake of my fucking life. It was when we were fixing to fly down to Spain to sort out Westie. Me and Tommy had a couple in a place in London. We got a bit hammered. I was twatting around. I admit it. Big-time London hit man, all that shit, you have to let them know you carry a bit of weight. To be honest I can't remember exactly how much I told him, but it would have been enough. He's got a brain, that guy. More than I fucking have.'

Winter turned away, then got up and went to the window. This was far, far worse than he'd ever imagined. Two million quid's worth of toot could put him away for an age. Add conspiracy to murder, and he'd be spending the rest of his life in some khazi of a prison. Possibly in Spain.

'You're sure about Peters?'

'As far as I can be. It all fits. It all makes sense.'

'Has he been in touch recently?'

'A week ago. That's when he got really heavy.'

'What did he say?'

'He said he'd hit us where it really hurt.'

'Us.'

'Us.'

Another silence, longer this time. Out in the darkness of the harbour, the lights of the Gosport ferry.

'Do we know where to find Peters?'

'Yes.'

'And you really think he'd burn that place down? With everyone inside? Abduct Johnny Holman? Nick the toot?'

'I'd put money on it, mush, if I fucking had any. The guy's a complete psycho. He wouldn't think twice about any of it.'

Winter watched Mackenzie get up and help himself to more Scotch from the bottle on the side. He seemed to have developed a limp.

'Tell me about Lou Sadler, Baz.'

Mackenzie put the bottle, uncapped, to one side. 'What's she got to do with it?'

'Just answer the question, Baz.'

Mackenzie hesitated, not liking any of this. Then he went back to the sofa.

Sadler, he said, was a Scummer. She'd once been mates with Misty. Mackenzie had met her a few times, way back, and as far as he knew she was now running a brothel somewhere on the Isle of Wight. Good-looking woman if you didn't mind a bit of weight. Fucking smart too.

Scummer was Pompey-speak for anyone from Southampton. Winter wanted to know whether Sadler might have had anything to do with the fire and the toot.

'No way. It's Peters, mush. I know it fucking is. The man's an animal. We have to get him off our backs.'

'And how do we do that?'

'You talk to him. You get him to level about the toot. Then we do a deal.'

'What kind of a deal?'

'Fuck knows. The way I'm feeling right now, I'm

gonna leave it to you. You sort it. You decide the split. You make it sweet enough for him never to come calling again. Otherwise . . .'

'Otherwise what, Baz?'

'Otherwise we might be back with the Westie solution. *Comprendes?*'

Winter said nothing. He studied his slippered feet, wondering where this conversation might go next. Then he heard the bathroom door open and he looked up to find Misty Gallagher standing beside the sofa, combing her wet hair. She was wearing Winter's dressing gown, open at the front.

'You coming to bed, Paul? Or what?'

Winter was watching Mackenzie. He got to his feet, drained the Scotch, headed for the door. Then he paused, turned back into the room.

'See you tomorrow, mush.' He nodded at Mist. 'Sweet dreams, eh?'

Chapter Thirteen

THURSDAY, 12 FEBRUARY 2009. *06.24*

Faraday was dreaming of Petra. It was the end of a long afternoon. He and Gabrielle had climbed away from the Valley of the Tombs and the endless shuffle of weary tourists. Away to the south, following their instincts through the trackless scrub, they found a perch among the rocks. Up here, in the clean winter air, they threw long shadows across the shale. Gabrielle had a sketch pad. She squatted beside a thorny bush, laid chalks in the dust, squinted into the dying sun. Her hands were powdered blue and green and violent crimson from the chalks.

She drew on her sketch pad while Faraday wandered among the shards of loose rock, pausing here, stooping there, gathering fragments for no purpose. In a while, his pockets heavy with stones, he found the very edge of the view. A thousand feet below was the bottom of a wadi. It lay in deep shadow. He braced himself, felt a tickle of sweat beneath his cotton shirt, lobbed one stone, then another, then a third, pausing each time to count the seconds before impact. The bark of the stones shattering on the dry riverbed echoed away down the wadi, becoming fainter and fainter, rubbed out by distance and by time.

Soon he had just one stone left. It was heavier and flatter than the rest. In some ways he wanted to keep it but knew he shouldn't. He knew it belonged to the wadi, to this bare biblical landscape, to the rough clatter of the stones he'd tossed before. And so he stepped to the very edge of the wadi and peered over before spinning the last stone into oblivion. The stone left his hand. He began to count. He got to ten. Twenty. Thirty. Nothing happened. Bewildered, he turned to shout to Gabrielle. But Gabrielle had gone.

From far away came another sound. Somebody knocking, somebody calling his name. Groggy, damp with sweat, he struggled up onto one elbow, fumbled for the light. The alarm clock he'd propped beside the bed told him it was half past six. He got out of bed and made it to the door.

It was Jimmy Suttle. He was standing in the dimness of the hotel corridor.

'Sorry, boss. I thought I ought to give you a

shout.'

'Why? What's happened?'

'They've found the Corsa. Or what's left of it.'

* * *

It was barely light when Winter woke up. He peered at the thin stripe of grey between the bedroom curtains, aware of a shape hanging over him. It was Misty. He could feel the warmth of her body, smell the scent she always wore. Obsession. Musky with a hint of citrus.

'You OK, Paul?'

For a moment he wondered why he shouldn't be. Then he remembered.

'I'm fine,' he muttered. 'Fine.'

'You want to try again?'

'What?'

She didn't answer. He lay back, his head on the pillow, his eyes closed. He'd never had a problem with Misty before, not until last night, but for reasons he couldn't explain it hadn't happened. Maybe it was the visit from Bazza. Maybe it was the prospect of the days that lay ahead. Maybe it was the realisation that this thing with Misty was suddenly theirs for keeps. He didn't know.

'How's that?' She'd ducked beneath the duvet. He could picture her fingernails. He could feel the hot scald of her tongue.

He grunted his approval, let out a tiny sigh.

'More?'

'More.'

Her face appeared, hooded by the duvet. She was smiling. She kissed him on the lips, on the chest. Then she disappeared again.

Minutes later, she was back beside him.

'Thank Christ for that.' She reached for a cigarette. 'I was beginning to worry.'

*   *   *

Faraday rode out to the site where they'd found the Corsa, Jimmy Suttle at the wheel of the borrowed Fiesta. They were in the south of the island, among the tangle of lanes that webbed the downland around the Brighstone Forest. A track led deep into the woods, and Suttle switched on the headlights as the trees grew thicker. Soon, ahead, Faraday spotted the flapping line of police aware tape. A couple of uniforms waved them to a halt. Beyond the tape Faraday could see the burned-out shell of the Corsa. The CSI who'd worked on Monkswell Farm was bending into the carcass of the vehicle, locked in conversation with a fireman. Faraday joined them.

What remained of the car had been reported by a local in search of foxes. He'd found the Corsa around half past three in the morning. The fire was out by then but the bodywork, he'd said, was still warm.

Faraday was looking at the remains. The rear windows had shattered and there were tendrils of rubber hanging from the wheel hubs. Scraps of charred fabric clung to the blackened seat frames and the plastic trim on the dashboard had largely melted.

'Accelerants?' Faraday was looking at the fireman.

'Yeah, big time. The FI's on his way, and it's his shout, but I'd say whoever did this knew what he was about. Cold night like last night, you'd never have the front windows down, would you?'

FI meant Fire Investigator. Winding down the windows before setting the fire guaranteed a draught.

'This guy with his foxes. He had a gun?' Faraday was looking at the CSI.

'Twelve-bore, boss. I've had it seized. Just in case.'

Faraday nodded. At the very best it was a punt, but twenty years on CID told him never to discount coincidence. Four bodies with gunshot wounds. Twelve-bore cartridges recovered from the scene. Now this.

Suttle had been talking to one of the uniforms. The Corsa was the closest thing they'd had so far to any kind of breakthrough. Faraday needed to get himself organised.

Suttle led him back towards the Fiesta.

'We need house-to-house, boss, as soon as. The guy I was talking to just now's happy to walk us through it. I'm thinking four two-man teams. The properties are well spread out. We've got at least three approach roads. CCTV-wise, we're pretty much fucked. In this immediate area there isn't any.'

Faraday was torn between gratitude and amusement. This was his call. These were his decisions.

'Have you finished?'

'Just trying to help, boss.' Suttle had no time for irony. 'You want to use the Airwave in the car?'

* * *

Winter took Misty breakfast in bed, a plate of toast loaded with her favourite marmalade. It was nearly nine by now and Misty had had enough of Radio Two.

'Are you joining me?'

'No, Mist.' Winter shook his head.

'Why not? Doesn't a girl deserve a bit of conversation?'

'Later, love.' He was standing by the door. 'What's the plan then?'

Mist gave the question some thought. She was in no great rush to get home. There was an early-spring sale at a few of the classier outlets in Gunwharf. She might wander across and check them out.

'All in good time though, eh?' Mist pushed back the duvet with her foot.

Winter hesitated. They were in new territory, and he didn't know quite what to make of it. Twenty-four hours ago he'd have bundled Misty out of the door ahead of another busy day with Bazza. Now she seemed to have rights of her own.

'I have to sort a couple of things out, Mist.'

'Like what?'

He looked at her and laughed. Like two million quid's worth of toot, he thought. And a London hit man who wanted to put him away for life.

'What's so funny?'

'Nothing, Mist. It's just business, that's all. Stuff I have to do.'

'You sound like Bazza.'

'I'm not fucking surprised. Just think of me when I'm gone, OK?'

'What's that supposed to mean?'

'Nothing,' he said again. He crossed to the

bed and gave her a kiss. She tasted of ginger marmalade. Happy days.

'So where are you going?'

'Out. I'm on the mobe if you need to get in touch. Back later, yeah?'

He left the bedroom without waiting for an answer. A mug of coffee he'd made earlier was still in the kitchen, untouched. He took it onto the balcony, looking out over the harbour, trying to foresee the kind of day that lay ahead. The priority just now was the cocaine. He'd need the details from Mackenzie: how much bulk was involved, where it had been stashed, what Holman might be doing with it now. As far as Tommy Peters was concerned, Winter wasn't convinced. While he bought Mackenzie's story about the extortion bid, he resisted the temptation to link Peters to the cocaine. It was too easy, too convenient. Bazza always joined the dots up far too fast. Just one reason why they were all in deep shit.

Winter swallowed the last of his coffee and took a final look at the harbour. Down below, on the promenade that skirted the front of the apartment blocks, he noticed a youngish guy in jeans and a leather jacket. He was taking his ease against the railings, studying a mobile phone. He'd been there earlier, when Winter had first pulled the curtains in the lounge. Funny, he thought, tucking the image away.

He took the mug into the kitchen, rinsed it and collected his briefcase en route to the bedroom. He put his head round the door, blew Misty a kiss. The lift in the corridor took him down to the parking lot in the undercroft. The sight of his new Lexus gave him a moment or two of regret. This was the second

Lexus he'd had off Mackenzie, top of the range, HDD navigation system, power moonroof, the lot, and sliding his bulk behind the wheel he knew he'd miss it. He turned the key in the ignition, amazed as always that he could barely hear the engine. A wide U-turn in reverse pointed him towards the exit. Seconds later, with an effortless surge of power, he was out in the thin drizzle, firing up the radio.

The guy in the unmarked Skoda watched him flash past. Silver-grey Lexus. Target at the wheel. He lifted his hand towards his mouth. The mike was taped to the buckle on his watch strap.

'He's left Gunwharf, boss. Out.'

* * *

Jimmy Suttle, at the MIR in Ryde, found himself looking at the overnight logs from the surveillance team that had Paul Winter plotted out at his Gunwharf apartment. Bazza Mackenzie, it seemed, had arrived mid-evening with a woman identified as Misty Gallagher. Gallagher was Mackenzie's long-term shag and had been first into Blake House. Mackenzie had parked his Bentley in the undercroft and the presumption was that he'd joined Gallagher inside. In the absence of real-time intel from the flat itself there was no proof that they'd been visiting Winter, but—in the dry prose of the reporting officer—it was reasonable to assume that this had been their intention. Either way, the Bentley had been clocked about an hour later, leaving Gunwharf at some speed. After that, there'd been no further movements to or from the apartment.

Suttle sat back. Parsons, as he now knew from Faraday, had secured authorisation at Assistant

Chief Constable level for a full intel rig at Winter's pad. For *Gosling* this was a significant tactical move, not something you'd undertake lightly, and Suttle could imagine Parsons making her case to the ACC. Winter, she'd argue, had the ear of Mackenzie. If they were talking a significant stash of cocaine at Monkswell Farm, and if some or all of that consignment belonged to Mackenzie, then Winter would be key to what happened next. On these grounds alone, she'd insist, the risks of a B & E would be wholly justified. Breaking and entering would put a couple of techies into Winter's apartment, and half an hour would be enough to give *Gosling* a front-row seat as Mackenzie's empire at last began to self-destruct.

So where did this leave his conversation with Winter last night? Suttle didn't know. Two pints of Abbot had been enough to persuade him to pick up the phone. The text from Winter had hurt and he wanted to put the record straight. Then had come the news that Winter and Mackenzie had parted company. Suttle couldn't possibly know whether Winter was being even more devious than usual but there had been something about him when they'd met in the pub that suggested he was telling the truth. Even for Winter it turned out there were limits. For whatever reason it seemed he'd had enough.

Suttle eyed the phone. Should he report last night's conversation? Cover his own arse and tell Faraday he'd fed Winter a name to see what might happen? Or should he hold his nerve and see how this thing played out? Winter, after all, was under surveillance. *Gosling* would know exactly where the bone he'd just been tossed might lead him.

Which sort of added Winter to the investigation's intelteam.

The irony put a grin on Suttle's face. It was, he thought, exactly the kind of tactic that Winter himself would have gone for in his CID days. As a young D/C new to the Job, Suttle had watched Winter on countless occasions playing both ends against the middle and emerging, as if by magic, with a result. That had been the man's MO. That's what had made him a detective of genius. Winter's way had never been ethical, and it frequently courted career suicide, but it had made him a star in the gathering darkness that was CID culture. That darkness, as Suttle knew only too well, was thickening by the year. People didn't make the moves any more. They kept risk at arm's length. Shame.

He got to his feet, pleased with himself. Winter, he thought. Back on the squad without even knowing it.

*   *   *

Faraday was thinking about Saturday. Saturday, he'd realised, was Valentine's Day, and with his foot hard down on *Gosling*'s throttle there was just a chance he might be able to swing a couple of hours off. Enough time, fingers crossed, to return to Salisbury, offer his apologies and start all over again.

The other night in the chill of the B & B he and Gabrielle had circled each other like strangers. Gabrielle could think of nothing but the child. Faraday was nursing wounds that seemed to deepen by the day. That tiny strip of territory they'd made their own, the long happy years of give and take, of getting along, of shared laughter at the general craziness of life, had been abandoned. Quite why, he didn't know. Maybe it was the accident. Maybe that's what trauma and shock and all the rest of it did to you. Maybe that kind of earthquake shook you to the very foundations and made you question pretty much everything. Certainly it felt that way—a numbness spiked with an acute sense of apprehension—but he was at a loss to know what to do about it. A mist had descended, impenetrable, all-enveloping. He felt, in a word, fogged-in.

He looked up from his desk to find Suttle looking at him. He hadn't a clue how long he'd been there.

'Sorry, boss,' he began. 'Am I interrupting anything?'

'Not at all.' Faraday rubbed his eyes. 'What do you want?'

'This address in Cowes we've got for the Estonian girl. It turns out to belong to Lou Sadler.'

Faraday was trying to concentrate. Kaija Luik, he told himself.

'I thought she'd gone home? Back to Mum?'

'She has, according to Sadler. But that's not the point.'

'It's not?'

'No. Sadler's still not come up with a photo of the girl, but I organised a spot of house-to-house.'

'And?'

'No one's seen any activity at the flat for weeks. A couple who live across the road seem to think it's been empty for a while.'

'No Kaija?'

'No, boss. And no Johnny Holman.'

*   *   *

Misty Gallagher told herself she must have been asleep again. She surfaced from beneath the duvet wondering what it was that had woken her up. Then came a noise, a knocking sound, and the low murmur of voices, men's voices, close enough to be in the living room.

She looked at her watch—nearly ten o'clock—trying to remember whether Winter had mentioned anyone dropping round—maybe someone to fix the Freeview box, which had gone wrong, maybe something else. But how had they got in?

She slipped quietly out of bed and reached for Winter's silk dressing gown, the one he'd nicked from the Al Burj in Dubai. Ideally, she'd have called him here and now, asked him what was going on, but she'd left her mobile in the living room. Unless she fancied going to sleep again and blanking the whole episode, her only option was to go next door and ask what the fuck these guys were up to.

She opened the door, hesitated. The voices were much clearer now. There seemed to be two of them. There was a problem about a tuning glitch, a brief discussion about wavelength. The Freeview box. For sure.

She stepped into the living room and found herself face to face with two youngish guys, both in white overalls. A silver metal case lay open on the carpet and one of the light fittings was dangling from the wall. She looked across at the TV. No one had touched the Freeview box.

Both guys were staring at her. She knew about guilt. She'd been round men for most of her adult life. She knew what to look for when a bloke found himself way up shit creek without a paddle. Whatever these two were doing was very definitely illegal.

One had the grace to smile.

'Lovely,' he said.

'Lovely?'

'The dressing gown. Very nice. My partner would kill for that.'

She ignored him. She was looking at the dustsheet spread beneath the light fitting. In the middle was a tiny curl of cable with a single glass eye on the end.

'What's that?' She nodded at it.

'Nothing.'

'Nothing, bollocks. Who the fuck are you? How did you get in?'

'Health and safety.' It was the other one this time. He was trying to keep a straight face. 'We have the magic key.'

She spotted her mobile, grabbed it. The taller of the two guys said there was no need to make a fuss. It was all cool. They were off. They were sorry to have bothered her.

'What about the light?' She was outraged.

'You want us to fix it?'

'Of course I fucking do.'

The guy shrugged and picked up a screwdriver while his mate repacked the box on the carpet. For the first time she realised who she was looking at. The haircuts. The attitude. Their bent little smiles. They way they looked at her.

'You're Filth, aren't you?'

'Charming. Do we get tea as well?'

'Fuck off out of here.'

'Pleasure.'

The light fitting was back in place. The dustsheet had been neatly folded and tucked away. Not a single clue remained.

'See, missus?' The tall one was shepherding his mate towards the door. 'We was never here.'

*   *   *

Winter was at the Trafalgar, looking for Bazza Mackenzie. The girl on reception said she'd seen him a few minutes ago, heading down towards the gym. The gym was in the hotel basement. Winter took the stairs.

At the bottom of the stairs, beyond the office Winter shared with Stu, a long corridor ran the length of the hotel. Pipework still hung from the ceiling but Mackenzie had made an effort with the rest of the decor, painting the rough plaster walls a startling white and hanging a series of cheerfully framed photos at one-metre intervals. Most of the photos came from Fratton Park, moments of glory from last season's winning FA Cup run, but towards the end he'd chosen a couple of shots from the boxing nights he staged on the pier: two young lads battering each other senseless, a classy black guy standing over the body of the Wecock Farm novice he'd just knocked unconscious.

The door to the gym lay beyond the photos. Winter peered through the square of wired glass. The gym was cavernous, running the depth of the building. Floor-to-ceiling mirrors lined three walls, offering endless views of the gym's only occupant. He was on the small side, not young. He was dressed in blue trackie bottoms and was belting the life out of a punchbag that Winter had never seen before. He moved the way a seasoned boxer moves, his head hunched between his shoulders, his face peeping out between his gloved hands, his eyes steady, focused on the bag. The blows came in quick flurries, *bam-bam-bam*, two lefts and a right, and in between he danced on his toes, bobbing and weaving, as if the bag might fancy a pokeback.

Winter watched him, fascinated, wondering how many four-star hotel guests had skills like these. Then his attention was drawn to the top half of the tracksuit neatly folded over a nearby rowing machine. On the back, in big white letters, Royal Navy.

'All right, mush?'

It was Mackenzie, standing behind him. Winter had no idea how long he'd been there.

'Who's that?'

'Mate of mine. Billy Angel.'

'Handy, isn't he?'

'Too right. Should be, too. He's a PTI down *Temeraire.* Been there a while.'

HMS *Temeraire* was the navy's School of Physical Training. Mackenzie eased Winter to the left and they both watched Angel for a while. He'd increased the tempo by now, maybe aware of the watching faces through the window, and Winter noticed tiny droplets of sweat spraying from his shorn scalp when he flicked his head. There were dark patches on the grey singlet too, and when he finally called it a day it was Mackenzie who pushed in through the door, grabbed a towel and tossed it across.

'Billy? Paul Winter, one of my team.'

The two men exchanged nods. Angel was sitting on the rowing machine, gently sliding the seat back and forth, sucking air into his lungs. Winter wondered whether to take issue with the word 'team' but decided against it. Angel had the scariest eyes he'd ever seen.

Mackenzie had evidently recovered since last night. There wasn't a hint of contrition in the way he bossed the conversation. He was in control again. This was his hotel, his world. People like Winter did his bidding.

Minutes later, back upstairs in Mackenzie's office, Winter wanted to know more about Angel.

'Guy's been around for years, mush. He runs on the seafront most mornings, calls in for a little sesh here when he fancies it. Makes a change from skinny fucking women wanting to look at themselves all day. Lovely bloke. Handy too.'

'Yeah?'

'Yeah. And I'd know, believe me.'

He gave Winter a nod, leaving the rest unspoken. Winter was tempted to ask about Kieron O'Dwyer. Was this the two-punch hero that had put the lad in hospital?

'What next then?' Mackenzie wanted to move on. He was playing the executive now, the busy CEO with a great deal on his mind. Since coming upstairs, his mood seemed to have darkened. Last night was plainly history. 'You'll need Tommy Peters' details, right?'

'Right.'

'Anything else? Only I've got no time to fuck about.'

'Lou Sadler?'

'Forget Lou Sadler. Lou Sadler's got fuck all to do with anything. I pay your wages, mush. You do what I tell you. And right now that means Tommy

Peters. Here.' He pulled open his desk drawer and slid a white envelope towards Winter. 'There's five hundred quid in there. Go to London. Talk to Peters. Buy him a meal. Give him a nice time. But get him fucking *sorted*, yeah?'

Winter looked at the envelope, then picked it up. He'd rarely seen Mackenzie this blunt, this aggressive. Last night he'd seemed on the edge of some kind of breakdown. Now he was back at full throttle.

'I meant what I said yesterday, Baz. This isn't for me any more. I'll do what I can about the toot, maybe Peters too. After that you're on your own.'

'You think it's that easy?'

'I think I've had enough.'

'Then think again, old son. And while you're about it, have a proper think about what happened with Westie down in Malaga. You know why? Because it isn't just Mr fucking Peters you should be worried about. It's me too. Like I said downstairs, we're a team. Someone wants out, that's a huge fucking problem.'

The silence hung between them. Then Winter's mobile began to ring. He looked at it. Misty Gallagher.

'You want to take that outside, mush?' Mackenzie nodded at the phone. 'Only I'm really busy.'

Chapter Fourteen

THURSDAY, 12 FEBRUARY 2009. *11.07*

Parsons was raging. Linked in by conference call, Faraday could imagine the scene in her office at Fratton nick. A D/S called Dave Michaels was responsible for the surveillance teams. He'd been hauled in from Totton for the full treatment.

'So what happened? Pretend there's some fucking excuse here. Talk me through it.'

Parsons never swore, hated the F-word. Faraday glanced up at Suttle. Suttle was grinning. This must be worse than bad.

'I talked to the guys on the night shift just now. As far as they're concerned, Mackenzie and Gallagher left last night.'

'You're telling me they saw her?'

'The Bentley went past in a pretty big hurry. The lighting wasn't great.'

'So *was* she in there? *In* that car? Did they *see* her?'

There was a brief silence. Michaels was an old hand, lots of experience, brilliant in interview. Not this one though. Not with Parsons about to throttle the life out of him.

'It might have been a question of inference.'

'*Inference?* Since when did obs have anything to do with inference? You lot cost us a fortune. The least we expect is you keep your eyes open. I can't sell inference to Mr Willard. Or a jury. Or anyone else for that matter. So tell me, D/S Michaels, what actually happened?'

'One of the guys thought she was in the car.'
'And the other one?'
'Caught short.'
'Christ. So let's go back to the first guy. He sees the car. It's a Bentley. It obviously belongs to Mackenzie. Right colour, right reg plate. It comes shooting past him with Mackenzie at the wheel, and because he's got shagging rights on Misty Gallagher he assumes she's in there as well. Am I right?'
'You could be, boss.'
'So what does that make your D/C? Apart from lazy and stupid?'
'Pass. I'll be having a word.'
'You bet your life. You know what happens now? You know what we have to do? Call off obs on Winter. That's great, isn't it? After just . . . what . . . *twelve hours*? Brilliant. Total result. Congratulations, D/S Michaels. I imagine Mr Willard may well be in touch.'
Faraday heard the scrape of a chair. Dave Michaels would take this on the chin. He'd doubtless been in worse scrapes and in a couple of months the scene at Winter's flat would have become the stuff of legend. Couple of techies caught in the act. Misty Gallagher all over them.
In the meantime, as Parsons had pointed out, surveillance on someone as astute as Winter would have to be abandoned. The way things were going just now he'd probably haul them off to court. Trespass with intent. Or some evil infringement of human rights legislation.
'Joe? Are you still there?' It was Parsons. Michaels had evidently dropped out of the conversation.
'Yep.'

'Pathetic, don't you think?'

'Not great.'

'Not *great*? Where have you been recently, Joe, apart from the inside of an Egyptian hospital? Winter's home free again. And this time he hasn't even tried.'

Faraday was looking at Suttle. Was now the time for Suttle to table his belief that Winter's days with Bazza Mackenzie were over? Suttle shook his head, put his finger to his lips. It had been Faraday's idea to invite him along to the conference call. Just now he'd prefer to stay anonymous.

'So what do we do, Joe? Any ideas?'

Faraday brought her up to speed on the burned-out Corsa. He had a POLSA team combing the woods. He had detectives on house-to-house in a slowly widening area around the forest. And he'd tasked another team to return to the CCTV centre in Newport, hunting—once again—for the Corsa. Their working assumption put the car somewhere to the north or east of the island, where most of the population lived. For the last couple of days it must have been in a lock-up of some kind. Given a glimpse or two on CCTV, and they might be able to narrow the search.

'And?'

'Nothing so far, I'm afraid. Early days though.'

'Nothing from the house-to-house?'

'Nothing.'

'What about intel? What about Suttle?'

'He's still building the picture. He thinks the key to this thing is Holman. And from where I'm sitting, he's probably right.'

'Great. Keep in touch, eh?'

The phone went dead. Faraday sat back in his

chair and looked at Suttle.

'Did that sound about right?'

'Perfect, boss.' Suttle was looking thoughtful. 'You're doing OK.'

*   *   *

Winter sat on the hovercraft, bouncing across the Solent towards Ryde. After a brief phone exchange with Misty outside Mackenzie's office, he'd just had a longer conversation. She'd told him about the guys in the white overalls and what they'd done to the wall light, and he'd known at once what they'd been up to. These were the sneaky-beakies you put into suss premises when you wanted the full SP. He'd worked with them on a few occasions himself. It meant that Major Crime had decided to target him big time, but thanks to Misty the whole thing had turned to rat shit. Misty, bless her, had a simpler take on all this. It was, she told Winter, a fucking outrage.

Winter knew he'd been lucky. So this morning's lone figure on the waterfront had, after all, been on obs. Quite how long they'd had him under surveillance was anyone's guess, but they'd been wasting their time so far, and now he was off the hook. Even Hantspol were bright enough to figure that from here on in he'd be careful where he put his feet.

The hovercraft roared up the ramp beside the Ryde terminal. Winter joined the dribble of disembarking passengers and sauntered along the seafront towards the cab rank. He waited until the first three cabs had gone before bending to the fourth and giving the driver an address in Cowes.

As the cab pulled away, he twisted round in the back seat, watching the road behind. Nothing. He turned back, making himself comfortable, enjoying the prospect of the next couple of hours.

Last night, in bed, Winter had asked Misty about Lou Sadler. According to Bazza, she and Sadler had once been mates. Was that true?

'Yeah. She was a headcase, that woman, but bright. She had a thing about jet skis too. She kept one down at Ocean Village, taught me how to do it. We used to bomb up and down Southampton Water, me on the back. She was nuts, Lou. She used to get behind one of those hydrofoils that go out to the island. If you ride across the wake and get it right you take off. Incredible. Shakes your arse to fucking pieces. Brilliant.'

Winter had asked her about Two's Company and she'd nodded. It was, she said, a makeover for a previous escort agency called Island Babes. Both operations had been Internet-based, with thumbnails of the girls on offer. Punters chose a tom they fancied, followed the prompts and turned up at one or other of the rented rooms. Payment was on a sliding scale depending on what you were after, and there'd been a limit of one hour for each session. Misty, who knew the guy behind Island Babes, thought it served the tackier end of the market. Some of the girls, she said, were real dogs, and if you were looking to make sensible money from this kind of investment then you had to take the business upmarket.

Lou Sadler, it seemed, had done exactly this. Two's Company was still an online operation, but the toms were far classier and Sadler made sure they kept their standards up. Many of them, according to Misty, had arrived from the old communist bloc, eager to sell their talents on the free market, and feedback from one punter she knew well had been enthusiastic. This guy, she explained, was a leading Pompey lawyer. He had money to burn, plus a raging coke habit, and had found the fuck of his dreams in the shape of a redhead from Minsk. She was funny as well as dextrous, and he was close to proposing something more permanent than busy afternoons in a Cowes motel.

Winter sat back, enjoying the journey. There'd been no sign of a Kaija Luik on the Two's Company website he'd checked this morning, but he knew these girls regularly changed their names. Word from Misty suggested that it was a happy ship and that they all knew each other. If that was true then his afternoon date might turn out more than helpful. Her name was Monique Duvall. Winter had chosen her because she had a pretty face and claimed to speak good English. A recent encounter with an Uzbek girl in Dubai had come to grief when a linguistic misunderstanding over her rates had threatened to land Winter with a four-figure bill. They hadn't even made it as far as bed.

The taxi dropped him outside a hotel on the outskirts of Cowes. He gave the driver a decent tip and ignored the wink. At reception, as instructed, he asked whether Room 18 was available. The guy behind the counter looked young enough to be a student. He had a light American accent. He gave Winter the room key, took an imprint of his credit card and told him that £200 bought him the girl for an hour, room included. After that, he said, he was on the meter.

Winter took the lift to the first floor. The room was clean if a little bare. The bowl of fruit included three bananas and he thought at once of Misty. In the early days, before they'd settled into each other, she'd taught him an awful lot about bananas.

He took off his jacket and his shoes, and wandered across to the window. The hotel was perched on a hillside above the Solent and he watched the long white stripe behind a departing car ferry slowly disappear. He was still thinking about Misty when he heard a knock at the door.

Monique was taller than he'd imagined but he'd got the smile right. She stepped into the room without a word of introduction and folded her raincoat carefully over the back of the chair. She was wearing the kind of white Lycra top that Winter had last seen in the gym at the Royal Trafalgar and a pair of tight jeans. The black leather belt was wide, with a silver buckle. Expecting an outbreak of bling, Winter was comforted by her simplicity. She had a single silver piercing in one ear and she'd barely bothered with make-up. Misty had been right. Classy women.

She beckoned him towards her, kissed him on the mouth.

'Hi,' she said.

Winter had been in two minds about what was going to happen next. He'd set off with the intention of getting down to a little chat but all of a sudden it seemed churlish to complicate things too early. They had an hour. Plenty of time to talk later.

She peeled his clothes off, one by one, then asked him what he'd like. Full service was in the price but she liked a man to tell her what he really wanted.

Winter said he didn't care. Her choice.

'You have a condom?'

'No.'

'I have.'

She led him towards the bed and then fetched her bag. Naked between the sheets, Winter watched her extract a couple of paperbacks before finding the packet of condoms.

'How many?'

'One's fine.' He gestured beyond the white hump that was his belly. 'All yours, love.'

The girl put the condom to one side. In the event, minutes later, Winter didn't need it. The girl smiled, wiping her chin.

'Maybe next time?' She was looking at the other condom.

Winter nodded, relaxing back against the pillow. The last occasion he'd met a girl like this was years ago, in a brothel in Old Portsmouth. Her name had been Maddox. Their relationship had begun in an interview room at Central police station and ended in bed, and they'd stayed very close for a while. She, like Monique, knew how to put a man at ease. She also devoured books, and went nowhere without a paperback or two.

'So what are you reading?' Winter nodded at her bag. If he still smoked, he thought, then this would be the perfect moment.

Monique laughed.

'Why do you want to know?'

'I just do. I'm nosy that way.'

'Nosy?' She touched her own nose.

'Curious.'

'Ah . . .'

She hopped out of bed and retrieved the books from her bag. She had the most perfect arse.

Catcher in the Rye and a book in French. He picked it up. Michel Houellebecq.

'Is this one a novel?'

'*Oui.* And *very* dirty.'

He thumbed through it. She'd turned over a page towards the end. Winter was wondering about the condom but knew he mustn't get carried away. First things first.

'Do you mind if I ask you something?'

'Go ahead.'

'There's a girl you might know.' He softened the question with a smile. 'Kaija?'

'Kaija? Kaija Luik?'

'Yes.'

'You want to meet her?'

'Yes.'

'Why?'

'Why do you think?'

Monique turned her head away. Winter couldn't work out whether the tiny pout signalled disapproval or disappointment. Why another woman so soon? Wasn't I good enough for you?

He found her hand under the duvet, gave it a tiny squeeze. He said he had a friend who went with Kaija.

'Who is he, this friend?'

'Just a friend.'

'You won't tell me?'

'It wouldn't be right.'

'But you ask me about Kaija. And I tell you. I say yes, I know Kaija. So why don't you tell me about your friend?'

'Because . . .' Winter feigned embarrassment. He was enjoying this. It was much, much easier than he'd thought and—God willing—he knew exactly where it might lead.

Monique was up on one elbow. She had small firm breasts and an all-over tan.

'This friend of yours, he's the same age?'

'As Kaija?'

'As you.'

'Yes. Pretty much.'

'And he . . .' She was looking deep into Winter's eyes, warier now. '. . . he sees Kaija a lot? Goes with her?'

'Yes.'

'A small man? Short? Little? Not so handsome here.' She touched Winter's face. 'Yes?'

Winter remembered the photo on the TV news the other morning. It was a shot from way back. These days, thanks to oceans of Stella, Holman was doubtless even more wrecked.

'That's him,' he said. 'His name's Johnny. Johnny Holman.'

'And you say he's a friend of yours?'

'He used to be.'

'But not now?'

'No.'

She nodded, thoughtful. Then she looked at her watch.

'He's horrible, this man. You know that? You know how horrible he is?'

'To you?'

'To Kaija.'

'So why does she go with him?'

'Because she's sorry for him. Because she's stupid. He's always drunk, this Johnny. And he smells.' She lay back against the bedhead and folded her arms. 'You're a cop, aren't you? I know cops. My brother's a cop. In Vilnius. You know Vilnius?'

‘I’m not a cop.’

‘No?’

‘No.’ Winter shook his head. ‘I used to be, but I’m not any more.’

‘A private cop, then. That’s why—’ she swung her legs out of bed and stood up ‘—you ask me all these questions.’

Winter was looking at her watch. He still had half an hour. He nodded down at the bed.

‘Are we going to do it again?’

‘No.’

‘Why not?’

‘I need a wash. I want to go.’

She disappeared into the bathroom and shut the door. Her bag was on the carpet beside the bed. Winter found her mobile beneath a ball of tissues. He reached for his clothes, pulled on his trousers, pocketed the phone. By the time Monique returned from the bathroom he was standing by the window, fully dressed.

‘So where do I find Kaija?’ he asked.

‘I don’t know.’

‘I don’t believe you.’

‘It’s true. I try to phone her on Sunday, Monday, Tuesday. She owes me money. I phone again this morning. She never answers.’ She shrugged. ‘So maybe she’s gone.’

‘Gone where?’

‘I don’t know. Home maybe?’ She offered a bleak smile. ‘Nice to meet you, Mr Cop.’

Chapter Fifteen

THURSDAY, 12 FEBRUARY 2009. *15.02*

The Scenes of Crime team released Monkswell Farm in mid-afternoon, a little later than expected. After nearly four days on site, examining every square inch of what remained of the property, sieving through a small mountain of sodden ash and miscellaneous debris, the Crime Scene Manager had bagged what little evidence he'd found and sent it over to the Major Incident Room in Ryde. All that remained for the team now was to tidy up the site, get rid of the police tape, hitch the SOC caravan to the tow vehicle, and make their way back to the car ferry. A call from the duty Crime Scene Coordinator had already put them on standby for a bloodfest in Aldershot. A squaddie returning three days early from Afghanistan had discovered his wife in bed with a fitness instructor. Happy days.

Meg Stanley too was returning to the mainland. She'd called into Ryde police station to say goodbye to the core management team who'd been driving the investigation since the weekend. Now she'd got as far as Faraday's office and was waiting for him to come off the phone. Last night she'd had a quiet drink with Jimmy Suttle and was a little wiser about his personal circumstances.

Faraday at last put the phone down. If you measured progress by the number of calls he was getting, he said, then *Gosling* should have been home and dry by now.

'You look much better,' she said at once.

'Really? What did I look like before?'
'Terrible. Pale. Exhausted. Not well at all.'
'Thanks.'
'I mean it. You know what was the giveaway?'
'Tell me.'
'Your hands. You were doing this all the time.' She made a washing motion with her hands. 'That's OCD in my book.'
Obsessive-compulsive disorder. One step along the road to madness.
'And now?'
She didn't say anything, just nodded at his hands. They were flat on the desk, totally motionless. Faraday looked down at them.
'So what does that say?'
'It says you're getting better.' She extended her own hand. 'It's been a pleasure. I just wish we could have been more help.'
Faraday shrugged. He didn't know what to say. Inside, where it mattered, he felt far from better, but he saw no point in complicating this courtly little scene with the truth.
The silence was becoming uncomfortable. Stanley nodded at the phone.
'All these calls . . . anything interesting?'
'Not really. We're still in the dark about the Corsa. We've got nothing on CCTV and the house-to-house was a waste of time. Your guys drew a blank too. Am I right?'
Stanley nodded. She'd called in another CSI from Shanklin. He'd spent a couple of hours crawling all over the little car but had found nothing in the way of useful evidence. For the second time in a week fire had defeated them. Another apology. Another nod at the phone.

'Nothing else?'

'Only a message from the CIU. They got the billing on Difford's mobile. The last call was to another mobile at 03.29 on Sunday morning. Since then no one's used it.'

For the Communications Intelligence Unit a two-day turnaround on billings was fast.

'By that time in the morning Difford would have been dead.' Stanley was trying to put this new development in context.

'You're right. Which probably puts the phone in Difford's car.'

'The Corsa.'

'Exactly.'

'Driven by Holman?'

'That's the assumption. There's no other way he could have left the premises.'

'And you say they've got the number he called?'

'Yeah. They've traced that too. It's a Pay As You Talk. Bought two months ago from a place in Reading.'

'Credit card?'

'Cash.'

'Shame.' A credit card would have left an audit trail: a name, contact details. A handful of notes for a Pay As You Talk left nothing.

'Have you contacted the store?'

'Of course.'

'And?'

'They've got the transaction details and the name of the girl who handled the sale, but it was just before Christmas and there's no way she's going to remember a face after that length of time.'

'Is she still there?'

'No. She moved to Manchester last week. I might

get someone up there. I haven't decided yet.'

Stanley nodded. Something else had occurred to her.

'We're assuming Holman took off with the cocaine, yes?'

'If we're right about the cocaine, it's certainly a possibility. The postman saw him on the Thursday. That's when he was working round the back of the property. He had all day Friday and all Saturday to lift the stuff out. He could have taken it elsewhere at any point. He had a big old Land Rover. Plenty of room.'

'I know. We boshed it.'

'And found nothing. We've been back to the ferry companies too, checking bookings in his name for Friday and Saturday.'

'And?'

'Nothing. But that proves sod all. If there *was* anything in that hole, and we're assuming there must have been, then he could have shipped it back to the mainland in any number of vehicles. We just don't know.'

'So it could still be on the island?'

'Of course. That's the whole point. If this stuff exists, it could be anywhere.'

'And you think it does exist?'

'Yes. The intel's circumstantial but it's bloody strong. Holman kept the right company. Times are hard. If you were babysitting a load of cocaine or whatever and you wanted to cash in, then now would be the time. Am I right?'

'Yes.' Stanley nodded. 'And who digs a hole for the fun of it?'

'Exactly. Which leaves us with a number of questions. Number one: where's Holman? Number two: what's he done with the goodies? Number three: how did he remove them from the farm? Personally, I think this guy is completely away with the fairies. The intelligence tells us his brain's shot to pieces. He's messed up big time with his stepdaughter. His life's in bits. I'd love to buy the theory that he's worked all this out, that he's planned it all, that he's done everything in the right order, made a decision, dug up the goodies, found a buyer, shipped the stuff out, then settled his debts with the rest of the family. But that's never going to happen. Like I say, the guy's stuffed. For my money, events overtook him. There's a trigger here. Something happened on the Saturday night, something that pushed him over the edge. The killings themselves seem pretty organised. At least he got that bit right. But we still don't know why he did it.'

'No intruders? No strangers in the property?'

'I doubt it. Holman's the guy we need to find.' He paused. 'Fifty blocks of cocaine? Could you get that kind of weight into a Corsa?'

Stanley gave the proposition some thought. Eventually she nodded.

'No problem,' she said. 'The back floorwell, the back seat and the boot would do it. You'd need a bit of time to fit it all in but it's perfectly possible.' She paused. 'But there's a problem here, isn't there?'

'Go on.'

'Holman's broke. Like you say, he's probably looking after the stash for someone else.'

'And?'

'Who *is* that someone else?'

'Good question, Meg.' Faraday, for the first time

in days, felt alive. 'And one we're eager to crack.'

* * *

Winter put another call through to Lou Sadler. Her number had been stored on the mobile he'd lifted from Monique's bag. The first time he phoned, there'd been no answer. Now came a female voice, someone busy, someone who resented this sudden interruption.

'Who's that?' Winter was using his own mobile. She wouldn't have recognised the number.

Winter introduced himself. He said he was making enquiries for a client.

'Enquiries about what?'

'I'd prefer to discuss this in person.'

'How did you get this number?'

'We can discuss that too.'

There was a brief silence. Then she came back on the phone.

'If you're wasting my time, Mr Winter, you'll regret it.' She named a car park at the back of Cowes High Street. She'd be driving a red Megane convertible. Half an hour. On the dot. The phone went dead.

Winter got to the car park with ten minutes to spare. Across the road was a parade of shops. It was getting dark by now and he found shelter from the wind in the doorway of a firm of undertakers, admiring the wicker coffin on display in the window. While he was waiting, a woman appeared at the door. She'd noted his interest in the coffin and said she had a friend in the Women's Institute who specialised in weaving flowers into the wicker bits. Winter thanked her and pocketed the contact card. A scarlet Megane had just pulled into the car park. He wandered across.

The woman behind the wheel opened the passenger door. Winter bent down.

'You're asking me to get in?'

'Yeah.'

Winter did what he was told. She was a big woman, her face framed in a tumble of auburn curls. Despite the weather she was wearing a rust-coloured singlet that showcased her chest. An elaborate rose tattoo coiled over one shoulder, and Winter glimpsed another plunging down over her right breast. She wore a heavy gold bracelet on one wrist and the ruby on her ring finger was the size of a walnut. This woman belongs in a fairground, thought Winter. Or on the door of a nightclub with a reputation for kicking off.

'What's this about?' She was eyeing Winter without much enthusiasm. 'And how did you get my number?'

'Misty Gallagher.'

'You know Mist?'

'Very well.' Winter offered his own mobile. 'Help yourself. Just press go.'

Sadler put the phone to her ear. Winter had already primed Misty to expect the call. When she answered, there was a brief exchange. Winter felt the woman's eyes looking him up and down.

'You need him to lose weight, Mist,' she said. 'He's way too fat.'

Winter heard Misty's cackle of laughter. Then Sadler was handing back the phone. She had ten minutes before she was due elsewhere. Whatever Winter wanted had better be quick.

'Kaija Luik,' he said. 'Where is she?'

'I've no idea. Are you the Old Bill, or what?'

'Used to be.'

'That's what Mist just said.'

'Then it must be true.'

Something about Winter seemed to amuse her. She put her head to one side, narrowed her eyes.

'I've seen you before, haven't I?' She was right. They'd met on the pier, one of Bazza's boxing evenings, last year or the year before. She'd been wearing a red spray-on dress, drawing whistles of approval from the sizeable crowd, and had arrived with a huge Dobermann which had cleared a path to her ringside seat. The ageing car salesman two seats along had spilled most of his lager with the excitement of it all.

'Never.' Winter shook his head. 'I'd remember someone like you.'

'You're lying.' At least she was still smiling. 'So why Kaija? You fancy it?'

'This isn't about me, love. It's about my client.'

'He fancies it?'

'He wants to get in touch with her. Old times, eh?'

'Really?'

'Yeah. Bit of a number, the way I hear it. Him and Kaija.'

'So what's his name? This client of yours?' The smile had gone.

'Johnny. Johnny Holman.'

There was a long silence. Sadler was studying Winter carefully.

'You know Johnny?' she said at last.

'Yes. Not as well as young Kaija, but yes.'

'So why doesn't he get in touch with her himself?'

'He can't.'

'Can't?' Her eyes were stony. She was fiddling with the ring. 'And why would that be?'

'I've no idea. He's been trying since Sunday. She's not answering.'

'You're sure about that?'

'That's what he tells me.'

'When?'

'When what?'

'When did he tell you that?'

'This morning. Over in Pompey.'

'Really? But Johnny's been missing for a while. That farm of his burned down. The Old Bill are trying to trace him. It's been all over the news.'

'You're right.'

'But you're telling me you know where he is?'

'Yeah.' Winter nodded. 'As of this morning, half nine, definitely.'

'Amazing.'

'Amazing how?'

'Just . . .' she shrugged '. . . amazing. You say you were Old Bill yourself?'

'That's right.'

'So why not do them a favour? Grass him up?'

'How could I? Johnny's my client.'

'He pays you?'

'Of course he pays me.'

'How come? He's skint. Johnny's always skint. Totally boracic.'

'Not any more.'

'What does that mean?'

'It means he's come into money. Lots of money. Am I getting warm, Lou?'

It was the Christian name that did it. Plus the bit about the money. Plus the matey smile, the sense of a shared secret, the acknowledgement that this coded conversation had come full circle. He could see it in her eyes, in the slight upward tilt of her head. She wanted this exchange to end. But not before she'd landed a punch of her own.

'You work for Mackenzie, don't you? That's where Misty comes in. You're the bent little Filth he took on board. You're the bagman, the guy who's supposed to keep him out of trouble. I was right all along. You were on the pier, along with his other toadies. Funny that.'

'Funny?'

'Yeah. You looked all right in a DJ.'

Winter held her eyes for a moment or two longer, then slipped the card from the undertakers out of his pocket and propped it on the dashboard.

'It's been a pleasure.' He shot her a smile. 'I'll be in touch.'

* * *

Faraday was on the point of leaving when Jimmy Suttle appeared at his open door. He'd just had a call from Parsons, good news as it turned out.

Suttle, scenting some kind of breakthrough, wanted to know more.

'She's called me back for the forensic management meeting tomorrow. Half ten at Fratton. She's in the chair, of course, but after that she's coming across to hold the fort until Monday.'

'Meaning?'

'Meaning I get the weekend off.'

'Great.' Suttle sank into the chair. He loathed Parsons. 'So how does that all work?'

'She got a call from Personnel. Apparently they told her to go easy with me. She's good at risk assessment. She had no choice.'

'And you're the risk?'

'So it seems.'

'So you're off *Gosling* completely? Is that what you're telling me?'

'Not at all. Back Monday. Sparrow fart.' He got to his feet and shot Suttle a grin. He felt immeasurably better. Then he realised that his intel D/S might have something to tell him.

Suttle nodded. He'd just had a call from Nadine Lorrimer, Kim Crocker's friend. Nadine, it seemed, had been brooding about Robbie Difford. The fact that Robbie's was one of the bodies recovered from the farm had changed everything. When she'd talked to them before, she'd missed one or two things out. Just in case she landed Robbie in trouble.

'Like what?'

'Like what really happened on the Saturday night.'

Faraday sat down again. He needed to hear this.

'And?'

'The police came round after the treble nine, just like Nadine told us. Robbie was already there. The uniforms did what they could then fucked off on another call. Which left the three of them again.'

'Remind me. Where was Mum and the sister?'

'Out somewhere. The point is, boss, that Holman got really stroppy, told Robbie to fuck off, told him he was an interfering little cunt, said he was making Kim really unhappy.'

'And was he?'

'Of course he wasn't. Not according to Nadine.'

'So what happened?'

'Holman lost it completely, took a swing at the

lad.'

'And?'

'Robbie decked him. Kneed him in the nuts and gave him a kicking.'

'Nadine's sure about this?'

'She's telling me it's gospel.'

'She'd be happy to repeat it in court? If she has to?'

'Better than that. She's saying it'd be a pleasure.'

Faraday nodded, pulled a pad from a drawer, wrote himself a note. This, he knew, was the trigger, the single episode that had—in all probability—set in motion everything that had followed.

'Can she remember the exact date?'

'It's on the file, boss. The uniforms logged it.'

'Of course they did. Remind me.'

'Monday 2nd February. That's ten days ago.'

'Excellent.' He wrote down the date, leaned back in the chair, went through the timeline. 'Monday, Holman has the ruck with Difford. Gets a kicking for his troubles. And all this in front of the stepdaughter. He's made a dick of himself already as far as she's concerned, but this makes everything worse. Next thing we know, he's up in London at a clinic for sexual dysfunction. Yes?'

'Yes.'

'Then he's back down again, back at the farm, desperate to get at whatever's in that hole of his. The Friday's still a blank. Saturday night the younger daughter goes into Newport. She's going to be kipping over with a mate but something kicks off and she wants to come home. Mum says no. Stay where you are. So we can reasonably assume things are getting tricky again at the farm.'

'Holman's pissed, bound to be.' Suttle took up the

running. 'Difford's up there, playing the white man, keeping an eye on Kim, maybe Mum as well.'

'Yeah, exactly. And by now we can assume that Holman has dug up whatever he needs to dig up.'

'Right.' Suttle nodded. 'So what happens next?'

'We don't know. Not for certain. But Holman's got access to a couple of shotguns. He's pissed again. He's had all week to stew about what kicked off on the Monday. These aren't his kids. Difford's humiliated him. Julie thinks he's a pervert. It writes itself, doesn't it?'

'Four bodies, boss? You really think that's enough for four bodies?'

'Maybe not. But add whatever was in that hole and it starts to look plausible, *n'est-ce pas*?'

Suttle tipped his head back. One of the reasons Faraday rated him so highly was the kind of attention he gave to propositions like this. He never took short cuts. He always asked himself the harder questions.

'It's still not enough,' he said. 'You're Holman. You're about to kill four people. You're about to torch the house of your dreams, everything you possess in the world. There has to be hope. There has to be light at the end of the tunnel. I know he's a fruitcake but he has to have a *plan.*'

'Like what?'

'Like Kaija Luik.'

*   *   *

Winter sat in a pub round the corner from the car park where he'd met Lou Sadler. She'd driven off without a backward glance, ignoring his cheerful wave of farewell. A working lifetime in the Job had taught him a great deal about guilt—what to look for, what it smelled like—and he had absolutely no doubt that Sadler had played some kind of role in what had happened at the farm. Jimmy Suttle had been right. A woman like that would have seen him off without breaking sweat. Quite what had happened to Kaija Luik was anybody's guess but Winter had found another stored number on Monique's mobile and was determined to find out.

The number, 07854 633524, was badged *K*. He'd tried it twice already. Both times it had rung and rung before the answering service cut in. Now he dialled it again, reaching for his bottle of Stella, wondering if pubs in Cowes were always so empty.

He was about to hang up when he heard a voice. It was an old voice, a woman's voice, an air of faint confusion.

Winter asked to talk to Kaija. He had to repeat the name three times. Finally, it registered.

'She's not here.'

'Do you know where she is?'

'No. Are you calling about her things?'

'Her things?'

'That bag of stuff she left? Only it's no use to me.'

Winter bent to the phone, his drink abandoned. He confirmed he'd be calling round for the bag. Kaija, he said, had asked him to pick it up.

The woman mumbled something he didn't understand. When he asked for an address, she didn't seem to hear. He repeated the question, louder, then louder still. The girl behind the bar stopped watching the Robbie Williams video, glanced his way.

The woman on the phone was back on the line: 6 St Andrew's Road. He'd have to be quick because she was going out any minute.

Winter was already on his feet, reaching for his coat. There was a list of taxi firms pinned up beside the door. He still had his mobile in his hand and he began to dial the first number but the girl behind the bar told him not to bother. There was a cab rank round the corner, she said, still watching the video.

Chapter Sixteen

THURSDAY, 12 FEBRUARY 2009. *18.04*

Colin Leyman was watching the early-evening news when he heard the knock at the front door. He hauled his bulk off the kitchen stool and glanced at his watch. His mate Chris was due at half six. Maybe he'd come early on purpose, he thought. Maybe he fancied a tinny or two before they got down to refighting Marshal Ney's late-afternoon cavalry charges against Wellington's redcoats.

The thought put a smile on his face. He'd spent most of the afternoon putting the finishing touches to his new troop of French cuirassiers. He'd bought them only last week, exquisite little mounted figures, and the painting had taken him an age to get right. He'd copied the uniforms from the best reference book he could find, a volume of engravings he'd picked up in an antiquarian second-hand shop in Albert Road, and he'd double-checked the results against some more prints he'd nailed down on Wikipedia. Chris, he knew, would love them.

The knocking again, more insistent this time. He shuffled along the narrow hall, hauling up his jeans. There was a blob of blue paint on one of the knees where he'd had an accident with the cuirassiers, and his fingers tracked absently down, scratching at the scab.

The door to the front room was ajar and he checked inside, making sure everything was exactly the way he wanted Chris to see it: Wellington's tightly bunched squares of infantry waiting for the French cavalry; the cuirassiers themselves preparing to charge; and the distant figure of Napoleon Bonaparte, caped in scarlet, mounted on a magnificent grey.

Satisfied, he turned to the front door and pulled it open. Expecting Chris's carefully trimmed beard, he found himself looking at someone shorter, more squat. There was another figure too, much bigger, standing beside him.

'Colin Leyman?'

'Yeah?'

'Your lucky day, son. Compliments of Mr M.'

For a split second Leyman thought these people were bringing him good news. Then, for no good reason he could fathom, a hand seized his throat and his world began to darken.

* * *

Winter told the taxi driver to wait. Number 6 St Andrews Road was a solid post-war semi-detached on the edges of Cowes. The curtains were closed on the ground floor but there was a light on upstairs. A decent patch of front garden was home to a water feature—a dolphin dancing on its tail—and someone had made an effort with the carefully tended flower beds. Early crocuses, Winter thought, and probably a stand or two of daffs to follow. Even in the gloom of a February evening this would be a nice place to come home to.

He rang again, then caught the *clump-clump* of footsteps coming downstairs. Seconds later the door opened. The woman was old, thick cardigan under a green anorak, plaid skirt, a wisp of grey hair escaping from beneath her beret.

'Yes?' She peered out at him.

Winter said he was a friend of Kaija. They'd spoken on the phone. He'd come to pick up her stuff.

The woman seemed pleased to see him. He stepped inside and lingered at the foot of the stairs. The door to the room at the front was open. From what he could see, it looked bare: a boarded-up fireplace, two utility armchairs, a fold-up table, not much else.

'She must have left her phone.' Winter nodded at the room.

'Who, dear?'

'Kaija. That's who I rang. You must have heard it.'

'I did.' She fumbled in the pocket of the cardigan. Kaija's phone was silver, an Ericsson. The woman handed it over. 'She left it under her pillow, silly girl.'

'Behave herself, did she? Kaija?'

'Nice girl.' She nodded. 'Very nice girl.'

'How long was she here? Only I haven't seen her for a while.'

'Not long. Christmas, she came. Yes . . .' she sucked her teeth'. . . definitely Christmas. I put an ad in the paper. She came next day. Lovely girl. You can tell her that.'

'I will.'

'Something else too.'

'What's that?'

'She hasn't came back for her deposit. A month's rent it was, £400. You can tell her that too.'

Winter nodded. The woman seemed glad to have company. So far so good, he thought.

'When did she go, Kaija? To tell you the truth I'm a bit confused.'

'So am I, dear. I got a phone call a couple of days ago.'

'From Kaija?'

'No, someone else. She didn't say who she was, just that Kaija definitely wasn't coming back, and if I wanted to rent the place out again then maybe I should.' She peered harder at Winter. 'You don't want a room, do you?'

Winter declined the offer. He wanted to know when she'd last seen Kaija.

The woman frowned, trying to remember.

'Saturday morning,' she said finally. 'We had a little conversation about how awful the weather's been.'

'And Saturday night?'

'I wasn't here, dear. I stay at my sister's sometimes, over in Newport. That's where I'm off to now.'

'And you didn't see Kaija after that?'

'No. I came back on Sunday but she'd gone.'

'Just like that?'

'Yes. She left me a little note. Said her mother had been taken poorly. Back home.'

Winter asked whether Kaija had any friends who

used to come round.

'Just one, dear.'

'Man? Woman?'

'A man. Much older than her. Shorter too. On the small side.'

'That would be Johnny.'

'That's right.' She nodded. 'Johnny.'

'Did he come round a lot?'

'Yes, often. She had a key cut for him. She asked me and I said yes. He used to let himself in, Johnny. He'd get shopping for me sometimes—little things, bread. Nice man.'

Without warning, she turned on her heel and made off down the hall. Seconds later she returned with a black plastic bin liner, knotted at the top.

'This was in the garden at the back,' she said. 'I found it behind the toolshed. It must be Kaija's.'

'How do you know?'

'It was the only thing they left.' Her eyes strayed to the empty front room.

'They?'

'Those other friends of hers. That woman I mentioned just now? The one who phoned? She was here yesterday. Took everything away with her. Except that.' She nodded at the bin liner. 'They must have forgotten.'

'You said "they".'

'There was a man with her—big fella, long hair, younger. I think he was foreign, like Kaija.'

'And the woman?'

'Tattoos.' She pulled a face and then touched her shoulder and chest. 'Here and here. Not right, is it? Not on a woman.'

Winter smiled, then nodded at the bin liner.

'So what's inside?'

‘I don’t know. I haven’t looked. You wouldn’t, would you? When it’s not yours.’

Winter agreed. Very wise. He extended a hand, said goodbye. The old lady said he was welcome, drop in any time, and she stood at the door watching while he carried the bin liner back to the waiting taxi.

Winter told the driver to park up round the corner. He was an islander, born and bred. On the way up from the rank they’d talked about the way foreigners were taking the place over. Even on the island, even here, there was something funny going on. The politicians never discussed it because they were scared, but it was happening just the same.

The taxi came to a halt. In the back Winter was wrestling with the knot. Finally he got the bag open. The driver was watching him in the rear-view mirror.

‘What’s that smell?’

‘Woodsmoke.’ Winter was grinning now. ‘That satnav of yours.’

‘Yeah?’

‘Place called Monkswell Farm?’

The driver said he knew it. Nice place. Lovely place. Until it burned down.

Winter was checking his leather jacket. The envelope Mackenzie had given him was still there. So far he’d spent nearly sixty quid on fares and other bits and pieces. He stared out at the estate. It was still barely seven o’clock.

He asked the driver for a price to Monkswell Farm, then on to the Ryde Hovercraft.

The driver gave it some thought. ‘Fifty-five, mate. More if you keep me hanging around too long.’

‘Have you got a torch?’

'Yeah. Two. Big one or a small one.' He stirred the engine into life. 'Take your choice.'

* * *

Colin Leyman's war-gaming partner, Chris Possett, was late getting across to Eastney. He jumped off the bus and hurried down the road. He was about to ring Leyman's bell when he realised that the door was open. He pushed at it, peered inside. The hall light was on and he could hear the TV from the kitchen at the back.

'Col?' He listened for a reply, heard nothing, called again. The One Stop was just round the corner. Thinking Leyman must have gone out for milk or whatever, he stepped inside and made his way down the hall. Then he heard the noise. It was a groaning noise, faint, slightly bubbly. It happened again, louder. It was coming from the front room.

Possett felt the first cold prickles of fear. Something had happened. He could sense it. Something terrible. He went back to the front door, called Leyman's name again, then turned to the door to the front room. A tiny strip of light down the side told him that this too was open. He pushed at it, feeling his pulse beginning to race. Leyman was face down, sprawled across the papier mâché battlefield, blood from the wreckage of his mouth pooling in the hollows around a tiny crossroads.

Possett knelt beside him, eased his head, made sure he could breathe.

'What is it? What happened? Talk to me for fuck's sake.'

Leyman's eyes briefly opened. The effort of trying to speak produced a thin dribble of vomit. Possett bent closer. A single word, he thought. Or maybe two.

'Again, mate. Try again.'

Leyman shook his head, closed his eyes. Then came a final effort.

'Help me . . .' he whispered.

* * *

Faraday was home by eight. He'd spent an hour with Parsons at Kingston Crescent, updating her on *Gosling*, and had been gratified to learn that the pit stop over the coming weekend had indeed been Personnel's idea and not her own. As far as she was concerned, Faraday was driving the investigation forward with his normal thoroughness. But if Personnel advised he ease up for a day or two, then she was happy to take the wheel herself. Tomorrow they'd be meeting for the forensic review. After that, she said, his time was his own.

The Bargemaster's House, after camping at the hotel in Ryde, truly felt like home. Faraday padded upstairs, threw off his suit, changed into jeans and a sweater, poured himself a drink. The last time he'd been here, banged up with his memories, haunted by what had happened to Hanif, bewildered by a partner who seemed to have disappeared, he'd been a headcase. Now, for reasons he didn't fully understand, life was beginning to slip back into focus.

Part of this transformation he put down to *Gosling.* Suttle in particular was playing a blinder, pushing hard on a door that might unlock the entire investigation, and as the narrative began to shape itself around the missing Kaija Luik he felt that buoyancy, that slowly building wave a Major Crime team can catch and ride. Faraday knew he was still woefully off the pace. He knew that his old sharpness, those instincts that had served him so well in the past, had yet fully to return. But he knew that inside he was still the detective he'd always been, and for that small moment of recognition he was profoundly grateful.

He'd stopped at the supermarket on the way home. He made himself a tuna and egg risotto and pulled the cork from a bottle of Côtes-du-Rhône. All he needed now, he told himself, was Gabrielle, the old Gabrielle, the Gabrielle who'd be watching him from the other end of the table in the kitchen, telling him about her day, enveloping him in her world, making kind noises about his burned rice, and finally, much later, taking him to bed.

This was the life they'd jigsawed together, a life that had successfully resisted the demons that plagued so many of his colleagues. It was a life they cracked open from time to time, spilling the richness of the yolk into the trips they made together. Travel, Faraday told himself, was the test of any relationship. Curiosity, a sense of humour and sheer guile would get you through, and in the shape of Gabrielle he'd found all three.

He thought of her now, sharing breakfast only weeks ago in a deserted Sinai village. From nowhere Hanif had found watermelon, honey, flatbreads and a jug of freshly made yoghurt. They'd squatted among assorted debris in the shade of a gnarled acacia tree beside the village well, tossing corners of bread to a stray dog, making lazy plans for an afternoon of birding in the mountains. During the day Gabrielle wore a wide-brimmed straw hat. It had been everywhere with her, folded into rucksacks, stuffed into crannies on countless buses, trailed through remote country markets where a white face was rare. Faraday had a thousand photos of that hat, and of the sudden smile that brightened the shadow it cast, but the image he treasured above all was the photo he'd taken that morning beside the well. They were themselves. They had each other. Life was blissfully simple. Yet that same night it was all going to end.

He took the remains of the bottle upstairs, stirred his PC into life and scrolled through his emails. He answered the handful he regarded as important and then stood at the window, staring out at the harbour. As far as he could judge, Gabrielle had yet to set foot in the Bargemaster's House since her return to the UK. Her clothes, her laptop, the books she'd been devouring were exactly the way she'd left them before their departure to the Middle East. Tomorrow he'd pack the kind of clothes she might need, sort out a few of the books, make sure he remembered her laptop. Then he'd take them over to the hospital on Saturday, spend the whole day with her, try and fathom exactly what kind of perch she'd found for herself. He smiled at his reflection in the glass of the window, his fingertips tracing the contours of the face that had been through the windscreen, then he tipped back his head and swallowed the last of the wine.

* * *

A puncture delayed Winter en route to Monkswell Farm. The taxi was deep in the countryside south of Newport, a succession of bends that came out of nowhere, when the driver brought the Subaru to a halt beside a farm gate. The steering, he said, was all over the place.

He and Winter circled the car, checking each tyre. The front onside was flat. Winter, who'd once owned a Subaru, held the torch while the driver wrestled with the jack and the wheel brace. Two of the nuts had rusted and they took turns trying to free them. It was Winter, in the end, who did most of the work, and by the time they'd swapped the dud tyre for the spare, nearly an hour later, they were mates.

'You're sure I'm not keeping you?' The driver was worried about the hovercraft from Ryde.

'No problem. If I have to, I'll stay over.'

'You're sure?'

'Yeah.'

They motored on in companionable silence. Then the driver, who said his name was Petroc, wanted to know what Winter did for a living.

'I'm a cop.'

'That's what I thought.'

'Really?'

'Yeah.'

'Why?'

'The way you handle yourself. Calling in on the old lady. The bag. Stands to reason.'

Winter laughed. Maybe he was right. Once a cop always a cop.

According to the satnav they were close now, barely half a mile to go. Winter leaned forward, his arms crossed on the back of the front passenger seat.

'Do us a favour, Petroc?'

'What's that?'

'We were never here, right?'

Petroc nodded, then hauled the taxi left. A farm gate loomed up at the bottom of the track. Winter told him to switch the lights out and wait until he came back.

'You'll need the torch.'

'Cheers.'

Winter eased the gate open and followed the beam of the big torch towards the remains of the farmhouse in the hollow beyond. The ground beneath his feet was muddy and wet, and twice he found himself on his arse. He could smell the fire by now: even five days later it left a damp bitter aftertaste in the back of his throat. At the house he stopped to flick the torch up, tracking the beam across the smoke-stained walls, the black oblongs where the windows had once been, the yawning gap that was the front door.

It was a cold night, and the wind blew rags of cloud across a full moon. With the torch off, Winter stood motionless, letting the house swim out of the darkness, feeling the wind on his face, hearing the call of an owl in the trees to his left. Then he started to pick his way forward again, skirting round the property, following what seemed to be a well-beaten path. Scenes of Crime, he thought, had done a good clear-up job. No crushed polystyrene cups. No forgotten scraps of paper. Not a trace of the dozens of men and women who must have tried to tease a story out of the remains of Monkswell Farm.

At what he judged to be the back of the property he paused and switched on the torch again. A patch of turned earth and a stand of canes indicated some kind of garden. Beyond was a trellis for runner beans. He turned round, getting his bearings, aware of the two brick chimneys, survivors from the fire, towering above the carcass of the farmhouse. Then he moved slowly away, out into the garden, sweeping the torch left and right. Beyond the runner beans was something that looked like a shed. Beside it, a yawning hole.

Winter approached it step by step, knowing that this was what he'd come to find. On the very edge of the hole he stopped. The light of the torch pooled at the bottom. Water, he thought. He half-closed his eyes, trying to gauge the shape of the hole, its depth, the storage possibilities it offered. How much earth would you pile on top? And how much space would that leave for whatever you wanted to stash underneath? He was crap at this kind of exercise. He didn't have the kind of brain that could compute figures and turn out any kind of decent result. All he knew was that it was a big hole. And that you didn't do this much digging without a bloody good reason.

He took a step back. The surrounding earth had been beaten flat with countless footprints but there was a sizeable pile of soil and something more matted beyond. He stepped across and gave it a poke with his shoe. Then he scooped up a handful and took a sniff or two. Horse manure. No question.

He was on the point of returning to the house when his mobile began to ring. He fetched it out. Bazza Mackenzie. He stepped back towards the hole, the torch off, the phone to his ear.

Mackenzie wanted to know where he was.

'London.'

'Seen Peters?'

'Not yet.'

'Tried?'

'Not yet.'

'Well fucking get on with it, mush. I didn't give you all that moolah for nothing. We have a problem here. I may have mentioned it. And you know what? The guy's onto me again this afternoon. He wants a meet. He wants to talk money. And I get the impression he's not dicking us around.'

'You still think he's the one?'

'Peters? Do I think he's nicked off with all that toot? Do me a favour, mush. Just fucking listen for a change. The guy knows I was holding. He's skint. He's not happy when I tell him to fuck off. And so now he's helped himself. Since when do I make all this stuff up?'

'So why does he need to talk to us?'

'Good fucking question. Why don't you find out?'

'But there'd be no point, would there? Not if he was sitting on all that toot. He'd just cash in and move on. Why bother with conversations he doesn't have to have?'

'Fuck knows, mush. Ask him.' The phone went dead.

Winter was still gazing at the hole. He could hear the soft moan of the wind in the trees. After a moment or two he turned back towards the house. Before he left he couldn't resist a look inside. He switched on the torch again and headed for what must have been the back door. The door itself had been torn off its hinges and tossed to one side, presumably by the firemen. Winter stepped inside the thick cob walls. Above his head, through a lattice of charred beams, he could see a star or two. The smell was stronger here, the smell that reminded him of the bin liner he'd collected from the old lady, and underfoot he could feel the greasiness of the sodden ash.

The beam of the torch settled on a pile of rubble that must once have been a kitchen. He recognised the bones of a fridge. An Aga. A circuit board that might have belonged to a telly. The torch found the gleam of a bottle, then another, then a third, and Winter tried to imagine what kind of life Holman must have lived here. The booze, in the end, had done for him. And now this was all that remained.

Winter shivered, all too aware that his own life was close to a disaster of this magnitude. Not because he'd necked too much Stella or hooked up with an Estonian tom, but because he'd let the likes of Bazza Mackenzie go to his head.

As a working cop, he'd always known that a decent criminal was constantly ahead of the game. With half a brain and access to the right advice, you'd be stupid not to make decent money. That's the way it worked. That's the way society was set up. You filled the courts with infant shoplifters and drugged-up inbreds, hit the right performance targets and took promotion with a smile on your face. Pretty soon you were fluent in bollock-speak and counting the weeks until you hit your thirty and could cash in that big fat pension. That's what the blokes were doing more and more. That's what got them through.

But Winter hadn't done that at all. No. Winter had been stitched up by the likes of Willard and Parsons and hung out to dry on a u/c operation that had nearly got him killed. Therapy had arrived in the shape of Bazza Mackenzie. With him had come good money and a few laughs. Bazza had trusted him. They'd all trusted him, the whole family. His name was dog wank among the people he'd left behind, but Winter hadn't cared a toss. He was cruising. He was at 30,000 feet. He had money, respect, a nice car. He even had stolen shares in Misty Gallagher.

So where had it all gone wrong? And what the fuck was he doing in some khazi of a crime scene, mud all over his Guccis, trying to figure out what to do next? He glanced up then ducked his head, feeling a flurry of rain, knowing that there were decisions, important decisions, he couldn't afford to postpone any longer. Staying with Bazza Mackenzie would put him away for the rest of his life. Either that or something worse.

He shook his head, trying to rid himself of a growing sense of helplessness, following the torch beam back towards the door and the darkness beyond.

* * *

An ambulance took Colin Leyman to A & E at the Queen Alexandra hospital. He was admitted to one of the bays in the major injuries area, where his condition was assessed by one of the duty nurses. When she tried to discover exactly what had happened, Leyman shook his head. He was pale with shock. His huge body was trembling. He was in acute pain. There was no way he could talk.

The duty nurse went to find the Registrar, who confirmed a double fracture of the jaw. Mr Leyman would have to spend at least one night on a ward pending an operation under general anaesthetic in the morning. Both fractures, as far as the Registrar could tell, were towards the back of the jawbone, one on the left, one on the right. Fractures that close to the joint were extremely difficult to repair with metal plates. In all likelihood Mr Leyman's jaws would be wired together for at least six weeks.

As Leyman was wheeled away to the X-ray department, the nurse drew the Registrar to one side. She'd been on duty a couple of days ago and had seen an identical injury, this time on a youngster. Double fracture, left and right.

The Registrar, deep in another patient's file, looked up. He too remembered the earlier case.

'You're right,' he said. 'Remind me to follow it up tomorrow.'

Chapter Seventeen

FRIDAY, 13 FEBRUARY 2009. *12.16*

DCI Gail Parsons took the midday hovercraft over to Ryde. She'd chaired the morning's forensic management meet, agreeing the schedule of samples to be submitted for further tests and pressing the new Crime Scene Coordinator for any inferences she felt able to draw from the pitifully meagre harvest of evidence retrieved from Monkswell Farm. Like most CSCs, Meg Stanley had been reluctant to commit herself beyond the known facts. Firstly, the fire had been deliberately set. Secondly, all four retrieved bodies had been dead before the fire caught hold. And thirdly, a large hole had recently been excavated in the garden to the rear of the property. The latter would suggest the removal of items that had been buried earlier, but there was no evidence to indicate what these items might be. Nor was there any confirmed link to the fire itself.

D/S Jimmy Suttle had volunteered to save Parsons the walk from the hovercraft terminal to Ryde police station. Now they were sitting in the office she'd taken over from Faraday, who had already briefed Parsons on the latest intel developments. She wanted Suttle's thoughts on the best way forward.

Suttle had been anticipating this conversation. Thanks to Faraday's state of mind, he'd never had such a free hand on a Major Crime job. The last week on *Gosling* had taught him a great deal about the challenges facing the SIO and her Deputy, and Suttle sensed that every fresh development offered a new fork in the investigative road. His own role had been limited to intel, but now, seeing the bigger picture, he realised what could be at stake.

Parsons was waiting for an answer. Which of *Gosling*'s many lines of enquiry deserved most attention?

'Lou Sadler,' he said.

'Because?'

'Because she knew Holman. Because she probably keeps dodgy company. Because she keeps stalling on a photo she owes us. And because she's lying.'

'Lying how?'

'She gave us an address for the girl Kaija Luik in Cowes. It seems to have been empty for weeks.'

'Who says?'

'We knocked on doors up and down the road. Like I say, no one's seen any movement there since

Christmas.'

'This is a flat?'

'Yeah. There's a flat upstairs as well. No reply there either.'

'Who owns this place?'

'Lou Sadler.'

Parsons nodded. She wanted to know more about the photo.

'This is a shot of the girl? Luik?'

'Yes. She must have at least one because the girl would have been up there on the website. I've phoned her a couple of times to get the thing pinged across but there's always an excuse. Her webmaster's still away. He's not returning her calls. Whatever.'

Parsons was frowning now. Why hadn't she been told about this before? She'd talked to Faraday only this morning.

'It must have slipped his mind, boss. We discussed it yesterday.'

'Really?' Parsons raised an eyebrow. 'So what are you suggesting?'

'I think Sadler's bullshitting us. I think the girl's been living at some other address, and for whatever reason Sadler doesn't want us to know where. That in itself is interesting. I could go back to her, press her for more detail, but from where I'm sitting, boss, there's a better way.'

'Which is?'

'We put her under obs.'

Mention of surveillance drew a wince from Parsons. Her battle with the D/S over the cock-up at Winter's Gunwharf apartment had now got as far as the Assistant Chief Constable. Twenty-four-hour surveillance would also cost a fortune.

'But where would it take us?'

'I've no idea, boss. If I knew the answer we wouldn't be having this conversation.'

'But your reasoning, Jimmy. Your rationale.'

Suttle began to relax. He was enjoying this conversation. Parsons rarely stooped to Christian names.

'Sadler is desperate to keep us lot at arm's length. That may be because of the business she runs. She says it's all legit, and she may be right, but in that case there's no point in feeding us all this stuff. Like I say, the address she gave us is bullshit. It's clever bullshit but it's still bullshit.'

'Why clever?'

'Because we'd be pushed to prove she was lying. We can demand rent receipts, run checks on the meter, talk to the utilities people, trace the postman—all that stuff—but in the end she'd just shrug and say the girl must have been kipping somewhere else. That's not a crime. That's not something we could have her for.'

'So why did she give you that address in the first place?'

'Because we caught her on the hop. She was in bed when we arrived.'

'A decent hour?'

'Midday.'

'And was she alone?'

'No. I've no idea who she was shagging but she made a big mistake letting us in. So—' he shot Parsons a grin '—you take advantage of that, don't you? Press all the buttons. Make it hard for her. She admitted she had the information there. So there was no way we were leaving without it.'

'Good work.' Parsons offered a nod of

congratulation. 'So talk me through the obs again. What *might* it give us?'

'I don't know. Not for sure. But my feeling is she has lots of fingers in lots of pies. She's that kind of woman. We need to know about her lifestyle, her mates, her business associates, where she goes, who she sees—you know, persons who might be of interest. All that.'

'And the time frame?'

'A couple of days for starters. See where it takes us.'

Parsons nodded, then looked at her watch. In principle, she said, she was prepared to run with Suttle's proposal. Was there anything else she should have been told?

Suttle shook his head.

'It's just a shame the sneaky-beaky screwed up in Winter's flat,' he said. 'He might have spared us all this.'

* * *

Winter, back in his apartment in Blake House, had double-locked the door and opened a couple of windows. After a decent breakfast he put on a pair of Marigolds from the kitchen and retrieved the bin liner from the bottom of the airing cupboard, where he'd stored it overnight. He'd spread an old sheet on the living-room carpet. Now he upended the bin liner and carefully emptied the contents onto the sheet. The smell again, stronger this time. Smoke. Definitely. He took a tiny step back, gazing down at the pile of clothes: jeans, red ankle socks with blue hoops, a white Bob Dylan T-shirt, a denim jacket, plus a pair of mud-caked baseball boots. On the small side, he thought. Johnny Holman's. For sure.

On his hands and knees, he sorted through the various items, examining them one by one, playing the CSI the way he'd watched them operate on job after job. The T-shirt was white, with the imprint of a young Bob Dylan on the chest. Below was a line of brown splatters that were almost certainly blood. There was more blood crusted on the jeans and the cuffs of the denim jacket. This, Winter knew, was a crime scene. There was evidence here that Jimmy Suttle and the rest of the Major Crime lot would kill for, DNA that would very probably link Johnny Holman to the bodies at Monkswell Farm. In investigative terms this was as good as it ever got, and the very fact that Winter had helped himself, without the slightest intention of handing it in, was yet another bullet for Willard's gun.

He went through the pockets of the jeans and the denim jacket, retrieving a handful of coins, a couple of petrol receipts, a slip for a £150 withdrawal from a cash machine, a small Swiss Army penknife and a disposable lighter. He gazed at the lighter for a moment or two, wondering if Holman had used it to set the fire at Monkswell Farm. Even now he could still smell the sour wreckage in what remained of the kitchen. Shame, he thought. Partner, kids, quiet life in the country. All gone up in flames.

Winter took a last look at the clothes, then bundled them back into the bin liner, trying to visualise what must have happened. As far as he knew from the media reports, the fire had happened early on Sunday morning. If all this kit belonged to Holman, which he assumed it did, then Holman must have been present when the fire began. The blood splatters suggested his involvement in the four deaths. At some point later he arrived at Kaija's place, took all his gear off, stuffed it in the bin liner. Presumably he'd had a spare set of clothes to hand. But what then? Where had he and Kaija gone?

Winter took the bin liner back to the airing cupboard and fetched a spray can of air freshener from the kitchen. It was getting chilly in the apartment with the windows still open and he sorted out a fleece for himself from the bedroom. Last night he'd left both Kaija and Monique's mobiles beside his bed. Kaija's, just now, was the one he really needed.

He settled on the bed and studied the numbers she'd stored on the SIM card. To his surprise, there were only five. Maybe she kept another mobile for regular punters. One of the numbers he recognised from Monique's directory. It belonged to *L*. Lou Sadler. Three of the other numbers were also capital letters. The fourth wasn't. He stared at it. *Max*.

*   *   *

Faraday couldn't wait. After he'd given Parsons a lift to the hovercraft he drove home, packed some things for Gabrielle, threw a change of clothing in for himself and set off for Salisbury. For the next couple of days he needn't devote a single minute to thoughts of *Gosling*. Parsons herself had said so.

He was in Salisbury by half past one. He found a car park near the city centre, bought flowers for Gabrielle and chocolate for the child. He also spent half an hour or so browsing in the Early Learning Centre, emerging with a wooden bridge and a pair of matching toy cars in bright reds and yellows. He'd no idea what might put a smile on the face of a five-year-old Palestinian girl, but the idea of a bridge seemed somehow fitting.

The hospital car park, early afternoon, was nearly full. Faraday found a space in a far corner and retraced his steps to the Burns Unit. The double doors were still locked, but when he buzzed, a cleaner appeared to let him in. The paediatric rooms, it seemed, were at the far end of the unit. He got as far as the nurses' station before anyone challenged him.

'So who have you come to visit?' The nurse was admiring the flowers.

Faraday mentioned Leila's name. She was a little girl from Gaza. His partner was helping to look after her.

'Ah, Gabrielle . . . So you must be the policeman.'

The nurse stepped into an office and whispered something to a woman sitting behind a desk. The woman got up and beckoned Faraday into the office. She was tall, blonde, nice smile. Faraday was aware of the door closing behind him. He introduced himself. The woman said she was one of the sisters in charge on the unit. Her name badge read nicole lewis.

'Your first visit, am I right?'

'Yes. I've been busy, I'm afraid.' Faraday wondered why he was apologising. 'How is she?'

'Gabrielle?'

'The little girl. I think her name's Leila.'

'Ah . . .' The smile again. 'Definitely better than she was, poor little mite. The grafts are certainly looking better than they were, and we think we've got the infection under control. I'm not sure how much you know about burns, Mr Faraday, but they can be very challenging, especially something like this.'

Leila, she explained, had suffered chemical burns from white phosphorus. Then she broke off.

'You were there, of course.'

'I was, yes—not in Gaza but at El Arish.'

'So you know all this?'

'Yes.'

'Then I'm sorry.' She studied him a moment. 'It must have been horrible. I know it's affected Gabrielle. So many kids in the hospital there.'

Faraday nodded. Horrible didn't do his memories justice. He still wanted to know about Leila. All he'd seen was a bundle of bandages in the ICU at El Arish. How badly had she been injured?

'Badly, I'm afraid. Normally we can cope with a 30 per cent burn but the phosphorus got into her system. It affects the liver and kidneys. Just that can be enough to kill you.'

'And Leila?'

'The doctors in Egypt did a remarkable job. We call it debridement. You pick bits out of the wounds. With phosphorus you have to be especially careful because it catches fire in contact with air and burns all over again. To be honest, I don't know how that little girl survived.'

'But you say she's getting better?'

'Definitely. She was burned on the chest and the back, as you probably know. The torso burns are deep, full thickness, but they're responding well. The real problem is her hands.'

She flexed her own hands as if grabbing at her upper body, trying to tear off her T-shirt.

'To be honest, Mr Faraday, they're pretty bad.'

'So what can you do?'

'We've done grafts, of course, and we've pinned a couple of fingers where there was tendon damage. Her problem will be what we call contractures. The fingers stiffen up like this—' her hands were claws '—so she'll need lots of physio to keep the fingers mobile. But all that's to come. For now it's enough just to keep her stable. This is no picnic, Mr Faraday. The pain can be intense, but children are very adaptable. They need to reach out to someone, as you might imagine.'

'Of course.' Faraday nodded.

The sister was looking at the flowers. She had something else she wanted to say.

'Gabrielle . . .' She gestured Faraday into the spare seat. 'It's not my place to ask, but I get the impression you two are close. Would that be right?'

'Yes. I like to think so.'

'Then maybe I ought to have just a tiny word in your ear.'

'Of course. Go ahead.'

'There's a translator here, did you know that? Her name's Riham. She and Gabrielle are doing a wonderful job with the little girl. To be honest, I'm not sure how we'd cope without them, especially Riham. The language would be a huge problem without her.'

'Go on.'

'Riham stays overnight. She and Leila have become very tight. It's obvious in a way, isn't it? Same culture, same language. Maybe Riham even looks like the little girl's mother. I've no idea.'

Faraday nodded. He knew exactly where this was going.

'And Gabrielle?'

'Gabrielle is . . .' she frowned '. . . passionate about the little girl. She wants to do everything for her. Everything. As you might imagine, that can sometimes be a problem.'

'For you.'

'For Riham. And most of all for Gabrielle.'

'Why?'

'Because she wants the little girl, *needs* her. It happens more often than you might think. People bond with children like these, especially women. With Riham it's different. She's less emotional. I gather she's had children of her own.'

And Gabrielle hasn't, Faraday thought. It was true. Every word this woman was saying made total sense. Gabrielle had always been passionate about more or less anything she regarded as important, and just now nothing would be more important than Leila. Not just a child hauled back from near-certain death, but a victim of the grossest injustice.

'You're telling me she's jealous.' His voice was flat. It was a statement of the obvious.

'Yes.' The sister nodded. 'That's exactly what I'm telling you. She wants little Leila for herself. She wants to keep her, adopt her, whatever it takes. And as far as I can make out, that will never happen. Not a child from Gaza. Not someone who can go back and live there.'

'Can or should?'

'That's not my decision, Mr Faraday. I'm just—' the smile again '—marking your card.'

'But what do you think? What's your opinion?'

'I don't have one. We make these children whole again. We love them, treasure them. Leila is no different. Sometimes it's the adults who have the problems, not the children. And maybe that's true in this case.'

Faraday got to his feet and extended a hand in thanks. In five short minutes this woman had shed a great deal of light on the last month of his life. No wonder Gabrielle had retreated to a place where no one could reach her. No wonder she was so obsessed, so strange, so utterly changed. She'd set out on a journey she could never complete. And maybe, deep down, she knew it.

'So where do I find them?' he said.

Chapter Eighteen

FRIDAY, 13 FEBRUARY 2009. *16.05*

Winter had fixed to meet Tommy Peters in the upstairs bar on Waterloo station. He wanted somewhere busy, public and within walking distance of the train home. He hadn't the slightest intention of staying in London for a minute longer than he absolutely had to.

He bought himself a tomato juice and found what passed for a quiet corner. From here he could see the station below. The rush hour had yet to begin in earnest but already there was a sizeable crowd beneath the bank of monitors on the concourse.

Peters was ten minutes late. Winter spotted him as he came up the last flight of stairs to the bar. He had his hands thrust into a brown leather jacket, and as he got closer, scanning the tables left and right, Winter realised how much he'd changed. The bullet head was still shaved, and Winter remembered the glint of gold around his neck, but the bulk that went with the air of quiet menace had gone. This was someone thinner, pale, visibly anxious. Maybe he's ill, Winter thought. Maybe he's got something really painful like bowel cancer. Maybe, fingers crossed, he's on the way out.

Winter gave him a wave, pushed the spare chair towards him with his foot. Peters didn't ask for a drink and Winter didn't offer.

'Great place to meet.' Peters sat down.

'Mackenzie sends his best. He's sorry he can't make it.'

'Yeah? So why didn't he try?'

'He's Mr Busy just now.' Winter spared him the details. 'Whatever you're after, I'll take it straight back to him. Mackenzie's good with decisions. He doesn't fanny around. He won't keep you waiting.'

'Keep me waiting for what?'

'A decision.'

'About what?'

'Whatever you've got in mind, Tommy.' He paused. 'Times are hard, yeah?'

Peters was finding it hard to look Winter in the face. His eyes kept wandering off. They seemed to have a life of their own. He was sweating too, which was strange when the weather people were forecasting snow.

'This is about you as well as him,' he said at last.

'Yeah?'

'Yeah.' Peters gestured Winter closer. His breath smelled like an ashtray. Monkswell Farm, Winter thought. Maybe Bazza had been right all along.

Peters was talking about Spain, the time they'd all flown down in the charter jet from Southampton. The immigration people still had the flight details logged in their system, including the passenger list.

'And that's a problem?'

'Yeah. For sure.'

'Why?'

'You remember Brett West?'

'Like yesterday.'

'And that girl of his?'

'Yeah.'

'Both bodies went to a guy I know in Malaga. I'd worked with him before, trusted him like a brother. He had loads of contacts in the construction business. The deal we had would put West and his lady in the foundations of a multi-storey car park up the coast.'

'And what happened?'

'West was fine. *No problema.* Job done.'

'And the lady?'

'Fuck knows. Maybe my guy got it wrong, maybe he didn't. Either way, it doesn't matter. A bunch of gypsies found her in a landfill site in Extremadura.'

Winter nodded, didn't say anything. His grasp of geography had never been brilliant but he thought Extremadura was a long way from Malaga. As for the girl, her upturned face pleading for mercy was another image that Winter would never forget. Her name had been Renate. Because she'd just watched her boyfriend shot to death, Peters had killed her too.

'They traced her in the end—name, details, the lot. This was a while back. When they had the chance they made a start on putting the story together. Where she'd been, who she'd hooked up with. Turned out she was an artist.'

Winter nodded again. She'd just opened a tiny gallery in Malaga, just a shop really. She'd been talking about it seconds before Peters had turned up to blow Westie away. Great timing.

'Have they linked her to Westie?'

'Yes.'

'And?'

'They started looking hard at passenger lists into Malaga, commercial flights to begin with. This is still a while ago. Then someone had a bright idea about business charters.'

'How do you know all this?'

'I've got a contact. Sort of mate. Happens to be a cop.'

'He's Spanish?'

'Of course he's fucking Spanish. And yes, he's highly placed, and yes, I bung him. And yes, I trust what he delivers.'

This was beginning to make sense. Last summer Winter had flown down to Vigo to pull Mackenzie's daughter out of a hole she'd dug for herself. At the airport he'd been smuggled past immigration by a guy called Riquelme because his name was on a police stop list. At the time it had shaken him. Now he knew why.

'So where are we now?'

'The spic *policía* are putting an extradition case together. My contact says it's still stoppable.'

'For a price.'

'Of course. Nothing comes cheap.'

'How much?'

'A quarter of a million. Doesn't Mackenzie *ever* fucking listen?'

Winter wanted to know who was in the frame. Peters said everyone on the charter flight. Winter tried to remember who else had been there. Peters saved him the trouble.

'There were five of us. The other two were mates of Mackenzie's, came along for the ride.'

Winter had them now. They'd both been Pompey scrappers from the old 6.57 days. One of them was called Tosh. The other drank nothing but Bacardi and Coke. Maybe they'd think twice about one of Bazza's jollies next time.

'My boss will need some kind of collateral,' Winter said.

'What does that mean?'

'Proof this guy of yours exists. That the dosh, whatever we settle on, will do the trick.'

'Settle on? How does that work?'

'Life's a negotiation, Tommy. This is Bazza talking, not me. You come up with that kind of price, he'll laugh in your face. Two hundred and fifty K? I tell you now, my friend, you're off your head.'

'Fine.' Peters stood up. The denim shirt was missing a button above the waistband. Definitely hard times.

Winter told him to sit down again. Peters didn't move.

'You've got a lot of attitude for a fat bastard,' he said.

'I'm asking you to sit down, Tommy. You want me to say please? Will that make it easier?'

Peters settled in the seat again. The bar was beginning to fill up.

'There's something else we need to discuss . . .' Winter began '. . . since you're here.'

Peters nodded, said nothing.

'Mackenzie thinks you've already been at it.'

'At what?'

'At a stash of bugle he's salted away.'

'You *what*?'

'He thinks you've got the hump. He thinks you've tootled down south and helped yourself. In fact he's convinced. So convinced he asked me to pop up and ask for it back.' Winter smiled. 'Politely, of course.'

'You're off your head.' Peters was staring at him.

'Bazza, Tommy. Not me. If all this is fairyland, it's down to Bazza.'

'But you're telling me he's serious?'

'Oh yes.'

'He thinks I've robbed him?'

'That's exactly what he thinks. He tells me you knew about the toot already. Why? Because he told you himself. Biggest fucking mistake the man ever made. His words, Tommy, not mine.'

'This is insane.' Peters checked round. He was really angry. 'I *kill* people for a living, mate. Straightforward contract. Honest day's pay for an honest day's work. I wouldn't touch bugle. Never. Not his. Not any other bastard's. Drugs are more trouble than they're worth. So do us a favour, yeah? Just tell him that. And just make sure he fucking understands.'

He sat back, outraged. Winter was eyeing the bar. A Stella would be nice, he thought.

Peters was on his feet again. He'd said his piece: 250K meant 250K. He'd talk to his Spanish contact about getting some kind of guarantee but he wasn't promising anything. The minute Mackenzie came up with the dosh, he'd get this thing moving.

Winter asked about the time frame. Was there any kind of deadline?

'Didn't I mention it?' Peters was staring down at him. 'The key meet's at the end of the month. After that, even 250K won't make a difference.'

*   *   *

Faraday sat in the hospital coffee shop. Out in the corridor, visitors were browsing the League of Friends bookshop.

Gabrielle picked at the wrap he'd just bought her, chicken tikka in a nest of lettuce. Her cappuccino was untouched.

'Well, *chéri*?'

'I think she's lovely. I think she's gorgeous. And I think she's very brave.'

'*Vraiment?*'

'Truly.'

His hand closed on hers. The tiny squeeze brought colour to her cheeks. She leaned across the table, beckoning him closer, kissed him on the mouth. A soldier at the next table, embarrassed, bent to his mobile.

'And you think . . .?'

'What?'

'*Alors* . . . you think I'm crazy? Bringing her all this way? Only sometimes that's what I think. I go home, back to that place down the road, and I lie there and wonder whether I was . . . you know . . . *dans le vrai*.'

Dans le vrai meant in the right. Faraday reached for both hands this time. He'd spent the best part of an hour beside Leila's bed, watching the little girl playing with Riham, amazed by how tiny she was. Riham was an older woman, late forties, early fifties. Her hair was beginning to grey and there was a hint of sternness when she talked to anyone but the child, but with Leila she was soft and playful, talking her patiently through a book of animal pictures, making the right noises for the lion and the elephant, then adding little asides, fragments of Arabic that occasionally drew a smile from the child.

Leila herself, to Faraday's surprise, looked almost untouched by what she had been through. Her face had been spared the phosphorus. Hide the bandaged hands and the dressings around her tiny torso, and except for her size she might have been any five-year-old. No wonder Gabrielle wanted to hang on to her.

'I'm sure you were in the right,' he said. 'I talked to the sister earlier. If you'd done nothing, she thinks Leila might not have made it.'

'*Ah oui?* What else did she say?'

'She told me about the treatment. About what they've done for Leila. She thinks you and Riham are wonderful.'

'No.' She shook her head. '*Il fallait le faire. C'est tout*.'

You just had to do it. That's all.

Faraday smiled, told her he was proud of her, of what she'd achieved, of the care and attention she'd conjured up for this tiny scrap of a girl. But how come Leila was so small?

'In Gaza there is no food, *chéri.* In Gaza there is no anything. Gaza is a prison. Everyone suffers. No one has enough to eat.'

Faraday knew where this was leading. Leila, in Gabrielle's view, belonged anywhere but home. He changed the subject. Told her about the stuff he'd brought over. How long was she planning to stay in Salisbury? How long before they could be back together again in the Bargemaster's House?

'You miss me, *chéri*?'

'Yes.'

'Very much?'

'Lots.'

'Then I hope you have patience.' Her smile was warm at last.

'So you're staying here a while? Is that what you're telling me?'

'*Oui.*' The smile had gone. '*Je dois.* I have to.'

Later, once the child had gone to sleep, Faraday suggested they went out for a meal together. Gabrielle lingered beside the bed, the back of her hand against Leila's cheek, while Faraday watched Riham prepare her evening meal. She kept her food in a special fridge in a room across the corridor, and she spooned hummus onto rounds of toast, adding slices of tomato on top. Faraday had already asked her whether she wanted to join them for supper, but she'd shaken her head with a ghost of a smile and said no. She had a Walkman to keep her amused, and plenty of books, and the nurses let her watch television if she was in the mood. Every day, she said, was the same, but she was happy to devote herself entirely to the child. After more than a week in the same room, Gabrielle admitted she knew virtually nothing about her.

Faraday had taken advice on where to eat. The sister in charge of the unit recommended a pub in a nearby village: good food, no hassle with parking and a choice of real ales. Gabrielle appeared not to mind where they went. She hung on Faraday's arm as they crossed the car park. She was clearly extremely pleased to see him.

The pub turned out to be an excellent choice. Friday night was obviously popular but they managed to find a table in the corner. Gabrielle liked the low oak-beamed ceiling and the lack of TV or canned music, and when she discovered her favourite, *coq au vin*, on the menu, Faraday decided to celebrate with a bottle of decent Burgundy.

Gabrielle wanted to know who was driving.

'I am.'

'But you've had beer already. You want me to drink the whole bottle?'

Faraday shook his head. The guest house where she was staying was a few miles down the road. He had no intention of driving any further.

'You want to stay with me, *chéri*? In my little bed?'

'Yes, please.'

'*Pas de problème*.' She smiled at him, the old grin. '*Avec plaisir*.'

They talked of Leila again, and of the world she'd left behind. Riham had been trying to coax out a little information about the girl's family. At first, said Gabrielle, Leila had refused to talk about her mother or father and the life she'd led at home, shutting her eyes and turning her head to the wall, but over the last couple of days it seemed she'd started to confront the memories she'd shut away.

As far as Riham could tell, she'd been living near the refugee camp at Jabaliya. Like many Gazan kids, she came from a big family—lots of brothers and sisters. The mortar strike and the shower of white phosphorus that followed had killed or injured lots of other civilians in the immediate vicinity, and Riham had the feeling that Leila's parents were among them. It was still far to early to pin down any of this stuff, but when Gabrielle talked about a feeling of lostness in the little girl's eyes, Faraday was inclined to believe her. Whatever the living conditions, the teeming slums of Gaza were a world away from the steady pulse of a UK hospital burns unit.

Faraday wanted to know why Riham had been chosen as the interpreter.

'The surgeon at El Arish knew her already. She's a friend of his sister's. He knew she spoke good English, and French as well. She'd studied at Cairo University. He said she'd be *parfaite*.'

Riham, she said, was also Palestinian, one of the thousands of refugees who had fled to either Jordan or Egypt. As a child she'd lived in Gaza, which made her even more perfect.

'So you met her in El Arish?'

'No. I met her here. At the hospital.'

'She came separately?'

'Separately how?'

'From you and Leila? She didn't come with you on the flight?'

'She did. That's exactly what she did. She came with Leila and with a nurse. They flew direct from El Arish to Southampton. Riham was on the plane with them.'

'So where were you?'

'I thought I told you, *chéri*.'

'Maybe you did. Maybe I've forgotten. Tell me again.'

Gabrielle looked at him a moment and Faraday thought he detected the tiniest flicker of alarm.

'Chartres,' she said. 'I was in Chartres. I went home. I know people, lots of people. I know people at the university in Orleans. *Il y avait beaucoup de manifs contre les Israéliens.* I met some Arab students. One of them was from Saudi. *Voilà*.'

Faraday had lost track. He'd simply asked where Gabrielle had been when the medical evacuation flight brought Leila and Riham to the UK. It seemed the answer was Chartres. Orleans was the nearest big city. With its endless street demos against the Israelis.

'And that's how you raised the money? From this Arab student at the university?'

'From his father, yes.'

'You met the father?'

'No, but I had photos of Leila in the hospital, and a letter from the surgeon, and more stuff from the people in Salisbury. I emailed everything. He lives in Riyadh. He's a rich man. It was very quick. Two or three days.'

'How much?'

'*Comment?*'

'How much did you need?'

'Eighty-seven thousand pounds.'

'And you raised that? In a few days?'

Gabrielle nodded. Faraday sensed her discomfort.

'Isn't this something you should be proud of? A huge sum like that?'

'Of course. But . . .' She shrugged.

'And that paid for what? The flight? The Burns Unit? Riham?'

'*Tout ça*.'

'Fantastic.' Faraday shook his head. 'Thank God for oil.'

'Oil?' Gabrielle was staring at him. She didn't understand.

'The Arab. The man in Riyadh. The one who gave you all the money. I'm guessing that maybe he works in the oil business . . .'

'*Dans le pétrole?*'

'Yes.'

'Yes, of course. That's where he works.' She frowned. 'I expect.'

'You don't know?'

'No. Not exactly. Why should I? He has the money. He wants to help. *Ça suffit, n'est-ce pas?*'

Faraday nodded, then apologised. Of course, he said. Of course it's enough.

She ducked her head and picked at her napkin for a moment or two. Watching her, Faraday was aware that a shadow had fallen over their evening. For whatever reason, she wasn't keen to discuss Leila's benefactor.

Moments later the food arrived. The waitress presented Gabrielle's *coq au vin* with a flourish. It looked, and smelled, delicious.

'*Santé*.' Faraday reached for his glass, trying to warm the atmosphere with a smile. 'Here's to oil.'

Chapter Nineteen

FRIDAY, 13 FEBRUARY 2009. *19.33*

Winter had asked Misty Gallagher to pick him up at Portsmouth Harbour station. It was pouring with rain again when he emerged on the station steps. Parked illegally among a line of cabs, Misty beeped her horn.

'Shit weather, Mist,' he said, climbing into her new Mercedes coupé.

They drove the half-mile to Gunwharf and Misty waited while Winter plunged into Blake House. He emerged minutes later carrying a large holdall, which he dumped in the boot of the car.

'Where next?' she enquired drily.

'Home, Mist. Yours, not mine.'

Misty lived on Hayling Island, a thirteen-mile trek onto the mainland and thence east. Mackenzie, back in the days when he had the time and the inclination to attend to her, had presented his mistress with a waterside house towards the bottom of the island with views of the Pompey skyline across Langstone Harbour. The gift had come with few strings attached, and Misty had made a life for herself among like-minded locals who spoke the language of poolside summer barbecues and drunken winter dinner parties. Winter had treated himself to the odd visit recently, episodes which Misty referred to as 'sleepovers'. The description amused Winter a great deal, not least because he enjoyed being mothered by the likes of Misty Gallagher.

Misty wanted to know what was in the holdall. Winter had slowly built up a modest wardrobe of clothes at Misty's, largely because he forgot to take them home with him. So why did he need more?

'They're not mine, Mist.'

'So whose are they?'

'Long story.' He gave her thigh a squeeze. 'Later.'

At home Misty was in the throes of something she called a primavera makeover. She'd picked up the idea from one of the endless DIY shows she watched on TV. Winter picked his way through the tangle of ladders, paint pots and dustsheets abandoned by the decorators Mackenzie had sent over. They were nice young lads, Misty said, but had left early to score some toot for the weekend.

'So what's primavera about, Mist?'

'Spring. You paint everything yellow. What do you think?'

Winter didn't answer. He had his head in the fridge. Misty kept a decent stock of Stellas for nights like these.

She joined him in the kitchen. Winter had dumped the holdall beneath the breakfast bar.

'You want me to take it upstairs?'

'No, Mist. I want you to hide it.'

'You're joking.'

'I'm not.'

'Like where? Why?' She was sitting on one of her mock-leather bar stools. She extended a foot and gave the bag a poke. 'What's inside?'

Winter poured her a vodka and pulled the tab on a fresh can of Coke. By the time he'd finished explaining about Johnny Holman, her glass was nearly empty.

'So what are you saying, Paul? You think Johnny killed them all?'

'More than possible.'

'But why? He was a darling, Johnny.'

Winter was debating how much of the story to share with Misty. Finally, in the spirit of their new relationship, he saw no point in holding anything back.

'Johnny had a problem, Mist. He drank too much.'

'We all drink too much. So far I don't remember killing anyone.'

'There are complications, Mist. Turns out Johnny was babysitting a whack of the laughing powder for your friend and mine.'

'I know.'

'You *what*?'

'I know about the toot Baz had with Johnny. I've known about it for years. Baz always said it was his little parachute. If things got too heavy, if it all went tits up and he had to bail out, then he'd cash in and fuck off. I thought at the time he'd take me with him but I think I was kidding myself. Deep down Baz is about Baz. End of.'

Winter felt the urge to applaud. No matter how much time he spent with Mist, she always came up with some new surprise.

'He trusted you with this stuff?'

'About the toot? Of course he did. There was no way I'd ever grass him up, and he knew that.'

'And now?'

'Now's different. That man's changing in front of my eyes. I never thought I'd hear myself say it, but since it's you . . .' She pushed her empty glass towards him. 'Not so much ice, eh? And don't be so mean with the Stolly.'

Winter reached for the vodka. He wanted to know more. And he wanted to compare notes. 'He's become more reckless, have you noticed that?'

'Definitely. And sometimes he loses it completely, just goes crazy. That Marie's never had an easy ride but now must be impossible. Take the other night, round your place. He was all over you. He'd have done anything to get you back. I hate to say it but the man was a serious embarrassment. That wasn't Baz, not the Baz I knew.'

'Yeah? You should have seen him the next morning. Different guy. Jekyll and Hyde. No wonder I'm jacking it in.'

'You're serious?'

'I am, Mist.'

'So what's he saying?'

'He's telling me I can't bail out. He's telling me to forget it. It's playground stuff, Mist. Once you're in his gang, you're stuffed.'

'He probably means it.'

'I'm sure he does.'

'So what will you do?'

'Fuck knows.' Winter stooped to the fridge for another Stella. The thought of a night with Misty Gallagher had rarely seemed so enticing. The front door treble-locked. Body oils at the ready. And a woman with a sense of humour to buffer him from thoughts of Bazza Mackenzie.

'Tell me something, Mist.'

'What, my love?'

'How did I ever get into this?'

'You thought it might be a laugh. He did too, when he wasn't pissing himself laughing at the stroke he'd pulled. He used to send your Filth ex-bosses little postcards to wind them up. How well he was treating you. How he'd doubled your wages. He couldn't help himself.'

'Really?' This was news to Winter. 'How do you know?'

'I posted some of them.'

'But how did he know their names?'

'You told him.'

'Did I?'

'So he said. But then he might have invented that bit. Fuck knows.' She ran a perfectly manicured finger round the top of her glass. 'Tell me again . . .' she said '. . . about getting out. Why now?'

This question had been troubling Winter all day. He couldn't rid himself of the memory of last night on the island, standing in the freezing darkness, surrounded by the wreckage of someone else's life.

Mackenzie in his current mood was someone you'd be wise to get away from. But how?

'I don't know, Mist. I know I've got to get out, but if you want the truth I haven't a clue what to do. A lot of it has been fun. I love some of the moves that man makes. I love the fact that he's clever as well as crazy. I like Marie as well. In fact from where I'm sitting, she's the one who's held it all together.'

'Big time.' Mist was gazing into her glass. 'But it was that way from the start. He treated her like shit but he'd be half the man without her. She knows that, of course. Which is why she hangs in there.'

'Loyal missus?'

'Nursemaid.' She looked up. 'All men are the same, my love. Come here and I'll show you how.'

* * *

Faraday and Gabrielle got back to Avon View just after ten. Her room, she'd warned him, was a mess, but after a couple of brandies on top of the Burgundy it didn't seem to matter. They made love in the narrow bed, conscious of something new in their relationship.

Afterwards, Gabrielle cradled beside him, Faraday tried to voice exactly what this something might be. It wasn't the crushing sense of abandonment that had stalked him during the days alone at the Bargemaster's House. Neither was it the fear that Gabrielle was pushing herself deeper and deeper into a situation that could only hurt her. It was something else. Something elemental. Something to do with need.

He tried to put it into words, failed completely.

'What do you mean, *chéri*?' Her head was on his

chest. 'I don't understand.'

He closed his eyes. In his mind he tried out one formulation, then another, each one carefully qualified in case it overstated the case he was trying to make for himself. Finally he saw no point in hiding from the truth.

'I'm nothing without you.' He said softly. '*Rien*.'

'*C'est absurde*.' Nonsense.

'Truly. I mean it. I've meant it from the start. And now it just makes the feeling stronger . . . all this . . .'

'All what?' A small, dangerous question.

'You . . . me . . . here . . .'

'And Leila?'

'Yes, her too.'

'You mean that?'

Faraday could feel the tension returning, the way her fingertips stopped tracing patterns across his chest, a stiffness all the more acute for being so physical.

'Tell me what you want to do,' he said.

'I want her to be with us for ever.'

'You want us to adopt her?'

'*Oui, bien sûr*.' Of course.

'And would that be easy?'

'No.'

'Difficult?'

'People say impossible.'

'Why?'

'Because . . .' She propped herself on one elbow and peered down at him in the darkness. 'You really want to talk about this? Now?'

'Yes, please.'

'Why?'

'Because it's important.'

'For me? For you?'

'For us.'

'You're right, *chéri . . . alors. . .*'

She tried to muster her thoughts, fogged in by the events of the past month and by too much wine. The hospital at El Arish, she said, had made her angry. So angry she'd scarcely known herself. And then Leila had arrived, and the moment she'd seen her on the trolley in the corridor, wheeled in by the ambulance men, all that anger had gone. Why? Because she'd known that here was a chance to *do* something.

'But why her? Why Leila?' The hospital had been full of kids.

'I don't know. Maybe because she was so small. Maybe because she wasn't crying. It was just something in her face. *J'sais pas.*'

Faraday nodded. The child's eyes were extraordinary. He'd seen it himself in the Burns Unit this afternoon. They were huge, almost black, and they followed you round the room, they sucked you in, they somehow made you accountable. We are the sum of all our choices, he told himself. And here's one that Gabrielle couldn't avoid.

'So . . .' She frowned at this effort of memory. 'You ask yourself what is it that I can do? Apart from sit with this child and listen to all the nurses whispering about her.'

'What were they saying?'

'I don't know. I don't speak Arabic.'

'What do you *think* they were saying?'

'They were saying she was going to die. I know they were. I could see it in their faces. But I didn't want that. I didn't want her to die. So that was something I could do. I could try and keep her alive. Not just alive, but make it possible for her to live again, properly—have a proper life.'

'And the surgeon? What did he think?'

'He spoke French. We had many conversations. He was a good man. And he was right too.'

'Right how?'

'She *did* live. Thanks to him. And after that it was my turn.'

My turn.

It was at this point, thought Faraday, that Gabrielle must have begun to think about treatment abroad, about what it would entail, how much it would cost, how she might be able to pay for it, but he'd been there once already this evening and he didn't want to return.

Instead, he asked her about adoption. Leila came from Gaza. Her parents may or may not be dead. She'd have aunts, uncles, extended family. Surely there were procedures here, hoops to jump through.

'Of course.'

'So what do you do?'

'You have to write to Gaza. You have to get permissions, many permissions. I'm still talking to the surgeon. It may be possible.'

'But he's in Egypt.'

'He knows people in Gaza, doctors like himself. There are lots of NGOs. Maybe the Red Crescent. Someone will be able to help.'

'And then what?'

'You have to talk to people here. People in Portsmouth. Social services people. They have to . . . *comment on dit*?'

'Assess you?'

'*Oui. Exactement.* Assess you. Lots more

questions. Why you want to do this thing. Where you live. Who you live with. How much money you have. *C'est très compliqué*.'

She said she had to find out more. She thought the process took a long time. It was expensive too, *très cher*. But that didn't matter. She had some money saved. And she couldn't think of a better way of spending it.

'On Leila?'

'On us. All three of us. In life, sometimes, you make *un investissement, n'est-ce pas*? All of you, all of what you have, everything. Something happens, something comes along, something unexpected, and you know what?'

'Tell me.'

'That makes you very lucky. Why? Because it only happens once, just once, and if you ignore it, if you let that something go, then it will never happen again.'

'You mean Leila.'

'*Oui*.' Her head settled on his chest again. '*Et toi, chéri*.'

Chapter Twenty

SATURDAY, 14 FEBRUARY 2009. *04.12*

Winter woke up in the early hours, groggy after an evening's drinking. Misty had always favoured king-sized beds and it took him several moments to realise that she wasn't there. He lay on his side in the darkness, trying to pin down what had roused him. Then, very faintly, he heard her voice. She was along the corridor somewhere, maybe in the bathroom, and she seemed to be having some kind of conversation. She's on the mobile, he thought vaguely, drifting off again.

It was daylight when he came to again. He reached out, feeling for Misty, finding a breast, half-remembering the earlier episode. She stirred in her sleep, rolling away from him, and he looked at the long curve of her back for a while before slipping out of bed and reaching for her dressing gown. He padded downstairs and put the kettle on. The breakfast bar was still littered with empty cans, and smears of Bolognese sauce had congealed on the hillock of spaghetti Misty hadn't bothered to finish.

He scraped the food into the waste bin and hunted for the tea bags. He was trying to work out where she kept her sweeteners when he heard the purr of an engine outside. From the front room he could see the half-moon of gravel that served as a drive. A small stocky figure was getting out of a dark blue Bentley. Mackenzie.

He let himself in. Winter was back in the kitchen. He wasn't sure whether he still had rights to Misty Gallagher but the teapot, he thought, could stretch to three cups.

Mackenzie didn't seem the least bit surprised to see him.

'Awright?' He settled onto one of the bar stools and nodded up at the clock on the wall. 'You've got fifteen minutes, mush. We're out of here by nine.'

'Why the rush, Baz?'

'Tell you later.' He nodded at the third cup. 'I'd let the old slapper kip on for a while if I were you.'

Winter showered and dressed. They drove back

towards the mainland. Winter had left Misty asleep in bed, disturbed by the realisation that the early-morning conversation that had woken him up must have been with Mackenzie. That's how he had known Winter was in residence. But why drive across?

Mackenzie was lighting a small cheroot. He wanted to know about Tommy Peters.

Winter described yesterday's exchange. In his view Peters was in deep financial shit and was calling in debts that didn't exist. The stuff about Brett West and the possibility of extradition proceedings was a clever move to put pressure on them both. There didn't seem to be a shred of evidence to back any of this stuff up, and 250K was a lot of money to give away for no good reason.

'You think he's making it up?' Mackenzie swerved to avoid a paper boy.

'Yeah.'

'A tenner says you're wrong, mush.'

'You believe him?'

'I do.'

'And you think we should bung him?'

'Tommy fucking Peters?' He shot Winter a look. 'Do me a favour.'

Winter was lost. Mackenzie appeared to know more about all this than he'd previously let on. What a surprise.

'What did he say about the toot?'

'He was outraged. He thought I was taking the piss to begin with. When he realised you meant it he gave me an earful. I get the impression he hasn't got much time for drug dealing. He thinks we're lowlife. Maybe he's right.'

Mackenzie looked briefly pained. Winter wanted

to know more about what was happening in Spain. Was Peters right about extradition?

'Yeah, but that's not the point. Down there these things are always more complicated than they look. The guys with the real power are the politicians. When you get something like this, the police often can't be arsed. They've got more crime on their doorstep than they know how to handle. The last thing they need is all the hassle that goes with trying to nail down people like us. It's mañana, mush. Bury the file. Forget it.'

'So how come it's still live?'

'Because there'll be some greedy little spic politician who's smelling money. Our money. Something like this, they can make life tough for us. They can lean on the police. They can talk to the papers. They can stir up a shit storm, push for extradition, exactly the way Peters says, until the moment comes when we bung them a whack of moolah and they call the dogs off.'

'That simple?'

'Sure.' He nodded. 'Believe me, I've seen it happen a million times in the property game. Planning consents. Water supplies. Access roads. Whatever. There's always a price, and unless you pay it you get fuck all. This thing's no different. But 250K's way over the top, and you know why? Because Tommy fucking Peters would skim a huge slice off the top.'

Winter nodded. In some ways, he thought, this rant made sense. No wonder Mackenzie wanted to become a politician.

'So what do we do, Baz?'

'We talk to Rikki. And we find out what kind of money they *really* want.'

Riquelme was the guy Winter had met last year, when he'd narrowly avoided arrest at Vigo airport. He lived out on the Galician coast, importing industrial quantities of cocaine, and now seemed to act as some kind of agent for Mackenzie.

'He knows these people?'

'Rikki knows everyone.'

'But that doesn't make sense, Baz. The last time I looked, Malaga was on the other side of Spain.'

'Doesn't matter. Rikki has the connections. He knows the way these things work. I trust the guy with my life, mush.'

Winter nodded, saying nothing, all too aware they might have to. They were back on the mainland now, heading west on the motorway. Was this the moment to talk about Lou Sadler? About Kaija Luik? About a black plastic bin liner that was, he hoped, still in Misty's loft? He thought not. Instead, he asked where they were going.

'QA.' Mackenzie indicated left for the exit road. ' We've got to pay a little visit.'

* * *

The Queen Alexandra hospital stood on the slopes of Portsdown Hill, with views across the city below. A recent makeover had transformed the place, giving it the look of a huge multi-storey hotel.

Mackenzie drew up outside the main entrance and told Winter to find a parking space while he dived inside and sorted out some flowers. When Winter wanted to know who they were visiting, Mackenzie grinned. Mate of yours, he said. Mate of mine too, once upon a time.

Winter slipped behind the wheel and took the

Bentley into the biggest of the parking lots. Minutes later he discovered Mackenzie prowling among the pre-wrapped bouquets in the atrium. Finally he went for an extravagant bunch of lilies.

'Here, mush.' He thrust the flowers at Winter. 'You do the honours.'

Ward D6 was up on the third floor. Winter stepped out of the lift and body-checked round a catering trolley, following Mackenzie, who'd already found the nurses' station and was bent over a pretty redhead finishing a conversation on the phone. He wanted to know where to find Mr Leyman. Winter stared at him, still holding the flowers, suddenly aware of what lay in store.

Leyman was in a bay at the far end of the ward. His bed was beside the window, and the brightness of the light threw his huge body into silhouette. Mackenzie, once again, was in the lead. He rounded the end of the bed, perched himself on the mattress and gave Leyman a little pat.

'Been in the wars, Col?'

Winter could see Leyman properly now. He was sitting upright in bed, the sheet tucked over the swell of his belly. His lower face was swollen, purpled with bruising. His teeth were wired together, stretching his mouth into an idiot grin, and when he tried to talk he could only manage a handful of noises.

'Well, mush?' Mackenzie glanced across at Winter, then nodded at the flowers. 'You gonna hand those over or what?'

Winter couldn't take his eyes off Leyman. I did that, he thought. I set him up. I took advantage. I squeezed out the pathetic scraps of gossip that earned him this beating.

He laid the flowers carefully on the bed. Leyman's hands plucked at the sheet. He was reading a magazine he must have picked up on the ward. *What's On In Hampshire.* Two years old.

'For you, Col.' Winter pushed the flowers towards him. 'All the best.'

Leyman couldn't take his eyes off Mackenzie. He was terrified. Winter could feel it, smell it. His eyes were huge in his head. He tried to say something. A thin trickle of pinkish saliva was the best he could manage.

'Give him a wipe, mush.' Mackenzie had spotted a box of tissues on the bedside table. 'Poor bastard.'

Winter didn't move. He knew exactly what Mackenzie was up to. Leyman was a warning. This is what happens, Mackenzie was telling him. This is where you'll end up if things get out of hand.

A cleaner had paused beside the bed. She thought the flowers were lovely. She'd go and find a vase.

Leyman was still staring at Mackenzie. Finally he managed what sounded like a sentence. Mackenzie shook his head. He hadn't a clue what Leyman was on about. He wanted him to try again. Winter spared him the effort.

'He's saying thank you, Baz.'

'Pleasure, mush.' Another pat. 'You mind if Paulie here takes a photo? Just you and me?'

Mackenzie had brought a little Nikon. He gave it to Winter, told him which buttons to press. Then he stood beside Leyman with the flowers between them and mugged a smile for the camera. Leyman, Winter knew, wanted anything but this. He sat in bed, his upper body sagging, the wreckage of his face frozen in the rictus grin. Beside him, on the little table, a single straw in a glass of orange juice.

Mackenzie wanted the camera back. Winter handed it over. It was his turn to pose beside the bed. Another shot. More humiliation.

'Ready, mush?' Mackenzie was waiting.

Winter looked at him for a long moment. Then he shook his head, gave Leyman's hand a squeeze and left. Only when he got to the ground floor did he realise he still had the keys to the Bentley.

* * *

The news about Kaija Luik found Jimmy Suttle in the tiny office that served as *Gosling*'s intelligence cell. It was nearly midday. In an hour or so, with Parsons' blessing, he'd be on the hovercraft back over to Pompey. His partner Lizzie was planning an expedition to Winchester. It seemed she had something special in mind.

'Here . . .' Parsons closed the door behind her and handed Suttle a printed email.

Suttle scanned it quickly, knowing that easyJet were the last airline to respond to *Gosling*'s request for passenger lists. According to their sales department, no tickets had been issued in the name of Luik for flights since last Saturday.

'So where does that take us?' Parsons had sat down.

'It probably means no one called Kaija Luik has travelled to Estonia over the past week.'

Suttle went through the various other carriers *Gosling* had contacted. Nothing from the coach companies. Nothing from the ferries across the North Sea. Nothing from SAS, Air Estonia, KLM and a host of other airlines. And now nothing from easyJet.

'Maybe she's using an assumed name,' said Parsons.

'I asked Sadler that. She said she couldn't remember seeing her passport.'

'Meaning Luik might not be her real name?'

'Yes.'

'Then we're stuffed, aren't we? She could be anyone when it comes to passenger lists. Plus she might have taken a different route. Or gone by train.' Parsons shrugged. 'It happens.'

'Of course it does, boss. But it's unlikely. And what's more important, it makes a pattern. Sadler's fending us off. She's keeping us at arm's length.'

'What about the photo she's supposed to be sending?'

'It still hasn't arrived.'

'So why? Why is she being so obstructive?'

'Because she doesn't want us to talk to the girl.'

'And why would that be?'

'I've no idea. We can tie the girl to Holman. We're still assuming Holman has absconded with whatever he dug up. D/I Faraday thinks he planned the whole thing with the girl in mind.'

'I know. He told me.'

'So maybe Sadler thinks that too.'

'Or knows it.'

'Giving her every incentive to throw us off the scent?'

'Exactly.' Parsons retrieved the email. 'So where is she now? This Kaija Luik?'

Suttle shook his head, said he didn't know. But that, in a sense, was secondary to a more important question. Just what had happened to Johnny Holman?

'This is a guy in a bit of a state. He's got a raging

thirst. He's totally chaotic. He may have killed four people. He may have burned his house down. A guy like that can't hide for ever.'

'Unless they've gone somewhere else.'

'Abroad, you mean?'

'Of course.'

Suttle nodded. It was a possibility. But the Border Agency had been sitting on his details since Wednesday. That still left a three-day window during which he could have fled the UK, but he'd still have been taking a sizeable risk.

Parsons agreed, then consulted her watch. She was due to conference with the local D/I in Newport. For the time being, she said, she was happy to keep Sadler under surveillance. Doubtless the time would come for a proper extended interview but the more they had to throw at her the better.

Suttle needed a catch-up on the surveillance. How was it going?

'Not much so far. It turns out the woman's got a bit of a thing about horses. She went out to some kind of stables this morning, treated herself to a ride.'

'Has anyone checked this place out?'

'Not yet. It's down as an action. If you want the details, talk to Outside Enquiries.'

She threw him a brief smile and left the office. Suttle waited until the *clack-clack* of her heels had disappeared down the corridor, then lifted the phone. He knew the relief skipper on Outside Enquiries from way back.

'George? It's Jimmy. Have you got a moment?'

*   *   *

Faraday returned to the Burns Unit at half past one, leaving Gabrielle at the guest house. Last night's modest celebrations had caught up with her and she wanted to snatch an extra hour or so in bed. Back at the unit, Leila was asleep. Faraday peered in through the glass panel in the door. Riham was in the armchair beside the bed. She was wearing headphones but also appeared to be dozing.

Faraday wondered whether to rejoin Gabrielle at the guest house but decided against it. The room depressed him—the muddy yellows on the wall, the faint smell of neglect—and now the sun was out again he fancied a stroll, lungfuls of fresh air to clear the last of his headache, maybe down by the river. At Riham's request, he'd bought a bag of olives and some halloumi cheese from the delicatessen Gabrielle had found, and he stepped into the treatment room where the patients' fridge was kept.

He put the olives and the cheese in the fridge and was about to leave when a nurse he hadn't seen before came in. She was carrying a box of toys, which she left on a chair. She was young, with a soft face and a twinkly nose stud.

'You must be Gabrielle's friend,' she said.

'Joe.' Faraday extended a hand. 'How did you know?'

'I was with Leila this morning. She was due for a change of dressings on one of her hands. She told me about your beard.'

'Through Riham? The translator?'

'No.' She smiled and shook her head. 'She's a very bright little girl. We talk in mime mainly but we talk. She's obviously got a problem with her hands but she does her best. She told me you had a beard.' She touched her own chin.

The thought that Leila could establish relationships like this hadn't occurred to him. He wanted to know more. How many other nurses did the little girl chatter to?

'I'm not a nurse. I'm what they call a play specialist. I'm the one who distracts them when all the nasty stuff happens. The older ones call me their Good Angel.'

'As opposed to bad?'

'Definitely.'

'And Leila? You're her Good Angel?'

'I am. She thinks I'm funny. I make her laugh.'

Faraday was eyeing the box of toys. He liked the idea of a Good Angel.

'So what do you think of our Leila?'

'I think she's amazing. Truly amazing. I know she's got a lot of support—the Arab lady, your Gabrielle—but the pain these children go through is horrible, and not having your mum and dad around must be very tough.'

'You think she's getting better?'

'Much.'

'You really see a difference?'

'A huge difference. I know part of that's down to all the treatment and stuff, but what matters is her and Riham. They're close, really close, you can see it. Children need one special person. They need to reach out. Maybe it's a trust thing, I don't know, but Riham has been there for her, twenty-four/seven. It gives her strength, confidence. Like I said, there's a smile back on her face.'

Children need to reach out. The sister had said exactly the same thing only yesterday. Poor Leila,

Faraday thought. Poor Gabrielle.

'And what about her future?' he said carefully.

'She'll go back. She'll have to go back.'

'I don't understand.'

'We had a little girl like this before. She came from Uganda. Once she was better we had to send her home. She had no family in this country. Just like Leila.'

'But what about . . .' he hesitated '. . . adoption?'

'That takes an age. I don't know enough about it. All I know is that the children first have to go back to where they came from.'

'And Gabrielle knows that?'

The play specialist looked at him. The question had thrown her.

'You're asking *me*?' she said.

*   *   *

Winter was back at Misty's place by two o'clock. He'd helped himself to the Bentley at the hospital, driven back down to Portsmouth and phoned her from Blake House, leaving a message asking her to get in touch. When she finally returned the call she said she felt vile. Too much vodka. Not enough sleep.

'Fine,' Winter said. 'I'm on my way.'

He floored the Bentley on the way out of the city, ignoring a succession of speed cameras. If Mackenzie ended up with a drawerful of speeding tickets, so much the better. He hadn't heard a word from him since leaving the hospital and he'd made no effort to get in touch. In some ways the scene at Leyman's bedside had reminded him of the afternoon Tommy Peters had wasted Westie and his girlfriend. The same passionless settling of a debt. The same cold application of carefully measured violence.

When he arrived at Misty's, she was taking a bath. He perched on the edge of the tub. She was right: she looked terrible.

She wanted to know how he'd got out to Hayling Island.

'I drove, Mist.'

'Drove what?'

'The Bentley.'

'That's what I thought. He wants it back.'

'I'm sure he does.'

The fact that Mackenzie had been in touch with her again told him everything he needed to know. No matter what he might have said about these new freedoms of hers, she was as tightly bound to him as ever. This had nothing to do with affection, he told himself. Only money.

'He's still there, isn't he, Mist?'

'Where?'

'On your back. All over you. You can't get shot of him. You don't *want* to get shot of him.'

'He owns this house, Paul. Life's not that simple.'

'Leave it. Walk away.'

'Where to? How?' She reached for a tumbler of something clear that Winter hadn't spotted before.

'What's that?'

'Vodka, darling. Are you my keeper?'

'Never. That's not what I want. Neither do you.'

'No? Then what *do* you want?'

'Excellent question, Mist, and if I knew the answer you'd be first on the list.' He paused. He'd never felt this kind of anger. Not with Misty Gallagher. 'What else did you tell him? As a matter of interest?'

'When?'

'At four in the morning. When you gave him a bell.'

'He called me. He's worried about you, Paul. We all are.' She nodded at the brimming tub. 'You want to share this with me?'

Winter ignored the invitation. He'd been crazy to think that circumstances would ever prise Bazza and this woman apart. That, he knew now, would never happen. Misty Gallagher, contrary to whatever fantasies he'd once had, was simply another bone Mackenzie had tossed his way.

'This man is sick, Mist. You understand that? Sick in the head. Clever? Yes. Handy? Yes. Ruthless? Yes again. But he's going to take us all down, Mist, all of us.'

'That's not what a girl likes to hear.'

'But it's true, Mist, and you know it.'

'So why didn't you tell me earlier? When you were enjoying it all? What's so special about now?' She reached for the glass. She looked, if anything, reproachful.

Winter gazed at her, risked a smile. Any moment now she was going to accuse him of losing his sense of humour, and he didn't want that. Not until he had this thing sorted. Not until he could see some way out.

He bent down, cupped her face with both hands, then nuzzled the wetness of her cheek. She responded, hauling herself upright in the bath, water sluicing down her ample chest. Winter felt the splashmarks spreading across his shirt.

'That padlock on the trapdoor up to the loft,' he said, 'where's the key?'

'In my purse. Kitchen drawer. You can't miss it.'

He nodded, stepped across to the door, paused. 'Something else, Mist. Be honest.'

'Always.'

'Did you mention the holdall to Baz?'

'No.' She submerged again. 'Trust me, eh?'

*   *   *

Lizzie Hodson drove an ancient Renault Clio with 130,000 miles on the clock. Suttle spotted it the moment he stepped off the hovercraft. She had the passenger door open by the time he emerged from the terminal building. He hadn't seen her for nearly a week.

It had taken the Outside Enquiries D/S to remind him it was Valentine's Day. En route to the hovercraft on the island side, Suttle had made a hasty detour to a florist at the bottom of Ryde High Street. She was nearly out of roses but let him have a bunch she'd prepared earlier for a client who hadn't turned up.

'Happy Valentine's.' Suttle kissed her, then again, properly. She looked at him a moment, nose to nose.

'You know something?' she said. 'Winchester's a really bad idea.'

'You're right.' Suttle produced a bottle. 'I got you this too.'

They took the champagne home. Their bedroom was at the back of the house, all the more intimate for being so small. Lizzie, who adored rich colours, had modelled the curtains on a feature she'd seen in a French magazine. She'd echoed the reds and purples in the bedding and spent a fortune on scented candles.

He put a match to them now, enjoying the light they cast. They drank the champagne, made love, had another glass or two, compared notes, caught up, emptied the bottle.

Then Lizzie rolled over, came very close. Suttle loved the smallness of her, the way she giggled when she was drunk, the things she liked to do to him, the sense she gave him that if everything else in the world turned to rat shit, it wouldn't begin to matter.

'My turn.' She licked his ear. 'There's something I forgot to mention.'

'Like what?'

'I'm pregnant.' Her eyes were gleaming. 'Happy Valentine's.'

Chapter Twenty-One

SATURDAY, 14 FEBRUARY 2009. *16.34*

For most of his life Winter had successfully resisted the temptation to think too hard about the passage of events. Like many police officers, he'd ridden the breaking wave of Pompey crime, anything from shoplifting to homicide, and largely enjoyed himself. There were rarely days without a challenge or two, and he'd completed more than twenty years in the Job with a number of decent scalps hanging from his belt.

His journey to the Dark Side had been conducted in the same spirit. He'd done his best to keep Bazza's little canoe in one piece as they plunged from one set of rapids to the next, and cherished some of the wilder moments en route. He'd known from the start that working for Mackenzie would never be dull and he hadn't been disappointed. Between them, they'd posted some famous victories. They'd also had a few laughs, and he could remember celebratory evenings around the table in Marie's kitchen that would stay with him for ever. But this was different.

In the Bentley it was a couple of minutes from Misty's place to the seafront. Hayling Island had escaped the development that had cluttered Southsea seafront. At low tide, beyond the sand dunes, the beach and the views seemed to stretch for ever, the grey winter light a pale gleam on the distant sea. Winter had always regarded this as a landscape for life's thinkers, troubled loners who worried too much about the bigger issues. That had never been Winter's way. Until now.

He walked east, his back to the distant Pompey skyline along the coast, trying to rid himself of the memory of Colin Leyman sitting in his hospital bed, the rabbit caught in Mackenzie's headlights. Inflicting that kind of damage, that kind of pain, made Winter deeply uncomfortable. Insisting on a trophy photograph afterwards verged, he thought, on the psychotic.

For whatever reason, Mackenzie had lost control of himself. Maybe, like many physically small men, he'd been in the business of compensation for most of his life. He'd had to try harder, run faster, think quicker, and stay on his toes longer than any other bastard. The world was a sweet shop, full of goodies, and he was determined to help himself. In many ways it had worked. He'd seized control of the city's cocaine trade and scored a fortune. He'd washed the money carefully and salted it away. He was much admired, much feared, and now—with Tide Turn—he was trying to cash in on that respect and build another little sandcastle on the Pompey beach. But that, maybe, was where it had all gone wrong. Not because he didn't have the talent and drive to do all this stuff, but because Bazza Mackenzie had never recognised the limits of what was possible. In his own view, Winter concluded, there was nothing that this person he'd become couldn't do.

Would that kind of raging ambition be enough to sink them all? Winter knew the answer was yes. Time and again, as a working cop, he'd collided with another man's life at the point when he thought he was beyond reach. Whether it was money, or drugs, or violence, these guys regarded themselves as immortal. Then came the knock on the door, or the intercept on the street, or the ambush on the motorway, and another stellar Pompey legend came plunging back to earth. Quite how it would happen to Mackenzie was yet to be seen, but Winter had an instinctive feel for the ebb and flow of advantage and knew Bazza's days were numbered. Not because Winter's ex-colleagues were especially bright. But because Mackenzie was going off his head.

So what to do? Winter, the master tactician, had dreamed up endless little schemes to keep them off the rocks, and so far, just, they were still afloat. But he knew that resolving the current situation—Tommy Peters, Johnny Holman, two million quid's worth of toot—was probably beyond him. And even if they survived, the recession was about to make the whole thing impossible. Bazza, he thought, couldn't have chosen a worse moment to play God.

Depressed by the prospect of the days to come, Winter returned to the car park. If nothing else, he thought, he could treat himself to one last taste of driving a 100K motor. He slipped behind the wheel of the Bentley and turned on the eight-speaker audio. It was getting dark by now, and he sat for a moment or two in the soft glow of the dashboard lights, listening to Five Live, Mackenzie's station of choice. The car was brand new, Bazza's second in as many years. It smelled of serious money. Enjoy.

At the top of the island Winter joined the stream of traffic heading west towards Portsmouth. Five minutes later, away to the left, he could see the floodlights at Fratton Park. He knew already from Five Live that Pompey were playing at home. Realising that the score might shape Mackenzie's mood for the evening, he listened for the result. The match had just finished. Doubtless to Bazza's satisfaction, Pompey had just beaten Manchester City 2–0.

Winter settled deeper in the seat, blipping the accelerator and enjoying the effortless surge of power. The motorway ran beside the creek at this point, and he glanced across at the blackness of the water before easing into the nearside lane for the Pompey exit. The long curve of the slip road opened out before him, feeding traffic south onto the spur motorway that crossed a corner of the harbour. Traffic from Fratton Park was flooding out of the city. He glanced at the soft orange dial of the speedo, wondered whether to ease up. The car handled like a dream. The last of the slip road was empty. He could barely hear the engine: 95 mph felt like walking speed.

He didn't see the van coming in from the right as he joined the motorway. Neither did he realise how quickly he was closing the gap with the big artic ahead. He had time to stamp on the brakes and flash his headlights before he felt the Bentley lurch sideways as it hit the van. There was a squeal of brakes and a sickening thump as the van spun sideways into the crash barrier. The Bentley too was out of control. For a brief split second, as the car began to turn over, Winter was aware of the looming bulk of the artic, the huge wheels, then he heard a strange roaring noise and the faintest tinkle of glass before the darkness and the silence bore him away.

After a while, he never really knew how long, he came to. He was hanging from the safety belt. Everything was upside down. The radio was still playing. He could smell petrol. He shut his eyes, opened them again. Definitely Gloria Gaynor. Then, to his faint surprise, came a voice from outside, a woman's voice. She wanted to know whether he was OK. She sounded frightened. His fingers were searching for the belt release. He asked her to help him but she refused.

'Wait,' she said. 'Wait for the ambulance.'

He did what he was told, wondering why nothing hurt. This was like a movie, he thought, the plot lines all tangled up, nothing making any sense. Then, from far away, the wail of a siren, something he recognised, something he could visualise. Just in time, he thought, feeling the first hot wave of nausea flooding up from his stomach.

He began to vomit, a horrible choking sensation. Then a gloved hand came in through the window, and a yellow high-vis cuff, and another voice, male, was telling him to take it easy. He threw up again, wondering vaguely when he'd have time to sponge out all the marks on the leather. Then, through the shattered windscreen, he thought he recognised the outlines of firemen. These guys have come to get me out, he thought. Thank Christ for that.

A little later the car had gone. He was lying on his back, staring up at a woman's face. He could feel movement, hear the swish of tyres on a wet road. Then came the siren again and a sharp movement to the left. When he tried to struggle upright, the woman restrained him. He became aware of other hands cupping his head. Strange, he thought vaguely. Whatever happened to Gloria Gaynor?

* * *

Marie took the call in the kitchen. Bazza was in the den, watching *Final Score.* Another three points took Pompey even further from the relegation zone. The season was beginning to perk up.

Hearing the door open, he glanced round. He knew at once something had happened.

'What's the matter? What's up?'

'That was the police. There's been an accident.'

Mackenzie was on his feet, reaching for his jacket. It was the Bentley. He knew it. Fucking Winter.

Marie told him what she could. There'd been a pile-up on the motorway into the city. There were a number of casualties. One of them, it seemed, was the driver of the Bentley. The car was registered to Mackenzie. Hence the call.

'They found ID on him,' Marie said. 'It was Paul.'

'Is he OK? Is he *alive*?'

'They think so.'

'*Think* so? Thank fuck for that.' Mackenzie pushed past her.

'Where are you going?'

'Where do you think.'

'Wait.' Marie hurried after him. 'I'll come too.'

They took her Peugeot up to the hospital. The motorway was closed beyond the continental ferry port and they joined a long slow queue of traffic winding up through the suburbs of North End. Mackenzie was fretting about Winter. He was a daft old cunt, he told Marie, but he'd hate to be without him. Marie said nothing. She had an overwhelming desire to cry. She'd got used to Winter, relied on him to some degree. He'd brought something extra to their lives, something that hadn't been there before. For one thing, he made her laugh. Now this.

At the QA she took the entrance that led up to A & E, joining yet another queue. She could see a line of ambulances at the top of the rise. There were police cars there as well. Mackenzie had the passenger door half open. He'd run up there. It'd be quicker. She shook her head.

'Leave it to me.' She stepped out into the rain. 'You find somewhere to park.'

* * *

Winter knew he'd been lucky. He was fully conscious now, lying on a bed in one of the treatment bays. He'd taken a crack on his head and he could feel scabs of blood on his temple above his right ear, but that was pretty much it. Maybe an ache or two in his right shoulder and a soreness across the chest where the seat belt had dug in, but nothing compared to the casualties he'd glimpsed in the neighbouring cubicles. One of them, an Asian guy, was groaning fit to bust. Seconds ago a doctor had come running, and now there was an urgent babble of voices from which Winter could coax little sense.

A nurse appeared, followed by another doctor. He was absurdly young, probably a teenager. He shone a light in Winter's eyes, took a hard look at the wound on his temple, asked him a series of daft questions about what day it was and whether or not he could divide eight by two. Finally he said that Winter would be kept under observation overnight after X-rays on his skull.

A third figure appeared, a uniformed policeman. He was carrying a breathalyser. When the doctor made room for him in the cubicle, he squatted beside the bed and explained the procedure. This was routine, he said. Every driver was being tested.

'How many's that?' Winter was still trying to get the last hour or so in some kind of order.

'Lots, sir. Do you mind blowing in this?'

Winter supplied a couple of lungfuls of air and waited for the result. He couldn't remember having a drink since last night but couldn't be sure.

'That's fine, sir. A few details now, if you don't mind. Then I'll be out of your hair.'

The officer already had his driving licence, a fragment of Winter's life that had somehow gone missing. Winter confirmed his address and date of birth. Yes, he'd been driving the Bentley. And no, he couldn't remember anything about the accident itself. This wasn't strictly true, but Winter saw no point in complicating the issue. Policemen dealt with amnesia every day of their working lives. Why make it easy for them?

'Many hurt?'

'A good few, sir, yes.'

'Badly?'

'Too early to say, sir.'

'And?' Winter looked him in the eye, sensing already that he'd been fingered as the guilty party.

'No, sir. No fatalities. Not yet, anyway.'

'Thank Christ for that.'

'Quite.'

The officer got to his feet. He said he'd be back tomorrow, once Winter had got his bearings. I don't doubt it, Winter thought. Odds on, you'll bloody arrest me.

He lay back, watching the officer pull the curtain closed behind him. The drama in the next cubicle appeared to have calmed down. Winter closed his eyes a moment, tracking back, trying to fit the pieces together, trying to remember the exact sequence of events that had taken him to the slip road and thence to disaster.

He remembered the lights of Fratton Park way off to the left. He remembered the car park at Hayling Island. He remembered the greyness of the afternoon, distant stick figures on the beach, a couple of dogs. Then an image of Misty came back to him, sprawled in the bath, the pinkness of her knees, the invitation to jump in that he might have been wise to accept. He smiled, wondering whether she'd pop across to Gunwharf over the next day or two. Bring him a bunch of flowers or a bottle of malt. Slap on a coat or two of that wonderful nail varnish.

The thought warmed him. Then, abruptly, he remembered something else. Before leaving Misty's place, he'd retrieved the holdall she'd stowed away in the loft. It had Johnny Holman's kit inside and it was still in the Bentley. If his new police friend or any of his mates laid hands on that, they'd all be stuffed. Unauthorised removal of evidence. Perverting the course of justice. Endgame.

He closed his eyes, shook his head in despair. He knew enough about road traffic accidents to picture exactly what would be happening on the motorway. The guys from the Road Policing Unit would be gathering evidence. Cameras would already have given them a clue or two about exactly what had happened. They'd collect witness statements, measure skid marks, examine impact damage. And finally the low loader from Boarhunt Motors would turn up and cart off the remains of the Bentley for further examination. In the boot of the Bentley was the holdall with Johnny Holman's clothes. The crime scene of Gail Parsons' dreams. Horrible.

*   *   *

It was gone eight o'clock by the time Marie got word that Winter had been transferred to a ward in the main hospital. Only too familiar with Bazza's impatience in situations like this, she'd finally managed to persuade him to take the Peugeot home. Alone in the big waiting room at A & E, she'd read an ancient copy of *Grazie* three times before her name was called by a nurse from the treatment area. Mr Winter was occupying a bed in the main hospital. She was welcome to pay him a visit.

Expecting something far, far worse, she found him sitting up in bed with a borrowed copy of the

Pompey *News.* The only real sign of damage was a bandage around his head. That, and a look of slight alarm when he caught sight of her making her way towards him.

'Baz?' he said at once.

'I've sent him home.'

'Thank Christ for that.'

'He's really emotional. I haven't seen him this way for a while.'

'I'm not surprised. It was a lovely car.'

'It's not about the car, Paul, it's about you.'

'Really?' Winter looked astonished.

He made room for her on the bed. She wanted to know how he felt. The miracle, she said, was that no one seemed to have been badly hurt.

'That's good.' Winter was pleased to hear it. 'Very good.'

He told her what he could remember about the accident. She knew him far too well to believe this was the whole truth, but Winter had a rare talent for finessing difficult situations, and she had no reason to think that this little episode would be any different.

'Are you telling me it was your fault?'

'It might have been. I can't remember.'

'But that's what they believe?'

'As far as I can tell . . .' He nodded. 'Yeah. The test comes tomorrow if I get discharged. Odds on, the cone heads will arrest me.' Cone heads was CID speak for the Road Policing Unit.

'And what then?'

'They'll interview me. If no one's died, it's not a huge deal. I wasn't pissed and the tox'll prove it. Hefty fine. Umpteen points. Job done.'

'You're sure?'

'Of course I'm not.' He gave her the old grin, then reached for her hand. Marie could feel the slightest tremble. Even Winter, she thought, was vulnerable.

'You matter to us, Paul.' She gave his hand a squeeze. 'You know that?'

'Yeah?' He still seemed uncertain.

'Of course you do. And in case you're wondering, it's not just me. I know Bazza can be a pain. Lately, I haven't a clue what's got into him. But he cares about you, he really does. And he knows how much we owe you too.'

This, to Winter, had the makings of a speech. Bazza might have put her up to it, but somehow he thought not. Marie, unlike the rest of the world, rarely did her husband's bidding. Neither was she frightened of him.

'Marie—' he beckoned her closer '—there's a problem with the Bentley.'

'I know. You've just written it off.'

He shook his head and explained about the holdall in the boot. One way or another, someone had to retrieve it.

'Why?'

'Because it could land us all in the shit.' He reached for her hand again. 'Big time.'

'You mean that?'

'I do.'

'You want me to tell Baz?'

'No. It'll only upset him.'

'Fine.' She smiled. 'So what do I do?'

Winter told her to phone Fratton police station. She'd need to talk to the road traffic guy in charge of this evening's little episode. She should explain that there was stuff in the Bentley that she needed and could she have it back? Items like mobiles they were bound to hang on to in case Winter had been on the phone when he crashed, but there'd be no reason to deny her access to a holdall.

'They'll take the car to Boarhunt Motors. That's the nominated garage. My guess is the skipper in charge will send some minion up there to fetch the holdall. Fingers crossed you'll get a call to collect it from Fratton nick.' He paused. 'Yeah?'

'So what's inside?'

'Bits and pieces of clothing. The stuff needs a wash. Badly.'

'You want me to do that too?'

'No way. Just give it to me. I'll sort the rest out.'

Marie gazed at him for a long moment but had the good sense not to ask any more questions. As an afterthought, Winter suggested she delay the call until tomorrow morning. Doing anything about it now might smack of panic.

'It's that bad?' She looked almost amused.

'No.' Winter shook his head. 'It's much, much worse.'

Chapter Twenty-Two

MONDAY, 16 FEBRUARY 2009. *09.35*

After a weekend of limited activity, Operation *Gosling* cranked itself up again. DCI Parsons, thanks to a full day with the Policy Book and associated files, had decreed a comprehensive intel review for the Monday morning. Like Faraday and Suttle, she thought that Johnny Holman, Kaija Luik and Lou Sadler probably represented their best pathways forward. There'd still been no sightings of either Luik or Holman, and two costly days of surveillance on Sadler had yielded very little beyond an evident passion for horse riding. The so-called golden hours on *Gosling* had come and gone. No sudden breakthroughs. No windfall bits of evidence. No signed confessions. From this point forward, the emphasis would be on graft.

The meeting took place in the SIO's office. Parsons had limited attendance to herself, Faraday and Suttle. Dribbles of intel had come in over the weekend and she pressed Suttle for an update.

Suttle wanted to concentrate on Lou Sadler. Land Registry and DVLC checks had confirmed ownership of two properties, her apartment in Cowes and the terraced house she'd cited as Luik's address. Experian credit checks had shown no outstanding loans against the red Renault Megane convertible or any other purchase. There were no entries against her name on the PNC, and Hantspol's Records Management System, a treasure trove of intelligence, simply carried a report from the Vice Squad on her stewardship of the escort agency Two's Company.

In Suttle's view the agency offered potential for money laundering, but without a full financial investigation this would be difficult to develop further. As it was, he'd tasked a financial investigator to use the Revenue and Customs gateway process to obtain details about her declared income and any other source of employment. That process, mounted on the back of terrorism legislation, was still incomplete.

'So what are you saying, Jimmy?' As ever, Parsons wanted the headlines.

'In broad terms, I think she's kept her nose clean. The Vice guys think she's running a decent business. The punters are happy, the girls are well paid, she keeps the books up, she's got a reputable accountant, she even pays her taxes. Based on this lot—' his hand rested on the file '—I'd say she wouldn't have much time for the likes of Mr Holman. The guy's chaos on legs. Too much hassle. Too much grief.'

'So why has she been lying to us about the Cowes address? And why is she being difficult about the photo of Luik?' This from Faraday.

'I don't know, boss. There's definitely a piece missing. There has to be.'

'Like what?'

'If I knew that, I'd tell you.'

Suttle had said exactly the same thing to Parsons. She smiled.

'What about Luik and Holman?'

'Still nothing, boss.'

'Media?'

'Zilch. The *County Press* published Holman's photo on Friday. I was hoping for something over the weekend but so far we've got sod all.'

Parsons was brooding. 'We need that photo, the one of Luik, right?'

'Yeah.'

'Do we have an address for this webmaster of Sadler's? The guy we assume is sitting on it?'

'No, but I can go back to Sadler.' Suttle paused. 'We threaten her with warrants? One for her? One for the webmaster?'

'Absolutely. And make sure she knows we mean it. Shake the tree first, Jimmy. See what falls out.'

Suttle made himself a note and checked his

watch. If Parsons had no objection, he'd like to spend the night in Pompey rather than staying over in Ryde.

Parsons said that was fine by her, as long as Suttle was back for Tuesday half eight. As an afterthought she asked if all was well.

'Never better, boss.' Suttle ducked his head, hiding a grin. Lizzie, his partner, would be back from the hospital by six. She was due, late-afternoon, for a scan.

'Nothing serious, I hope?'

'Christ, no. It turns out she's pregnant. We're having a nipper.'

'Really?' Faraday was beaming. 'Terrific news, Jimmy.'

* * *

Paul Winter was arrested at 10.37, moments before his discharge from the QA. The uniform, a P/C called Dave McCutcheon who'd recently transferred to Hantspol after ten years policing in the West Midlands, had spent a peaceable hour or so at Winter's bedside while he waited for a final visit from his consultant. They'd talked about Pompey mostly—where to eat in Gunwharf, the comprehensives to avoid for the uniform's eleven-year-old and the iniquity of shelling out £700 for a season ticket at Fratton Park. By the time Winter had the all-clear from the consultant—nothing broken, no evidence of brain damage, no need for outpatient visits—he and Dave were close to becoming mates.

A traffic car took him into the city. Winter sat in the back as they swung south onto the M275, gazing out at the harbour, trying to match this familiar stretch of road with the crazy paving of images from Saturday night. One of the nurses at the hospital had taken a hard copy of the accident report from the *News* website. The Saturday edition of the paper had been too late to cover the incident and the next edition didn't appear until noon on Monday, so this brief summary was all he had in the way of reference. There was a photo alongside the text, and Winter had taken a moment or two to recognise the upturned Bentley, nestled alongside an enormous French container truck en route to the ferry port. Among the surrounding wreckage there were two other cars and a white van. The police spokesman had reported no life-threatening injuries and the headline spoke of 'miracle escapes', a phrase that took Winter back to the photo of the Bentley. That was me in there, he'd thought to himself. That could have been my tomb.

At the Central police station, Winter stood in front of the custody Sergeant as they shuffled through the booking-in process. He'd been arrested on suspicion of driving without due care and attention, a charge that was unlikely to end in a prison sentence. It was highly unusual for his ex-colleagues to go to these lengths for a due care, but Winter had the sense that old debts were being settled. In his CID days Winter had posted a number of victories in this same custody suite, bending the procedural rules to suit himself, and he failed to raise even a flicker of a smile from the custody skipper. Potentially, he grunted, the incident had been extremely grave. Under the circumstances Winter was lucky not to be facing a charge of causing death by dangerous driving.

The duty solicitor, whom Winter knew well, took the same view. They had half an hour together in a side office before the interview. When Winter asked about disclosure, the brief took him through the witness statements the traffic guys had gathered at the scene. The information, as ever, was carefully rationed, but the brief left Winter in no doubt that a Not Guilty plea was going to be extremely difficult to sustain. All four drivers, plus a couple of passengers, had described the moment when the Bentley joined the motorway from the slip road. The driver was going way too fast. He hadn't a clue what he was doing. No one else had a chance.

'Dickhead? Would that be fair?'

Winter agreed. In their shoes he'd feel exactly the same way. Problem was, he couldn't remember a thing.

'You mean that?'

'Yeah.'

'And that's what you've been saying all along? At the hospital?'

'Yeah. First thing I know is hanging upside down in the Bentley wondering what the fuck's going on. It's still a bit woolly after that, but ask me how I got there and I wouldn't have a clue.'

The brief looked at him a moment, knowing perfectly well that Winter was lying, then shrugged. Using amnesia instead of going No Comment was a rational defence. He'd used it once himself.

'Fine.' He got to his feet. 'Thank Christ you're still in one piece.'

The interview itself lasted barely half an hour. In the absence of tox results from the blood sample and a detailed examination of the Bentley, the RPU officers were simply after Winter's version of events. Winter, with an air of faint bemusement, talked them through what little he said he remembered. He'd been on Hayling Island for most of the afternoon. He'd been returning the car to its owner. He must have been joining the M275 from the westbound dual carriageway. End of.

Pushed for more detail, Winter simply shrugged. He was aware of accounts from other witnesses. He was perfectly prepared to believe that he'd got it wrong. No, he didn't make a habit of using his mobile at the wheel, though they were welcome to check his billing records. And no, he couldn't remember having a drink. He was sorry about all the grief he'd caused, and if any of this stuff came back to him then they'd be the first to know. In the meantime, though, he'd be happy to cop a Guilty plea.

The lead interviewer, a sergeant on the RPU, didn't believe a word.

'You make it sound like it was someone else,' he said.

'Nicely put, skipper.' Winter shot him a smile. 'A bit of your life goes missing, it's the weirdest feeling.'

'Really? I'd call it carelessness . . . and that's being kind.'

The brief was about to lodge a protest—oppressive behaviour—but Winter put a hand on his arm.

'No hard feelings, skipper. Like I say, I got it wrong. Do what you have to do. Be my guest.'

'Thank you.'

'My pleasure.' Winter smiled again. 'As ever.'

*   *

At about the same time, Marie went to Fratton police station. She'd had a call from a P/C Collinson just after breakfast and phoned Winter to tell him, but his mobile was on divert. The holdall, said Collinson, was ready for collection. She was to present herself at the front desk and ask for him by name. He'd pop down with the bag and ask her to sign a form. Simple.

Marie got to Fratton just after two. She'd never much liked this part of the city—the sudden plunge into discount stores, burger bars and clusters of fat women keeping a weary eye on their kids—and she'd taken a cab to spare herself the hassle of trying to find a parking space. Steps led to a pair of doors at the front of the building. She'd made a bit of an effort with a nice skirt and blouse and had added a dab or two of Coco Chanel. What she needed, above all, was confidence.

The tiny reception area smelled of new paint. She lingered for a while, flicking through a copy of the giveaway force newspaper, *Frontline*, while a distressed-looking man in his sixties reported the theft of his bicycle. Finally, she got the chance to ask for P/C Collinson. By now mild nervousness had become dread. Winter never spelled out these things but the contents of the holdall were clearly of enormous importance. Why *clothes*, for God's sake?

Collinson was young, fresh-faced and had just read the manual on customer relations. The holdall was black and had seen better days. Collinson put it on the counter.

'Is this the one, Mrs Mackenzie?'

Marie hadn't got a clue. Winter had never

described it.

'That's it,' she said brightly.

'Do you mind having a look inside? Just to check everything's there?' Marie hadn't been expecting this. Collinson sensed her hesitation. 'It's more for our sake than yours, Mrs Mackenzie. Nothing personal, but you'd be amazed at the strokes some people try and pull. The money they say's gone missing? All that nonsense? I'm afraid we just have to cover ourselves.'

Marie gave him a warm smile. Of course she understood. She unzipped the holdall. Inside was a black bin liner. She took it out.

'You want me to check this too?'

'Please. If you don't mind.'

'Not at all.'

Marie opened the bin liner and began to pull the contents out. Jeans, a T-shirt, a fleece, a pair of mud-caked baseball boots. There was no hiding the bitter, acrid stench that came with this stuff. Marie pulled a face. She'd never had to think so fast in her life.

'Sorry about this . . .' She waved a hand under her nose. 'My husband's been helping a friend clear his garden. I know he likes bonfires but this is ridiculous.'

She had the jeans now and she began to go through the pockets, aware that Collinson was watching her.

'Everything in order, Mrs Mackenzie?' He had the form ready for her signature.

Marie was stuffing the clothes back inside the bin liner. 'It's a set of house keys I'm after. That's why I wanted the holdall back.'

'You're sure they were there?'

'No, I'm not. Sometimes I think my husband's brain dead. He must have left them somewhere else.' Another smile. 'Are men just born stupid or what?'

She had the bin liner back in the holdall by now. She reached for the form, pretended to read it, then signed at the bottom. Mercifully, someone else had just stepped in from the street, pissed as a rat.

Collinson had lost interest in the holdall. He muttered something to the desk officer then shot Marie a quick farewell smile.

'Our pleasure, Mrs Mackenzie. Anything else you need, just give us a ring.'

Chapter Twenty-Three

MONDAY, 16 FEBRUARY 2009. *11.05*

D/S Jimmy Suttle drove across to Newport, then took the road north towards Cowes. The rain had cleared at last. It was cold—ice on the roads overnight—but the mist was clearing ahead of what promised to be a flawless day.

Upcourt Farm lay at the end of a track to the west of the Cowes road. On the surveillance logs the D/C in charge had been less than precise about the layout. Operational difficulties had restricted his field of view, but he thought the stables must lie beyond the farmhouse. What was beyond dispute was the target's passion for riding. Both days, over the weekend, she'd driven up here and spent a couple of hours in the saddle.

Suttle bumped the Fiesta up the drive and parked

beside a barn. He'd phoned Lou Sadler about an hour ago, telling her that he needed the missing photo as soon as. To his surprise, she said that her webmaster would be sending it across this morning. She'd even apologised for the delay, explaining the guy had been having problems retrieving the image from his system. Even in e-space, it seemed, Kaija Luik was hard to find.

The farmhouse lay across the yard from the barn. The track continued towards a paddock at the back and Suttle could see a straggle of outhouses that might, he thought, serve as some kind of stable. Beyond the outhouses was a caravan with a black four-by-four parked outside. The rest of the paddock was grazed by sheep.

Suttle walked to the farmhouse and knocked on the door. The place looked dingy, unkempt. No one had touched the square of front garden for months and the wood around the windows was beginning to rot. Inside he could hear someone singing, a woman's voice. Finally the door opened.

The woman was in her forties, thin, striking, with a yellow bandanna around a mass of jet-black hair. She looked South American, brown skin, flattish face. Twenty years earlier, Suttle thought, she'd have been a crowd-stopper.

'So who are you?' Heavy foreign accent.

Suttle introduced himself. She studied the warrant card with some care, then looked up at him, smiling.

'Nice photo.'

Suttle explained that he was making enquiries about stables.

'Why? Have we done something wrong?'

'Not at all. You have stables?'

'We have horses. Not me, not my horses. But horses that live here. With us and the sheep. Up there, you can see.' She took him by the arm, a tight bony grip, and walked him back towards the sagging gate. She smelled of joss sticks, a thick heavy scent that took Suttle back to Valentine's Day.

'So whose horses are they?'

'A friend of mine.'

'Does she have a name? This friend?'

'Of course she does. Everyone has a name. You want coffee? Come.'

Suttle felt the pressure on his elbow again. Inside the house was dark. He'd been right about the joss sticks. They were everywhere, masking a heavy smell of dog. The living room was a mess. He spotted a guitar on the sofa beside a pile of magazines. A single candle was burning among the scatter of bills on the mantelpiece and a cat was dozing among the wreckage of the only armchair. The kitchen was at the back. Suttle stepped over a mountain of washing—men's clothes mainly—jeans, T-shirts, towels, bedding.

'I'll need your name, please.' Suttle had produced his notebook.

'Ximena. It's Spanish.' She spelled it for him.

'And your surname? Family name?'

'Gomez.'

'You live here alone?'

'No. You want milk?' A pot of coffee was bubbling on the stove. Beside it, in a big saucepan, she was boiling underclothes.

Suttle was waiting for more details. She poured coffee into a mug and nodded at the fridge for milk.

'Sugar?'

'No, thanks.' He was looking at the clothes.

'You've got a partner, maybe?'

'A friend. She's upstairs. Why do you want to know all this?'

Suttle explained about the fire at Monkswell Farm. She may have read about it in the paper. Four people dead.

'So?'

'We're making enquiries. This is one of them. The horses belong to your friend upstairs?'

'Eva?' She laughed. 'Eva is seventy. Eva hates horses. And you know something? The horses hate her too. Because of her dog. No, the horses belong to another friend. You want her name? Her name is Lou. Lou Sadler.'

Suttle hesitated. For some reason he'd assumed Sadler hired them from someone else. Not true.

'You look after the horses for her?'

'No.' A shake of the head. 'Lou has a friend. The world is full of friends, no?' She laughed and poured another mug of coffee before disappearing back into the living room. Suttle heard the clump of footsteps on wooden stairs and then a murmured conversation overhead. He was looking at the washing again when she reappeared.

'Lou's friend is called Max. Max lives in the caravan. You know the caravan?' A jerk of the head towards the paddock. 'Max looks after the horses, and a little bit the sheep as well.'

'And that lot?' Suttle nodded at the jeans on the floor.

'Max. You're right. Very good. Very clever. You want something to eat? Toast maybe?'

Suttle shook his head. The coffee was vile.

'Were you here on Saturday night?'

'No.'

‘Where were you?’

‘I was in Ventnor. You want me to prove it? *No problema.* I sing in a pub. You know the Spyglass Inn? Many people come. You should talk to them all. Many clappings. Much applause.’

‘And afterwards? You came back here?’

‘No. I have a friend as well. He lives in Shanklin.’

‘You spent the night with him?’

‘Of course. Why not?’

Suttle asked for his name and contact details. Pete Rafferty. A road near the seafront. Ximena watched him write it down.

‘You gonna check him out? He hates the police. He’s a mad guy sometimes.’ She laughed, a full throaty cackle, her head tossed back. ‘Me? I love this man. Go and see him. *Muy guapo.*’

Suttle wanted to know about Eva. Where was she on Saturday night?

‘Eva? She sleeps. She sleeps like sometimes you think maybe she is dead. A deep, deep sleep.’ She mimed it, put her head on her clasped hands. ‘So, you want to talk to Max, you go up to the caravan. Maybe he’s there, maybe not. This week he works all the time, cleaning and cleaning. It’s springtime, no? So—’ she nodded at his brimming mug ‘—my coffee is shit? Is that what you think?’

Suttle made his way out. As he closed the door behind him, Ximena was singing again, something bouncy and feel-good that told him this visit of his hadn’t bothered her one jot.

The caravan was at the top of the paddock. Suttle paused beside the row of outhouses. These must once have been storage of some kind, and one was still home to a biggish trailer. The next two units had been converted to stables. The doors had been crudely sawn along a horizontal line with the top half hanging open.

Suttle paused and looked in. As a kid back in the New Forest he'd grown up with animals and he had no fear of horses. This one, a big bay, eyed him for a moment before lumbering towards the door. Suttle extended a hand to give it a pat and it sniffed his palm for a moment before tossing its head and rolling an eye. Suttle loved the smell of horses and the bigness they brought with them and for a split second he found himself wondering whether, rather than staying in Pompey, he and Lizzie might somehow raise the money to find themselves a place in the country. Somewhere like this maybe, a bit neglected, a tad shabby, somewhere not too pricey where they could put down roots, raise a few chickens, hide away from the madness of the city.

This evening, by the time he got home, Lizzie would have had the results from the amnio. They'd discussed whether they wanted to know the sex of the child ahead of the birth and they'd both agreed yes, though they differed when it came to preference. Lizzie quite fancied the idea of a boy while Suttle was already convinced it had to be a little girl. He'd get her a pony to begin with, he told himself. Then something like this fella when she was a bit bigger.

'Who are you?'

The question took Suttle by surprise. He glanced round, understanding now why the horse had stepped back so abruptly.

The guy was big, in shape, late twenties, maybe older. He was wearing jeans, boots and a heavy leather jacket against the cold. The fall of long black hair and a startlingly white T-shirt gave him the look of a rock star. Max, Suttle thought. Has to be.

Suttle produced his warrant card. The guy scarcely spared it a glance.

'A cop?'

'Yeah.'

'What do you want?' The tone was businesslike. A foreign accent again.

Suttle asked his name.

'Max,' he said. 'Max Oobik.'

'And you live here?' Suttle nodded at the caravan.

'Yes.'

'It belongs to you? The caravan?'

'No.' A brisk shake of the head. 'What is this? What do you want?'

Suttle explained about the fire at the farm. He was making enquiries, needed a conversation.

'Now?'

'Yes, please.'

'I have stuff to do. Later maybe?'

'Now, if you don't mind.'

'Sure.' He gave Suttle a hard stare. 'You think it's that important, why not?'

They walked the twenty metres to the caravan. There was another horse in the stable beside the bay. Despite the recent rain, everything looked neat and newly tidied.

Inside, the caravan was equally immaculate: everything squared away, room to move about, even a vase of early daffs beside the heavy-metal CDs on the folding table. Suttle's footsteps rang hollow on the metal floor as he made his way towards the couch at the end. There was a pile of newly ironed shirts on it and a poster of somewhere Suttle didn't recognise Blu-tacked to the wardrobe door. A view of the sea was framed between pine trees. A couple of kids were playing on the otherwise empty sand dunes. In the far distance the faint white triangle of a sailing boat, barely a shadow in the haze.

'So where's that?' Suttle nodded at the poster.

'Sarema. It's an island in the Baltic.'

'And that's where you're from? That area?'

'Yes.'

'Which country?'

'Estonia.'

'Do you have a passport here?'

'Of course.'

Suttle said nothing, just waited. Oobik didn't move.

'You want to see it?' he said at last.

'Yes, please.'

He shrugged. The passport was in a rucksack under the table. Suttle made a note of the details, carefully transcribing the passport number and taking a good look at the photo. A couple of years ago Oobik had been a skinhead.

At length he looked up. There was a smell in the air and he'd only just recognised it. Bleach, spiked maybe with something else.

'Do you know a woman called Lou Sadler?'

'Yes.'

'Well?'

'Yes.'

'And she comes up here to ride the horses?'

'The horses belong to her. I look after the horses.'

'I see.' Ximena had said the same thing. 'So how would you describe the relationship?'

'With the horses?'

'With Mrs Sadler.'

'Ms Sadler.' The smile was icy. He was making a

point, answering the question. *Ms* Sadler. No one else's property but her own.

Suttle reached for his pen again, taking his time.

'So are you close?'

'Yes.'

'Not just the horses then?'

'No.'

'OK.' Suttle sat back, enjoying the thin warmth of the sun through the window. 'There's someone else I'd like to ask you about. Her name's Kaija Luik. Do you know this person?'

'Sure.' He shrugged. 'She's Estonian, like me. We talk a couple of times.'

'So do you know where I could find her?'

'No. I think she went back home. I don't know.'

'When? When did she go?'

'Recently. Maybe last week.'

'Do you know why?'

'No.'

'But she's definitely gone? Is that what you're telling me?'

'Yes . . . I think so.'

'Do you have an address for her in Estonia?'

'No.'

'Not even a city? Or a town?'

'No.'

Suttle nodded, his eyes returning to the poster. Max wanted him out of here. The man was acutely uncomfortable. Suttle could sense it.

'So where was Kaija living before she left?'

'In Cowes. She had a flat.' He mentioned a road but said he couldn't remember the number. Suttle made another note. Darcy Road was where Lou Sadler had the property. Same place. For sure.

Suttle looked up again.

'Do you know someone called Johnny Holman?'

'No.'

'Kaija never mentioned him?'

'No.'

'Did she ever mention having an English boyfriend?'

'No.'

'What was she doing? Kaija?'

'She was . . .' Oobik studied his bitten nails '. . . a girl, an escort girl. She worked for Lou.'

'Do you mean a prostitute?'

'I mean an escort girl.' The voice had hardened.

'Same thing, isn't it?'

The big head came up, the face curtained by the fall of hair, and Suttle glimpsed the anger in his eyes. The question seemed to have touched a nerve.

'Lou has a good business. She employs good girls. She looks after them—good pay, good conditions. Kaija met interesting people, nice people. So—' it sounded like a warning '—she was *not* a prostitute.'

'Was?'

'Sure. Like I say, she went home.'

Suttle let the moment pass. This was the guy in Lou Sadler's bed, he told himself, the morning he and Patsy Lowe called in for a chat.

'So you work for Lou Sadler, is that it?'

'Yes.'

'Doing what?'

'Looking after the horses. I told you.'

'And the girls too?'

'No.' That same curt note of irritation. 'The girls look after themselves.'

'And she owns all this? The stables? The horses?'

'Only the horses. The buildings, this place . . .' he waved a huge hand around the interior of the caravan '. . . belongs to the farm.'

'To Ximena?'

'You know Ximena?'

'Yes.'

'No.' He shook his head. 'To someone else. Ximena is like me, like Lou—we rent.'

At Suttle's prompting he managed to remember the name of the owner. He was English. He had lots of businesses. His name was Martin Skelley.

'You have an address? A phone number?'

'No.'

'And yet you pay him rent?'

'I pay rent to Lou. Lou passes on the money.'

'So whereabouts do you think he lives? Is he on the island?'

'I don't know.'

'London?'

'Maybe . . . yes . . . I don't know.'

Suttle bent to his pad. This was shaping nicely. For the first time in a week *Gosling* was threatening to take off. He looked up again.

'I want you to remember what you did on Saturday night,' he said carefully. 'Think about it, Mr Oobik.'

'I was . . .' he paused '. . . in Cowes.'

'Whereabouts?'

He named a couple of pubs. He'd been drinking with friends. Afterwards they'd gone for a Chinese. He gave Suttle their names. Suttle wanted contact details from his mobile. With some reluctance, he complied, chasing down the numbers on his directory. The mobile was a Nokia. Suttle made yet another note.

'And afterwards?'

'I went to Lou's place.'

'Was she there?'

'No. I have a key. She'd gone to Southampton. She got back after me.'

Suttle nodded. Sadler had attended a fund-raiser for Down's syndrome. Back on the last hydrofoil.

'And you stayed there that night?'

'Yes.'

'With Mrs Sadler?'

'With Lou, yes.'

'And Sunday morning?'

'I can't remember.' He shrugged. 'We got up.'

'At what time?'

'I don't know. Ten? Eleven? Not early. Then I came back here.'

'Alone?'

'Yes. Maybe, no.' He was thinking hard. 'Ask her. Ask Lou.'

'I will.' Suttle pocketed his notebook. 'Do you mind if I have a look round?'

'Where?'

'Here.'

'No, sure.' The shrug again. 'Of course.'

Suttle stepped out into the chilly sunshine. The caravan was parked a metre or two from the paddock fence, and when he went round the back he found himself looking at a motorcycle. It was big, low-slung, a Chinese rip-off of a Harley. Beside it, half-tucked beneath the caravan, was a petrol can.

Suttle found a wad of tissue in his pocket. He flattened it out, then knelt to the can and lifted it up, not letting his fingers touch the bare metal of the handle. The can was empty.

Hearing a movement in the wet grass, Suttle looked up. Oobik was standing by the corner of the van, watching his every move. In the low slant of winter sunlight he threw a long shadow.

'When did you last fill this up?' Suttle nodded at the can.

'I can't remember.'

'Was it recently?'

'No.'

'Do you use it for the bike?'

'Sometimes.'

'What else then? The four-by-four?'

'Yes.'

'So why isn't it inside? Inside the four-by-four?'

'I don't know. It just isn't.'

Suttle nodded, wiping his fingers on the tissue. Still on his hands and knees, he peered under the caravan. All he could see were a couple of empty wine bottles and the frame for what must have been a sunlounger, the fabric gone.

He got to his feet again. The burned-out Corsa had been reported in the early hours of Thursday morning.

'Where were you on Wednesday night?'

'When?'

'Last week.'

'I was with Lou.'

'Here?'

'Her place. Always her place.'

'No point asking whether anyone else was there, I suppose?'

Suttle let the question hang between them. The irony was lost on Max. Suttle shrugged, then did a careful circuit of the outhouses. At the far end he found a pile of horse manure. He gazed at it for a long moment, wondering why he hadn't spotted it before, then checked out the trailer he'd seen earlier. Oobik was still watching him, still tracking his every movement.

'What's this for?' Suttle nodded at the trailer.

'It belongs to Lou.'

'That wasn't my question. What's it for?'

'I don't know.'

'A boat, maybe? Does she go sailing?'

'I don't know.'

Suttle shot him a look, then shook his head before stepping across to the four-by-four. He made a careful note of the registration, before turning to Oobik again.

'Yours?'

'Lou's.'

'Has she had it long? To your knowledge?'

'I don't know.'

'But since you've known her, maybe?'

'Maybe.'

'So how long's that?' He smiled. 'Or can't you remember?'

Oobik wasn't going to tell him. He'd had enough of this game, of these baited questions, of this remorseless dissection of his private life.

'I have to go,' he said. 'Maybe some other time, eh?'

'No problem.' Suttle shot him a grin this time. 'I look forward to it.'

* * *

Early afternoon, Winter took a cab to Sandown Road to pick up the holdall. Marie was sitting in the kitchen with Bazza. This was the first time Winter had laid eyes on Mackenzie since the accident and he realised he hadn't the least idea what to say.

To his relief, Bazza seemed pleased to see him. 'Sorry would be in order, you old cunt.' He stood up and gave Winter a hug. 'You know what you've just done to my insurance premiums?'

Winter apologised. Under the circumstances it was the least he could do.

Marie asked him about the interview with the traffic guys at Central. Winter shrugged it off. He'd had a quiet word with the duty solicitor afterwards. A thousand-pound fine and six points sounded about right. Maybe less if the brief could put a decent buff on his reputation.

The thought of a plea in mitigation made Bazza laugh.

'A bent ex-cop? Working for the likes of me? They'll change the law, mush. Put you away for ever.'

Winter was wondering what could possibly account for Mackenzie's high spirits. He hadn't seen him so cheerful for weeks.

'So how's it going, Baz? Been made Mayor yet?'

'One day, mush. One fucking day. Shame you missed the Solent piece.'

Radio Solent was the local BBC station. It seemed they'd visited Sandown Road and invited Mackenzie to air his views on local democracy. Leo Kinder, said Baz, had had a shrewd idea about the line of questioning they would pursue and had thoroughly prepped his would-be candidate. For once in his life, buoyed by Kinder's suspicion that some of this stuff might find its way onto network radio, Baz had listened, and the results, as even Marie agreed, had been impressive.

Local democracy, according to Bazza Mackenzie, belonged in the same knacker's yard as local accountability, grass-roots participation, community involvement and all the other New Labour bollocks. He wasn't blaming them exclusively because you could be sure the other lot would do exactly the same thing when their turn came round, but until the locals—you and me—were trusted to raise and spend their own fucking money then nothing would ever happen. All this local democracy tosh was nothing more than a sound bite, a smokescreen to hide what was really going on. And what was really going on was a royal shafting for one and all. As if people didn't know already. As if we were all that stupid.

'But he didn't say fucking.' It was Marie. 'And he didn't say bollocks.'

'No, I fucking didn't, mush.' Mackenzie was still eyeballing Winter, still making his point. 'But you know something? That Leo was right. Sunday evening. Last night. Radio Four. *Pick of the Week*. Yeah . . . right. Little *me*.'

Winter saw the pride in his eyes, the bantam cock strutting his stuff. Not just king of the Pompey hen coop but, maybe somewhere down the line, of a bigger playground still.

Marie got to her feet. She had to get round to Ezzie's to look after the kids. She gave Winter a kiss and told Bazza she'd be back later. Bazza waited for her to leave. He wanted to know about the holdall Marie had brought back from Fratton nick.

'It's black, yeah? Tatty old thing?'

'That's right. Tell me you haven't looked inside.'

'Of course I fucking have.'

'Touched it?'

'*Touched* it? I had the lot all over the kitchen

floor.'

'Great.'

'Is that a problem, mush?'

'Yeah.'

Winter explained about the old lady's house in Cowes, Kaija's place, the way the girl had suddenly disappeared and what she'd left behind her.

'Who's this Kaija?' He pronounced it 'Kaiser'.

'She's Johnny Holman's special girl. One of Sadler's toms.'

'He was knobbing her?'

'Big time. Paying her sometimes. Sometimes not.'

'The old dog. And you say she's disappeared?'

'Yeah, along with Johnny.'

'Shit.' Bazza was staring at the holdall. It was tucked behind the vegetable rack, clearly visible. 'You're telling me that could be Johnny's gear? All smoky?'

'Exactly. And you know what's all over it? Apart from your DNA?'

'Tell me, mush. I never looked that hard.'

'Blood, Baz. That's the gear he must have been wearing when the kids were killed, and Julie, and the other lad. And after that, from where I'm sitting, a tenner says he torched the place. You don't have to be a cop to suss any of this.' Winter nodded at the holdall. 'All you need is a sense of fucking smell.'

'Johnny did all that?' Bazza couldn't believe it. 'Little Johnny Holman?'

'Yeah.'

'But why would he?'

'Fuck knows. The guy was a fanny rat. He was off his head. Stella does weird things to a man.'

'Not Tommy Peters then?'

'No, Baz. Johnny H.'

'Johnny . . . Johnny . . .' Mackenzie rolled the name round his mouth, trying to get some kind of purchase on this alarming new development. Then he looked up, the last piece of the jigsaw falling softly into place. 'So Johnny did Julie, the kids—right?'

'Right.'

'Dumped his gear. Did a runner. Right?'

'Right.'

'With the girl?'

'We assume so.'

'Right.' He shook his head. 'So where's my fucking toot?'

Chapter Twenty-Four

MONDAY, 16 FEBRUARY 2009. *12.41*

Faraday was still talking to Gabrielle when one of the intel D/Cs working with Jimmy Suttle appeared at his office door. He mimed a waiting phone call, indicated it was urgent. Faraday tapped his watch, held up two fingers. Give me a couple of minutes, eh?

Gabrielle sounded excited. She was still in Salisbury. She'd been talking to a woman in Social Services. The lady ran the Adoption Team. She understood now what they had to do. It wouldn't be simple, but the lady in Portsmouth thought it might be possible. It would take a long time. Best to start now.

'Start what?'

‘We have to be assessed. They have to send someone round, a social worker. They need to know everything about us. We have to do it, *chéri*. It’s for the little one.’

The thought of unzipping his private life for the benefit of some social worker filled Faraday with dread. What kind of questions did these people ask? Were they as intrusive and remorseless as the *Gosling* team? Given the fact that a life was at stake he presumed the answer could only be yes.

‘So when is this supposed to happen?’

‘As soon as we like. I told her this week.’

‘This *week*?’

‘How about Thursday, *chéri*? Would that be OK?’

The D/C was still at the door, still waiting. Faraday bent to the phone again, grunted something noncommittal and hung up. The D/C disappeared to have the call transferred. It was Jimmy Suttle.

‘Boss?’

Suttle sounded excited. He described his visit to the farm. The key, he said, was a guy called Oobik, Max Oobik.

‘Spell it.’ Faraday pulled a pad towards him, wrote the name down. ‘So why is he so special?’

‘Number one, he’s shacked up with Lou Sadler, kips with her, minds bits and pieces of the business. Number two, he’s Estonian, so there’s no way he doesn’t know this Kaija Luik.’

‘Is he denying it?’

‘No, boss. But he makes it sound like they rarely met.’

Faraday asked whether Oobik was still in touch with her. An address? A mobile number?

‘Nothing, boss.’

'And Holman?'

'He says he's never heard of the guy.'

'But Sadler admits Holman was a regular punter of hers.'

'Exactly. And it gets better. The guy looks after a couple of horses for Sadler. So guess what I found beside the stables?'

Faraday gave the question some thought.

'Horse manure,' he said at last.

'Yeah. And where did we last see any of that?'

Faraday smiled. Suttle was right. *Gosling* was at last revving up.

'You're thinking Monkswell Farm?'

'Of course I am, boss. The hole at the back of the place was covered in horse shit. Holman's all over the Estonian girl. The Estonian girl's working for Sadler. Sadler owns a couple of horses. And—hey presto—she's at it with this guy Oobik. Who just happens to be Estonian. Call me slow, boss, but do we smell a pattern here?'

Faraday was trying to work out the science of *Gosling*'s next move. How would you match one set of horse shit with another and make the results lawyer-proof in court? Meg Stanley, he thought.

Suttle hadn't finished.

'Three more little items . . .' he said.

He described the empty petrol can he'd found half-hidden behind the caravan. Robbie Difford's Corsa had been torched a couple of days back. Why not blitz garages across the island, spread the guy's mugshot around, seize CCTV footage?

'To establish what?'

'That the guy's filled the can up recently.'

'What would that prove?'

'That he's lying. He told me he'd last filled it ages

ago.'

'Ah . . .' Faraday bent to his pad. 'And what else?'

'There's a trailer up there, quite a hefty thing. He says it's Sadler's. We need to find out what belongs on that trailer. And where she keeps it.'

'You're thinking transportation?'

'Exactly.'

'Some kind of boat?'

'Yeah.'

'To get rid of whatever?'

'Of course. And here's the clincher, boss. A guy called Martin Skelley. According to Oobik, he's a businessman. He owns the farm where the horses are and seems to know Sadler. Ask one of my guys to run him through PNC. Along with Oobik.'

Faraday had already written the name down. He glanced at his watch. Suttle's news had turned the caravan and the stables into a potential crime scene. He needed to get a SOC team out there as soon as possible, and for that he needed a search warrant.

He bent to the phone again, thinking about Max Oobik. The name rang a bell and he couldn't work out why.

'Has this Oobik come up before, Jimmy?'

'No, boss.'

'So where are you?'

'Still at the farm. Sitting right on top of him.'

* * *

It was Bazza's idea to go to SAS. Safe And Sure was a storage company on an industrial estate at the top of Portsea Island. Mackenzie had had a couple of run-ins with the guy who owned it, chiefly because he wanted to buy the business, and knew he ran a tight operation. For a very reasonable fee, Winter could put Misty's holdall beyond the reach of any interested party.

Winter booked the bag in and bought a padlock with two keys. Any time during business hours he could nip up and retrieve it. He strolled back to the Lexus and rejoined Mackenzie in the car.

'I'm buying you lunch, mush. The Churchillian OK?'

The Churchillian was a pub on the crest of Portsdown Hill. To Winter's knowledge it had never been a favourite of Bazza's, but it had panoramic views over the city below and served decent food. On a fine day like today you could practically touch the Isle ofWight.

Their route up the hill took them past the QA hospital. Winter was driving, Mackenzie sitting beside him. He turned in his seat to watch a pretty nurse emerging from the main entrance.

'You must be sick of the place, mush. Maybe we should have gone somewhere in town.'

Mackenzie rarely bothered himself with this kind of chit-chat. Winter wondered whether he was trying to apologise again.

'What do you mean, Baz?'

'The accident. All the grief you must have gone through afterwards. I hate hospitals. Can't bear them.'

'I thought you meant Leyman.'

'Col?' He seemed genuinely surprised. 'He's out, mush. Safe back home. I popped round yesterday. Made it right with him. Mates again. Like always.'

'Made it right how?'

'Gave him some money.'

‘How much?’

‘A grand.’

‘A *grand*?’ This was unprecedented. ‘Why?’

‘I knew you were upset, mush.’ He patted Winter’s thigh and shot him the old grin. ‘No hard feelings, eh?’

The Churchillian was packed. Winter managed to find a table at the back, away from the pensioners beside the window enjoying the view. Mackenzie took the food order to the bar and returned with a couple of pints of Stella. He had something on his mind.

‘It’s Johnny Holman, mush. We need to get one or two things straight.’

He beckoned Winter closer. Holman, he admitted, had become a bit of a liability after his motorbike accident. Bazza had naturally felt sorry for him and had done what he could to help, not least because he’d always had a soft spot for Julie Crocker.

‘I always thought Jules was made for Johnny,’ he said. ‘She was the only one of all that lot who made the time to go up and see him.’

Holman had been in hospital on the Isle of Man. Julie, he said, had nearly lost her bar job on account of the time off she took for the journeys north. Baz had bunged her a few quid to help out with the fares, and when Johnny came home and started looking for somewhere half-decent to live, it had been Bazza’s idea to try the Isle of Wight.

‘I knew Jules would love it there. She’d had enough of Pompey by then. She couldn’t wait to get her and the kids out of the place. Then Johnny found the farm and they were sorted.’

By now, said Bazza, his own business interests

were mostly legit. Various enterprises were turning over a tidy profit and he'd put his hands-on cocaine dealings behind him. But then he'd got a phone call from Rikki in Cambados. The guy was offering sixty-four kilos of Colombian White at a guaranteed 83 per cent purity for a silly price.

'How much?'

'Three K a kilo, 175K the lot.'

'So when was this?'

'Three years ago.'

Winter nodded. In 2006 he'd still been in the Job. If he remembered right, cocaine was then selling at around eight quid a wrap. A wrap was a fifth of a gram. Forty quid a gram meant £40,000 a kilo. And this after you'd stamped hard on the original consignment, adding all kinds of shit to make a kilo go a lot, lot further. No wonder Bazza had been interested.

'So what happened?'

'I said yes. Rikki did the business at his end and we got the lot trucked through Pompey with a load of fruit and wine. The driver was delivering somewhere upcountry. We did the offload in the back of beyond and stored the toot in a lock-up in Gosport. There was no way I was keeping it there because even then I fancied something long term, just in case. Turns out I was right too, mush. No other fucker saw this lot coming. Not then.'

Winter assumed he meant the credit crunch. Mackenzie had been right: it had been a smart move.

The meals arrived. Bazza tucked into steak and ale pie and a mountain of chips. Winter had ordered fish and chips but had doubts about his appetite. Since the accident he'd barely eaten anything.

He glanced across at Mackenzie, wondering where all this was going.

'So you shipped the toot across to Johnny? Right?'

'Right. Once he and Jules had moved into that farm of theirs, I knew they had the space. I thought Johnny was sound, solid, even then. And I knew he could use the rent.'

'Rent?'

'On the bugle. I paid him by the month. A straight grand. Like you would. Turns out most of it went down his throat.'

Winter picked at a chip. Twelve K a year sounded a lot for babysitting sixty-four kilos of Colombian White, but given the current market price of—say—four million quid, a consignment like that would put you away for a very long time if the men in blue arrived.

'Did you check on him at all?'

'No, mush. But recently I started getting these calls.'

'What calls?'

'From Jules. She was worried about him. She said he was up to all sorts. What she really meant was he'd gone off his head.'

'So what did you do?'

'Nothing, mush. Fuck all. I buried it, blanked it, told myself the daft old sod would realise how lucky he was and sort himself out. Turns out I was wrong.' He paused to swallow a mouthful of Stella. 'Tell you the truth, I still can't believe it.'

Winter shrugged. His years on CID had taught him a great deal about human nature, about the journeys so-called friends can make, about the strokes they can pull, and not much surprised him any more.

'You sure you've got this right?' Bazza had abandoned the steak pie. 'He killed them all? Burned the place down?'

'That's the way it looks.'

'No one else involved? Just him? Little Johnny?'

'We can't be sure, Baz. If I was sitting in Major Crime just now I'd be looking very hard at Lou Sadler and I'd be moving heaven and earth to find the girl.'

'That tom of Johnny's?'

'Yeah. Men follow their dicks. You might have noticed. Find the girl and you might find Johnny too. Find Johnny and . . .' He shrugged, leaving the thought unfinished.

'The toot, you mean? We'd find the toot? I know the market's flat just now but even two and a bit mill is a lot of money.'

'It is, Baz. Which is one of the reasons why looking for Johnny might be harder than we think.' He pushed his plate away.

There was a long silence while Mackenzie brooded further on what might have happened. Finally he voiced the obvious conclusion.

'You think he's dead, mush? You think someone's had him?'

'Maybe.' Winter reached for his glass. 'Cheers, Baz. Here's to crime.'

* * *

Faraday had Meg Stanley on the phone. He'd belled her earlier and she'd taken her time calling back, blaming yet another series of meetings.

Faraday gave her a heads-up on the developing scene at Upcourt Farm. The SOC team were driving over from Shanklin, and he'd no idea whether Stanley would be joining them.

'Of course I am.' She sounded cheerful. 'What's the strength?'

Faraday described Max Oobik and the relationship with Lou Sadler. In his view they had to be linked to the missing girl, Kaija Luik. Which in turn put them alongside Johnny Holman.

'You think?'

'I think.'

'Anything else?'

'Yes.'

Faraday told her about the pile of horse manure. How could they establish a match with the stuff her SOC team had forked off the hole at Monkswell Farm? Stanley gave the proposition some thought. Finally she confirmed it was doable.

'How?'

'We take a blood sample from each of these animals. That'll give us a DNA profile. Then we wait.'

'For what?'

'We wait for them to poo. We swab the surface of the dung, recover a sample from the stuff at Monkswell. If you want to be technical, we're interested in the fibrous structure. Then we submit the lot to FSS. Job done.'

'As it were.'

'Quite.' Faraday could hear her laughing.

'So we seize the horses? Is that what you're saying?'

'Absolutely. And good luck, eh?'

Faraday put the phone down to find himself

looking at Gail Parsons. She'd just arrived on the early-afternoon hovercraft, her face pinked from the climb up the hill from the seafront. She must have run, Faraday thought. Couldn't wait to join the party.

'Well?'

Faraday gave her the headlines. The warrant was en route to Upcourt Farm. The Scenes of Crime team had just left Shanklin. Meg Stanley was driving to Southampton to take the hydrofoil across to Cowes. And Jimmy Suttle was still keeping an eye on Max Oobik, awaiting further orders.

'Where is he? This man Oobik?'

'In his caravan. Suttle thinks he's a flight risk.'

'And you, Joe?'

'I'd arrest him.'

'For?'

'Sus homicide. Keep it simple. Give nothing away.'

He went through the grounds for arrest. There was nothing conclusive but the circumstantial evidence was beginning to heap up.

'Motive? Apart from the cocaine?'

'Hard to say. We need to know more about him. Anything from forensics would be a huge bonus, though Jimmy thinks he's done a good job cleaning up.'

'Cleaning up?' This seemed to swing it for Parsons. 'Tell Jimmy to nick him.'

*   *   *

Mackenzie was at the Royal Trafalgar when he took the phone call from Lou Sadler. He closed his office door, then returned to the desk.

'Lou. Long time, eh?'

Sadler clearly wasn't in the mood for conversation.

'There's a guy working for you,' she said at once. 'An older guy, fat, ex-cop.'

'Might be, love. What's the problem?'

'He's been over here. I met him myself the other night, had one of those cutesy-cutesy conversations. I got the impression he was trying to deliver some kind of warning.'

'About what, Lou?'

'About Johnny Holman.'

'But what did he say?'

'He said he'd met Johnny over in Pompey.'

'When?'

'Earlier this week. Monday, maybe? Tuesday? Fuck knows.'

Mackenzie began to tread carefully. Winter rarely did anything without a purpose.

'So maybe he did meet Johnny. Is that any kind of big deal?'

'It is when half the world's looking for him.'

'Including you, love?'

'Fuck off.'

'Is that a yes?'

There was a silence. Then came an abrupt change of subject. Lou had been employing a girl called Kaija Luik. Before she decided to jack it in she'd been living in a flat in Cowes.

'And?'

'She left some stuff. I went round just now to pick it up and guess who beat me to it. Same age. Same fucking waistline.'

'You mean my guy?'

'Has to be, Baz. So here's my question: when do

we get it back?'

'We?'

'Me. When do I get it back?'

Mackenzie looked at the phone a moment, then he hung up. Winter, he thought. Total fucking genius.

Chapter Twenty-Five

MONDAY, 16 FEBRUARY 2009. *16.34*

Max Oobik was arrested just after half past three and taken to the custody centre at Newport police station. He asked for a lawyer and was put in touch with the duty brief. In an office upstairs, Parsons and Faraday had summoned a Tactical Interview Adviser from the mainland, a veteran called Ian Whatmore. Parsons was beginning to fret that *Gosling* might outgrow the facilities at the satellite MIR, but a transfer to Fratton at this stage in the proceedings was deemed impossible. For one thing, the Fratton Major Incident Room was already busy with a Buckland lad who'd been kicked to death the previous evening. For another, events were moving too fast. So Ryde it had to be.

For the last hour Faraday had been in constant touch with Jimmy Suttle, who was still at the scene at the back of Upcourt Farm. Suttle, watching the SOC team robing up beside the caravan, was waiting for Meg Stanley to arrive from the mainland. Until Faraday made time to come over from Ryde, Suttle would be responsible for drawing up the outlines of a forensic strategy for the coming day or so: how to divide their resources, how to structure the search, how to arrive at agreed priorities.

In the meantime, as Suttle was only too aware, there were a million other boxes to tick. Oobik's four-by-four needed to be seized, pending a full SOC examination. Someone had to come up with a decent local map. Someone else had to establish ownership of the surrounding fields, liaise with the duty POLSA officer, agree parameters for the first sweep, scope out local house-to-house opportunities, organise parking on site, food, shelter, plus the thousand and one other items to keep the *Gosling* Outside Enquiry teams plunging on.

Thanks to Faraday's trust in him, this was the closest Suttle had ever been to the driving seat of a Major Crime inquiry at full throttle, and already he was finding the experience totally engrossing. As the daylight began to fade it was his job to cast the investigative net as wide as possible, then haul it in, hand over hand, constantly aware that a poor decision or a single missed opportunity could jeopardise everything. In these situations the overwhelming priority was to crack on. But cracking on blindly was to invite disaster.

Meg Stanley arrived by cab from the hydrofoil at Cowes. She wanted to know about the PACE clock. Suttle said he'd arrested Oobik just over an hour ago and had him shipped over to Newport nick. By this time tomorrow, unless granted a twelve-hour extension by a uniformed Superintendent, they had to charge him or let him go.

Suttle was leading her across to the stables. She told him already that she'd alerted a local vet to come and take blood samples. A fresh dung swab would obviously depend on the horses. Either way, according to the FSS laboratories at Chepstow, they'd still be looking at a sizeable time gap before they could establish a DNA match.

'How long?'

'Weeks.' Suttle wasn't surprised. Nor would Faraday be. Suttle wanted to know whether anyone had been up to Monkswell to take a sample of the dung at the back of the Holman property.

'Not yet.' She nodded at the caravan. 'First things first, eh?'

The CSI was approaching, a grey ghost in the gathering dusk. Suttle had already asked him for a hot intel search, looking for anything obvious in the caravan before the full forensic examination began. The only item he'd come up with was a B&Q receipt.

'Mobile?'

'Afraid not.'

'Where's he put it then?'

'Haven't a clue.'

On arrest, Suttle had asked for Oobik's Nokia. There'd followed a pantomime search and the news that it seemed to have gone missing. The guy was taking the piss. No doubt about it.

'My guess is he threw it into the next field.'

'And the SIM card?'

'Tear the place apart. Chemical toilet, isn't it?'

'He might have swallowed it.' This from Stanley.

'Great.' Suttle was thinking about the horses. 'That's another arsehole we've got to watch.'

Stanley laughed. She liked Suttle. The CSI had something else on his mind.

'This guy's been cleaning up,' he said. 'Big time.

You can see it, smell it. He's been using bleach and doing a spot of painting as well. The carpet's gone too, and we've found a couple of cans of metallic gloss at the bottom of the wardrobe, both half empty.'

In the fading light Suttle did his best to read the B&Q receipt. One-litre tin of acrylic latex metal paint, a pack of cheap paintbrushes, a litre of white spirit, two litres of bleach, two rolls of dustbin liners, one roll of gaffer tape. He peered at the date.

'When was the eighth?'

'Sunday.'

'Shit. That's a week ago. The day after the fire.'

'Exactly.'

* * *

Winter met Mackenzie at his daughter's house in Craneswater. Neither Ezzie nor her dad had a clue what was going on. Winter led Mackenzie into the big living room at the front of the house, switched on the lights and pulled the curtains shut. Then he turned round.

'Door, Baz.'

'What the fuck are you up to?' Mackenzie shut the door.

'Tell me again.'

'Tell you what?'

'About Sadler. What exactly did she say?'

Mackenzie went through the conversation word for word. It didn't take long.

'So she'd been round to the girl's place? The flat where she'd been staying?'

'Yeah.'

'Looking for the bin liner?'

'Yeah.'

'Great. That means something's kicked off. I don't know what but I can guess.'

'And?'

'They've nicked someone. When I picked up Holman's gear, the old girl said a couple of the girl's friends had come round and taken her stuff away. The mobile was under her pillow so they missed that, and my guess is Johnny had dumped the bin liner in the garden. One of these mates was Sadler. Perfect description. The other guy was younger, foreign, heavy-looking. Maybe they've nicked him, taken a hostage, given the tree a shake, and now's the time it dawns on Sadler that they forgot to look for the bin liner. Either way, Baz, the Major Crime lot are going to be onto that property pretty fucking quickly. Which is when it gets tricky.'

'Who for?'

'Us, mush.' Winter had been waiting years to turn the tables. Now was a perfect time.

Mackenzie still didn't see it.

'OK. You're Faraday. Or Jimmy Suttle, Or any detective with half a brain. One way or another the next couple of hours are going to open a lot of doors. One of them will be that property, take my word for it. They're going to talk to the old dear I met. She's going to tell them all about that nice young tom she had downstairs and that rat-arsed bloke she sometimes brought home. They'll probably have mugshots. She's a tom, for fuck's sake. She made her living from the Internet.'

'And?'

'And they'll ask her more questions, make her go through the whole thing. They're thorough that way. They don't miss a trick. And at some point in that conversation they're going to want to know about her gear, her possessions—what happened to them.'

Mackenzie was frowning. 'You're telling me Sadler went round there? Collected most of her gear?'

'Yeah. For sure.'

'And forgot the bin liner?'

'Obviously.'

'No wonder she's bricking herself.'

'Quite, Baz, and so am I. Why? Because the old dear will describe me. Nice man. Charming. Going bald. Nice leather coat. These guys aren't stupid. They know me. They know who I work for. They'll have us down for the cocaine. And you know what? They'll come calling . . .'

Mackenzie, to Winter's astonishment, was grinning. He reached out and gave Winter's arm a little squeeze.

'That's good,' he said. 'I like *us.*'

*　　*　　*

The photo of Kaija Luik dropped into Faraday's in-box at 17.34. By now the *Gosling* Outside Enquiry team had dispersed on action after action. A handful of D/Cs were conducting house-to-house, tasked to log Oobik's movements over the last week. Another two-man team was interviewing Ximena and her elderly friend upstairs, trying to nail down the same information. What Oobik had been up to over the weekend of the fire. Whether or not they'd noticed a red Vauxhall Corsa. And what might have happened the night the little car had been torched. As each of these lines of enquiry snaked out, the suspicion was beginning to harden that *Gosling* might be dealing not with four deaths in a house fire, nor even a fifth in the shape of Johnny Holman, but perhaps one other.

Faraday was looking at her now, trying to imagine what lay behind the knowing smile and the lazy eyes. Kaija Luik was blonde. She had lovely bone structure, a face perfectly sculpted by genes and exercise, and there was no doubt that she'd be a dream date for a visiting businessman with time and money on his hands. But what on earth had persuaded her to turn paid encounters with Johnny Holman into something more personal? And just how much had this bizarre choice of partner cost her?

Faraday forwarded the photo to the intel cell with instructions to print and circulate it to the Outside Enquiry teams. Any time now Parsons would be demanding another conference, and aside from agreeing a strategy for Oobik's first interview, there'd be the issue of the media. In return for help on getting Luik's photo out there, Faraday was inclined to offer a moderately helpful briefing, but he knew that Parsons regarded reporters with the deepest suspicion.

He scribbled himself a note, looking up at the screen again. Luik's face hung there, curiously disembodied, as if she was already dead, and as he gazed at her he realised that its final arrival raised another question—not about Luik but about Lou Sadler.

Parsons had precisely the same thought. She'd stepped into the office and joined Faraday in front of the screen.

'Why now?' She was frowning. 'Why does she send it now?'

'Because she'd promised.'

'Of course, Joe. But now's different, isn't it? She knows the shit's hit the fan. Oobik would have phoned her. He had at least an hour before Suttle arrested him.'

'Then she's playing Mrs Helpful. Getting in the credits before we knock on her door.'

Arresting Sadler had been a possibility for the last two hours. On Faraday's advice, Parsons had agreed to hold off, not least because Sadler was still under surveillance. Whatever she was up to now might offer all kinds of ammunition for the forthcoming series of interviews.

'Have the obs guys called in yet?'

'Yeah.' Faraday consulted the Policy Book. 'I got a call about an hour ago. She paid a visit to an address on the edge of Cowes. Stayed about ten minutes. Drove away again.'

'So who's going to action that?'

'Jimmy Suttle.'

*   *   *

Thanks to his satnav, Suttle had no problem finding the address. According to checks through the *Gosling* intelligence cell, the property belonged to a Mrs Nancy Percival. Suttle was still admiring her dolphin water feature when she answered the door. He introduced himself and showed her his warrant card. She peered at it in the light from the hall and then asked him to come in.

'My goodness—' the gnarled old hands kept knotting and unknotting '—you must have come about that sweet young girl. I *am* popular.'

* * *

Winter got Mackenzie to make the call. They were still in the big front lounge at Ezzie's. She'd just come in to put a match to the fire and offer them a drink. For once in his life Winter said no.

Bazza was bent over his mobile. Finally, a voice answered. Lou Sadler.

'I've got your favourite man with me, Lou. I think he wants a chat.'

Baz handed over the mobile without a word. Winter found himself listening to Sadler. She sounded icy.

'That was you in the car park, right?'

'Right.'

'So what do you want?'

'I want you to tell me about Kaija Luik.'

'What do you want to know?'

'I want to know what kind of gear she wears.'

'You mean dresses?'

'I mean whatever she wears.' He paused. 'Think of the last time you saw her. What was she wearing?'

'Why?'

'Just do it. Right?'

'What's your name again?'

'Winter. Paul Winter.'

'Then listen to me, Paul Winter. I don't know what the fuck you're up to, but I didn't like you from the start and now's no different. In fact now's a whole lot fucking worse. Do you want to end this call or shall I?'

Winter rolled his eyes. Mackenzie was getting

visibly twitchy. Even Ezzie was taking an interest.

'Just listen to me, eh? I know what's in that bin liner and maybe you do too. Otherwise you wouldn't have gone round to pick it up. But that's not the point, Lou. The point is this. The old lady you talked to this afternoon doesn't. She told me she never looked inside and I believe her. So that just makes two of us. You and me.'

'Go on.'

'Pretty soon my ex-colleagues are going to be knocking on my door. I won't bother you with the small print, Lou, but they're going to want that bin liner. That bin liner could land you and me in deep, deep shit. So there has to be another bin liner. With something else in it. Am I getting warm here?'

'Kaija's stuff?'

'You've got it.'

There was a brief silence on the line, then Sadler was back again. She seemed to have made a decision. She seemed to have understood.

'Size ten,' she said. 'Kaija loves blue. She's got excellent taste. Frocks from Whistles. Jeans by Armani. Hobbs blouses. Converse trainers.' She paused. 'Have you got all that?'

Winter made her go through it again. This time he wrote it down. Ezzie had stepped across and was standing behind the sofa.

'The trainers again?'

'Converse.'

'OK.' He peered at the list. 'What am I missing here?'

'Height. She's tall for a woman. I'd say five eight.'

'Waist?'

'Size ten. Slim. Work it out.'

'Up top?'

'I beg your pardon?'

'Her tits, love.'

'Thirty-four C. She was a popular girl.'

'Is that right?' Winter couldn't be sure but he thought he heard the whisper of a chuckle.

'Anything else you want to know?'

'Yeah. Where is she now?'

'Fuck knows. And that's the truth.'

'What about Johnny Holman?'

'Holman?' The voice had hardened again. 'Holman was an arsehole.'

The line went dead. Mackenzie, greatly relieved, patted Winter on the thigh. Ezzie was still studying the list.

'It's all upstairs,' she said. 'Be my guest.'

* * *

Faraday and Parsons were at Newport police station, conferencing with the Tactical Interview Adviser. D/C Ian Whatmore had made a name for himself force-wide in the dark arts of interview management. How to invite a suspect to divulge more than he ever planned. How to spot the cracks in that first account interview. And how to feed in morsel after morsel of carefully gathered information that would tighten the investigative noose until even the suspect realised he'd been kippered. Whatmore was good at this stuff, so good Parsons had pulled every string to get him sprung from a training course at Southwick Park and whisked at high speed to the Southsea hovercraft terminal.

Whatmore was up for this. Faraday could see it in his face. At forty-nine, a little portlier than his former self, he was close to calling it a day, but like every ageing cop he relished the chance to take another scalp or two.

Already Faraday had outlined what they had to throw at Oobik, but like every good cop Whatmore was more interested in gut feeling.

'You think he did it? Killed Holman?'

Faraday exchanged glances with Parsons.

'Yeah. Ninety-five per cent that's exactly what he did.'

'And the girl? Luik?'

'Ditto.'

Now Whatmore was interested in the disclosure they had to make ahead of the interview to Oobik's solicitor. He was looking at Parsons.

'Oobik's asked for the duty brief. To be honest, we haven't got a great deal. The account he gave Jimmy Suttle is all over the place. We know he's lying, but we've still got to prove it.'

Whatmore nodded. He wanted to know about the duty brief.

Faraday named a Newport-based solicitor. Whatmore knew him well.

'He'll tell this guy to go No Comment. Bet your life.'

'Why?'

'Because he's good, sharp, shrewd. He'll be thinking what you're thinking. And if we give him the impression we've got fuck all, there's no way he's gonna let Oobik open his mouth.'

'So what do we do?'

'We give him short rations. Just enough for him to advise his client. That way he might think we're playing the incremental disclosure game, that we know more than we really do. It's a bit of a punt but it might work.'

Faraday had spotted another problem. This first interview was open account. That meant it was largely down to Oobik. If he chose not to say anything at all, they'd pretty soon run out of questions. And once that happened, the brief would have grounds for drawing the whole thing to a close. 'Diligent and expeditious' was a phrase that had come to haunt every interview room. If the thing wasn't moving on, then stumps would be drawn.

'Not a problem.' Whatmore had a plan. 'The guys we're putting in with him have worked this trick before. Patsy Lowe is brilliant at the touchy-feely. She's the one to find the sweet spot, what turns him on, what he's been proud of in his life. Angus can save the charm for later. I'll tell him to keep his mouth shut.'

'Until the challenge phase.'

'Of course, boss. We want the truth or provable lies, right?'

'Right.'

'Then we spend tonight getting the lad onside.'

Faraday had no problem with Patsy Lowe. Her long years as a Family Liaison Officer had taught her how to build a bridge to pretty much anybody. Angus McEwan too had the knack of looking a man in the eye and winning his trust. He was a big man, physically imposing, with five kids and a wife who was a genius in the kitchen, and his soft Scots accent masked a great deal of guile.

Whatmore looked from Faraday to Parsons.

'Are we through here? You want to policy this thing up?'

'Sure.' Faraday reached for his notes. More

typing. More layers of armour plate.

Whatmore got to his feet and put his jacket on. Then came a knock at the door. It was Suttle. His mop of curls was plastered to his skull. It must have started raining again.

He looked first at Faraday.

'You're not going to believe this, boss.'

Chapter Twenty-Six

MONDAY, 16 FEBRUARY 2009. *18.37*

It wasn't in Mackenzie's nature to wait. He sat on the sofa, still at Ezzie's, still in the big front lounge, aware of the murmur of conversation upstairs. Winter was with him, buried in Stu's copy of the *Financial Times.* The credit squeeze was tightening by the day. More bad news from Dubai.

A peal of laughter caught Winter's attention. Marie, definitely. Summoned by phone, she'd come round to give her daughter a hand. There was more laughter, louder as a door opened, then came the patter of footsteps on the stairs and the two women were back in the lounge.

Ezzie was carrying a black plastic sack. She looked pleased with herself.

'You want a peek? Make sure we've got it right?'

She emptied the contents of the bag on the carpet and Winter found himself looking at a jumble of clothes: a patterned blue skirt, a couple of halter tops in pinks and yellows, a pair of denim shorts with a rose embroidered on the arse, two pairs of rope sandals. Ezzie knelt on the carpet and dug around, extracting a thong in black mesh. She held it up, suspended on one finger.

'What do you think, Dad? Does this fit the bill?'

Mackenzie had the grace to muster a grin, all too aware that Winter was in charge now. He understood the rules of this strange new game. He seemed to know the moves they had to make to head off disaster.

'That's great,' Winter said. 'Have you got a torch?'

Marie stuffed the clothes back in the bin liner while Ezzie fetched a torch. The back garden was surrounded by a high brick wall and there was an area at the far end shielded from the neighbours. It was pouring with rain again and the square of newly turfed lawn was soggy underfoot. Perfect, thought Winter, following the beam of the torch towards the rear wall.

Here, at the back end of last year, Stu had begun a compost heap with piles of raked leaves. Since then he and Ezzie had added hedge cuttings, rose trimmings and sundry garden waste. Winter stirred the edges of the compost with his foot, then stooped down for a handful of the soil underneath and smeared it all over the bin liner. The soil was wet from the rain, and bits of fibre from the compost stuck to the black plastic. He gave it another coating then headed back indoors.

Mackenzie was in the kitchen, helping himself to Stu's malt. Winter left the soiled bag beside the door and went to find Ezzie. He was back in moments, drying himself with a towel. Then Ezzie came in.

'This OK?'

She offered Winter the hairdryer. Winter plugged

it in, hauled the bin liner onto the breakfast bar and began to hose the black plastic with hot air. Slowly, the pebbles of rain disappeared, leaving brown smears of soil.

Marie had joined them in the kitchen. She'd seen the bin liner Winter had brought back from the Isle of Wight. She understood exactly what was going on.

'You're an artist, Paul.' She reached out for the towel. 'You think they'll come looking?'

'I know they will.'

'But what about the other one? The one I picked up from the police station? I told them Baz had been giving a friend a hand in the garden. I said they'd done a bonfire together.'

'Perfect.'

'We stick to that?'

'Absolutely.'

'But what if they want to check? What if they want to see all that stuff?'

'You threw it out. It was disgusting. You're a woman with standards. A rare breed these days.'

'And the friend?' It was Mackenzie. He was getting the hang of this.

Winter gave the question some thought.

'Misty,' he said. 'Leave it to me.'

* * *

Lou Sadler was arrested at 20.17 by two D/Cs from the Outside Enquiry team on suspicion of murder. Suttle was parked on the Cowes promenade in front of the apartment block, waiting for one of the off-duty Crime Scene Investigators to arrive from Shanklin. The decision to scoop up Sadler had been

Parsons', with heavy backing from Faraday.

Suttle's own inclination had been to let her run and see what developed. The obs team were still sitting on her every move and her visit to Nancy Percival had already produced a breakthrough. She must have known exactly where Kaija Luik had been living, and her eagerness to lay her hands on the bin liner opened a line of enquiry that was deeply promising. What had the bin liner contained? And was it pushing supposition too far to agree that the overweight charmer at Mrs Percival's door must have been Paul Winter?

That, he knew, was Parsons' assumption. It was now an article of faith that a quantity of narcotics had been removed from Monkswell Farm. Johnny Holman was a close associate of Bazza Mackenzie. A remote property on the Isle of Wight was exactly the place you might choose for a stash. Winter had already been sniffing around the investigation. With his nose in *Gosling*'s trough and his mastery of the dark arts of detection, would it be a surprise if he wasn't, in some respects, ahead of their game?

Suttle smiled, amazed as ever by Winter's MO, a mix of guile, low cunning and sheer bravado. Removing vital evidence that might turn out to be a crime scene could earn him a hefty prison sentence, but Suttle knew Winter far too well not to understand that this decision would have been carefully weighed. In the Job, Winter had always tried to lay hands on the single clue that would unlock an entire investigation, and in the shape of the bin liner, thought Suttle, he might have found exactly that.

The big door in the front of the apartment block swung open and Suttle peered out through the teeming rain as the two arrestingD/Cs hurried Lou Sadler into the waiting car. He got out of the Fiesta and stepped across. One of the D/Cs handed him the key to Sadler's apartment.

'Fourth floor,' he said. 'Number 8. Help yourself.'

Suttle nodded, said nothing. Lou Sadler was sitting in the back of the squad car, looking up at him. Her face was impassive, not a flicker of emotion. Parsons was right, Suttle thought. She's been sitting up there waiting for us.

* * *

It was Faraday's idea to summon reinforcements from the mainland to give the investigation a fighting chance. Parsons was now sharing his borrowed office at Newport police station, squeezing herself behind the spare desk and demanding flowers to brighten the place up. One of the civvy inputters in the Ryde MIR, underimpressed by Parsons' slightly regal air, had quietly coined a nickname that was threatening to catch on: Her Bustiness. Or, more simply, HB.

Faraday, bent over the Policy Book, was mentally reviewing developments over the last couple of hours. The Outside Enquiry team was fully stretched on action after action, racing against the clock to find fresh bullets for *Gosling*'s gun. A trawl of Mrs Percival's neighbours to establish whether anyone had information about visitors in the small hours of Sunday morning. Flat-to-flat calls in Sadler's apartment block. Marina enquiries to try and establish whether or not she owned a boat of any description. A wider intel trawl to build a picture of Martin Skelley. Already the

PNC had yielded a number of convictions, two—in his youth—for GBH. Since then he appeared to have built a substantial business empire but the details were still imprecise. More Googling. More Facebook. More calls.

With Sadler en route to Newport from Cowes, the task now was to prepare for another set of interviews. Because *Gosling*'s D/Cs were fully occupied, Faraday was suggesting a couple of names from the Major Crime team back at Fratton. Both he knew well. D/C Bev Yates was a career detective, a veteran forty-something. His private life was never less than chaotic, but his sleepy eyes and Italian good looks had won him a series of victories in the interview room, often against women. D/C Dawn Ellis was younger but no less shrewd. Pale, slight, passionately vegan, she carried an air of boyishness which she used to great advantage. Pre-Christmas there'd been rumours that she'd begun to lose the plot—talk of man trouble—but Faraday mistrusted canteen gossip and was glad to have her on the team. Some serious criminals had made the mistake of underestimating Ellis and had regretted the consequences.

Faraday was worrying about the PACE clock. It was already gone half eight. Sadler had yet to arrive. The booking-in process would take at least half an hour. If she wanted the services of her own lawyer, it might be midnight before all the consultations with the brief were complete. By that time Sadler would be due the stipulated eight-hour rest period, pushing the first interview into the following day.

Parsons dismissed Faraday's reservations. Making a fresh start tomorrow morning, she said, had lots of advantages. For one thing they'd have time to agree a proper strategy with Ian Whatmore and the interview team. For another, the overnight enquiries, plus forensic developments at the caravan and Sadler's apartment, might well affect the whole thrust of the investigation. At last, she said, *Gosling* appeared to be in the driving seat.

'Yates and Ellis then?' Faraday had them on standby.

'Yep. Get them over now.'

'And Winter?'

To Faraday's surprise, Parsons hesitated. Thinking she couldn't resist this golden chance to at last get even, he'd assumed she'd want detectives knocking on his door as soon as possible. On the contrary, she appeared to favour caution. She was wary of Winter. She wanted to make sure they weren't walking into yet another cleverly baited trap.

'Who knows him best, Joe?'

'Suttle, without question. Winter trained him. He knows exactly the way the guy ticks.'

'And we trust Suttle?'

'Completely.'

'Then send him over.'

'To do what?'

'Have a chat.'

'And if Winter admits removing the bin liner?'

'Then we arrest him.'

'For what?'

'Perverting the course of justice. This is page one, Joe. The man's trying to make things hard for us.'

Faraday nodded. She was right. Winter was definitely on a nicking.

'So when do you suggest we action this?'

'Tonight.' She glanced at her watch. 'As soon as.'

* * *

Jimmy Suttle stepped into Sadler's apartment, leaving the door open for the Crime Scene Investigator, who'd just arrived from Shanklin. The lights were on and he waited for the CSI to join him. He was an older man, overweight, and he came puffing up the stairs complaining about the supper he'd had to abandon. Steak and kidney pudding. His wife's own recipe. Criminal.

They started in the kitchen, a brief scan of the shelves, a cursory poke through the drawers, looking for anything obvious that might help the interview teams over the next twenty-four hours. According to items pinned to the corkboard on the back of the door, Lou Sadler owed two weeks' worth of milk and fancied a recipe for prawns in a coconut and chilli sauce. The contents of her fridge betrayed a weakness for crème fraiche and eclairs, and she was manic about hanging on to Sainsbury's bags.

The bedroom looked more promising. There were two dressing gowns folded over the foot of the big double bed and a whole drawerful of men's clothing, chiefly jeans and T-shirts. The T-shirts were large; the jeans thirty-six in the leg. On the table beside the bed was a framed photo. Sadler sat at the wheel of a biggish rigid inflatable, grinning at the camera. It was a glorious day, not a cloud in the sky, and the background matched the view across the Medina from West Cowes. Riding pillion in the RIB was a bigger figure, Max Oobik—blue anorak, knee-length olive-green shorts. He too was enjoying himself. Suttle gazed at the photo, knowing that this was probably the boat that belonged to the trailer at Upcourt Farm. He put the photo to one side and had started going through the twin drawers in the dressing table when he got a call from next door.

The CSI, looking for a second bedroom, had found Sadler's office. Venetian blinds on the single window. PC on the desk. An Ikea filing cabinet in the corner. Very neat. Not a single concession to sentiment or unnecessary decoration.

Suttle slipped behind the desk. The PC was still live and a face hung on the screen. It was the girl, Kaija Luik, exactly the same shot Suttle had seen earlier in Faraday's office, and Suttle stared at it, wondering if this little gesture was deliberate, an electronic *adieu* from someone who, after a full week, still remained a total mystery.

The CSI was going through the filing cabinet. So far he'd found detailed records from the business including bank statements, tax computations, VAT printouts, profit and loss accounts, payment schedules, remittance slips and a couple of spreadsheets offering a glimpse of where Two's Company might be heading next. Suttle knew at once that he'd need financial specialists to make proper sense of all this. There was doubtless more on the PC's hard disk, but time was short and overnight he'd only have time for a brief trawl for relevant material before the interview team got a proper crack at Sadler. He was asking the CSI to bundle up all this material when his mobile began to chirp. He checked caller ID. Faraday.

'Parsons wants you to talk to Winter.'

'About the bin liner?'

'Yeah. And the girl's phone he took.'

'When?'
'Now.'
'Where?'
'We're assuming Pompey.'
Suttle was watching the CSI pull yet more paperwork from the filing cabinet. If the two D/Cs manning *Gosling*'s intel cell were expecting a night's sleep, they were in for a shock. Faraday was waiting for an answer. Suttle told him about the intel haul and asked about the hovercraft shedule. Faraday told him to seize the paperwork and the RIB photo and send it back with the CSI. As for the hovercraft to Southsea, there was no crossing after 20.20. Best, therefore, to take the 21.15 RedJet catamaran to Southampton and then cab it across to Pompey.
'Done, boss,' Suttle said, checking his watch.

* * *

Winter had settled in for a night in front of the telly. By half ten, coshed by a plate of beef in chilli noodles delivered from the Water Margin, he was ready for bed. For once in his life he hadn't had a drink. The videophone buzzed at 10.47. Winter, half-asleep in front of *Newsnight,* struggled to his feet. They're late, he thought, checking his watch. He padded down the hall and checked the screen. To his surprise, he found himself gazing at Jimmy Suttle. The boy looked soaked.
'You,' he grunted, buzzing him in.
'Me,' Suttle agreed, ducking out of the rain.
Winter had the door open and a towel ready.
'You'll catch your death,' he muttered. 'Me? I was just off to bed.'
'Yeah?' Suttle was drying his mop of red curls. 'It

could have been worse. It could have been me and the Ninjas.'

Ninjas was cop-speak for the Force Support Unit, the house-entry guys in full body armour, who were rarely in the mood for conversation. Winter felt pained by the very thought.

'She wouldn't be that spiteful, would she?' He was looking at the row of lagers he'd readied in the fridge.

'Who?'

'Parsons.'

'She might.' Suttle tossed him the towel, refused a bottle of Stella. 'Where do you want to do this?'

'Do I have a choice?'

'Yeah. Here if you don't fuck around. Otherwise it's the Bridewell.'

'You'd have to arrest me.'

'Absolutely my pleasure.'

'D'you mean that?'

'Yes, I fucking do. What are you up to, Paul? First you turn up in Ryde, picture of fucking innocence, just happen to have heard about a fire or something. Next thing we know, you're poking round a key witness then nicking off with what you know might be a crime scene. Am I right here? Or have I missed something?'

Winter was amused. Master and pupil, he thought.

'Sit down, son. And don't shout. The neighbours hate it. It might be news to you but we pay a fortune for peace and quiet in this neighbourhood.'

Suttle stared at him, then took a seat in the corner of the sofa. Winter settled in the armchair. He hadn't touched his Stella.

'In your place, son, I'd have gone for open

account first,' he said. 'I'd have asked me to explain my movements, every single one, and then I'd have listened very hard until I tripped myself up.'

'But you won't, will you? You won't trip yourself up.'

'So why are you here? Apart from the apology you're about to make?'

'Apology?' Suttle looked blank.

'For the techies. For the sneaky-beaky. I don't know whether it's budget cuts but we used to be quite good at B & Es. In-out, bish-bosh, job done. You know about rule one?'

'Tell me.'

'Always check the bedrooms.' Winter lifted his bottle. 'Cheers. Mist sends her love. Here's hoping those guys are still in a job.'

Suttle smothered a yawn and rubbed his eyes. Winter knew exactly how he felt.

'Long day?'

'Yeah.'

'Getting anywhere?'

'Don't be a twat, Paul. Just give me credit, eh?'

'Fine, son. So how can I help you?'

Suttle was half-watching the television. Jeremy Paxman was getting indignant about overpaid bankers. Winter reached for the remote and turned the set off.

'Well?' he said.

'You went to see Nancy Percival, right?'

'The old lady in Cowes? The one who rented the room to Luik?'

'Yeah.'

'That's right.' Winter nodded. 'I did.'

'Why?'

'Because I had grounds for thinking the girl had

been there. And as it transpired, I was right.'

'Stop talking like a cop.'

'I was a cop, son.'

'Then tell me why the girl was of any interest. What was Luik to you lot?'

'Was?'

'Is.' Suttle shrugged.

'You think she's dead?'

'Just answer the fucking question, Paul. And stop twatting about.'

'You *do* think she's dead.'

Suttle gave him a hard look, made a point of checking his watch.

'I can have a car here in five,' he said. 'It'll take a while to get you booked in because no one down there likes you very much. Then there's the brief. Then there's disclosure. And then you've got eight hours straight on one of those poxy mattresses in one of our nice new cells before we even begin to get down to the business.'

'I know.' Winter nodded. 'I was down there yesterday.'

'At the Bridewell?' Suttle was at sea again.

Winter explained about the crash on the M275: 90 mph in Bazza's Bentley and a photo from one of the ANPR cameras to prove it. This was plainly news to Suttle.

'Did you kill anyone?'

'No, thank fuck.'

'Injuries?'

'Minor.'

'And you?'

'Me, son? I was lucky. I'm still here, talking to you.'

Suttle went back to Kaija Luik. He wanted to

know why Mackenzie thought she was so important.

'Mackenzie didn't. I did.'

'Why?'

'Because Luik was screwing Johnny Holman, and Holman is very definitely important to Mr M.'

'In what way?'

'In every way. They go back years, centuries, for fucking ever. You'll have seen the file. You'll have done the association chart. You know Bazza. He can be a handful sometimes but deep down he's loyalty on legs. Holman was having a rough time—his own fault mostly, but you don't look too hard when you've been mates. Then the guy gets burned to death, and that pisses you off somewhat, then it turns out that he wasn't in the house at the time, and that starts you thinking.'

'About what?'

'About what's going on with your mate Johnny. About exactly what's happened to the old cunt. And about the various ways you might be able to make life a bit sweeter for him.'

'Very touching.' Suttle didn't believe a word.

'But true, as it happens. So guess who gets the sharp end of all this? Guess who finds himself on that fucking hovercraft *again*?'

'Surprise me.'

'Yeah, son. Little me. Why? Because I've got to find Johnny. And how do I do that? I go looking for his girlfriend. And how do I know her name? Because *you* told me.'

'I did.' Suttle nodded. 'You're right.'

'OK.' Winter nodded, his point made. 'Next?'

Suttle wanted to know how Winter got to Nancy Percival's place. Winter explained about his hour with Monique Duvall. Suttle shook his head in disbelief.

'That was on expenses?'

'Of course.'

'And?'

'Lovely. Outstanding.'

'I bet. So the mobile you nicked took you to Luik?'

'To the old girl. That was luck on my part and shit work on Lou Sadler's. Luik had left her mobile under the pillow. Like I said just now, always check out the bedroom.'

'So you paid the old girl a visit?'

'Yeah. We had a little chat, like you do, and she gave me the rest of the stuff.'

'The bin liner?'

'Yeah.'

'And the mobile?'

'Yeah.'

'Which you took away?'

'Of course.'

'Why?'

'Because it might take me a step closer to Luik. And if that happened, I might even lay my hands on little Johnny.' He held his hands wide, an expression of the purest innocence. 'Job done.'

'So what was in the bag?'

'Clothes.'

'What kind of clothes.'

'Her clothes. Luik's clothes. Or so I assume. You want to look? Give me a receipt and take the fucker off my hands? Only you're more than welcome, son.'

Suttle studied him for a long moment.

'The old lady told me she found the bin liner in the garden. Why would that be?'

'I've no idea, son. I'm not a detective. D'you want this sodding bin liner or not? Only it's way past my bedtime.'

Suttle gazed at him. Winter wondered whether the last five minutes was worth a round of applause. The boy looked exhausted.

'There's something that really interests me,' he said at last, 'something about you and Mackenzie.'

'And what's that, son?'

'I think you've had enough.' He glanced at his watch and then reached for Winter's bottle of Stella. 'Would that be right?'

Chapter Twenty-Seven

TUESDAY, 17 FEBRUARY 2009. *05.17*

Faraday awoke before dawn, aware that something seemed to have changed. The tenement at the back of the hotel was in darkness. Beyond, he could see the orange glow of the Ryde street lights. From miles away, out in the Solent, came the *parp* of a ship's hooter; closer, the whine of a car changing down through the gears for the roundabout. He rolled over and checked the alarm clock beside the bed.

He rubbed his eyes, wondering why he felt so fresh, so rested, so free from the constant tug of anxiety that had shadowed him since the accident. Then he had it: *Gosling* had turned a corner and he was back at the controls of a machine for which he had a profound respect. Get the next twenty-four hours right, he told himself, and his life might be his own again.

He sat on the edge of the bed, gazing down at the carpet, aware that since Oobik's arrest he hadn't spared Gabrielle a moment's thought. He'd been too busy, too alert, too aware that he couldn't afford a single distraction. In the past this degree of concentration had been a huge mental drain; now, for reasons he couldn't fathom, it seemed to have revived him. He reached for the towel he'd abandoned on the nearby chair. A shower, he thought, then an early start.

*   *   *

Winter, at about the same hour, was lying in bed listening to the growl of an early Fastcat as it made its way down-harbour for the crossing to Ryde Pier. Jimmy Suttle had left before midnight, pocketing Luik's mobile but scarcely bothering to inspect the contents of the carefully soiled bin liner. They were both aware that this was an artful piece of theatre, and Suttle was wise enough to know that Winter would have taken every possible precaution to shield himself and his boss from any kind of charge, but the essence of the evening had come later.

Suttle, to Winter's quiet satisfaction, was a detective of quality, mindful of the investigative possibilities that lay in the friendship that had somehow survived Winter's journey to the Dark Side. He'd probed the older man with care and, Winter thought, genuine concern. He'd wanted to know why the buzz of working for Mackenzie had begun to fade. He'd gently suggested that the guy had some seriously vicious habits that no amount of money or political ambition or gruff Pompey wit could disguise. And he'd pointed out that sooner or later, come what may, Mackenzie would crash and burn. Did Winter want to be part of that? Was the prospect of getting old in a prison cell *that* enticing?

At first Winter had kept him at arm's length. How could Suttle possibly assume that anything had soured between him and Bazza? And what kind of betting man would take a serious wager against Mackenzie going from strength to strength? Serious criminals, he told Suttle, were in a different league to the Men in Blue. The best of them, class acts like Mackenzie, were perfectly equipped for the cut and thrust of business. They were bold, they knew the moves, and they weren't afraid to pay good money for the best advice. In a bare handful of years they could emerge untainted from the mud and bullets they'd left behind. No more racing round Pompey, chasing up drug debts. No more strong-arm tenant evictions to free up this property or that. Just a busy, diligent, civilised ascent to fame and fortune.

Suttle had laughed at this and wished Winter luck. Then, getting to his feet, pocketing Kaija's mobile and then picking up the bin liner, he'd said something else. He and Lizzie were going to have a baby, a little girl. And if everything worked out, they'd be honoured if Winter would consent to be a godfather.

If everything worked out.

Winter lay in the half-darkness, listening to the distant roar as the Fastcat picked up speed, wondering exactly what the lad had meant.

*   *   *

Faraday was at his desk in the SIO's office by six

o'clock. Soon he'd have to drive over to Newport for the interviews, but for now he needed to review overnight developments. On top of the pile of paperwork on his desk was an interim report from the intel cell on Martin Skelley. One of the D/Cs must have worked half the night to get this thing done, Faraday thought, wondering whether the seized accounts from Sadler's office had got the same treatment.

He fired up Parsons' coffee machine and settled down to read the report. Martin Skelley was a Scouse bad boy from a big Catholic family in Toxteth. By his late teens, according to intelligence reports from the Merseyside force, he'd been running a tyro protection racket, extorting weekly insurance 'premiums' from terrified local shopkeepers. One Sikh, braver than the others, had told Skelley to get lost, an act of neighbourly defiance that had put him in hospital with injuries described in the intel report as 'briefly life-threatening'. Violence on this level had provoked a robust CID response, and Skelley—who'd personally inflicted the bulk of the damage—got a hefty stretch for GBH. He'd served the early part of this sentence at HMP Parkhurst on the Isle of Wight, then a tough Category A prison. He'd held his own against the usual army of bully boys and assorted psychotics and had emerged virtually intact.

Criminality plagued his twenties, but prison had taught him a great deal about not getting caught again. His talent for violence and his taste for the good life took him into drug dealing—mainly cannabis and cocaine—and by the end of the 90s he'd managed to wash and invest a serious amount of money. Some of it went on the purchase of a successful car auction franchise, operating nationwide. The rest bought him a fleet of refrigerated vans, from Transits upwards, which became the backbone of a company called Freezee.

Faraday broke off to pour himself a coffee. Skelley's genius lay in realising the potential of the regular, reliable and above all cheap delivery of cut-price fast-food packs nationwide. This was the kind of stuff that went to roadside burger stalls, fairground outlets and the tens of thousands of inner-city caffs that made a living by dishing up this crap. These people always dealt in cash. There were no hassles about credit terms or unpaid invoices. Either you paid for the stuff on the spot or the van drove away. If Skelley could undercut the opposition, and he could, then he was perfectly placed to make a second fortune.

And so it had proved. Freezee had gone from strength to strength, and the corporate website now boasted of more than 170 vehicles nationwide. Treat yourself to a cheapo burger in Aberdeen or Penzance, and the chances were that the thin greasy disc of beef and gristle had been delivered by Martin Skelley.

According to the intel D/C, Freezee had bought Skelley the lifestyle of his dreams. The company was run from a trading estate near a major motorway junction outside Manchester. Skelley had a trophy penthouse in one of the city's new canalside apartment blocks, plus a sprawling house tucked away on the shores of Derwent Water in the Lake District. He got around in a brand new Porsche Carrera and kept a decent-sized day cruiser on a private mooring at his lakeside home.

But it was his first property purchase that caught Faraday's eye. In 2002, with Freezee gobbling up more and more of the market, he'd bought nine acres of the Isle of Wight in the shape of Upcourt Farm.

Faraday helped himself to a refill, spooned in more sugar, aware that this was the link he'd been after. Suttle had already established that Lou Sadler rented the stables from Skelley. It was therefore reasonable to suppose that these two knew each other. They were business people. They were used to operating on the margins of what was legal. And Faraday could well imagine Sadler offering some kind of discount on her escort girls when Skelley was trying to win new business. That's the way these people worked. If you spotted an opportunity, you could share it. And if you suddenly found yourself in the shit, then all you had to do was pick up the phone.

Faraday smiled and reached for a pen. He was still scribbling himself a note for the Outside Enquiry D/S when he heard a light tap at the door. He looked up. Meg Stanley.

It was barely half past six. She was on her way across to Upcourt Farm from the hotel and had intended to drop a summary of last night's forensic developments on Faraday's desk. Since he was here, she could go one better.

She confirmed that the examination of the caravan was virtually complete. As Suttle had suspected, someone—presumably Oobik—had given the place a thorough clean prior to repainting. Tiny shreds of fabric where the floor met the sheet-metal sides of the caravan indicated the recent removal of a carpet, and there were confirmatory screw holes along the edges of the floor where someone had removed lengths of carpet gripper. Neither the sink trap nor the chemical toilet had yielded anything of forensic interest, nor were there any traces of blood, hair or skin scrapings. In summary, she said, an impressive job.

'But definitely a clean-up?'

'Yes. The CSI told me about the B&Q receipt. If we need to, we can match the new paint in the van to what's left in the tin. That means the clean-up happened last week after the purchase time.'

'Anything else?'

'Yes.' She nodded. 'Oobik bought two rolls of dustbin liner. There are twenty sacks on each roll but we can only find thirteen sacks left. That means he must have used twenty-seven sacks. Which is a lot for a bit of carpet and whatever else he wanted to get rid of.'

Faraday extended a hand for the summary. She handed it across.

There was more, she said. At first light the CSI was going to make a proper start on the area outside the caravan, but last night, under floodlights, he'd had a preliminary look round.

'And?'

'Interesting. There are three outhouses. Two serve as stables, the other one is a kind of garage for the boat trailer. The CSI had a good look at the last one and thinks there might be two sets of tyre marks. Nothing evidential, but indentations. He looked outside too and got the same impression.'

'Meaning?'

'Meaning we might be dealing with two separate items. The trailer obviously and something else, maybe a small car.'

Faraday nodded. The Corsa, he thought. If you wanted to hide it, an outhouse like that would be perfect.

'One other thing, Joe.' Stanley still hadn't finished. 'It's pretty exposed up there, and the caravan is tied down at each corner. We're talking guy ropes, basically, secured to anchor points. I took a shot of one of them.' She nodded at the summary. 'It's on page seven.'

Faraday found the photo. It had been taken at night. A big metal eye had been sunk into a crude concrete block. A rope secured through the eye disappeared vertically out of shot.

'How much do these things weigh?' Faraday was trying to imagine them.

'They're heavy. They have to be.'

'Too heavy to carry?'

'No way. Not if you're someone like Oobik.' She gestured at the photo again. 'Now turn over.'

Faraday went to the next page and found himself looking at another guy rope, secured this time to a thick iron stake.

'This is from the caravan too?'

'Yes. And the really interesting thing is the grass around it. Here.'

She dug around in her bag. The sight of a magnifying glass put a smile on Faraday's face. She passed it across.

'Take a look at the grass,' she said.

Faraday did what he was told. The outlines of what could have been a block were clearly visible.

'You're thinking someone's taken the block?'

'Yes, definitely.'

'When?'

'It has to be recent.'

'How recent?'

'Not more than a week. The pattern's survived because it's winter. In summer we'd have lost it within a day or so. Too much growth.'

Faraday nodded. This, he sensed, was hugely significant. First the suggestion of a car in the outhouse. Then the need for all those dustbin liners. Then the clean-up. And now the removal of a hefty chunk of concrete with a handy fixing on top.

'OK.' He leaned back, hands clasped behind his head. 'So how do you read this?'

'What do I think happened?'

'Yes.' He nodded towards the pot. 'Coffee first?'

* * *

Winter arrived at Misty Gallagher's in time for breakfast. She was in the kitchen, wrestling a collection of pans from the dishwasher. Alone in the house, with the central heating at full blast, she made do with a silk dressing gown. Recently she seemed to have lost the belt.

'How did you get in?' She gathered the dressing gown around her.

'You gave me a key, Mist.'

'Did I?'

'Yeah. You want it back?'

She gave him a sharp look, then shook her head.

'Come here,' she said. 'Give me a kiss. Tell me we're friends again.'

Winter put his arms around her. She let the gown hang loose and held him tight. She said she'd missed him. She said they were too old to worry about all the stuff that might or might not happen. He made her laugh and he wasn't bad in bed when he made an effort, and to be honest they'd had some good times so what, exactly, was the problem?

Winter laughed. She never failed to stir him.

'What are you after, Mist?'

'You, my love. Do you think you can manage it? Just one more time?'

She caught his hand and put it on her breast. Then she kissed him properly before sinking to her knees. Winter watched her kissing him through his trousers. He'd never been quite sure what love meant but moments like these might be quite close.

'Here or upstairs?' She was looking up at him.

'Your call, Mist. But you'd better stop doing that.'

She took him up to the bathroom, ran a tubful of hot water, tipped in a generous slurp of scented bubbles, soaped him like a baby until Winter smelled of pine needles.

'I've always wanted to fuck a lumberjack,' she murmured, giving him a little squeeze.

She led him, pink and newly towelled, through to her bedroom. The bed was still warm from her body. At Misty's insistence, Winter lay back while she dribbled oil between her breasts. Then she knelt between his open thighs and planted a row of kisses across the swell of his belly, swooping lower and lower until he shut his eyes and began to move against her. He felt her breasts on either side of him, cupping him, and after a while, longer than usual, he gave in and let it happen.

'Good boy.' He opened his eyes. Her face was inches from his. 'Better now?'

She fetched a tray of coffee and croissants from the kitchen. This could be Paris, Winter thought, except better. They were sitting side by side under the duvet, like an old couple on a bench enjoying the view. Winter wondered whether he should feed the seagulls.

'You need to know about that bonfire you had,' he said instead. 'Baz gave you a hand. We're talking about the week before last. Lots of smoke. Baz got changed afterwards and left his gear here. You stuffed it in a bag and gave it to me on Saturday. You got all that?'

'No problem, Mr Lumberjack.' Misty's fingers were at work again under the duvet. 'You want to do it again? Properly this time?'

* * *

It was nearly half past seven before the Outside Enquiries D/S stepped into Faraday's office. Expecting Parsons to turn up any minute, Faraday fetched a spare chair from the incident room. The D/S, a veteran, had been a probationer on the Isle of Wight and knew it well.

Faraday was looking at the check list on his clipboard. It wasn't very long.

'So what have we got?'

The D/S gave him the headlines. Enquiries along Mrs Percival's street had drawn a blank on movements in and out of her house in the small hours of Sunday morning. No one had been awake after midnight and no one could remember any disturbance. Further along the Newport Road, the same house-to-house team had visited every property within sight of Upcourt Farm. Oobik and Sadler were familiar figures to various neighbours. Oobik was a permanent fixture on the farm and

Sadler arrived often, always in the red convertible, mainly at weekends. As far as last week was concerned, no one reported anything out of the ordinary. The weather had been dreadful, too wet and windy to venture out, and most afternoons it had been dark by five.

'Little red Corsa? First thing Sunday morning?'

'No chance, boss. One thing though.'

'What's that?'

'There's an elderly woman who lives on the farm. Her name's . . .' his eyes went down to the clipboard '. . . Eva Gonzalez.'

'And?'

'It seems she's got a dog, big old thing. She takes it out for walkies every morning, goes up the field where the sheep are, has to keep it on a lead. Our guys pinned her down to last week. She says from Monday through to Wednesday there was a biggish boat trailer out on the grass in front of one of the outhouses by the caravan. She'd never seen it there before, which is why she remembered.'

'And the outhouse itself?'

'The door was closed. She couldn't see inside.'

'And Thursday?'

'The trailer was back inside. With the door half open.'

Faraday was drawing the timeline. The burned-out remains of the Corsa had been reported pre-dawn on Thursday morning. Perfect.

He looked up, nodded at the clipboard.

'What else have you got?'

'All negatives, I'm afraid, boss. We've knocked on doors in that apartment block of Sadler's. Half of them are empty—second homes or holiday lets. A couple on the floor below pass the time of day with her. Think she's fine, no problem. We've also been looking for that inflatable of hers. We're assuming it's registered in her name. Since start of play we've done just over half of the Cowes marinas. So far, nothing.'

Faraday scribbled himself a note. This would need to be an early question for Sadler in interview. He looked up again.

'Done?'

'Yep.'

'Good.' He sorted through his paperwork until he found the intel summary on Martin Skelley. He slid it across to the D/S.

'There's a delivery firm called Freezee. It's all in the report. We need to know if and when they had any vans over here last week. If so, we need full details: driver, drop-offs, ferry bookings, the lot. OK?'

'Priority?'

'Urgent.'

'I'll get it actioned, boss.' He looked at his watch. 'Right away.'

Faraday reached for the phone. Both of the D/Cs in the intel cell were already at their desks.

'Is D/S Suttle with you?'

'No, boss.'

'Who's going through those accounts we seized from Sadler?'

'Me, boss.'

'Got a moment?'

The D/C was young, scarcely three years in the Job. Prior to joining up she'd worked in a building society and knew her way around financial paperwork. Her name was Coleen. She needed to lose a lot of weight.

'How are you doing?'

'Fine. Assuming the data's OK, this woman kept excellent records. Very neat. Very thorough.'

'And what does it tell us?'

'She's got a good business here. The spreadsheets map it all out. Lots of growth over the past couple of years and pretty ambitious forecasts after that.'

'How many girls?'

'So far I've identified thirteen. The standard rate is £200 an hour. Twenty quid of that goes to the hotel for the room hire and Sadler seems to take 40 per cent off what's left. The girls get to keep the rest.'

'Is that standard? Generous? Mean?'

'I'm sorry, sir.' A hint of colour in her cheeks. 'I've no idea.'

Faraday was doing the maths: £110 an hour felt like a decent rate.

'We're in the wrong job, Coleen. Ever think that?'

'No, boss.'

'So how many tricks are these girls turning?'

'On average you're looking at a couple a day, sometimes more. So most of the girls would be on around £220-plus a day. Some choose to take a couple of days a week off.'

'I'm not surprised.' He was looking at the buff folder on her lap. 'What about Luik?'

'That's the problem, boss. She doesn't appear to exist.'

'There's no mention of her at all?'

'None.'

'Why do you think that is?'

'I've no idea. Maybe Sadler sanitised the files before we got to them.'

'Would that be easy?'

'The way the software's set up, yes, it would. But why bother when we know she exists?'

'Quite.' She hesitated, a tiny frown of concentration on her face.

'Go on.'

'There's another name I recognise.'

'Which is?'

'Oobik.'

'Really?' Faraday blinked. 'And he's on the payroll?'

'Yeah. Exactly the same pattern as the girls. Couple of clients a day. Good steady earner.'

'You think he's turning tricks too?'

'Must be. Why not? Women pay for sex, especially older women. And he might tom for men too.'

It was true. In theory there was absolutely nothing to stop Two's Company marketing male escorts alongside the girls. Suttle had described Oobik as a fit young guy with a bit of an attitude problem, but that was probably a turn-on to a certain kind of client. On the other hand, why would Lou Sadler be selling the sexual services of the bloke she was kipping with? Unless this too carried a certain kind of frisson?

'Have you checked the website? Two's Company?'

'Yeah.'

'And?'

'He's not featured. No mugshot, no details, no come-on—nothing.'

The photo of Kaija Luik lay under the pile of paperwork. Faraday fetched it out and gazed at it for a long moment. There was still something snagging in the deep recesses of his brain, something about the name Oobik, but for the life of him he couldn't tease it to the surface.

Coleen wanted to know whether they were through. D/S Suttle had just arrived back from the mainland, and she had a mountain of stuff to sort out.

'Fine, Coleen.' Faraday nodded at the file. 'Thanks for that. Tell Jimmy he's on parade at nine with the interview teams, yeah?'

Chapter Twenty-Eight

TUESDAY, 17 FEBRUARY 2009. *08.39*

Misty was proposing a day's shopping in Guildford. Winter wasn't keen.

'What would I buy, Mist? I hate all that stuff. For one thing it costs an arm and a leg. For another I don't need it.'

'That's because you live in Gunwharf. You're spoiled, Paul. Factory outlets, silly prices. Guildford's a cut above. You can escort me. You can carry my bags, buy me lunch, make me laugh.'

She was already playing with her car keys. Winter, with absolutely nothing to do, knew he was doomed. He'd tried to make contact with Lou Sadler but without any success. Odds on she'd been arrested, along with anyone else Parsons and Faraday deemed relevant to the inquiry. All he could do now was wait.

They rode north, Winter folded into Misty's Mercedes coupé. Guildford was an hour away. After a while Misty asked him about Bazza. He'd known the question was coming but was still uncertain how to play it.

'What about him, Mist?'

'Have you kissed and made up?'

'Don't be daft.'

'I mean it.'

'Why? Why is it so important?'

'Because it is. Because you're important, and Baz too in his funny little way.'

'All friends? All mates together?'

'Yeah. Exactly. Is that so terrible?'

Winter didn't answer. For one thing he was uncertain how much of these conversations found their way back to Mackenzie. For another, he was genuinely perplexed by where events were taking him. Suttle, he thought, had put it rather well last night. You can't rely on luck for ever, he'd said. And Winter, with some regret, was beginning to suspect he was right.

'I've been trying to calm him down, Mist,' he said at last.

'Impossible. The man doesn't do calm. Never did. Never will.'

'Exactly, so where does that leave me?'

'Sure . . . and me, and Marie, and Ezzie, and Stu, and all the rest of them. We're a family, Paul. Hasn't anyone ever told you that?'

Winter shook his head, retuned the radio. Another mile sped by. At last he saw no point in not voicing what was on his mind.

'Does the name Colin Leyman mean anything to you, Mist?'

'No. Never heard of him.'

'He'd like to think he's a face from the old days, the 6.57 days. If you want the truth, they took the piss out of him most of the time, but I don't think he ever understood that. He's a sweet guy, a simple guy, takes stuff on trust. He's putty, Mist, you can bend him any way you want.'

'And?'

'I bent him. Big time.'

'Surprise me.'

'Sure, but it didn't stop there. Bazza got the hump. Had him taken out.' Winter described the injuries, the careful application of extreme violence.

'Horrible,' she agreed. 'Vile. Completely over the top.'

'Exactly. And my fault.'

'Why?'

'Because I should have seen it coming. Not to me. To him.'

'And you didn't?'

'No, Mist. That either makes me slow or stupid or as psycho as Mackenzie. As it happens, I'm none of those things.'

'So what are you?'

'I'm wrong.'

'*Wrong?*'

'Yeah.' Winter nodded, glad to have settled on the truth. 'It's a moral thing, Mist. I just shouldn't be doing this kind of stuff.'

She said nothing. Ahead were a couple of big artics. She passed them both, settled down to seventy again. Then she spared him a glance.

'You never told me that,' she murmured. 'Right?'

*   *   *

Faraday convened the pre-interview meet for nine o'clock at Newport police station. The D/I in charge of the island's CID had found them a room downstairs big enough to accommodate the key players. Ian Whatmore, the Tactical Interview Adviser, had been talking to the two interview teams for the past hour. Ellis and Yates had yet to start with Lou Sadler but last night's session with Max Oobik had been deeply disappointing. As expected, he'd gone pretty much No Comment on everything. Apart from acknowledging that he lived in the caravan at Upcourt Farm and had a relationship with Sadler, even Patsy Lowe had failed to break his silence.

'He's got a lot of anger, boss.' It was the big Scot, Angus McEwan. 'You can see it in his face. There's heaps he's not telling us, but it doesn't stop there. Could he have done them both? Holman and Luik? Physically, the answer has to be yes. He's a powerful guy. But *would* he have done them? I'm not persuaded. Even for a squillion quid's worth of toot it's a big ask.'

Patsy Lowe agreed.

'He's a child, boss. A boy. He thinks we're all ganging up on him, and he's dead right, but so is Angus. There's a button we need to press, but I'm buggered if I know where to find it.'

Faraday said he understood. He'd spent the last hour or so reviewing *Gosling*'s progress and he wanted to offer a sequence of events that might underpin the conduct of both sets of interviews. Oobik's, in particular, had now moved into the challenge phase, and he wanted to be clear what was available to throw at the man.

'First off,' he said, 'we think from seized business records that he's being paid as a tom. That's what the documentation's telling us. Two tricks a day, presumably with the ladies, though maybe not. A grand and a half a week. Decent money. Next, I think Patsy's right. I think we need a timeline to throw at him. A lot of this will be supposition, but that doesn't matter. We've got to shake his tree, big time, so here goes . . .'

On the Saturday night, said Faraday, Johnny Holman flees the fire at Monkswell Farm. He's nicked Robbie Difford's Corsa to muddy the waters, and he's carrying a hefty stash of cocaine in the back. Difford's phone is in the Corsa, and the last call on Difford's mobile billing is to Kaija Luik, the Estonian girl. Why? Because Holman's nuts about her. And because he has nowhere else to go.

'OK so far?'

Suttle had just joined them. He too was nodding.

'So Luik gets the call from Holman. He's driving. He's probably pissed. Plus he's in a right state because he's just shot four people to death and burned his own house down. When he arrives at Luik's flat, at God knows what hour in the morning, he's all over the place. So what does the girl do? She phones Lou Sadler. And what does Sadler do? She wakes Max. They both turn up at Luik's place. They see the state Holman's in. This is a guy who must be reeking of smoke. He may have blood all over him. We don't know. But outside in Difford's car is a whack of toot. It may be that Sadler already knows about it. It may be that Max helped Holman dig the hole at Monkswell. All that makes sense. Why? Because Holman's already known to Sadler. And because we can probably tie the shit from her horses to the stuff at Monkswell Farm. So, gentlemen. . .' Faraday glanced round '. . . we probably agree that Sadler has the lead here. She's the boss. So what does she do next?'

'She gets Holman out of there.'

'Right. And where do they take him?'

'The caravan. Along with the Corsa.'

'Right again. That takes care of the toot. Makes perfect sense. And then what?'

'Max kills him.' This from Suttle. 'Probably strangles him. He's a huge guy. Holman's a runt. Plus he's given up. The caravan was never a bloodfest. A ligature or a manual strangling would account for it.'

'Fine.' Faraday nodded. 'And the body?'

'He wrapped it up in bin liners. You just leave them on the roll. The guy ends up like a mummy, rolled and taped.'

'Exactly.' Faraday named a serial killer caught and convicted by Major Crime back in the 1990s. He'd pulled exactly the same trick before dumping the corpses in the country. 'So now you have a body. It's Sunday. It's probably in the caravan. How do you get rid of it?'

Bev Yates raised a hand. The RIB inflatable, he said. It belongs to Sadler. She can ship the body out to wherever and chuck it overboard.

Faraday smiled. This was working beautifully.

'But you'd need some kind of weight,' he said. 'Which is where this comes in.'

He'd had Meg Stanley's shots photocopied. Now they passed from hand to hand. More nods. More smiles.

Faraday, conscious of time passing, pressed on. At some point after the Sunday, Holman's body is disposed of. Early on Thursday morning the Corsa is found burned out in the woods. By now the crime scene in the caravan has been cleaned up and the boat trailer is back in the outhouse beside the caravan.

Minutes before this meeting Faraday had tasked the Outside Enquiries D/S to start a house-to-house sweep of properties adjoining Newtown Creek. On the assumption that Sadler and Oobik wouldn't take the risk of dragging the body through a marina, the nearby creek, with its relative remoteness, would have been near-perfect.

Patsy Lowe had a question. She wanted to know about Kaija Luik. Had she been murdered too? Had there been a couple of carefully wrapped corpses in Oobik's caravan?

Faraday said he didn't know. The girl definitely represented a risk as far as Sadler and Oobik were concerned. She probably knew about the cocaine because Holman would have told her, and she probably knew that something terrible had happened back at the farm.

'But is that enough, boss?' Ellis wasn't convinced.

Again, Faraday hedged his bets. *Gosling* had made extensive booking checks on routes to Estonia without any success. The Estonian police appeared to be in the dark about her. Nor had the Borders Agency logged her out of the country.

'But she could be anywhere,' insisted Lowe.

'You're right. You're absolutely right. But as far as Oobik's concerned, it may be to our advantage to suggest he killed her too. Let's just try it and see what happens.'

Lowe nodded, still unconvinced, and Ian Whatmore, the TIA, took over. On the basis of Faraday's exposition, Lowe and McEwan would move through the timeline, pressing him on point after point. Interviews like these, regardless of the steady drumbeat of 'No comment,' often proved far more volatile than you'd ever expect. With luck Oobik might crack. At which point *Gosling* would take a giant step forward.

McEwan stirred. 'And if he doesn't, boss?'

'We're off the clock at three. If necessary, I'll go for an extension, but there's no guarantee we'll get one.'

McEwan nodded. These days uniformed Superintendents were extremely wary about granting PACE extensions that simply turned into fishing expeditions. A properly organised inquiry moved steadily forward. Hence the need for meticulous preparation.

There remained the opening interview with Lou Sadler. Last night she'd asked to be represented by a south London lawyer she used regularly. Faraday, conscious of the precious time he might lose, had insisted she phone him at once and get him down early the following day. This she'd done, telling Faraday that Benny Stanton would be on the 8.15 RedJet catamaran from Southampton. The crossing took twenty-three minutes. So far, at nearly half past nine, there was no sign of the man. Sadler herself, according to the turnkey, had spent a peaceful night in her cell and had tucked into beans on toast for breakfast. Not a good sign.

Yates wanted to know whether Oobik and Sadler were each aware of the presence of the other in the custody unit. Faraday nodded. He'd made sure to have Sadler escorted slowly past Oobik's cell. There was no way they wouldn't know that one story would be carefully matched against the other.

'That's why he's gone No Comment,' Suttle said.

Faraday nodded. Dead right. He turned to Yates

and Ellis. It would be their job to let Sadler run, mindful all the time of the evidence that *Gosling* had managed to establish. When it came to the challenge phase, they'd do their best to stress-test her account to breaking point, but this first interview would be largely devoted to establishing her own version of exactly what had happened.

'You OK with this?' Faraday nodded at the notes he'd made.

'No problem, boss.' Ellis shot him a smile. 'And thanks for the invite.'

*   *   *

The interviews were due to start at ten. Suttle accompanied Faraday back to the SIO's office. Parsons had at last turned up, accompanied, to Faraday's surprise, by Detective Chief Superintendent Geoff Willard. Willard had been Head of CID for some time now, a lengthening pit stop on his passage to ACPO rank. A big man with an air of slightly forbidding command, he'd won the respect of detectives force-wide. Parsons adored him.

Faraday gave Parsons a swift heads-up on the morning's developments. Much would now depend on the coming interviews. Parsons began to fret about the PACE clock. Willard interrupted.

'How are you, Joe?'

'I'm fine, sir, thank you.'

'Head OK?' Willard tapped his own skull. 'I heard about the accident.'

'Ah . . .' Faraday smiled.

There was a brief silence. Then Willard turned to Suttle.

'DCI Parsons tells me you interviewed Winter last night.'

'I talked to him, sir.' Suttle nodded. 'Yes.'

'And?'

'He admitted removing a bin liner from Mrs Percival's property. There was some of the girl's stuff inside.'

'And why did he do that?'

'He claimed he was helping out, sir. He meant to hand it over to Sadler in case the girl ever came back. He had the girl's mobile as well.'

'He's aware this constitutes interference in a crime scene?'

'He says he wasn't.'

'I bet he does. Where are these items?'

'I seized them. The clothes are downstairs. The phone's gone to the CIU for billing.' He paused, looking from one face to the other. 'There's something else . . .'

'Regarding?'

'Winter.'

'And?'

'I think he's had enough.'

'Of what?'

'Mackenzie, sir. And everything that goes with him.'

Chapter Twenty-Nine

TUESDAY, 17 FEBRUARY 2009. *09.57*

The second interview with Max Oobik began a couple of minutes after ten o'clock. By now Benny

Stanton had phoned to alert his client that he'd been held up on the journey down from London and wouldn't get to Newport until 10.15 at the earliest. This delay, Faraday knew, was tactical, taking a hefty bite out of the interview time available on the PACE clock. Under the rules of engagement he could lodge a protest on grounds of unreasonable delay, but he realised that this piece of gamesmanship on Stanton's part could play to *Gosling*'s advantage. They needed to squeeze everything from Oobik before tackling Lou Sadler.

In the absence of video from the interview suite, Faraday was obliged to rely on an audio feed. He settled in the downstream monitoring room with Jimmy Suttle while Patsy Lowe date-and-time-tagged the interview for the benefit of the recording machine. Faraday and Suttle had glimpsed Oobik minutes earlier in the corridor that led from the cells. He'd chosen not to shave, and lack of sleep had darkened the bags beneath his eyes. He had walked slowly, pausing from time to time, making the turnkey wait for him. When one of the custodyP/Cs asked whether he'd like to take a coffee from the machine into the interview room he barely acknowledged the question, and the moment he set eyes on Suttle there was something in his face that spoke of a deep anger.

Patsy Lowe had finished. Angus McEwan got the interview under way. Earlier they'd decided to try and wrong-foot Oobik from the start. Faraday had calculated Oobik's average earnings at more than £1,300 a week. McEwan, sweetly reasonable, suggested that this was good corn.

'Corn?' Oobik obviously didn't understand.

'Money. Good money.'

'What money?'

'Nearly one and a half thousand pounds a week, Mr Oobik—I just told you. Was that only with the ladies? Or were you on offer to anyone who fancied it?'

'You think I sleep with people? For money?'

'Yes, Mr Oobik. In fact we know you do. My question is what kind of people? Women? Men? Both?'

There was a silence. So far, in less than thirty seconds, McEwan had dug more out of Oobik than at any point during last night's interview. The man sounded outraged. Maybe the interview strategy was working.

'There's no confusion here, Mr Oobik. All you have to say is yes or no. Men? Yes?'

'You're crazy.'

'Not men?'

'I'm getting out of here.' There was the scrape of a chair.

'Sit down, Mr Oobik.' A brief pause. 'Thank you.' The question again. Do you sleep with men?

'No comment.' Oobik had obviously got himself under control again, though his voice had audibly thickened.

'Do you sleep with women?'

'No comment.'

'Do you sleep with anyone?'

'I sleep with Lou.'

'And is she the only person you sleep with?'

'No comment.'

'So you might sleep with women? And you might earn all this money?'

'No comment.'

The interview, once again, was bogging down.

Careering down a hill he hadn't expected, Oobik had hauled himself into the escape lane and brought everything to a halt. Patsy Lowe took over, trying to play to Oobik's softer side. Sleeping with women for money wasn't an offence, she pointed out. As police officers, in this and every other respect, they were simply trying to get at the truth. Given the disappearance of two individuals, Johnny Holman and Kaija Luik, might Oobik be able to offer them a little help?

'No comment.'

Mention of Kaija Luik was McEwan's cue to take over again. The allegation that he slept with men had clearly got to Oobik. Now was the moment to clarify the seriousness of his plight.

'We're investigating what we believe to be murder, Mr Oobik. Not just one murder but two. In the first place we believe that Holman drove to Luik's flat very early on that Sunday morning. We know that Luik had a relationship with Holman. We believe that Holman was very distressed. Who would Luik phone? She'd phone Lou Sadler. And what would Lou Sadler do? She'd talk to the person beside her in bed. That was you, Mr Oobik, am I right?'

'No comment.'

'You weren't in bed with Lou Sadler?'

'No comment.'

'But yesterday you told D/S Suttle that you were.'

'No comment.'

'OK. Let's assume you weren't lying to D/S Suttle. Let's say you were telling the truth. Lou Sadler has Kaija Luik on the phone. Kaija's very upset. Why? Because Holman is there with her and it's very early in the morning and he stinks of woodsmoke and he's probably drunk. Are you with me here?'

'No comment.'

'OK.' McEwan had endless patience. 'There's something else too. Holman tells Luik he's got lots of drugs in the car outside, lots of cocaine. It's worth a great deal of money, millions and millions of pounds. He wants to drive away with Luik. He wants to drive to a better place where everything's going to be fine again, where he and Kaija can live happily ever after, and nothing will ever go wrong again. It sounds wonderful, doesn't it, Mr Oobik? Except Kaija didn't believe a word of it.'

There was a silence. Faraday could imagine the scene in the interview room, Oobik immobile in his chair, his face expressionless, his big hands lying in his lap. He didn't even have to bother with another 'No comment.' All he had to do was pretend he was deaf.

'So, Mr Oobik, you're both there, you and Lou Sadler, and as it happens, you know about the cocaine already. Why? Because you've been over at Holman's place, the farm, Monkswell Farm, earlier in the week. Isn't that true? You don't believe me? You don't remember being over there? Helping Johnny dig that great big hole in his back garden? No?'

'No comment.'

'Ah . . . no comment. You're still with us then. Good. And you know why? Because now it gets very interesting. It's Sunday. It's four o'clock in the morning. Sadler tells you to get up. You take her car. You both drive over to that flat of Kaija's. And you know what? She's right. Holman's there. And he's in exactly the state that made Kaija make the call in the first place. He stinks of woodsmoke.

And outside in a little red car is the cocaine. How do you know it's cocaine? Because Johnny told you so himself. When you dug it up for him. When you asked. Isn't that true, Mr Oobik? Isn't that the way it happened? No? Then tell me what *did* happen?'

Again there was no response from Oobik. McEwan, undeterred, pushed the story forward. How Lou Sadler knew that they had to get Johnny and the cocaine away from the flat. How she'd told Oobik to put Johnny in the little red car and drive him to Upcourt Farm. Hide the car, Max, she must have said. Put it in the outhouse. And hide Johnny too. In fact, worse. Get rid of him.

'And so you did, Mr Oobik. That's exactly what you did. You put Johnny in the car and you drove him back to your caravan, and you wheeled the trailer out of the outhouse, and you hid the car. But once you'd done that, you still had a problem. And you know the name of that problem? Johnny Holman. Am I right, Mr Oobik? He's there in your caravan. He's probably drunk. He's probably in a terrible state. And so now you must do your mistress's bidding. Am I getting close, Mr Oobik? Or are you telling me you don't remember?'

This, Faraday knew, was the moment *Gosling* might falter. So far everything linked perfectly together, but was it really credible that Max Oobik would kill another human being simply because his mistress wanted to tidy things up?

Oobik had grunted something incomprehensible. Faraday bent to the speaker, trying to smuggle himself into the room. Was he on the point of confession? Had McEwan, in his quiet Scots way, piled up the pressure of events until Oobik could no longer hide behind silence? Was this the moment

Gosling crested the hill and began to motor towards its day in court?

'No comment.'

'I don't believe you, Mr Oobik. I don't believe you don't remember. I believe you remember only too well. I believe you remember killing Johnny Holman. I believe you made a quick, simple job of it. I believe he didn't struggle, didn't bleed everywhere, didn't make it hard for you. I believe Johnny Holman was dead before it got light, before you drove back to Cowes, and I believe something else. I believe you killed the girl too. I believe you killed Kaija Luik.'

'No.'

Faraday blinked. A response. Sharp. Emphatic. And deeply, deeply angry. Not just anger. Outrage.

'No?' McEwan's innocent response hung in the air. Tell me more. Tell me what's so suddenly got into you. Show me which nerve I just touched.

Oobik appeared to have opted for silence again. McEwan wasn't letting go.

'You didn't kill Kaija Luik?'

'No.'

'Why not?'

'No comment.'

'Tell me, Mr Oobik. Tell me why it was so important *not* to kill Kaija? After everything you'd just done to wee Johnny?'

'No comment.'

'But it *was* important, wasn't it? Not to harm the girl? Not to kill her? That's what you just told me. That's what you said. You said no. You said you didn't kill the girl. That means you *wouldn't* kill the girl. The question is why. Why did you say that? Why should I believe it? Why is it true?'

Faraday sat back, shaking his head. He'd suddenly realised what it was he'd been missing about Oobik. Suttle was still sitting beside him, a tiny frown of concentration on his face, trying to slot this tiny lowering of Oobik's guard into everything else they knew and didn't know about the events of last week.

'The name, Jimmy.'

'Whose name, boss?'

'The girl's. Kaija's. The other day you told me Luik means swan.'

'That's what Sadler said, yes.'

'OK.' Faraday nodded, excited now. 'And you know what Oobik means? In Estonian?'

'Tell me.'

'Nightingale. It means nightingale. I've known it from way back. *Rossignol* in French. *Ruiseñor* in Spanish. *Usignolo* in Italian. And *Oobik* in Estonian.'

'So?' Suttle was lost.

'Luik is the girl's working name, her stage name if you like. She's not Luik at all. That's the name she chose. Another bird. Another beautiful bird. No longer a nightingale but a swan.'

'So she's really Kaija Oobik? Is that what you're telling me?'

'Exactly.' Faraday nodded at the speaker. 'Which makes her this guy's sister.'

* * *

Faraday called a halt to the interview several minutes later. While Oobik's solicitor fetched a coffee for his client, the interview team plus Faraday, Suttle and the TIA, Ian Whatmore, squeezed into the monitoring room. They couldn't be sure until they started on Lou Sadler, but in Faraday's view it was a reasonable assumption that Max Oobik and Kaija Luik were brother and sister.

'Where's her passport, boss?' This from McEwan.

Faraday glanced at Suttle.

'We never saw it,' Suttle said. 'And Sadler told us she hadn't either.'

'Credit cards? Any other ID?'

'The girl's disappeared. We never had a chance to look.'

McEwan nodded. This kind of oversight happened more often than you might expect, but it took Faraday to draw the straightest line between the obvious dots.

'This is why you rattled him over all the money he was supposed to be earning,' he said to McEwan. 'It wasn't his money at all, it was his sister's.'

'Right, boss. I get you.'

'And just now, when you hit him with the second murder, the girl's, that's why you shook him again. He wasn't having it. No way would he kill his own sister.'

'So why doesn't he just tell us that?'

'Because Sadler's told him to go No Comment. That's why she's so relaxed. As long as he does what he's told, they're going to have no problem getting their stories straight. She's obviously worked out what to tell us. All he has to do is tell us fuck all. That way it's seamless.'

There was a brief silence. On the speaker, they could hear Oobik's brief returning with the coffees.

'You've got to be right, boss.' It was Jimmy Suttle. 'This gives him the motive, doesn't it? Oobik doesn't like Holman at all. He's all over his sister, he's pissed most of the time, he's pretty disgusting in every way you can imagine, and lately he's not even paying her. Fuck, she might even have fallen in *love* with the old dosser. So suddenly, middle of the night, our Max has the chance to make everything right. And how does he do that? By taking the arsehole out. End of.'

There was a knock on the door. The uniformed inspector who ran the custody centre wanted Faraday to know that Sadler's brief had finally arrived, a full ninety minutes late. Before talking to his client he was demanding disclosure.

'Believe me, Joe,' he said, 'you're going to love this guy.'

*   *   *

Benny Stanton was waiting in a side office reserved for visiting solicitors. He was early thirties, squat, loud, aggressive, gelled hair, ear stud, chalk-stripe suit, chunky watch. In the sleepy calm of the island's only custody centre, he was deeply exotic.

'So what have you got?' He'd already helped himself to a coffee, didn't bother with formal introductions.

Faraday took the other seat across the table. He said that Lou Sadler had been arrested on suspicion of homicide. She had lied with respect to Kaija Luik's real address, had been slow in producing important evidence and had a relationship with the other person suspected of murder. In the shape of a suspected consignment of cocaine, she had a motive for the killings, and in the shape of a rigid inflatable boat, she had the means of disposing of the body or bodies involved.

Stanton was barely listening. When Faraday had finished, he smothered a yawn.

'And that's it? Fuck me, I should have stayed at home.'

'Early start, was it?' Faraday said heavily. 'Bit of a struggle getting down here?'

'Yeah.' He shot Faraday a grin. 'Where is she then? The old slapper?'

* * *

The interview with Max Oobik terminated at 12.19. Every challenge from both McEwan and Patsy Lowe had been met with a stony 'No comment.' He wasn't interested in their belief that Kaija Luik was his sister. Nor that he'd killed Johnny Holman to rid her of his attentions. Nor that he'd wrapped Holman's body in dustbin liners, disposed of it at sea and returned to clean up the caravan. At the end of the interview, advised that a full account of what had really happened might work to his benefit in court, he'd simply shrugged.

'No comment,' he'd muttered, getting to his feet.

Faraday had borrowed an office up on the first floor. The interview team gathered for a debrief, joined by Ellis and Yates, who were preparing for their first session with Lou Sadler. By now she'd been closeted with Benny Stanton for the best part of two hours.

Faraday knew that he had to go for a custody extension on both suspects, an extra twelve hours that might enable him to feed in new material unearthed by the Outside Enquiries teams. In Oobik's case this would give him the late afternoon and the evening for as many as two extra sessions.

Sadler, on the other hand, was more problematic. Her thirty-six hours would run out at eight o'clock in the morning. Interviews rarely stretched beyond eleven o'clock at night, at which point Sadler would be permitted eight hours' sleep. Effectively, Faraday would be left with a tight last-chance three-hour window if the first two interviews hit a brick wall.

He went round the room, wondering what two sessions with Oobik had won them.

McEwan was the most optimistic. He'd been within touching distance of Oobik. He'd been watching the man very carefully. He'd seen what everyone else had seen: that Oobik was proud, angry and full of attitude. But he'd also sensed something else: that loyalty to Kaija probably came before loyalty to anyone else, even Lou Sadler, and that this hairline crack in his defences might be worth further exploration.

Faraday wanted to know whether McEwan accepted the suggestion that Luik was probably Oobik's sister.

'Absolutely, boss. It makes perfect sense.'

'Good. Everyone else happy with that?'

Heads nodded around the room. Pressing Sadler on this small detail would be a priority, but in the meantime Luik's photo and assumed new surname had gone to the Estonian police tagged urgent. Maybe, fingers crossed, she was already on file. Maybe not.

Faraday moved on to Outside Enquiries. Early reports from the house-to-house team combing the handful of properties around Newtown Creek had been disappointing. No one remembered any night-time activity on or off the water over the past week, nor had the Harbour Master logged anything out of the ordinary. This of course didn't rule out the transfer of a body from some other location but it certainly began to narrow the options.

Bev Yates had a question about this first interview with Sadler. Did Faraday and Whatmore want Sadler hit from the off?

'With what, Bev?'

'With the girl's real name? And whether or not she really owns a RIB?'

'Absolutely. We've got to nail this stuff down. Otherwise the Outside Enquiries guys are running round in circles.'

The interview with Sadler started at 12.41. Faraday was back in the monitoring room, with Suttle once again beside him. A text from Gabrielle on Faraday's mobile had gone unanswered.

Benny Stanton took his MO into the interview room. He wanted ice cubes in the glass of water for his client plus an understanding that any hint of oppressive questioning would jeopardise his client's absolute preparedness to cooperate to the fullest. Ms Sadler, he said, would have happily attended any police station of their choice for an extended interview. The fact that they'd insisted on arresting her was, in his view, both aggressive and unnecessary.

Faraday's heart fell. He'd met this kind of tactic before. It often came with out-of-area briefs, especially from London. They stamped hard on the nearest throat and did their best to intimidate the opposition from the off. Neither Bev Yates nor Dawn Ellis was easily cowed, but Faraday knew that Stanton had already laid down an important marker. The next couple of hours, as he remarked to Suttle, were going to be far from easy.

Bev Yates took the lead. He wanted to know whether Kaija Luik was the girl's real name.

'No.' Sadler's voice was low. Yates asked her to speak up. 'I said no.'

'So what was her real name?'

Stanton objected at once. He said that Yates' choice of tense was a gross supposition. This girl was alive and kicking unless anyone had the evidence to prove otherwise.

'So what *is* her real name?' Yates sounded weary already.

'Oobik.' Sadler was laughing.

'And her first name?'

'Maarika.'

'And does she have a family relationship to Max Oobik?'

'Yes. She's his sister.'

'So why didn't you tell us that to begin with?'

'No one asked me.'

'That's not true, Ms Sadler. Detective Sergeant Suttle asked you on . . .' there was a shuffle of paper '. . . Wednesday of last week.'

'Did he? I must have been distracted at the time.'

'How come?'

'Your Detective Sergeant arrived at an awkward moment. I was otherwise engaged.'

'She means she was shagging.' It was Stanton. 'She's a bit shy that way, our Lou.'

'So why did you let D/S Suttle in?'

'I thought he was someone else.'

'Would that have made a difference?'

'Yes.'

'Need I ask why?'

'Ask whatever you like.'

'Then why?'

'Because I was expecting an important parcel.'

'I see.'

Faraday shut his eyes. Yates had lost his thread. This was turning into a nightmare.

'But why didn't you clarify the girl's name later?'

'I've been too busy. No one asked.'

'And the address you gave for her? The address in Darcy Road?'

'That was different.'

'In what way?'

'Some of my girls are sensitive. They get easily upset. Maarika was one of those girls. In that situation you don't want them put under any kind of pressure.'

'So you lied about her address? When you knew she was living somewhere else? Is that what you're saying?'

'Exactly. And I'd probably do it again under similar circumstances. In fact I'm sure I would. I'm like a mother to some of them. Certainly to Maarika.'

'But she's got a brother, hasn't she? Or that's what you've just told us.'

'Max is a man. I'm not. That can be important to a woman.'

'Fine, Ms Sadler. I understand that. So tell me something else. Where does she live in Estonia?'

'I haven't the faintest.'

'You don't know where her home is? When you're telling me you're like a mother to her? You expect me to believe that?'

'I do. Because it's true. And if you can spare the time, I'll tell you why.'

Faraday nodded. This was getting better. Yates had revived, dragged himself off the ropes, started delivering the odd counterpunch. Sadler was a fluent liar, without either shame or fear, and had doubtless spent the last couple of hours rehearsing this little exchange. She'd yet to drop a single stitch, but these were still early days.

Ellis had taken over. She wanted to know about Sadler's interest in water sports. Did she by any chance own a RIB?

'Yes.'

'Where is it?'

Sadler named a marina in Cowes and a berth number on one of the inner pontoons where the inflatable was moored. She said it was a Ballistic 6.5 with an Evinrude Etec 250 outboard.

Suttle was writing down the details. When he'd finished, he phoned the Outside Enquiries D/S and passed on the information. He wanted a couple of guys out there sharpish. Above all he wanted to know about CCTV.

Yates saved him the trouble.

'Does it have CCTV? This marina?'

'Of course. That's one of the reasons I chose it. For the money those people charge, you expect decent security. Eighteen grand's worth of outboard? There are bad people everywhere, my love. Even here.'

'And a GPS system? You've got one of those on the RIB?'

'Yep. Max gave it to me for Christmas. It's a Lowrance, state of the art. Beautiful little thing.'

Suttle made another note. The latest GPS kit, as long as it was switched on, kept a record of the last outing. If Sadler had taken the RIB anywhere over the previous week or so, then the details might be easily accessed.

Faraday was looking sombre. From this kind of information, freely volunteered, you could only draw one inference: the RIB hadn't left the marina for at least ten days.

Ellis appeared to have reached the same conclusion. Her questions about the boat had come to an end. Now she invited Sadler to account for her movements since Saturday night. She was to take her time, share everything.

'Of course.' There was amusement in her voice again. 'My pleasure.'

On Saturday night, she said, she'd been over in Southampton helping out a friend at a fund-raiser. She'd taken the last RedJet back to Cowes and been home by quarter past midnight.

'Was anyone else at your flat that night?'

'Max was there. He has a key.'

Max, she said, was already in bed. She'd joined him. Next thing she knew it was four in the morning and she had Maarika on the phone.

'The girl was out of her head.'

'What do you mean?'

'She sounded terrified.'

'Why?'

'She said she'd had a lot of hassle from a man.'

'A punter?'

'Must have been. She wouldn't say.'

'What happened? What had he done?'

'He'd come round and thumped her. Beaten her up. It happens sometimes. Not often, not with my class of girls, but it happens.'

'So what did you do?'

'I asked his name, obviously.'

'And?'

'She wouldn't tell me. All she'd say was she wanted out.'

'You couldn't check her bookings? Whatever records you keep?'

'Not at four in the morning. And in any case, he might not be in the system.'

'So what did you do?'

'We went round there.'

'We?'

'Me and Max. This guy might have come back. He might be waiting outside. We'd no idea.'

'And what did you find when you got there?'

'Just Maarika. She was in a terrible state—shaking, trembling, crying her eyes out. He'd done a good job on her, whoever this animal was. She just wanted out, and I must say I didn't blame her.'

'And Max?'

'Max tried talking her down. He sat beside her, put his arm round her. He wanted a name, obviously. No kidding, he'd have killed the guy.'

'And did he get a name?'

'No. She was just sat on the edge of the bed there, head in her hands. Get me out, she kept saying. Just please get me out. I want to go home. I want to get out.'

Faraday glanced at Suttle. This was bullshit. Stanton must be pissing himself.

Yates took over. He wanted to talk about Johnny Holman.

'You know this guy?'

'Yes. Not well but . . . yes.' She frowned. 'What's Holman got to do with any of this?'

'Just answer the question, please.' He paused. 'How did you get to know him in the first place?'

'He got in touch a while back. He was a client. He wanted to buy company.'

'And?'

'I recommended Maarika. Or Kaija as she called herself.'

'Why?'

'Because she was new at that time—she'd just joined us. And because Johnny fancied the look of her on the website.'

He bought a couple of sessions, she said, and tried her out. He liked what he'd paid for and became a regular client. Johnny was happy, Maarika was £110 a session better off, Sadler was making a decent commission. Result all round.

'Then what?'

'Then it got messy.'

'What does messy mean?'

'I think Johnny started laying stuff on her, personal stuff, stuff about his marriage, about his life in general. This is more common than you might think, and Maarika never told me everything, but I think they must have started seeing each other, you know, socially.'

'So what was in it for her? For Maarika?'

'Good question. To be honest, I don't know. Some of these girls can be really vulnerable, and I think that was the case with Maarika. She was round to my place a couple of times, floods of tears. Holman was a manipulator. He knew which strings to pull. God knows why, but she'd fallen in love with him just a little bit. Maybe not love, maybe more pity. D'you know what I mean? Either way, it was in her interests to get rid of the guy. Which is exactly what I told her to do. Forget him. Blank him. Don't answer his calls. Even if he offers to pay again, tell him to fuck off.'

'And she didn't?'

'Obviously not. Like I say, I don't know the details.'

'But he was another nightmare punter?'

'Yeah . . . in his own way . . . yeah, definitely.'

'But not the guy on Saturday night?'

'No, I don't think so.'

'You don't *think* so? *Might* he have been the guy on Saturday night? The guy that beat her up?'

'I doubt it. Holman's an arsehole but he doesn't get heavy.'

'And what about her brother? Max? What did he think?'

'About what?'

'About Johnny?'

For the first time Faraday sensed a whisper of caution in Sadler's voice, the tiniest bump in the road, a couple of cobblestones, no more.

'Max didn't like Holman, didn't like the stuff he was laying on his kid sister. You can understand that, can't you?'

'You're telling me Holman abused her?'

'Not physically, no, not as far as I know. But psychologically, that's exactly what he was doing. And that kind of abuse, believe me, can be evil. Maybe that's what Max saw happening.'

'So why didn't Max do something about it?'

'I've no idea. The boy's a puppy. He might try and look like Marlon Brando, but underneath he's like Maarika, really sensitive, really soft.'

Faraday threw a glance at Suttle. More bullshit.

Ellis got the interview back on track. She wanted to know what Sadler and Max did that night, once they'd calmed Maarika down.

'I made her get dressed. We threw a few things into a bag—toothbrush, change of clothes, all that. Then we took her home.'

'To where?'

'Back to Cowes, my place. Where else?'

'And the mystery visitor? The guy who'd done all the damage?'

'Max had a look around outside, just in case, but the guy had gone.'

'Did Maarika mention a car at all?'

'Nothing. She wouldn't talk about him. We didn't know what he looked like, how old he was, what colour he was, absolutely nothing. She'd just blanked him, rubbed him out of her life.'

'Really?'

'Really.'

Yates wanted to know what had happened on the Sunday. Sadler said that Maarika had kipped on the sofa. They'd all got up late. Maarika had friends in London and she wanted to get up there as soon as possible. From London, said Sadler, she'd make her way home.

'So who were these friends?'

'I've no idea. She wouldn't tell me.'

'And afterwards? Back in Estonia?'

'Pass. Sunday afternoon I gave her a grand in notes and put her on the ferry. She was a bit better by then.'

'And that was that?'

'Exactly. Until your nice detective came along with his auntie, asking all his questions.'

There was a long silence. Suttle, still sitting beside Faraday, chuckled at the reference to Patsy Lowe. Then someone cleared their throat, maybe Stanton.

'That it then, boys and gals? Only we're busy

people . . .'
Yates told him to sit down. In a moment or two they'd take a break, but in the meantime he had one last question. Surely Maarika had relatives in Estonia?
'Of course she does.'
'Do you have an address?'
'No.'
'Does Max?'
'I'm sure he does. Ask him.'
'We have.'
'And?'
'He won't say a word.'
'Ah . . .' Amused again. 'Shame, eh?'

Chapter Thirty

TUESDAY, 17 FEBRUARY 2009. *16.50*

Alone in his borrowed office at Newport police station, Faraday found time to contact Gabrielle. Hours ago, before the start of the first interview with Lou Sadler, she'd sent him a text: *Jeudi seize heures? Chez nous?*

The terseness of the message told him everything he needed to know. He was to report to the Bargemaster's House at four o'clock on Thursday afternoon, presumably for some kind of preliminary chat with the social worker about the prospect of adopting Leila. No sense that this might present some difficulty for a working detective up to his eyes in a multiple homicide. No awareness that he and Gabrielle had yet to explore the real implications of prising open their lives and making room for a damaged little girl from a culture more foreign than they could possibly imagine. Just a curt tap on the shoulder from someone whose life had shrunk to a tiny bundle of neediness.

Gabrielle answered on the second ring. Faraday could imagine her in the Burns Unit, probably at Leila's bedside, doubtless sharing her bedside duties with Riham in the daily tussle for the girl's attention.

'Chéri? C'est toi?'

Faraday asked her how things were going. She said they were fine. Leila had spent a couple of hours out of bed, tottering down the corridor to the kids' playroom, making body-language friends with an older girl from Portsmouth with terrible scald injuries. Life was on the move again, she said. Just like Leila.

She sounded sunny, optimistic, positive, and Faraday wondered whether it was really his job to cast a shadow over all that. The butterfly in Gabrielle's life, this exquisite little creature she'd cherished and protected for weeks now, was at last emerging from its chrysalis of pain and torment. Things, Gabrielle was saying, could only get better.

Faraday looked up to find Suttle at his door. The D/S held up a single finger and tapped his watch. The all-important second interview with Lou Sadler was about to start. Everyone was waiting for him.

Faraday ducked to the phone again.

'I'll be in touch,' he mumbled. *'À bientôt.'*

* * *

Winter had spent most of the day wondering when to phone Jimmy Suttle. A brisk lunch with Bazza at the hotel had finally convinced him that his boss had swapped reality for the land of dreams. *Newsnight* had at last aired its piece about electoral stirrings in the Pompey undergrowth, and this had sparked more interest from the London broadsheets. The tone of the TV report had been decidedly tongue-in-cheek, and even Bazza had acknowledged that they'd come close to taking the piss, but Leo Kinder had assured him that every particle of airtime was gold dust, and in the shape of multiple enquiries from *The Times* and the *Daily Telegraph* he was undoubtedly right. Both papers were after interviews, seeking to put the possibility of a Pompey referendum in a wider national context, and Kinder had said yes to both.

As far as Winter was concerned, Bazza had lost the plot, and over a sandwich lunch in his office he'd told him exactly that. Lou Sadler was probably under arrest. Faraday and Parsons had the time, money and manpower to take their investigation in any direction they fancied. A hefty whack of Bazza's precious toot was there for the finding, and once they'd laid hands on it, which they undoubtedly would, then it would only be a matter of hours before they came knocking on his door. In short, two decades of gleeful criminality were about to come to an end. Did Bazza understand that? Or had the prospect of one day becoming Mr Pompey left him *totally* brain-dead?

Bazza, typically, had barely listened. Things were on the up, he said. Winter was a wily old dog and had as much to lose as everyone else. There'd be a way out of this, because that's the way it had always been, and this was no time to lose your fucking nerve. At the end of the snack, Winter's sandwich barely touched, Bazza had told him to sort it. He'd got the police thing wrong. It wasn't a question of waiting for those bastards to come calling. He wanted Winter to find all that toot, turn it into money and have a big fat cheque ready for next week.

Next week? Winter hadn't a clue what he was talking about.

'Thursday, mush. Rikki's found the spic politico we need to pay off. I'm flying her over and, believe me, she won't expect to go home empty-handed.' Bazza was on his feet, preparing himself for yet another confab with Leo Kinder. '*Comprendes?*'

Back in his apartment, Winter eyed the phone. Jimmy Suttle, he told himself. Has to be.

* * *

Suttle joined Faraday for another session in the monitoring room. Lou Sadler had spent most of the last forty minutes with her brief. Faraday had glimpsed them a couple of times in the glass-walled office reserved for visiting solicitors and had been struck by the rapport between them. Under difficult circumstances, Benny Stanton had the knack of making her laugh, something she clearly appreciated.

Now she was back in the interview room waiting for Yates and Ellis to sort themselves out. After failing to breach Oobik's defences, Faraday knew that a great deal hung on the next couple of hours.

Ellis launched the first salvo of questions. She wanted to be clear about the boat trailer housed next door to the stables at Upcourt Farm. Where was it normally kept?

'In the empty shed next to the horses.'

'And why was that?'

'Security.' Faraday sensed a shrug. 'Protection from the weather.'

'So was it always in there?'

'Normally, yes.'

'So why was it out in the open last Monday? And last Tuesday? And the day after that?'

Faraday shot a look at Suttle. This information had come from Eva, the elderly woman from Upcourt Farm who walked her dog every morning. Suttle was convinced that the trailer had been wheeled out to make room for Robbie Difford's Corsa.

Lou Sadler offered a different interpretation. The same fluency, the same easy lies.

'This time of the year we pull the RIB out for a refurb,' she said. 'It's all weather-dependent, obviously, but I asked Max to have the thing out and ready in case I came up to tow it away and he wasn't there.'

'But it was out in the open three days running.'

'I know. The weather was shit.'

She was right. For most of last week it had never stopped raining. Faraday shook his head. Even the elements were on her side.

'So what happened on the Thursday?' Ellis hadn't given up.

'I asked Max to put it back under cover. I was busy from then on. The RIB would have to wait.'

Suttle was on the phone to Meg Stanley. Sadler's Megane had been seized last night for full forensic examination. He'd seen it himself in the car park behind her apartment but he needed confirmation that the cabriolet had a tow bar.

'And?' Faraday was looking at him.

'She'll check and phone back.'

'Good lad.' Faraday patted his arm, bending to the speaker again.

Ellis had moved on to the issue of Oobik's caravan. It seemed he'd spent a great deal of time giving the inside a thorough clean. Recovered evidence indicated that he'd even got rid of the carpet. Why might that have been?

Sadler laughed. She enjoyed questions like these. She couldn't wait to play the housewife.

'Did you ever see that carpet?'

'Obviously not, Ms Sadler.'

'It was vile, a kind of mustardy colour with blotches. I always wondered whether he'd spewed all over it and never bothered to clean up, you know what I mean?'

Ellis didn't. She asked about the rest of the work Max had done.

'I've no idea, love. I think he probably started with the carpet and then got the bug. It's spring, isn't it? You have a clear-out, splash a bit of paint around, brighten things up. And you're right, he did an incredible job. I was amazed. I told him he could start on my place next, but I don't think he was that keen. Funny about men, isn't it? They never last the pace.' She laughed again.

'We think he used twenty-seven dustbin liners.' It was Yates this time.

'Really? Who's counting?'

'We are, Ms Sadler. The question is, why?'

'You'll have to ask him.'

'We're asking you.'

'No idea. He had a load of stuff in that caravan aside from the carpet.'

'What kind of stuff?'

'Just stuff, general stuff, clutter—you know, the kind of crap none of us notice until it gets on top of you. Maybe it was that.'

'You haven't answered the question, Ms Sadler. I want you to be specific. I want you to remember the inside of that caravan. Tell me the way it was before he had the clear-out.'

'To be honest, I can't.'

'Why not?'

'Because, like I just said, I never went in there with a pencil and paper and wrote it all down. That wasn't the way it worked. You just get a general impression. The place was a mess. To be honest, I never fancied it. Not compared to my place.'

'Fancied it?'

'For sex. For friendship. For being together. Why freeze your arse off in that khazi of a caravan when you've clean sheets and central heating down the road? Doesn't make sense, does it?'

Faraday shook his head. Yates had done exactly the right thing, pressing her to be specific, hoping she'd trip up over tiny details, praying she'd expose this glib little fantasy for what it really was: a tissue of lies. But every time Yates or Ellis threatened to lay a hand on her, she simply danced away, wrapping this life of theirs in cosy generalities that were difficult to challenge. No wonder she'd spent so much time rehearsing with Benny Stanton. No wonder he'd put a smile on her face.

Yates had moved on to the visits Sadler had made to Mrs Percival's place. The first, with Max, had been to rescue Maarika from her mystery attacker.

The second had taken place days later. Yates wanted to know why.

'We went to pick up the rest of her stuff.'

'What kind of stuff?'

'Clothes, a few books, some shoes.'

'Had she asked you to do this?'

'Yes.'

'But you say she left for London almost immediately.'

'She did. But there was always a chance she'd be back. Or that's what she said.'

'No, it's not, Ms Sadler. You told us earlier that she just wanted to get away.' Faraday heard the rustle of paper as Yates consulted his notes. '*Get me out, she kept saying. Just please get me out. I want to go home. I want to get out.* That's what you told us.'

'It's true. That's exactly what she said.'

'Then how come she'd ever want to make time to come back? Just for a bunch of old clothes?'

'Because she might. These girls are volatile. They change their minds all the time. We'd helped her to get out of the place. The least we owed her was to make a proper job of it.'

'Did you know exactly what you were looking for? At the time?'

'Of course not.'

'Did she ever mention a mobile she might have left behind? Or a bag full of clothes?'

'No. We just went round to clear out what we ...ld see. The old lady who owned the place ... to re-let, obviously. That was another ...ving the place empty.' She paused. ...hing here? Is it a crime to be

Yates ignored this. 'There was a third visit, wasn't there? Yesterday afternoon?'

'That's right.'

'And why was that?'

'I realised the old lady would still be holding Maarika's deposit. I hadn't thought about it before.'

'So you picked it up?'

'Yeah. Four hundred quid. If Maarika comes back, no problem. If she doesn't, I'll give it to Max.'

'Keep it in the family?'

'Exactly.'

'And was there anything else you needed to pick up?'

'Like what?'

'I'm asking you.'

'No.' She frowned. 'Not that I can remember.'

'Not a bin bag full of clothes?'

There was a silence. Suttle was bent towards the speaker. He'd talked to Mrs Percival yesterday. According to her, Lou Sadler had wanted to know about the bin bag.

'Oh, that . . .' Sadler was laughing. 'She said someone had come round for it.'

'Someone?'

'She didn't know his name.'

'And did that bother you?'

'Christ, no. I assumed it was some friend of Maarika's. Saved me having to hang on to the stuff in case she ever came back.'

'One more chore off your list?'

'Exactly.'

Yates' question had a flipness born of desperation. Faraday didn't blame him. This woman was running rings round them. At the pre-interview meet they'd agreed to concentrate on six points of potential weakness. Already they were halfway down the list and had yet to lay a glove on her.

Ellis asked about the blocks of concrete Oobik used to steady his caravan in high winds. Faraday could picture the bemusement on Sadler's face.

'Concrete blocks?' she queried. 'Is there some kind of problem?'

'One's missing.'

'Is it?'

'Yes, Ms Sadler. And we think it may have been removed recently.'

'Why? Why would anyone want to do that? In this weather?'

'Exactly.'

'And you're asking *me*?'

'Yes.'

'But how would I ever know? I live in an apartment in Cowes. I'm a businesswoman. I've got shitloads of stuff to get through every working day of my life. Why would I ever be worrying about concrete blocks?'

'Because we think one of them was used to dispose of a body.'

'Whose body?'

'Johnny Holman's.'

There was a moment of silence. Then Sadler began to laugh.

'This is mad,' she said. 'This is crazy. Tell them, Benny. Tell them they're off their heads.'

...nton murmured something Faraday didn't ...n Yates asked her to think again about ...nd Max had arrived at Maarika's ...day morning. Had the girl

'Of course she was. Who else would have been there? I told you before. The guy had gone.'

'Whoever he was.'

'Yeah. Exactly.'

'You never got a name? You're sure about that?'

'Absolutely.'

'Maarika never told you?'

'No.'

'But you'd have asked? You and Max?'

'Yeah, of course we did. Maarika's his sister. He wanted to know.'

'And?'

'She wouldn't tell us. We asked and she wouldn't say. That's what happened. That's the way it was. Don't you guys understand plain English? Do I have to tell you *again*?'

There was a long silence. Yates and Ellis were plainly waiting for more but Sadler didn't say a word. Yates cleared his throat. He wanted to return to the missing concrete block. The question threw Sadler for a moment or two. She seemed to have lost her thread.

Yates reminded her about the blocks that held down the caravan. One had gone missing. In his view it would be perfect if you wanted to dispose of a body at sea.

Sadler at last understood.

'This is bizarre,' she said. 'First you seem to be suggesting I might have something to do with killing Johnny Holman. Now you're telling me I've got rid of his body. At sea. So how do I do that? Tie him to your precious concrete block and chuck him off my RIB? Dead of night? Is that what happened?'

'It's a possibility.'

'Fine. Go down to the marina. I've given you the

details. Check out the boat. Look at the CCTV. Do whatever you have to do.'

'We just did.'

'And?'

'You're right. It hasn't moved for weeks.'

'Thank you. Thank you very much. Might an apology be in order? Or do I have to put up with any more of this shit?'

She sounded really angry. Fantastic performance. Yates wasn't giving up. He still wanted to know how she explained the missing concrete block.

'How do *I* explain it? Are you guys thick or something? Don't you *listen*? I know fuck all about concrete blocks. Neither do I make a habit of killing people, or disposing of them, or any of this other rubbish you're trying to pin on me.'

'What other rubbish, Ms Sadler?'

'Dustbin liners, for a start. Listen. Max takes it into his head to do a spot of spring cleaning. What do I do, except applaud? You've got to get a grip, guys. This is a waste of time, mine and yours. It's the tax from people like me that pays your wages, don't forget. And if this is the best you can do, I'm going to start wondering about a refund.'

Faraday was trying to imagine the expression on Benny Stanton's face. Lou Sadler must be nearly home and dry, he's probably thinking. Nearly time for a bevvy or two.

Dawn Ellis wanted to move on to Wednesday night. Someone had driven a red Vauxhall Corsa out to woodland on the south of the island and set fire to it. Ellis believed that was the car Johnny Holman had used early Sunday morning when he'd fled from the burning farmhouse. She wanted to know where Sadler had been on that same

Wednesday night.

'In bed. At home. With Max.'

'Convenient, wouldn't you say?'

'Convenient?' Sadler was off again. '*Convenient?* Listen, my love. I can tell you a lot about Max. I can tell you what he does to me, for me, in me, whatever you like. We can go into that in great detail. My pleasure. As it happens, I can tell you a great deal about Wednesday because we were both a bit pissed, and that can help no end in all kinds of ways. If you want the truth, we fucked each other stupid most of the night. That was great. That was the kind of night a girl really appreciates. But was it *convenient*? I think not. You know what you guys should do? You should get a life. It's not too late. I promise.'

Faraday heard a chuckle. Stanton, he thought.

Yates took over. He had one card left to play. It was the name on the bottom of Faraday's checklist.

'Let's talk about Martin Skelley,' he began.

'Of course. Whatever.' Sadler was recovering her breath.

'You know this guy?'

'I pay him rent. On the stables.'

'That wasn't my question. I asked you whether you know him.'

'Then the answer's yes.'

Faraday glanced at Suttle. There was something new here, a tiny hint of wariness in Sadler's voice that hadn't been there before. Suttle had heard it too. And so had Yates.

'So how well do you know him?'

'I've met him on social occasions a couple of times.'

'How many times?'

'God knows. I never count.'

'Try.'

'Half a dozen? More? Less? Fuck knows.'

'What kind of social occasions?'

'Business functions, mainly.'

'Here? On the mainland?'

'Mostly on the mainland. I met him here once. He came down to the farm. We had tea together.'

'So what sort of a guy is he? This Martin Skelley?'

'He's . . .' she hesitated '. . . late forties, bit older than me, nicely dressed, smart/casual. Brilliant businessman—spotted an opportunity, got in there, did it well, earned himself a fortune. You can still do that in this country, believe it or not.'

Faraday was waiting to see where this line of questioning went next. Suttle's D/Cs had been trying to develop the intel on Skelley's company all day, so far with little result. Urgent requests for the movements of Freezee delivery vans at the beginning of last week had so far been blanked.

Ellis had taken up the running again. There was a hint of irritation in her voice. She wanted to know how familiar Sadler was with Skelley's past.

'I know he's been inside, if that's what you mean.'

'And do you know why? What for?'

'Haven't a clue. It's not the kind of question you ask, believe it or not.'

'GBH,' Ellis said quietly. 'A particularly brutal attack.'

'Really?' Sadler didn't seem the least bit interested.

'Yes. Does that put the man in a new light?'

'Not in the slightest. I'm not sure what you're trying to tell me here.'

'I'm trying to suggest, Ms Sadler, that you know

Skelley a great deal better than you say you do.'

'And why would that be?'

'Because good friends, *close* friends, friends with lots in common, often help each other out.'

'That's true.'

'Especially when they're in trouble.'

'That's true too.'

'On Sunday night, Ms Sadler, we believe you were in serious trouble, big, big trouble.'

'Not me, love. Maarika.'

'And you too, Ms Sadler. Why? Because you'd landed yourself with a body. Or to put it more accurately, *Max* had landed you with a body. We don't know how he killed Holman, not exactly, not yet, but the overwhelming probability is that he did. And so the pair of you had to make a decision.'

There was a silence. Both Faraday and Suttle knew that Dawn Ellis had gone way off-piste. This second interview was still meant to be coaxing a clear account from Lou Sadler. Only later would she be challenged with an alternative interpretation of events.

'This is bizarre,' she said. 'You're telling me it was Max who killed Holman? Is that it?'

'Yes.'

'But why would he do that?'

'Because he hated what Holman had done to his sister.'

'So he *killed* the man?'

'Yes. And that gave you a problem, because afterwards you had to decide what to do with this body, how to get rid of it. First off, we thought you might have used the RIB. Now we have to accept you didn't. So there had to be another way, a better way, and what better way than giving your old mate

Martin Skelley a ring?'

'To do what?' She laughed. 'Turn Holman into burgers and flog him to some caff or other? Get real, love. Why would he do that?'

'Because you phoned him and asked him. And because you said you were also sitting on a huge consignment of cocaine.'

'Of what?'

'Cocaine. Bugle. Toot. Lots and lots of it.'

Sadler was laughing again. She seemed to be enjoying herself.

'This is fabulous. So now I'm the cocaine queen?'

'Yes.'

'This is the purest bollocks. I know nothing about any cocaine.'

'I don't believe you.'

'Fine. That's your privilege. You think I made a phone call to Martin Skelley? You prove it. You think I'm trying to flog him a couple of tons of toot? Same answer. Prove it.'

'The cocaine belonged to Johnny Holman. We believe it was in the back of the Corsa. We believe the car was outside Maarika's place when you and Max arrived from Cowes. And we believe that Holman was there inside the flat.'

'Bollocks. Total bullshit. What are you guys on, for fuck's sake?'

Ellis ignored the jibe. 'We believe Max drove the Corsa up to the caravan that Sunday morning, hid the car in the spare outhouse and killed Holman. We believe he wrapped him in a roll of dustbin liners and probably kept him in the caravan. Two problems, Ms Sadler. What to do with the body and what to do with the toot. And you know the sweetest answer? Phone Martin Skelley.'

'But why? Why would I do that?'

'Because Skelley runs delivery vans all over the country. They come here, to the island. They drop stuff off. They go home empty. Plenty of room inside, Ms Sadler, for Johnny Holman and all that toot.'

'Fine. So what are you telling me?'

'We're suggesting, Ms Sadler, that one of Skelley's vans called at Upcourt Farm, probably last Monday afternoon, probably late, probably after dark, and solved your little problem. Not just Holman. Not just the toot. But a big fat concrete weight as well. You know where Skelley calls home? He's got a lovely little place up in the Lake District, bang on Derwent Water. Perfect, wouldn't you say?'

There was a long silence. It wasn't hard to imagine Sadler tipping her head back, letting the slow smile spread and spread. Ellis wanted to know whether she had any comment to make.

'Yes. I think it's rubbish. And that's being kind.'

'You're still denying it?'

'Of course I am.'

'We don't believe you.'

'Fine.' Sadler smothered an audible yawn. 'So why don't you prove it?'

Chapter Thirty-One

TUESDAY, 17 FEBRUARY 2009. *18.57*

It was the TIA, Ian Whatmore, who tore into Dawn Ellis. In twenty years of conducting CID interviews he'd never seen a working detective throw away so many cards. In his view she'd opened the doors to *Gosling*'s fragile store of inner secrets and invited Sadler, the prime suspect for fuck's sake, to help herself. Already, she and her spivvy brief were aware of how hard the detectives were all having to work to climb the evidential mountain. Now, in barely a couple of minutes, Ellis had made that task, that ascent, all the tougher. Ellis, chalk-faced, tight-lipped, was still convinced the punt had been worth it. The woman was guilty as fuck. Plus she was taking the piss. Two perfectly good reasons to give her a bit of a shake.

'Didn't work though, did it?' This from Whatmore. 'So thanks for fucking nothing.'

This second interview with Lou Sadler ended a couple of minutes before seven in the evening. After Ellis had gone for broke, Yates had done the bulk of the work. He'd pressed Sadler's account time and again, revisiting moments of potential crisis, challenging her on this detail or that, alert for the merest hint of hesitation or doubt, the tiniest suggestion that she might trip herself up or give herself away. But none of the usual strategies had worked. Whatever combination of punches he threw at her, she simply ducked or parried. She had immense stamina and self-confidence, and afterwards, in the debrief, even Yates had come close to admiring her performance.

'Dawn's right,' he said glumly. 'She's guilt on legs. But that's not enough, is it?'

Dawn Ellis had nothing to say. She seemed to have lost interest in *Gosling.* Faraday was about to voice the obvious but Parsons saved him the trouble.

'This is becoming a disaster,' she said. 'At this rate we're going to be struggling to even get an extension.'

Application to the island's uniformed Superintendent was due within the hour. Unless Parsons could demonstrate that the ongoing investigation was, in the parlance, 'diligent and expeditious', then Sadler would walk free. In the light of his non-cooperation, an earlier application for a twelve-hour extension on Oobik had been grudgingly granted, but Sadler's continued detention, when she was only too willing to offer and defend her account of events, was a different matter entirely. As a law-abiding citizen without a blemish on her name, she had rights in this matter, and it was the job of the Superintendent to uphold them.

These last few days Parsons had developed a habit of bypassing Faraday in meetings like these, and now was no exception.

'Jimmy,' she said, 'I'm pleading our case in ten. What do I tell the Superintendent? What have we got left?'

Suttle, it seemed, had been anticipating exactly this question.

'It boils down to Martin Skelley, boss. As far as last week's concerned, we have to link Sadler to

Skelley, and to do that we need two things. One of them is billing on whatever phone she used, and the other is proof that he had a delivery van on the island.'

'When?'

'My money's on Monday. Sunday they get their bearings, tidy up, make the call to Skelley. It may be that he had a van down on the island already. In which case she's home free. Or he may have jacked up something special, just for her. In which case we're in with a shout.'

'He'd cover his tracks,' Faraday pointed out. 'He'd invent deliveries, bend arms, concoct some kind of schedule. He understands all this stuff. He'd know what we'd be after.'

'I know, boss. But at least it gives us a chance, something to get stuck into, something to unpick. Plus . . .' Suttle turned to Parsons '. . . it gives you something for the Superintendent.'

'Sure, Jimmy.' Parsons nodded. 'But we're talking twelve hours. That takes us to breakfast time tomorrow morning, which means we'll have to jack something up for this evening. Are you really telling me you can get that information within—say—a couple of hours?'

Suttle shook his head. No chance, he admitted.

'What about the phone she used?' It was Faraday again.

'That's interesting. She obviously doesn't care a fuck about her phones—landline or mobiles—which tells me she probably used Oobik's mobile.'

'Which he says he's lost.'

'Exactly.' Suttle checked his watch. 'I was there on the farm for the hour or so before he was arrested. I was sitting in the car in the drive with line of sight to the caravan. If he was going to get rid of the phone he'd have had to do it then, because he was searched in the custody suite. He definitely came out of the caravan a couple of times and went round the back, and he also went into one of the stables. He could have binned the phone in the field behind the caravan, dug a hole, fed the SIM card to one of the horses, anything that took his fancy. We could blitz it now, throw loads of guys at it, whatever.' He shrugged, looking at Parsons. 'Your call, boss.'

'But how do you know he had the phone when you arrived?'

'He looked up some numbers for me. Corroboration for what he'd been doing on Saturday night. It was a Nokia.'

'Was it Pay As You Talk or was he on some plan or other?'

'He won't tell us.'

'Shit.' Parsons rarely swore.

'Exactly, boss.'

The silence was broken by a cackle of laughter from the office down the corridor. Benny Stanton.

Finally Parsons made a decision. She'd press the Superintendent for a twelve-hour extension. They'd throw everything they had at the caravan and its surroundings. And they'd pray to God that this last desperate toss of the investigative dice would work to *Gosling*'s advantage before they interviewed Oobik and Sadler for the last time.

* * *

It didn't.

Faraday mustered as many D/Cs as he could from

the MIR at Ryde. The local duty Inspector supplied half a dozen more hands, mainly P/Cs. In the wet darkness, on their hands and knees, they combed and re-combed every square inch of turf behind the caravan, looking for signs of recent disturbance. Climbing the fence, they worked methodically outwards, fumbling among the tussocks of wet grass, the same fingertip search, until they'd gone beyond what Suttle calculated as a throw radius. Nothing.

Inside the caravan, meanwhile, a separate search team tore the place apart, dismantling the wardrobe, unscrewing the tiny kitchen unit from its brackets, examining every inch of the mattress in case Oobik had managed to slip the mobile inside. Ninety minutes later the search team beat a retreat. Again, nothing.

The interviews were a formality, no more. Oobik, after a day and a half's rehearsal, had perfected the art of going No Comment, while there was almost a hint of sympathy in Lou Sadler's performance. Her faith in the script she and Benny Stanton had concocted never wavered for a moment. No, she hadn't seen Johnny Holman for weeks and weeks. No, she hadn't asked Max to kill him. And no, she hadn't arranged for one of Martin Skelley's vans to pick up his remains. As for the cocaine, she expressed mild surprise that Johnny Holman had either the money or the wit to have acquired a decent stash and suggested that Yates and his mates look elsewhere for the real owners.

'Try Pompey,' she'd said as the interview came to a close. 'They love the stuff over there.'

Back in Ryde, dead on his feet, Faraday had a quiet word with Dawn Ellis, expressing his disappointment at the way she'd handled Sadler in the interview suite. She accepted responsibility for what she'd done, offered neither an apology nor an explanation, but said she had to be back in Pompey as soon as she could be spared. Watching her leave the office, Faraday could only assume she'd been overwhelmed by some personal crisis. Maybe he should listen to canteen gossip more carefully in future. Maybe he wasn't the only Major Crime detective to be cornered by his demons.

When Suttle appeared, minutes later, Faraday suggested a drink. He wasn't at all sure where *Gosling* might be headed next but Parsons had decided against application to the magistrates for yet another custody extension and both Sadler and Oobik would be released on police bail by eight o'clock the following morning. Suttle had pressed Parsons to maintain obs on Sadler, but *Gosling* was gobbling up budget by the day and Parsons was reluctant to have her name attached to an expensive failure. Sadler, as she'd demonstrated so amply, was a class operator. Even if Dawn Ellis had kept to the script, there was no guarantee they'd have got any kind of result. Now, with all their immediate leads exhausted, that possibility was even more remote. Sadler now knew the case they had to prove. As Parsons pointed out, it was unlikely she'd make it easy for them.

Even Suttle had to admit that Parsons was probably right. Tomorrow he and Faraday would be driving up to London to put a little pressure on Martin Skelley. Whether the delivery information they were after would offer a pathway forward was anyone's guess. Skelley, like Sadler, obviously knew his way around the criminal justice system and would already have taken steps to make it hard for them. Meanwhile, to his regret, Suttle had yet another downer to share with his boss.

'What's that?' Faraday had just sunk a pint of Goddards and was waiting for a second.

'I talked to Meg Stanley again. She's having second thoughts about matching the fresh stuff from Sadler's horses to the manure at Monkswell Farm. Apparently the manure they shifted at Holman's place is too wet. There's fuck all left to analyse after the rain we've been having.'

'Shit.' Faraday sucked the head off his fresh pint.

'Exactly.'

'This woman's luck is beyond belief.'

'It is, boss. But she's played it well too. Like Bev said.'

'So what haven't we done? Apart from charge them?'

'You tell me, boss. You think we *could* charge them?'

'No chance. The CPS wouldn't wear it for a second. Circumstantially, it looks like a stone bonker. But we need something more.'

Suttle nodded. Faraday had collapsed again. All the air had left his fragile balloon. Maybe it was the accident. Or maybe it was a lot more than that.

'You want to share it, boss?'

'Share what?'

'Whatever's got to you?'

'You mean apart from all this crap? Five murders, four bodies, two prime suspects and no fucking clue what to do next? You mean apart from all that?'

Suttle laughed. This was better, he thought. Genuine despair, in his experience, never had much to do with the Job.

‘There’s something else, isn’t there?’

‘I’m not with you, Jimmy.’

‘Something’s happened. Something’s got to you. Big time.’

Faraday reflected on the question, then took a long pull at his beer.

‘Yeah . . .’ he said at last ‘. . . it has.’

He told Suttle about Gabrielle, about the Burns Unit, about the ongoing tussle for the little girl’s affections. He’d sensed for weeks that something had changed in Gabrielle, and now he knew the consequences that lay in wait for all three of them.

‘Like what?’

‘Like we sit at home, whenever, and have some infant social worker crawl all over us, all over our private lives, all over our family histories, everything. Like we try and make space for a little girl who will never, *never* be able to come to live with us. It’s a fairy tale, Jimmy, total make-believe, and the shame of it is that I seem to be going along with it. Why? Because I’ve been up to my neck in all this crap. Why *really*? Because I can’t, for the life of me, work out how to stop it.’

‘Just say no.’

‘And lose her?’

‘But you just told me it’ll never happen.’

‘I meant Gabrielle.’

‘Really? You’re serious?’ Suttle’s surprise was genuine.

‘Yeah, I think I am.’ Faraday nodded. ‘It’s not something I’d say lightly, but I think it’s probably the case. This little girl’s sweet. And she’s vulnerable. And all the rest of it.’

‘So why don’t you go along with it? Adopt her?’

‘Because it’s impossible. Because the minute she

gets better, they'll fly her back to Gaza. Because the system just won't permit it.'

'But *should* it permit it?'

'That's a different question. I'm just telling you it'll never happen. How do I know? Because people at the hospital, people who *do* know, have had a quiet word. Why? Because they want to save Gabrielle from being hurt.'

'You mean from hurting herself?'

'Yeah, exactly. Well put. Me? I just want us back again. Does that sound unreasonable?'

Suttle shook his head, only too aware that his own relationship, with a baby on the way, probably made it worse for Faraday. No dramas about adoption. No visits to the Burns Unit. No anguished conversations in Isle of Wight pubs. He was still trying to work out how to voice all this when his mobile beeped.

He fetched it out, glanced at caller ID. Winter again. Second time today.

He glanced at his watch then slipped off the bar stool.

'I'll be back in five, boss. Mine's a lager.'

*   *   *

Suttle took the call on the seafront, across from the pub. Winter, he knew at once, had been drinking.

'Son . . .'

'Me. What is it? What do you want?'

'I've got something to tell you.'

'Like what?'

'Lots of stuff. Good stuff. Better than good stuff. Stuff that'll make you—' He broke off.

'Make me what?'

'Wet yourself, son. This is crazy. The whole thing's crazy. You know what?'
'What?'
'It's crazy.'
The line went dead. Suttle gazed across the road towards the pub, wondering how best to pursue this last slim hope.

Chapter Thirty-Two

WEDNESDAY, 18 FEBRUARY 2009. *09.47*

It was Faraday, oddly, who raised the issue of Winter. He and Suttle were on the mainland, heading north on the M3. Two hours earlier Sadler and Oobik had both been released on police bail, while Martin Skelley had agreed to make himself available for interview at his Brentford distribution centre at half eleven. On the phone he thought there was a reasonable prospect of having the information they needed.

Faraday wanted to know more about Suttle's last conversation with Winter.

'You mean in Pompey? When I went over on Monday night?'
'Yes.'
'Like I told you, I think he wants out.'
'But why?'
'I think he's had enough. I think it's dawned on him that he's in a bad place.'
'He's right.'
'Of course he's right, boss. The real question is what he does next.'

'From our point of view, you mean?'

'Yeah. Winter's a player, always has been. Just now my guess is that he's in a big, big hole. If he can get himself out more or less intact, then that's exactly what he'll do. But he may need us to help him.'

Suttle had ghosted this idea past both Willard and Parsons on his return to Ryde, but Willard had dismissed it out of hand. He was disappointed that no grounds existed for arresting Winter for the removal of the girl's clothes and her phone but he was confident that one day, hopefully soon, Winter would make himself a sitting target for the fate he so richly deserved. No way would Willard deny himself the satisfaction of putting the man away for good.

'So where's the advantage?' Faraday eased into the fast lane.

'For us, you mean?'

'Yes.'

'As far as this job's concerned, I'm not sure. Assuming the cocaine exists, it may well be linked to Mackenzie. If that's true, then Winter would know about it. How much he'd know is down to how much Mackenzie's told him. These guys are canny. Information's gold dust. They hate sharing it around.'

Faraday laughed. 'Sounds like Winter,' he said.

'Exactly. Same MO. Ferrets in a sack. No wonder he wants out.'

Faraday nodded. The next question was obvious.

'You're telling me he might grass Mackenzie up?'

'Yeah, I think he might.'

'On this job? On the cocaine?'

'Yeah.'

'You think it's worth a shot? Some form of approach? Another conversation?'

'Absolutely.' Suttle sat back, gazing out at the traffic. 'Where else do we go?'

*   *   *

Winter awoke to the buzzing of his video entryphone. It was late and he had a headache. Naked, he made his way to the hall. Mackenzie's upturned face hung on the tiny screen, demanding to be let in.

By the time he made it up to the third floor, Winter had wrapped himself in a dressing gown, filled the kettle, opened the door to the apartment and retreated to the bathroom to swallow a handful of ibuprofen. He was still trying to remember why he'd necked so much malt last night when he joined Mackenzie in the big living room.

Mackenzie, as ever these days, was on a tight schedule. The media were like kids, he told Winter. They needed constant attention otherwise they lost interest.

'A whole day without an interview?' Winter rubbed his aching head, trying to massage the pain away. 'God forbid, Baz.'

'You think that's funny?'

'I think it's mad.'

'Why?'

'These people will bite you on the arse one day. They're not kids, they're animals. One sniff of blood and they'll be all over you.'

'Bollocks, mush. Me and Leo sort out the music. All the other monkeys do is dance.'

He perched on the edge of the sofa, ignoring

Winter's offer of coffee.

'You gonna sit down and listen to me or what, mush?'

Winter did his master's bidding. Mackenzie's suit was new, quiet, nicely cut. Marie's choice, Winter thought.

Bazza was talking about Lou Sadler. He'd belled her half an hour ago.

'Why?'

'Because we need a little chat.'

'About what?'

'My toot, mush. I wasn't kidding about the spic woman. Her name's Alisa. She's due next week, Tuesday.'

'You told me tomorrow.'

'Change of plan. She's flying into Gatwick. We meet her at the airport. We do the business. We give her the cheque. *Problema* sorted.'

Winter assumed they were talking about the hit on Brett West. He was right.

'But what about Tommy Peters?'

'He's the middleman. We've just cut him out.'

'And if he objects?'

'We whack him.'

'*Whack* him?'

'Yeah.'

'You've told him that?'

'No, mush. Not yet. First things first, eh?'

Mackenzie went back to Sadler. She said she'd been away for a couple of days. On business.

Winter laughed. His headache was beginning to recede.

'Did she tell you where?'

'I never asked, mush.'

'I bet. What else did she say?'

'She said yes.'

'To what?'

'To my invitation. You're buying her lunch.'

'Where?'

'Here. She's coming over on the hovercraft. I said La Tasca, half twelve.'

'And she agreed?'

'Like a shot, mush. Can't wait to meet you again. Shake you by the throat. Sweet lady. Get her in the right mood, she might even bung you a freebie. See what you can do. Anything less than a million, we're not interested.'

'A million?'

'For my toot, mush. She's got it and, if she agrees a respectable price, she can keep it. Two hundred and fifty K of what she pays goes to our new Spanish friend. The rest is ours. So . . .' he got to his feet, cracked his knuckles '. . . start high. Anything over a million, you're on 10 per cent. How does that sound?'

He checked his watch and headed for the door, not bothering to wait for an answer. Then he paused.

'One other thing, mush.'

'What's that, Baz?'

'Today's *Telegraph.*' He flashed a smile. 'Fill your boots.'

*   *   *

Freezee's southern distribution depot lay on the edge of a west London trading estate beside the M4. Rows of white refrigerated vans and lorries were parked beyond the chain-link fence and a couple of security guards bent to Faraday's borrowed Fiesta to check his ID. His name was evidently on the list of expected callers. The guy with the clipboard was black.

'You suppliers? Customers? Or what?'

'Neither. Where do we find Mr Skelley?'

'Over there, mate. Ask the lady on reception.'

Faraday parked. The girl behind reception was young, neatly turned out, beautiful eyes. Suttle did the honours.

'Mr Skelley's expecting you, gentlemen.' She had a flat London accent. 'Can I get you a coffee?'

Skelley kept them waiting more than half an hour. Suttle helped himself to a copy of the *Sun* from the selection of tabloids on the low glass table while Faraday watched the comings and goings. Business, it seemed, was brisk. Cut-price burgers were clearly weathering the recession.

Skelley came out in person to collect them. He was a big man, carrying a stone or two of extra weight, but he moved with the grace and lightness of a ballroom dancer. One look at his face told Faraday that there must be West Indian blood in his family: the skin colour, the tiny button ears, the tight whorls of greying hair, the blackness in his eyes. His handshake was firm. There was no warmth in his smile.

'You guys OK for coffee?' He was looking at the empty cup.

'Fine, thanks.'

Faraday and Suttle followed him down a long corridor to an office at the end. A couple of secretaries stepped carefully aside to let him pass. He acknowledged neither of them.

The office was modest: a desk, a small conference table, no windows. On the plain white wall behind

Skelley's chair hung a framed photograph. Faraday had once been to Derwent Water on a birding expedition. He recognised the distant whale hump of Skiddaw.

'Nice.' He especially liked the gleam of silver grey on the water. 'Fantastic light.'

Skelley wasn't interested in small talk. Nor did he apologise for keeping them waiting. He wanted to know how he could help them. He had a light Scouse accent and his habit of twirling a pen between his fingers spoke of a deep impatience.

Faraday briefly described the thrust of Operation *Gosling.* He and D/S Suttle were exploring various lines of enquiry. Whether or not Skelley had any Freezee vans on the Isle of Wight within a certain time frame was one of them.

'Why?' The question was blunt.

'I'm afraid I'm not prepared to discuss that, Mr Skelley. We're simply after the information we discussed on the phone.'

'And if I don't give it to you?'

'Then we'll continue the conversation elsewhere.'

'Down the nick?'

'Yes.'

He nodded, unsurprised, and pulled a drawer open. Moments later Faraday found himself looking at a complicated spreadsheet tallying the movements of various Freezee vehicles.

'My PA's highlighted the one you want in yellow,' Skelley said.

Faraday followed the yellow band. The vehicle in question was a long-wheelbase Transit. It had left the London depot at 06.15 on Monday morning, driven down to Portsmouth, crossed to Fishbourne on the car ferry and spent the whole day on the Isle of Wight. By 23.18 on Monday night it was back in Brentford.

'Do you have a delivery schedule for the island?'

'Next page.'

Faraday turned over. The list of drop-offs began in Ryde, after which the driver had made calls in Sandown, Shanklin, Ventnor, Freshwater, Totland, Yarmouth, Newport and finally Cowes.

'You've got addresses for this lot?' Faraday tapped the list.

'Obviously.'

'Can we have them?'

'That might take a while.'

'We're happy to wait, Mr Skelley.'

'I'm sure you are.'

He held Faraday's gaze for a moment or two, then lifted the phone and murmured instructions.

'Half an hour,' he said, replacing the phone. 'You're in luck.'

'What about timings?'

'You'll have to go round and check.'

'Doesn't the driver keep a log? Can't you ask him?'

'Sadly, no.' The same mirthless smile. 'The guy's Polish. He left us at the end of last week.'

Suttle produced a notebook and jotted down the details. Guy called Pavel Beginski. Worked for Freezee for eleven months. Lived at a couple of addresses in west London, most recently in Shepherd's Bush.

'Is he still in the UK?'

'No.'

'Where did he go?'

'No idea. He didn't tell me.'

'Then how do you know he's not around?'

'Because he said he'd had enough of us. The money was good when the pound was strong. Nowadays the pound's shit so . . .' he shrugged '. . . guys like him go looking elsewhere. France? Germany? Somewhere in Scandinavia? Depends how hard you want to look.'

Faraday nodded. This was turning into a repeat performance of the interviews with Lou Sadler. Immigrant labour again, always on the move.

Suttle wanted to know about the booking-in process. Skelley was watching him carefully.

'I'm not with you, son.'

'What happens when these vans come back?'

'Empty, you mean?'

'Yes.'

'We give them a bit of a sweep-out.'

'Who does that?'

'The driver.'

'Pavel?'

'In this case, yes. There's a hose too, and scrubbing brushes and all sorts if he fancies it. You get inspected in this business. Those guys can be evil, believe me. Any complaints—' the edge of his hand came down on the desk '—the driver gets the sack. There and then. On the spot.'

Faraday nodded. He'd spotted CCTV cameras on the gate. How long did Freezee keep the recorded pictures?

'Four working weeks.'

'So last week . . .?'

'We've still got them. You're telling me you want them?'

'Yes, please.'

Skelley nodded. His hand reached for the phone again, then paused.

'Anything else? Before I drive the poor fucking woman mad?'

'Yeah . . .' It was Suttle. 'You say this Polish guy, Pavel, left on Friday last week. Right?'

'Right.'

'So he worked the rest of the week, yes?'

'I assume so.'

'And you'd have a schedule of the jobs he did?'

'Of course.'

'Yes, please.' Suttle nodded at the phone.

Skelley made the call. Faraday's eyes were on the photo of Derwent Water. It was some small comfort that Suttle was way, way ahead of the game.

Skelley was off the phone. He had a meeting scheduled any time now. He wanted to know what else they wanted.

'Lou Sadler . . .' It was Faraday this time. 'Do you know her, by any chance?'

'Of course I know her. She's a tenant of mine. She and those horses of hers.' He paused. 'You know something? That little farm was the first property I ever owned in my life. And you know why? Because I spent the best part of a year and a half in the nick down the road, Parkhurst. My cell was up on the fourth floor. If I stood on tiptoe I could see clear over the prison wall. There was countryside all the way over to Cowes—fields and little farms—and I told myself that one day I'd buy myself a bit of that. And you know something? That's exactly what happened. It took a bit of time but I did it. Upcourt Farm. Nothing special. Nothing fancy. But mine.'

'You know Upcourt Farm?'

'Of course I do. I just told you.'

'But you know Upcourt Farm in the context of

this inquiry?'

'All I know is the rents get paid. There's a South American woman lives in the farm itself. Colombian lady. Mad as a box of frogs. Nice though. Makes you laugh.'

'And Lou?'

'What about her?'

'You know her well?'

'Well enough. We've met socially, if that's what you mean.'

'Do you speak regularly? On the phone maybe?'

Skelley hesitated, recognising the trap that Faraday was trying to lay. Most phone calls were a matter of record. Call billings could offer rich pickings in a situation like this.

'Of course we talk on the phone. Do I remember the last time that happened? No, I don't. This is a multi-million-pound business. By six o'clock most days my brain's exploding. When did I last talk to Lou Sadler? Sorry, guys, can't help you.'

'But you're close.'

'I like to think we're friends. Where I come from there's a difference.'

There was a knock on the door and a woman in her fifties came in. She handed Skelley an A4 envelope and whispered something in his ear. He checked his watch and nodded. Then she'd gone.

'I've got someone waiting for me downstairs.' He flashed the smile again. 'Can't keep them hanging around.'

He gave Faraday the envelope and hoped their journey up hadn't been in vain. Anything else they needed, just give him a ring.

'And this?' Faraday gestured at the envelope.

'All the stuff you were after. Good luck, eh?'

*　　*　　*

Back in the Fiesta, the envelope still unopened, Faraday asked for Suttle's assessment.

'We attack him on the fine print, boss. Go to all those drop-offs on the island, build a timeline, check the ferry bookings, cross-match them with the CCTV, establish just when he could have dropped off the radar for an hour or so and nipped into Upcourt Farm. Logic says it has to be after dark. In, bosh, out again. Job done.'

'And afterwards?' Faraday was gazing round the big asphalt apron. 'Up here?'

'My guess is this guy Pavel locked the van, left it here, got his head down, then pushed on next day.'

'Where?'

'Take a look.' Suttle nodded at the envelope. 'My money's on somewhere way up north.'

Faraday opened the envelope and shook out the contents. The information he was after was on the second sheet of paper. Pavel Beginski's last-ever job for Freezee had been on the Tuesday of last week. After that he'd taken three days' paid leave in lieu of holiday and disappeared.

'So where did he go on the Tuesday, boss?'

Faraday glanced across. His finger was still anchored on the spreadsheet.

'Carlisle.'

Chapter Thirty-Three

WEDNESDAY, 18 FEBRUARY 2009. *12.35*

Lou Sadler was already at La Tasca when Winter arrived. A grey day in February was a strange time to be wearing dark glasses but Winter imagined she'd probably had enough of being eyeballed. Major Crime interviews could be seriously intrusive. And the cuisine in most custody centres was frankly crap.

Sadler had been studying the menu. Winter shed his leather jacket and sat down.

'You're late.' She didn't look up.

'My apologies. It's a bit of a hike from my place.'

'Really?'

'Yeah.' He knew the menu by heart. 'Those big prawns in chilli and garlic are brilliant. So are the *Patatas bravas.* Me? I'd eat in here every day of my life. Misty's the same.'

'How is she?'

'Fine. Sends her best. Hoped you didn't let all those hairy men get to you.'

'What hairy men?'

'The Major Crime lot. The ones who can read can be good company. The rest . . .' Winter shrugged and then signalled to a waitress.

'And you'd know, would you?'

'Yeah. I used to be one.'

'So I understand. So what was that like?'

'OK. Multiple homicides were the best. You'd be amazed what people get up to.'

The waitress had arrived. Winter ordered a San

Miguel. Sadler wanted a glass of white wine. Then she turned to Winter again.

'Let's get this thing done,' she said.

'Thing?'

'Don't. I've been fucked around enough as it is. Frankly, I could have done without all this.'

'I bet.'

'Right. So just tell me.'

'Tell you what?'

'Tell me what's in that fucking bin liner. The one you nicked. The one you've stashed. The one you talked to me about on the phone. And do me a favour, yeah? Don't take me for an idiot.'

Winter did his best to look contrite. Thirty-six hours with Major Crime obviously did nothing for your sense of humour.

'Johnny Holman must have appeared at your girl's place. Right?'

'Wrong.'

'The guy looked a wreck. Stank of smoke. Stuff all over him, some of it blood. Yes?'

'You're making this stuff up.' She was laughing now. 'You're like the rest of them. No wonder you were a cop.'

Winter ignored her. 'You told him to get changed, ' he said. 'Maybe he had clothes there already. Maybe he and the girl were that cosy. Maybe she lent him a dressing gown. Fuck knows. But either way you got those clothes off him.'

'And then?' The laughter had gone. She was listening at last. She gestured for Winter to carry on, but he shook his head and just looked at her.

'You tell me,' he said at length. 'You tell me what happened next.'

'You found the clothes, didn't you?'

'Johnny's gear?' Winter nodded. 'Yes, I did. Just like I told you on the phone the other day.'

'I didn't believe you.'

'Big mistake.'

'I thought it was a bluff.'

'Wrong. I'm good at this stuff, believe it or not.'

'So where is it, Johnny's gear?'

'Silly question.'

'Somewhere safe?'

'Somewhere very safe.'

'And what next?'

'Good question.'

He let the silence between them lengthen. Then he asked her where she thought Holman's dirty clothes had gone that night.

'I think he must have bagged them up. I've no idea what happened after that. The whole thing was a nightmare.'

'So he *was* there?'

'Of course he was there.'

'And you came back soon after? Picked up the rest of her things?'

'Yeah.'

'But not Holman's gear?'

'No. We assumed the old lady must have found them and chucked them out. Turned out I was wrong.'

'Shame.' Winter shook his head. 'Rule one, never assume *anything*.'

'Don't be a smart-arse. Just tell me again you're sitting on this stuff.'

'I am.'

'So what was he wearing? Describe the T-shirt.'

'Bob Dylan. A mug shot, black on white. Plus that line about the Joker and the Thief. Very apt.'

Winter smiled at her. 'Happy now? Believe me?'

'So what do you want?'

'A cut of what you've made on the cocaine.'

'What cocaine?'

'Don't fuck about, Lou. I don't know what you've done with it, and I've no idea where it is, but Misty tells me you're really, *really* good at spotting opportunities. And if two and a half million quid's worth of my boss's toot isn't an opportunity, then you tell me what is.'

'Two and a half *million*? You're having a joke, aren't you?'

'We're talking street prices, Lou. Baz is good at adding up. He's one of those guys who can count in their sleep. When he tells me his mate Johnny was sitting on sixty-four kilos of the pure stuff, the wholesale stuff, then I believe him. And when someone comes along and digs a fucking great hole to get it all out, I buy that too. Why? Because I bimbled along and saw the hole for myself. The night after they released the scene.'

'Don't put a foot wrong, do you?' Winter sensed she was impressed. Either that or she was taking the piss.

'Never, love. Not then. Not now. So say we accept you've sold it on. Say some other monkey stamps on it and bangs out all those little wraps. You'll still be looking at around two and a half million quid. And all that for nicking someone else's toot. Ours, as it happens.'

She nodded, said nothing. The drinks arrived. Winter swallowed a mouthful of San Miguel. Sadler's wine remained untouched.

'One thing I forgot to ask.' It was Winter. 'Did Max give Johnny a hand to dig that hole?'

'What makes you think that?'

'Because the way I hear it, Johnny was a little runt. He'd have needed that kind of help. Big time.'

She shook her head. She wasn't having any of this. Winter helped her out.

'I'm serious, Lou. It had to be Max, didn't it? That's how you got to know about the toot in the first place. Unless shitface told you first.'

'Shitface is Holman?'

'Yeah. That comes from way back. A tribute to his thirst. Tell me something else too. Shitface was putting it about that he got freebies off you. Is that right?'

'Off the girl, not me.'

'Kaija?'

'Her real name's Maarika. So yes, it's true. God knows why, but she put out for him, gave him pretty much everything he wanted. I told her she was nuts. I told her it would all end in tears. As it turned out I was wrong: it was much worse than that. Like I say, total fucking grade-A nightmare . . .' She reached for the glass at last.

'So who killed Johnny?'

'I'm not telling you that.'

'But he was killed, right?'

'Yeah. Dead man walking. Maybe someone did him a favour.'

'Like Max?'

She smiled a tight little smile, said nothing. In the interview room, thought Winter, I'd have her kippered in no time at all. He'd rarely seen a franker admission of guilt.

She was toying with her glass now. She wanted to know what would happen if she simply got up and walked away. It was a possibility. She could do it.

What then?

'Then I phone a friend.'

'Like who?'

'Like the guy who's driving the intel cell for Major Crime. I think you've met him.'

'Tall guy? Curly red hair? Early thirties?'

'Yeah.'

'He was all right. Had a brain on him.'

'Exactly. And you know what he'd do with that bag? All that gear of Johnny's? Once I'd filled him in about how I came across it?'

'Surprise me.'

'He'd do his best to link it to you. Maybe you handled it. Maybe you stuffed it in the bag. Or maybe Max did. Either way, we're talking DNA. And why does that matter? Because by now you'll have told him all about rescuing the girl, and for my money you'd have left little Johnny out of it. Why? Because you want to keep the little twat at arm's length. He was nothing to do with you. You hadn't seen him for weeks. And he certainly wasn't with the girl when you and Max turned up. This stuff isn't rocket science, love. In your place I'd have run exactly the same story. You got a call, right? In the middle of the night, right?'

She nodded, said nothing.

'The girl was upset. She couldn't tell her arse from her elbow. Johnny's probably fed her all this shit about a brand new start in tootle-land. The guy's covered in blood. He smells like a bonfire. He's probably pissed. So what's a working girl going to do? Run away with a headcase like Holman? No way. She phones you. Am I getting warm?'

Sadler was looking at her glass. She said nothing.

'So you arrive. With Max. You assess the scene.

You know you're looking at a disaster. You have to make some decisions pretty fucking fast. This guy Holman is sitting on a great fat whack of toot. Plus he's probably got a shotgun in the car. You might even had had a peek inside the car because it's sitting out there in the road. And even if you can't see all those kilo bricks, the girl's probably mentioned them already. All part of the nightmare. Yeah?'

'It's worse.'

'How?'

'Max is her brother.'

'Whose brother?'

'Maarika's.'

'Fuck. So Max isn't at *all* pleased.'

'No—' she shook her head '—he wasn't.'

'You want to tell me the rest?'

'No.'

'You understand what I can do with Johnny's gear?'

'Yes.'

'What next then?' Winter grinned at her. 'Your call.'

*   *   *

Faraday and Suttle didn't go back to the island that afternoon. Instead, they drove to Portsmouth and checked into the Major Crime suite at Fratton police station. Parsons was at her desk, preparing an interim report on *Gosling* for Willard. Stony-faced, she listened to Faraday's account of the interview with Martin Skelley. At the end of it she seemed just a little brighter.

'You're right, Joe,' she said. 'We test Skelley's

account to breaking point. Every single link in that chain. Start on the island, like Jimmy's suggesting. Track the delivery van. Draw up a timeline.'

'And the van itself?'

'Seize it. Bosh it. One dead body? Loads of cocaine? No one's forensically perfect.'

'It's been a while, boss.' This from Suttle. 'They've got steam-cleaning equipment at the depot. We saw it.'

'Doesn't matter. People make mistakes.' The light was in her eyes again. She drew a brisk line through her draft report. 'Get people up to London. Take a look at his place in the Lake District. Do some work on his comms. Analyse the billings. Put them alongside Sadler's. New start, Joe. Just get it done.'

Faraday retired to his office and phoned the satellite MIR at Ryde. After this morning's release of Oobik and Sadler, more than half of Faraday's detectives had been returned to the mainland with the result that the investigation was running at half-throttle. Now *Gosling* had to be cranked up again.

The Outside Enquiries D/S was still at his desk. Faraday told him that Suttle was on his way over with the new brief. He himself would be staying on the mainland overnight and returning first thing tomorrow.

'Eight a.m.,' he said. 'Squad meet.'

He put the phone down to find Parsons standing at his open door. She'd had Personnel on again, wanting an update on Faraday's well-being.

'You look knackered, Joe. Do whatever won't wait, then have an early night. Mr Willard sends his best, by the way. I've told him everything's in hand again.'

* * *

It was gone seven when Faraday returned home. The lights were on in the kitchen and one of the windows was open upstairs. Gabrielle, he told himself. She must have come back.

He parked the CID Fiesta behind his ancient Mondeo and let himself into the house. The kitchen was empty but Gabrielle's laptop was open at the end of the table she often used for work. He stepped into the living room, wondering whether she might have fallen asleep on the sofa, then carefully made his way upstairs. The bedroom door was ajar. He could hear the familiar rise and fall of her breathing. He eased the door open until he could see her slender shape under the duvet. Her face on the pillow was turned towards him. In the soft spill of light from the hall she looked utterly at peace, the old Gabrielle.

He smiled, gladder than he knew that she'd come home at last. A small toast, he told himself. A glass or two of something decent in celebration. He found a bottle of Rioja in a cupboard downstairs. He uncorked it and poured himself a glass. Then he took it through to the kitchen, gazing at the stove, wondering whether to get something ready for when she woke. Would she be hungry? Did he have anything fresh he could knock into the kind of alfresco meal they'd always enjoyed together?

He decided that could wait. For the time being he'd just settle down and enjoy the wine. He sank into the chair at the end of the table. Then his eyes strayed to the laptop and he began to read. He was looking at Gabrielle's in-box. She must have been reading the email on the screen. It was in French. It had arrived a couple of hours ago.

Ma petite, it went. *Je suis si heureux de savoir que tout va bien pour toi. Tes photos de la petite Leila sont extraordinaires. Je suis très fier de toi et de tes efforts. Tu as toujours été courageuse, toujours tenace, mais maintenant plus que jamais. Ca me fait énormement plaisir de te donner un peu d'argent. Ca a été merveilleux de te revoir après toutes ces années. Reviens à Paris une fois de plus. Et reste plus longtemps. Je t'embrasse. Philippe.*

Faraday, still nursing his glass of wine, read it again. This was somebody who knew Gabrielle very well. His name was Philippe. He'd seen photos of Leila that Gabrielle must have sent him and he wanted her to know how proud of her he was. It had been great to see her after all these years, and it had been an absolute pleasure to give her a little money. She must come to Paris again. And this time she must stay longer.

Faraday looked up, trying to focus on the clock above the stove. 'A little money' was clearly an understatement. This was the man who had made Leila's transfer to the UK possible. This was the guy who'd given her £87,000. Only days ago, over the meal in the pub, Gabrielle had told him the money had come from a rich Arab she'd met through a friend at the university in Orleans. Not some old flame from Paris. She'd been lying to him. And now Philippe couldn't wait for her return.

For a while he did nothing. He could hear the tick of the clock and the sigh of the wind in the trees beside the harbour. Then came the distant cry of a solitary curlew, way out in the darkness, haunting, almost spectral. Gabrielle's bag was on the floor in the corner of the kitchen. Everything that mattered to her was inside it. If this sudden glimpse into her private life wasn't to tip him back into a kind of madness, then he knew he had to find out more.

The wallet she used for money and credit cards and scribbled notes on scraps of paper was at the bottom of the bag. He began to go through it, item by item, methodical, driven, fearful of what he might find. In some respects, he thought, this is a crime scene. You steal into someone's secrets. And then you steal out again.

The card was tucked behind her blood donor details. Philippe Stern. A Paris address in the 8th arrondissement. Maybe a shop of some kind. *Objets d'art et tapisseries.* Faraday carefully noted down the details, then slipped the wallet back into her bag. The clock on the wall told him it was quarter to eight. He emptied his glass, re-corked the bottle and replaced it in the cupboard.

Then he got to his feet, checked to make sure he'd left no trace of his visit and left. An hour later he was on the top deck of the Isle of Wight car ferry, hanging over the rail in the windy darkness, thinking about the curlew again.

* * *

Mackenzie didn't get back to Portsmouth until gone nine. He got off the train at the harbour station and walked the half-mile to Blake House. Winter let him in on the second buzz. He was watching *Nature's Great Events.*

Mackenzie stood in front of the set. A meet with yet another journalist had put an extra spring in his step. She was Irish, he said. And she just loved the way he was taking a chainsaw to the British constitution.

'Was that her phrase or yours, Baz?'

'Hers, mush.'

'What does it mean?'

'Fuck knows. She was a good drinker though. Jameson. No ice. Leo fancied the arse off her. In fact he's probably still at it.'

Baz wanted to know about Lou Sadler.

'You met her?'

'Yeah.'

'So why didn't you phone me? Afterwards?'

'I didn't think it was necessary.'

'Why not?'

'She's talking silly money.'

'How much?'

'Two hundred and fifty grand. She says that's all she can manage.'

'She's got it then. She must have.'

'The toot? Of course she has. God knows what she's done with it by now. Sold it on, I imagine.'

'Yeah? Who to?'

'Haven't a clue, Baz.' Winter smothered a yawn. 'She'll be well connected, that woman. Big client base. Loads of the right kind of punters. London? Southampton? Bournemouth? Poole? I wouldn't know where to start.'

Mackenzie nodded. To Winter's surprise he hadn't tossed his toys out of the pram.

'What about Johnny?' he asked.

'They nailed him. Definitely.'

'Who's "they"?'

'She's got a friend, a big guy half her age, Max. Turns out Max is the brother of the tom Holman had been shagging. Our Johnny was way out of line.

Plus he was sitting on all that toot.'

'My toot.'

'Yes, Baz. Your toot.'

'So they killed him? Is that what you're saying?'

'Yeah. Must have done a nice job too. Class woman. Very canny.'

Mackenzie was having a think. Winter asked him to move. A line of grizzly bears was stationed at the top of a waterfall, scooping up salmon after leaping salmon.

'You're right, mush,' Mackenzie said at last. 'Two hundred and fifty K's a joke. So what do we do?'

'We let her sweat. Give it a day or two, she'll come back, I know she will. But there's no way we're going to get anywhere near a million.'

'We have to.'

'It won't happen, Baz. I'm telling you now.'

'How much then?'

'Maybe five hundred grand? It depends what's happening down the line. She may not have done the deal yet. She's been busy the last couple of days, tucked up with my ex-colleagues.'

'She told you about that?'

'Yeah. She's done pretty well so far. They've bailed her and lover boy, all the usual bollocks, so they definitely haven't given up.'

'But you think she's home safe?'

'Yeah. Unless we grass her up with Holman's gear. In which case she's probably fucked. It's odds on that stuff has her DNA on it. Or maybe Max's.'

'And mine?'

'Yes, Baz.'

Mackenzie nodded, his eyes turning to the screen. The biggest grizzly had just nabbed another salmon. Mackenzie was looking thoughtful.

'She understands we're serious?' he said at last.
'Oh yeah. She understands that.'
'Excellent, mush.' Mackenzie stepped towards the door. 'I'll leave you to it.'

Chapter Thirty-Four

THURSDAY, 19 FEBRUARY 2009. *08.02*

Faraday launched what he called the second phase of Operation *Gosling* at the morning squad meet in Ryde. Thanks to some determined lobbying by Parsons, Willard had OK'd the return of the D/Cs who'd been stood down the previous day. It now fell to Faraday to get them re-motivated.

It was obvious to everyone in the room that something had happened to him overnight. He was paler than ever, the bones of his face starting to show, and his voice had dropped to a near-whisper. Twice, people at the back of the room had to ask him to speak up and both times he seemed to have difficulty understanding the request. Suttle, standing near him, began to wonder whether there was a graceful way of taking over.

It wasn't necessary. Faraday kept his remarks to the minimum. Oobik and Sadler, he reminded everyone, had been released yesterday morning on police bail. Oobik had surrendered his passport and both of them were obliged to report weekly to Newport police station. As far as the interviews were concerned, they'd both been pressed hard, but *Gosling* still lacked the evidence to make the decisive breakthrough. In his view both remained prime suspects for the murder of Johnny Holman and for associated narcotics offences, but the difficulty lay in proving it. The kind of information that would have justified an application to the magistrates for a warrant of further detention simply wasn't available within the specified time limits. Hence their release.

The job now, said Faraday, was to take a longer, harder, more considered look at *Gosling*. A lot of this work would be intel-based: trying to establish the exact pattern of person-to-person contacts that webbed the events of last week. Nailing this stuff down, drawing up a timeline, making it lawyer-proof would take a great deal of effort and patience, but before they confronted Sadler and Oobik again, it had to be done.

The most promising line of enquiry, he said, related to the disposal of the body. In that respect a company called Freezee would be investigated, and on the basis of information already acquired that work would start at once. Some detectives would be making calls around the island. A small task force, backed by a Scenes of Crime team, would be heading for west London. Still further north there were enquiries to be made in the Lake District.

He looked around, squinting in the fierce throw of morning sunlight through the window, and Suttle realised how old he looked, and how suddenly lost.

'Coffee, boss?' he said, taking him by the arm.

* * *

To Winter's immense satisfaction, Sadler belled him mid-morning. There was no way she wanted to have a conversation on the phone. She was working her arse off trying to sort out a couple of business problems and suggested he come over to the island. She'd be free around one. She had a new proposal in mind. She might even buy him lunch.

Winter, far too canny to take any of this at face value, got in touch with Mackenzie. Under the circumstances, meeting Sadler alone was a risk he wasn't prepared to take. They were already talking serious amounts of money, and he'd no desire to be taken hostage as part of ongoing negotiations. In his view, he told Bazza, these were people who'd already killed once. The stakes were high and getting higher. So what did Bazza suggest?

'Leave it to me, mush. Ring me again when you're ready to leave. You want company? I'll sort something out.'

*   *   *

Billy Angel was waiting in the hovercraft terminal when Winter arrived. He was wearing a suit with a crested blue tie and there was a new-looking leather briefcase on the seat beside him. A white raincoat was folded over his lap. He didn't bother to get up.

'How come you guys get so much time off?'

'Time off what?'

'The job. *Temeraire*, isn't it? That's what Mackenzie told me.'

'I binned that a while ago. I'm part time now. Holiday relief, like.' He had a nasal Brummie accent which somehow matched the pale face and the dead eyes. He didn't smile much.

A queue was forming at the door. Winter bought a ticket and rejoined Angel as the passengers shuffled out into the breezy sunshine. Curls of seaweed blew across the big ramp that led down to the sea. The hovercraft was less than half full. Winter squeezed himself into a window seat. Angel joined him.

A roar from the turbo-diesels lifted the hovercraft as it pirouetted sideways down the ramp. The pilot kicked it straight and there was a tiny jolt as it settled on the water and began to accelerate away. Winter was aware of Angel beside him. He had an almost animal presence, something you could probably sense in a darkened room, and Winter watched while he stooped for his briefcase, knowing that he didn't like this man at all. The bitten nails. The small stubby fingers. The diver's watch. The way he was always moving, shifting his weight, looking round. Winter was wondering whether Mackenzie had any more little errands in store for him when Angel pulled a newspaper out of the briefcase and passed it across.

'Page 6,' he muttered.

Winter had forgotten about yesterday's *Daily Telegraph.* He opened the paper and flicked through it. The main story on page 6 was headlined would-be mayor reclaims the streets, beneath it a photo that chilled him to the marrow. Colin Leyman was sitting in his hospital bed, the huge face frozen in a rictus grin. Beside him, mugging for the camera, was Bazza Mackenzie.

'I took that shot,' Winter muttered. 'That was me.'

His eyes skated through the text that followed. Pompey's favourite son had decided to draw a line in the sand. Violence, he said, was disfiguring the city he loved. Pompey folk, both old and young, were frightened to go out at night. The police were too busy form-filling to do anything about it. And so the time had come for people to stand up and be counted. Why? Because even in your own home you could no longer be safe from attack. There followed an account of an unprovoked assault on Colin Leyman. The fact that he was unprepared to even talk about the incident was, to Mackenzie, proof that things were falling apart. Someone comes knocking at your door. You let them in. Next thing you know, they've broken your jaw. Not once but twice. What kind of society puts up with stuff like this? What kind of city surrenders itself to the law of the jungle?

Winter read no further. Billy Angel must have been through this piece a thousand times, and even now he couldn't resist another look. Winter folded the paper and gave it back. He felt dirty beside this man. He felt a surge of overwhelming disgust.

'All your own work, eh, Billy?'

Angel grunted something he didn't catch. Then he told Winter that Mackenzie must have a pair of bollocks the size of melons.

'Why?'

'*Why?* Is that a serious question?'

'I'm afraid it is.'

'You don't get it?' He nodded down at the paper. 'To have me take the guy out and then pull a stunt like that?'

'You think that's clever?'

'I think it's hysterical.'

'Yeah? So what else turns you on?'

* * *

They took a taxi from Ryde to Cowes, barely

talking. Sadler had given Winter directions to a restaurant near the waterfront. She said she was coming alone and added that she knew the people who owned it. They'd have a discreet table slightly apart from the main dining area. The food, she'd said, was great.

Winter had already told Angel that he wanted him posted outside for the duration of the meal. To his intense disappointment it was still sunny. A couple of hours in the rain, thought Winter, would have served the bastard right.

Lou Sadler was already in the restaurant when Winter arrived. He made sure she knew he had company, then settled himself at the table. Despite the low ceiling, the place was bright. They offered a decent selection of bottled lagers, and the smells from the kitchen were decidedly promising.

'So who is he?' Sadler was still watching the squat figure of Billy Angel. The net curtains gave him a slightly portly look as he shifted from foot to foot, like a figure from a child's cartoon.

'Mate of Mackenzie's,' Winter explained. 'Total animal.'

'Don't you trust me?'

'Not one bit.' He flashed her a matey grin and reached for the menu. 'Is this lot still on you?'

They both went for the leg of lamb *en croute*. Sadler, to Winter's delight, was surprisingly good company. She told him a number of stories about her least favourite clients, some of whom Winter knew. One of them, a successful accountant with a Portsea-born wife and a tribe of kids, liked nothing better than a chapter of *Christopher Robin* and a sound thrashing. Another, an ex-Wren officer who'd made it to the upper reaches of IBM, always ordered at least two girls in her hunt for the ultimate orgasm.

When Winter was still in the Job, tales like these had often brightened chatter in the canteen, and now he found himself digging up one or two war stories of his own. How he'd led a raid on an Old Portsmouth brothel, only to fall into the arms of a student who turned tricks to pay her way through a PhD on some obscure French poet. How he'd specialised in kippering a long line of informants, only to get totally kippered himself by this very same tom.

'She was wonderful,' he said. 'Smashing girl. Totally off her fucking head.'

He laughed at the memory, picking at the remains of his lamb. Sadler, her glass of Sauvignon still untouched, wanted to talk business.

'Fine.' Winter reached for his napkin, wiped his mouth. 'How much?'

'Three hundred and fifty K.'

'Why so soon?'

'Because we need to get this thing sorted.'

'*You* need to get this thing sorted.'

'Too right.' She held his gaze. 'So what do you say?'

Winter took his time. He sensed this was close to the limit of what Lou Sadler would probably pay, but he sensed something else as well. He no longer had the remotest interest in screwing any deal for the likes of Bazza Mackenzie. Sitting on the hovercraft, reading the latest instalment of his grotesque assault on the foothills of the mayorship, he'd had enough. He was in bad company. He no longer had the taste or the time for people like the guy in the road outside. Billy Angel was vermin.

Bazza Mackenzie was off his head. People like that belonged in someone else's life. All he wanted now was a safe way out.

'That's fine,' he said. 'So how do we do this?'

Sadler didn't bother to hide her surprise.

'You can agree? Just like that?'

'Yeah.'

'You don't have to take it back to the boss?'

'No. All I need are the details. Are we talking cash?'

'I'm afraid so.'

'Large-denomination notes?'

'Fifties.'

'We want it in euros. Preferably five hundreds. We'll call the exchange rate parity. I make that . . .' he frowned '. . . seven hundred notes. A hundred notes in each bundle, that's seven bundles.'

'Euros might take a while.'

'We need it by Monday of next week. Latest.'

'That could be a problem.'

'Yeah?'

Winter was trying to work out the implications. A transaction like this would have to be washed through somebody's books to get round all the money-laundering legislation. That told him a great deal about where the cocaine might have gone. Some kind of company, he thought. Not small.

Sadler wanted to know about his end of the deal. Winter smiled. In the end it was very simple, he said. She'd give him the money. And in return he'd give her two padlock keys and the receipt for a storage compartment. In case she had any worries, he was happy to come with her to collect Holman's gear.

'How do I know you haven't kept anything back?'

'You don't. You have to trust me.'
'And why should I do that?'
'Because deep down I'm quite a straight guy.'
'You're kidding me.'
'No.' Winter shook his head, eyeing Angel again. 'Sadly, I'm not.'

She studied him for longer than Winter felt comfortable with. Then she reached for her bag. The meal was over. She wanted the bill.

'You remember a girl called Monique?' she said. 'Monique Duvall?'

'Very well.'

'She asked to be remembered. She said you were sweet.'

'I'm flattered.'

'She said something else too.'

'What's that?'

'She'd quite like her phone back.'

* * *

Suttle finally got hold of Parsons after lunch. She'd been in meetings all morning and hadn't been picking up.

'It's Faraday,' he said. 'I don't think he's very well.'

'Like how?'

'Like he's not communicating.' Suttle wouldn't go into details.

'If you think you're being loyal, Jimmy, forget it. I need to know how bad he is.'

'He's bad, boss.'

'And that's all you're going to tell me?'

'Yes. I'm not sure he can make decisions any more. I'm not even sure he wants to.'

There was a silence at Parsons' end. For all his odd little ways, both she and Suttle knew that Faraday had never been frightened of making the tougher calls.

'Do you think this has to do with the accident?'

'I've no idea, boss. I assume it can't be a coincidence, but I'm not a psychiatrist.'

'A psychiatrist? You think it's that bad?'

Suttle didn't say anything. In a way he regretted the term but he couldn't think of anything better. In his view, a fuse had blown deep in Faraday's brain. A couple of minutes ago he'd found him in his office, staring at his mobile. There was a stack of calls from Gabrielle, recent calls, and none of them seemed to have been answered. When Suttle offered to help, maybe call her himself, make some excuse or other, Faraday had just looked blank. He couldn't cope any more. Didn't see the point.

'You need to come over, boss,' he told Parsons. 'You need to sort this thing out.'

* * *

Bazza Mackenzie was conferencing with the Leader of the Council when Winter and Billy Angel returned from the Isle of Wight. Ignoring the DO NOT DISTURB notice hanging on Mackenzie's office door, Winter knocked and stepped inside. The Leader of the Council, a plump woman with some bold ideas on community involvement, was becoming a regular visitor to the Royal Trafalgar. Mackenzie looked up, visibly annoyed.

'What is it?'

'I need a word, Baz.'

'Later, mate. Like it says on the door.'

'Now, Baz.'

Mackenzie blinked. This was no way to address a future mayor. Especially in this kind of company. He was about to have the full ruck but thought better of it. He pushed a plate of biscuits towards the councillor and got to his feet.

There was another office, smaller, that Mackenzie reserved for more intimate conversations. A huge blow-up photo of David James adorned one wall. *A Safe Pair of Hands* was currently under consideration for use in Bazza's projected poster campaign. Along with *The Real Thing* and *Clean Up Pompey.*

'Who the fuck do you think you are, mush?'

'Shut the door, Baz.'

'You shut the fucking door.'

'Fine.' Winter pushed it shut with his foot. 'She's offering 350K.'

'What the fuck are you on about?'

'Lou Sadler.'

'Three hundred and fifty? She's having a laugh, isn't she?'

'I don't think so.'

'So what did you say?'

'I said yes.'

'You said *what*?'

'I said yes. I agreed it, Baz. I did the deal. We need that money by Monday. There's no point fucking about.'

'But three fifty's a steal. It's outrageous. It's blind fucking robbery. There's no way she's getting away with that.'

'Fine.' Winter shrugged. 'Have you got a quarter of a million handy? For your Spanish friend?'

'*Our* Spanish friend, mush. And no, I haven't.'

'Then three fifty it is. You want the good news? She'll pay in euros.' He shot Mackenzie a cold smile and stepped past him. The door open again, he turned. 'Something I forgot to mention, Baz. When I go down on the due care charge, they'll lay a grand fine on me. You're looking at a hundred grand change from Sadler.' Another smile, warmer this time. 'Any chance?'

* * *

Parsons was on the Isle of Wight by late afternoon. She stepped into the SIO's office without knocking. Faraday looked up, surprised to see her. After the best part of an hour spent tidying up, his desk was bare.

'Boss?'

'How are you, Joe?'

'Fine,' he said vaguely. 'You?'

She smiled at him, uncertain, then sat down.

'Seriously?'

'Seriously.'

'So how's it going?'

'How's what going?'

'Everything . . . *Gosling.*' She frowned. She'd just noticed the whiteboard on the wall. Yesterday it had been littered with reminders, phone numbers, names and the odd scrap of heavily underlined information that badged major inquiries force-wide. Now, like the desk, it was wiped clean.

Faraday was telling her that everything was fine, just fine. Suttle, he said, had been kindness itself.

'How?'

'Little ways, important ways. It's not easy sometimes, boss. You know something about that lad? He understands.'

'Understands what?'

'Me. This. The Job. Pretty much everything, really.'

Faraday leaned back and gazed up at the ceiling. He had a tiny smile on his face, as if he was privy to some joke or other, but then his head came down again and Parsons recognised the glint of tears in his eyes. He stared at her, forcing the smile wider. The tears were running down his cheeks now, and she stood up, edging her bulk around the desk, putting her arms around him, telling him everything was going to be all right. Then the door opened, admitting Suttle.

'I've got a car round the back, boss,' he said quietly. 'You want me to give you a hand?'

Chapter Thirty-Five

THURSDAY, 19 FEBRUARY 2009. *17.28*

Faraday was back at the Bargemaster's House by half past five. Suttle had accompanied him across on the hovercraft and organised a taxi from the Southsea terminal. Now, he walked him up the path to his front door. Faraday had the keys in the pocket of his anorak but told Suttle to ring the bell.

'She'll be in,' he said. 'We've got a meeting.'

Suttle rang the bell, waited, rang again. Nothing. He got the keys from Faraday's pocket and opened the door. Faraday stood in the hallway, uncertain in the darkness. Suttle found the light switch and called Gabrielle's name. Again, nothing. The house smelled damp and unloved. No one's been here for a while, Suttle thought, and it's beginning to show.

In the kitchen, propped against the teapot, he found the note. It was terse. *Merci pour rien*, it said. Suttle didn't read French but caught the gist. No name. No scribbled kiss. Just the savage biro strokes of someone with a lot to get off her chest. Gabrielle was angry. And she'd obviously gone.

He stuffed the note in his pocket, not wanting to upset Faraday any further.

'So what was the meeting about, boss?'

Faraday was standing in the open doorway, gazing round, an expression of mild curiosity on his face. This house might have belonged to someone else, Suttle thought, and in a way it had.

'Meeting?'

'Yeah. You mentioned a meeting just now, you and Gabrielle . . .'

'Ah, yes. The social worker.'

'*Social* worker?'

'About the child, Leila. Maybe I've got the wrong day. Maybe that's it.' He started worrying about what day of the week it was, and when Suttle confirmed that it was Thursday, he checked his watch and sighed.

'Funny,' he said. 'Odd.'

Suttle gazed at him. In truth, he hadn't a clue what to do next. Should he take this boss of his to his GP? Get him checked out? Or should he risk a bit of a short cut and ring the people at St James and get him sectioned? Parsons, clearly out of her depth, had earlier told him to ring Personnel for advice, but Suttle knew she was only covering her back. This man needed more than advice. He needed a bit of a cuddle.

He stepped across, put his arms round Faraday and held him tight. Faraday stiffened at once, an instinctive act of resistance, but then he began to relax and moments later Suttle felt a head settle on his shoulder.

'You're a good lad.' His voice was a murmur. 'A good lad.'

Suttle said it was nothing. Faraday had been a terrific boss. He just needed a bit of time, a bit of peace.

'"Have been"?'

'Are. This is just a blip, boss. A pit stop. You know something? You should have left it a bit longer before you came back. Going through a windscreen isn't something you can rush. You need to work it through.'

'Really?' Faraday was looking at him now, his eyes shiny again.

'Yeah, for sure. You want a drink? Something to eat?'

'Yeah.' Faraday nodded at the fridge. 'You're going to join me?'

'Of course.'

Suttle fumbled around in the fridge. He counted eight cans of Kronenbourg, not much else. He was still looking for glasses when his phone began to ring. He fetched it out, checked caller ID. Winter.

'You mind, boss?'

'Go ahead.'

Winter said he was in his Lexus on the seafront. He wanted to come across to the island. He had something on his mind.

'Like what?'

'We have to talk, son. Properly. Just this once, eh?' He sounded needy, almost plaintive. Fuck me,

Suttle thought. Two of them.

'I'm not on the island, Paul.'

'You're not?'

'No, I'm back in Pompey.'

He half turned, catching Faraday's eye. Faraday had guessed who it was on the line. His slow smile was the first faint glimmer of sanity Suttle had seen all day.

'Get him round, Jimmy.' Faraday nodded at the fridge. 'Party time.'

*   *   *

Winter was knocking on the door minutes later. Suttle let him in, wondering how much to say about Faraday. In the end he opted for nothing. Winter, he knew, could scent frailty or a weakness within seconds. He'd draw his own conclusions.

Faraday was tucked up on the sofa, nursing his second glass of Kronenbourg. Winter made himself comfortable in a nearby armchair. He was gazing at the hi-fi stack. Faraday's choice of music had always been a total mystery.

'Richard Strauss. *Four Last Songs.*' Faraday tipped his glass in salute. 'Cheers.'

Suttle returned from the kitchen. A single glance told him that Winter had sussed it all. The blanket tucked round Faraday's knees. The slightly manic smile. The way his face had changed.

Winter threw a look at Suttle, an eyebrow raised a millimetre or two, and Suttle just nodded. A couple of years back he and Winter had been in countless situations like this, needing to check the rules of engagement without putting anything into words. Suttle's nod meant fine, go ahead, no problem.

Winter swallowed a mouthful of lager, plucked at the crease on his trousers, decided to direct the thrust of what he had to say to Faraday.

'It's about me,' he began, 'and Mackenzie.'

He talked for maybe twenty minutes. At the end of it Suttle knew a great deal about what Winter had been up to with Mackenzie these past couple of years, where their various adventures had taken them, and he had a very clear notion of what might be up for grabs. Nothing spelled out. Nothing he could statement, record, turn into evidence. But something deeper and altogether more personal. Winter and Mackenzie had come to a parting of the ways.

'Does Mackenzie know this?' The question, to Suttle's surprise, came from Faraday.

'No, boss.' Winter shook his head.

'Then I'm glad.'

'Why?'

'Because now you can do it.'

'Do what?'

'Screw him.'

'No, boss.' Another shake of the head from Winter. 'We. *We* can screw him.'

There was a long silence. Suttle was suddenly grateful for Richard Strauss. This stuff caught the mood beautifully. Something was dying. And about time too.

'You mean that?' Suttle this time.

'Absolutely.'

'When?'

'You'll have to give it a while.'

'Why?'

'Because I have to sort one or two things out.'

'But why not now? Why not just give us

everything? Everything you know? That'll put Mackenzie away for a very long time. The rest we can discuss.'

'Like what?'

'Like what kind of deal the bosses might cut. You'll need that, Paul.'

'You mean witness protection? New ID? New start? All that bollocks?'

'Yeah.' Suttle nodded. 'Otherwise he'll have you.'

'He's had me already, son, in ways he doesn't even realise.'

'What does that mean?'

'You go so far, and then you go a little further, and then something happens, something horrible, and you realise what kind of animal you've become. That's bad enough, son, but when it happens twice you know you've got to do something about it.'

'And that's what's brought you here? That's what this is about?'

'Yeah.'

'Care to share it?'

'Not really. Not yet.'

'But you will share it?'

'I'll have to.'

'And I can take that as gospel? When I talk to—' he shrugged '—whoever?'

'Willard.' It was Faraday again. 'You'll have to talk to Willard.'

'That won't be easy.' Suttle knew exactly how much trust Willard was prepared to put in Winter. He'd been burned too often, Faraday too.

'What do you think, boss?' Suttle turned to Faraday.

'About what?'

'About this. About Winter. About what he's

offering us.'

Faraday's head went down. For a moment Suttle thought he was going to cry again, but he was wrong.

'I think he probably means it,' he said at last. 'I think here and now it makes perfect sense. The problem with all of us is tomorrow. Why? Because we never know.'

There was an exchange of looks. Winter's sense of timing had never been less than perfect. He leaned forward, his voice soft, sympathy on legs, probably genuine.

'What's the matter, Joe?' He'd never used Faraday's Christian name in his life, something that sparked a small nod of appreciation.

'I got something badly wrong,' he murmured after a while. 'And I'm supposed to be a fucking detective.'

Chapter Thirty-Six

FRIDAY, 20 FEBRUARY 2009. *08.12*

Suttle stayed overnight at the Bargemaster's House. Winter had left around ten o'clock, no less determined to bring his association with Mackenzie to an end, and Suttle had been the one to see him to the door. Winter had paused outside in the throw of light from the hall, the Lexus keys already in his hand. He wanted Suttle to know that he was serious. Suttle had nodded.

'You'd better be,' he said. 'Because this is your last chance.'

'You think I don't know that?'

'No, I think you do. And I think that's why you came.'

'Good call, son.' Winter had given him a little pat on the arm. 'Someone must have taught you well.'

Suttle and Faraday had talked a little longer. Faraday was exhausted—Suttle could see it in the sag of his shoulders—and it was at Suttle's suggestion that he took himself off to bed. Alone, still downstairs, Suttle had wondered whether to drive home but in the end decided against it. Lizzie wasn't expecting him back. She'd assume he was still on the island. Best to kip over on the sofa in case Faraday did anything silly. Tomorrow, he told himself, I'll phone Gabrielle. If anyone knows what to do with the old boy, then it's probably her.

* * *

He made the call from the hovercraft terminal the following morning. He'd spent a comfortable night on Faraday's sofa, made him tea at daybreak and told him to have a lie-in. The sight of Suttle at his bedside didn't seem to surprise Faraday in the slightest. Nor did he appear to have any interest in what might be happening with *Gosling.* After thirty years in the Job, the light he kept in that special place, the candle that had always lit the pathways forward, had been snuffed out. He asked how many sugars Suttle had put in the tea. And when Suttle said one and a half, like always, he seemed pleased.

Gabrielle answered almost immediately. She'd met Suttle on a number of social occasions and knew how close he was to Faraday. Suttle told her what had happened. Her man wasn't himself.

He'd been taken off the current inquiry. There was no question of him returning to work for the foreseeable future, certainly not before he'd had help.

'What kind of help?' Gabrielle sounded shocked.

'I'm not sure.' It was the truth.

'Is it something physical?'

'No, not really.'

'What then?'

Good question. Suttle was watching a seagull chase a fragment of bread roll across the landing ramp. Faraday, as far as he could judge, had suffered a crisis of belief, but how would you ever put that into words?

'I think he's a bit lost,' Suttle said.

'Lost, how?'

'He doesn't know who he is any more. He doesn't trust himself. He can't make decisions. In our business that can be a problem.'

'*Bien sûr.* So where is he?'

'At home. In bed.' Suttle was about to suggest she got over there, saw him for herself, made up her own mind, but Gabrielle beat him to it.

'I'm in Salisbury,' she said. 'I'll get the train home.'

* * *

Faraday left the Bargemaster's House at half past nine. He'd checked out Paris flights from Southampton airport and knew that the next one left early that afternoon. After a peaceful night's sleep he told himself he was in the mood for some serious detective work. Not because he couldn't bear the thought of Gabrielle having a fling with some old boyfriend, but because he wanted to know who this person might be. Reading the email on her laptop had broken his heart. Now he was left with nothing but the vaguest sense of curiosity. Shame, he kept telling himself. Just such a shame.

Car parking at the airport presented him with a challenge: short or long stay? He went for the latter, not caring any more where the next few days might take him. He took the shuttle bus to the terminal building and studied the destinations board. The FlyBe flight to Orly was already showing. He bought a single ticket, browsed the bookshop, wondered about a paper, decided against it. The flight left at 14.45, giving him four hours to kill. Maybe a nap, he thought, heading across the concourse towards a distant row of seats.

* * *

Suttle had to wait until late morning before he could get in to see Parsons. With Faraday off the plot, she'd had to take hour-by-hour command of *Gosling* herself, something that Suttle knew she'd resent. Over the last couple of years Faraday had been the most reliable of Deputy SIOs, a trusty backstop who'd been more than happy to take on the bulk of the work. Now, as Parsons was about to discover, that pressure could be crushing.

She was alone in the office vacated by Faraday. The news from west London was less than brilliant. Martin Skelley was away in the north on business. His sidekick, a woman, had been difficult about giving the Scenes of Crime team access to the van that had toured the Isle of Wight. In the end she'd had no choice, but neither Parsons nor Meg Stanley anticipated any kind of forensic result. It was ten days since the van had been on the island, ample time—in the words of one D/C—to steam-clean the arse off it.

Parsons wanted to know about Faraday. Suttle told her about taking him home and about staying the night, and managed to steer her away from any referral to Personnel. Faraday, he said, was now being looked after by his partner. She, surely, would know what to do.

Parsons agreed. She'd already had a word with Mr Willard about the situation. In due course, given a thumbs up from the appropriate medical authority, it might be possible for Faraday to return to active duty in one capacity or another. He still had a year to serve before he could retire on a full pension, and these were early days to bring his career to a premature end. On the other hand it would be unrealistic not to accept that his days on Major Crime were probably over. Maybe something on the community involvement front, she murmured. Or maybe a stint talking to kids in schools.

Her hand was reaching for the phone. *Gosling* was grinding ever onward. She wanted Suttle back at his desk, developing the intel on Skelley, looking for any tiny cracks that *Gosling* might explore. Suttle lingered, not wanting to leave.

'You heard about Stanton?'

'Who?' Parsons was only half listening.

'Benny Stanton. Sadler's brief. The guy from London.'

'What about him?'

'It turns out he represents Skelley as well.'

'Really?' He'd got Parsons' attention at last. 'Are

we sure about that?'

'Positive. I got it from a Met source. It tells us nothing that we didn't know before, boss, but it makes that link with Sadler all the more important.'

'Good. You're right, Jimmy. Excellent.' She paused. 'Was there anything else?'

'Yes.'

'What?'

'I've had a long conversation with Winter.'

'Another one?'

'A different one. This time I think he's serious.'

'About what?'

'About giving us Mackenzie.'

'Really?' She was listening again.

'Yeah, really. And you know who might be the key to all this? Assuming we've got it right?'

'Tell me.'

'Martin Skelley.'

*   *   *

Gabrielle was at the Bargemaster's House by midday. Thinking Faraday might still be in bed, maybe even asleep, she let herself in very quietly and made her way upstairs. The bedroom door was wide open, a scatter of Faraday's clothes on the floor.

'Joe?'

She called his name again, went from room to room, stepped back outside, looked in the garden, went to the front of the house, eyed the rising tide, felt a choking wave of panic deep inside her. Something terrible had happened. She knew it. For a moment or two she wondered whether to get her bike out and ride up the waterside path towards the bird reserve at the top of the harbour in case he'd gone for a walk, but then she remembered Jimmy Suttle on the phone, only hours ago. She knew cops always favoured understatement. In which case Faraday very definitely had a problem.

She hurried inside again and dug in her bag for her mobile. She'd logged Suttle's number from the previous call. He took a while to answer.

'Jimmy?' By now she was tearful. 'He's gone.'

* * *

Faraday landed at Orly in the last embers of a sensational sunset. Away to the left of the aircraft, as it wobbled down the approach path, the middle of Paris was necklaced with lights in the gathering darkness. Before joining the departures queue back at Southampton, Faraday had bought a map of the city. The address he wanted, rue du Faubourg Saint-Honoré, was within walking distance of Charles de Gaulle—Étoile on the Metro. A shuttle bus from the airport would take him to the RER station. From there it was a short hop to the middle of the city.

He was emerging from the Metro by half past five. The Champs-Elysées was thick with rush-hour traffic. He ducked across on a green pedestrian light, heading for the avenue de Friedland. He didn't know Paris well but realised at once that this was an affluent area: four-star hotels, extravagant pavement displays outside florist after florist, suited waiters hurrying from table to table in expensive-looking café-bars.

The rue du Faubourg Saint-Honoré ran north-west. The address he was after lay on the left-hand side. Opposite, of all things, was a police station. Faraday stood on the pavement for a moment or two, watching a couple of detectives in dark suits deep in conversation at the foot of the station steps. They were laughing together, sharing a joke and a cigarette, another long day coming to a close. That was me once, he thought.

The address on Philippe Stern's card, as Faraday had imagined, belonged to an antiques shop. It was closed. There was no light on inside the shop, and he stepped close to the plate-glass window, peering in. The objects on display spoke of Africa, maybe some long-forgotten outpost of the French empire: two wooden carvings of what looked like lions, a handful of brass pots, a native drum with a bold motif in thick black zigzags around the top, a fold of carpet in rich blues and reds. He wiped the glass, trying to get a better view, trying to penetrate the darkness inside. The shop seemed somehow neglected. There were no prices on display, no sign of the hard sell.

He was still trying to imagine what kind of man would own a place like this, and what kind of living he might make from it, when his attention was caught by a handwritten card he hadn't noticed before. It was crudely taped to the glass door of the shop. *En Cas d'Absence, Votre Contact au* 06 03 144 045. He stared at it, fumbled for his mobile, then had second thoughts. He made a note of the number, stepped back.

Next door to the shop was a bar-brasserie. Unlike the places he'd passed earlier, it was narrow and slightly scruffy. A wall-mounted TV was showing horse racing. There were a couple of punters at the bar, laying tote bets. An older man at a table near the back was reading a copy of *L'Équipe* and picking at a bowl of *frites.* He too had the look of a cop. The way he'd glance up from time to time, scoping the faces around him. The way his hand lingered on the barely touched *demi* of lager beside the plate.

Faraday found an empty table and ordered a beer. He still had the phone number from the shop next door. For the first time he wondered exactly what he was going to do about this man. Did he want a conversation? Or would it be enough to come back tomorrow, stake the shop out and wait until Stern arrived so he could at least put a face to his raging fantasies?

If that was the case, then maybe he'd go into the shop and spend a while browsing, watching all the time for tiny clues that might explain this sudden revival in Gabrielle's interest. Her last birthday had been a couple of months ago, just before Christmas. She was still only thirty-seven. Was Philippe Stern someone of Faraday's age? Did she have a thing about older men? Or had she originally bedded him because of his youth? Because of his vigour and vitality? Because he drifted from day to day in this select little quarter of Paris—handsome, arty, rich, untroubled by the need to earn a proper living?

Knowing that he had no idea, Faraday decided to defer the decision. Tomorrow seemed an age away. He'd have something to eat and find a hotel nearby. Expensive, maybe, but what the fuck. He was suddenly very tired.

* * *

Willard summoned Suttle to an evening meet in

the Major Crime suite at Fratton nick. For the second time in two days Suttle found himself on the hovercraft, bouncing back across the Solent, wondering just what lay in store. Not for a moment did he underestimate the implications of the decision he was asking his bosses to make. Over the last couple of years, since turning his back on the force, Winter had destroyed the last shred of any trust they might once have had in him.

This latest initiative, as Suttle would be the first to admit, reeked of self-interest. Pompey's rogue ex-cop was clearly in the shit and desperate for a deal that would keep him out of prison. The prospect of a long sentence for Winter was the answer to Willard's prayers, yet the payback for keeping him out, as Winter knew only too well, was huge. Bazza Mackenzie. Pompey's top face. On a plate.

None of this, as it turned out, was lost on Willard. He was waiting in Parsons' office. Of Parsons herself there was no sign.

He asked Suttle to go through what had happened last night. He wanted no embellishments, no omissions, just a bare account.

Suttle obliged. The fact that the meet had taken place at Faraday's house raised an eyebrow or two.

'How is he? Faraday?'

'Bad, sir. And he's disappeared.'

'So I understand. Do we know where?'

'No, and neither does Gabrielle. She's his partner.'

'How's she taking it?'

'Not well. I get the impression things haven't been great between them lately. I think she's blaming herself.'

'Has she any idea where he might have gone?'

'None. I think that's part of the problem. She's everything to him. He's not a man with many friends.'

'And she knows that?'

'Yeah. Which is why she feels so guilty.'

'Is there someone else then?'

Suttle hesitated. The someone else, he guessed, was the little girl, Leila. But that, just now, was a complication too far.

'No, sir,' he said. 'Not as far as I know.'

Willard went back to Winter. How could he be sure that the guy was on the level?

'He's not, sir. He's never been on the level. But that, with respect, isn't the question we should be asking.'

'So what is?' Willard was attentive. He wanted to know. This was easier than talking to Parsons.

'From where I'm sitting, sir, Winter's had enough. I know the guy. He trained me. Believe it or not, I owe him lots. Deep down he's a decent man. Stuff has been happening, he won't tell me what, but it's definitely got to him. You'll probably laugh at this, but he still knows right from wrong. Just now he's in a very bad place.' Suttle paused. 'Does any of that make sense?'

'It does, Jimmy. And I'm not laughing.' Willard looked away for a moment, deep in thought. 'So what's worst case?'

'Worst case is he fucks us about again. In which case I suggest he's on a nicking.'

'For?'

'Perverting the course of.' He risked a grin. 'Plenty of previous too.'

'Best case?' Willard wasn't smiling.

'Best case?' Suttle took his time. 'We set a trap. We point Mackenzie at Skelley, and we see what happens.'

'But who sets a trap? Who are you talking about?'

'Winter, sir. With a little help from us.'

*   *   *

Gabrielle, after an exhaustive search of the house, was close to despair. She'd been looking for any tiny clue that Faraday might have left, any hint of a destination or plan. To simply disappear without leaving a note, without leaving *anything*, was so totally out of character that she was beginning to understand the seriousness of whatever it was that had happened.

The last couple of times they'd been together, after the trauma of the accident and everything that had followed, had seemed like the old times. They'd been close. He'd made her laugh. He'd been supportive too about her plans for Leila, and although she knew he had reservations about adoption, she was convinced she could talk him round. The little girl needed a home, a future. And that's exactly what they could give her.

If only.

Even Gabrielle was beginning to admit to herself that this thing was close to impossible. She'd had to cancel the social worker's initial visit to the Bargemaster's House, his opportunity to get a feel for the kind of couple who wanted little Leila so badly, because Faraday hadn't replied to any of her messages. That was frustrating, of course it was, but even worse were the costs involved. She'd yet to share any of this with Joe, but the bill for the local authority assessment—without which nothing could happen—could be more than £15,000. So far she hadn't paid a penny because the process had yet to start, but the Portsmouth Social Services Adoption Team wanted the money up front. In principle that was OK. She had modest savings, and she could think of no better investment than Leila, but there was yet another problem.

Leila had been admitted on a short-stay visa. If she had had relatives in the UK, this could be extended, but since she didn't she'd be sent back to Gaza the moment she was discharged from the Burns Unit. This, to Gabrielle, made no sense at all. What about outpatient treatment? What about physio for her precious hands? This, it seemed, was of little consequence. Aftercare was assumed to be available in Gaza. And so Leila could only return to the UK if the Gazan authorities said yes and Gabrielle and Faraday were judged to be suitable adoptive parents. That was a process that would take at least eight months, and just now that felt like an eternity.

Gabrielle glanced at her watch. Nearly nine. She gazed round the kitchen, wondering where she hadn't looked, what she hadn't checked, then she realised where—God willing—she might find a clue.

She hurried upstairs. Faraday kept his PC on a desk in the bedroom. She fired it up and went online. A couple of keystrokes took her into his recent browsing history on the Internet. She rubbed her eyes, willing the ancient machine to speed up. Then, quite suddenly, she was looking at what he'd done with the machine before he'd left. At 07.47 he'd logged on to the Air France site in search of flights. His chosen destination? Paris.

She stared at the computer screen for a long moment, piecing it all together. Then she reached for the phone, dialling a number from memory.

After a while the number answered.

'Philippe?' she said. '*C'est toi?*'

Chapter Thirty-Seven

SATURDAY, 21 FEBRUARY 2009. *08.17*

Faraday was dreaming. He emerged from the Bargemaster's House on a sunnier day than he could ever remember. He stood on the path beside the harbour, gazing out, wondering where the water had gone. The gleaming mud stretched clear across to the distant smudge of Hayling Island. He clambered carefully down to the thin ribbon of pebble beach, picked his way between the scatter of driftwood, wisps of fishing net, curls of tarry rope, wondering why there was no smell to any of this stuff. Then came a tug on his arm and he turned to find himself looking at his son, Joe Junior. J-J, after a lifetime of silence, had shed his deafness. He had a strange accent, foreign, but there was no problem shaping the words.

'There, Dad.' He was pointing towards the far horizon. 'There . . . Look.'

Faraday followed him onto the mud. Expecting to sink ankle deep, as usual, he found himself supported by a delicate crust, solid, weight-bearing, treacherous, slippery. It felt like brown ice underfoot. Father and son glided seawards, towards the breaking line of surf across the harbour mouth, hand in hand. A band was playing, miles away, and J-J's thin frame swayed and bent with the lilt of the music. Then he came to a halt, catching Faraday in his arms as he began tofall.

'There, Dad,' he said again, pointing down this time.

Faraday followed his bony finger, lost but happy. A cormorant lay on its side on the glistening mud, limp, sodden, the long yellow beak half open. J-J bent to it, got down on his knees, put his mouth beside the sleekness of the bird's head, asked about the time, then looked up, raising his thumb.

'It's gone, Dad,' he whispered. 'It's dead.'

A police siren cut through the dream, and Faraday awoke to find himself looking at the ceiling. He rubbed his eyes, wondering vaguely where on earth he was. Then he saw the Ibis notepad on the table beside the bed and the tiny pile of euros he'd pocketed in change from the brasserie. Paris, he thought. Time to get moving.

* * *

The receptionist at the Royal Trafalgar had a message for Winter when he arrived. The new sauna, she said, was at last ready. Later that morning there was to be a formal opening. Bazza had laid hands on a couple of Scandinavian air hostesses who were prepared to pose for publicity shots in return for a free weekend. In the meantime he was trying out the new facility for himself. Winter was welcome to join him. The invitation had the force of an order.

Winter hated saunas. The last couple of years

had done nothing for his waistline and he had no intention of sharing lungfuls of scalding air with anyone, least of all Mackenzie. On the other hand he had an hour to get back to Lou Sadler before the rest of her day put her out of reach. She wanted to come over tomorrow with the money. She was suggesting a handover around noon. She needed a rendezvous and an assurance that everything was in place.

The sauna was in the basement, alongside the gym. Winter tugged on the heavy wood door and let himself into the tiny changing room. Mackenzie's jeans and leather jacket were hanging on a hook, middle of the row. He appeared to be alone. There was a window in the door that led to the sauna itself. Winter stepped across and took a look. Bazza was sitting on the bench on the far side, a white hotel towel folded over his lap. His eyes were closed and his head was back against the wall. Sweat had beaded on his face and Winter could see the slow rise and fall of his chest, but there was an oddness in the way his body had slumped to one side.

Winter hauled on the door, knowing something wasn't right. The heat enveloped him, thick with resin.

'Baz?' he shouted. '*Baz?*'

Mackenzie didn't move.

*   *   *

Faraday was back in the rue du Faubourg Saint-Honoré by half past nine. The shop was still closed. He stood on the pavement for a moment or two, wondering what to do. Keeping obs outside a police station, he told himself, was an invitation to get arrested. The French were picky about stuff like this. If he wanted to get close to Philippe Stern, he had to be patient.

He walked to the big traffic intersection at the end of the street, eyed the gleaming mass of parked scooters, then began to browse the line of shops that led towards the Parc Monceau. High-class kitchen equipment. A *clinique vétérinaire.* A huge canvas in the window of an art gallery, an angry swirl of blacks and whites. He wandered on, intrigued by the emptiness of his head. He didn't feel angry any more, or even upset. Gabrielle had come and gone, taking everything with her. All that was left were these few precious moments in the thin Parisian sunshine.

The park took him by surprise, appearing suddenly to his right, a frieze of winter trees beyond a wrought-iron fence at the end of an avenue. The houses on either side of the avenue were grand, heavy security, shuttered windows, and a maid cleaning the brass on one of the big front doors paused to watch him wander by.

In the park he settled peaceably on a bench, wishing he'd brought something for the marauding squirrels. There were joggers doing circuits, and Faraday shut his eyes, waiting for the soft, steady *lap-lap* of their trainers on the wetness of the sandy path. There were young Asian women too, pushing prams. They looked Thai, and Faraday had a brief vision of himself and Gabrielle on the bus in the mountains, the hot afternoon they'd first met. He could remember exactly what she was wearing, every detail, and he remembered too the single ring she wore on her left hand. It was thin, silver, delicate. Once they were living together she'd taken it off, and he never saw it again.

He tipped his head back, enjoying the warmth of the sun on his face. Could you ever really know another person? Could you ever be sure about them? Be certain? Could you make a little parcel of yourself and hand it across for safe keeping? Or was this single act of trust, so absolute, so reckless, bound to end in betrayal? He didn't know, and the realisation that he didn't much care any more brought a smile to his lips. He'd once met a Buddhist monk on a ferry on the Mekong river who'd talked of the lightness of being, of the mistake we make in looking for significance in a waste of emptiness. Maybe he was right, he thought. Maybe that's where this journey ends. Back in the mountains. Back on the bus. Back in the steamy heat of the jungle.

* * *

The ambulance was at the Royal Trafalgar in minutes. Winter had sent the receptionist to find one of the hotel's freebie towelling robes, and the paramedics wheeled Mackenzie out through the lobby, wrapped in powder blue, still unconscious. Winter had phoned Marie, and she drove up to meet him at the hospital. Early word from the resus crew at A & E indicated a stroke, a diagnosis Marie found hard to accept. She was pale with shock.

'He's still in his forties, Paul. That doesn't happen.'

Winter didn't know what to believe. Half an hour earlier he'd been assuming some kind of heart attack, probably mild, probably triggered by a night on the tiles and far too long in the sauna. Bazza had always attacked life, seizing it by the throat and giving it a good shake, and a mild heart attack would have been life's way of answering back. A stroke, on the other hand, was something very different. A stroke could empty your head. A stroke could put you in a wheelchair for the rest of your life. A stroke could turn you into a serious dribbler.

Winter went across to the machine to fetch a coffee for Marie. He was fumbling for the right change when his mobile began to peep. It was Lou Sadler. She was still waiting for an answer.

Winter glanced back at Marie. She was sitting in a puddle of sunshine beneath one of the big plate-glass windows, staring into nowhere. Someone had to take charge of this thing, he told himself. Someone had to start making decisions.

'Tomorrow, Lou. Twelve noon. Come to the hotel.'

* * *

By midday, the shop was still closed. Faraday had a beer in the brasserie next door then stepped back onto the street to make the call. The beer had made him light-headed. It felt like a bird in his chest, an odd fluttering sensation, not unpleasant. He was wondering what kind of bird it might be when the call finally answered. It was a male voice, slightly formal, clipped, precise French. To Faraday it spoke of a world where people were expected to state their business. Who are you? What do you want?

Faraday gave his name. He said he wanted to talk to Monsieur Philippe Stern.

'Un moment, s'il vous plaît.'

Another voice, older, softer.

'Oui, monsieur?'

Faraday stared at the phone. This wasn't working out the way he'd anticipated. He stumbled in French, had trouble with the simplest phrases, couldn't work out what he wanted to say.

Stern seemed to understand. His English was heavily accented.

'Come round,' he said. 'Come round and see me.'

He gave Faraday directions. He lived in an apartment block in the Rue Monceau. Number 14. On foot it was less than five minutes away. Press the buzzer for Flat 8. It was on the top floor. How wise of Mr Faraday not to bother with a car.

Stern rang off.

Number 14 was a four-storey building next to a school. The shutters needed a coat of paint and there was a rain-soaked poster for a Christmas organ recital on the shabby green doors. When Faraday crossed the street for a better view, he noticed the eruption of flowers on one of the top-floor balconies.

The buzzer opened the door at once. Faraday stepped inside. A lift awaited him behind an old-fashioned grille. The grille made a clanking noise when he slid it back. Inside was a full-length mirror, gilt-framed. Faraday studied himself as the the lift creaked upwards. He looked old, broken, used-up. There was a fleck of something yellow on the front of his shirt which smudged when he tried to get it off. No matter, he thought. *Tant pis.*

As the lift came to a halt on the fourth floor, he became aware of a tall figure waiting for him in the shadows. He slid the doors open, robbed of any idea of what to do next. In his previous life this was the moment when he confronted the prime suspect. There'd be a procedure, a form of words, the comfort of knowing that his job was nearly done. Now he could barely put one foot in front of theother.

The face was ageless, maybe early fifties. He was wearing jeans and a collarless grey shirt. A couple of days' stubble darkened his chin. Firm handshake. Bewildering smile.

'You are welcome. Please call me Marc.'

'Marc?'

'Come.'

Faraday followed him into the flat. The apartment was enormous, flooded with sunshine. An elderly man was sitting beside the window, a copy of *Le Monde* folded on his lap. He was wearing a pair of baggy old corduroy trousers, and the heavy roll-neck sweater looked hand-knitted. He had a bony indoor face, blotched with liver marks, and he badly needed a haircut.

'My father, Philippe.'

The old man waved Faraday into the nearby armchair. There was a jug of coffee on the table between them and a couple of cups.

'You like cakes? My son makes fine madeleines. Marc . . .?'

Marc disappeared into the adjoining room. Faraday heard the discreet clatter of plates. His sense of direction had deserted him. Who was Marc? How come Philippe was so old? And why did they seem to be expecting him?

'You are with Gabrielle? No?'

'No.' Faraday shook his head. 'I'm here alone. By myself.'

'I mean . . . *donc* . . . in life. You and Gabrielle are

together, *n'est-ce pas?*'

Absurd, Faraday thought. A film script. Surreal. He needed to get his bearings. He needed to play the copper again. Just one more time. He needed to *find out.*

'You know Gabrielle?'

'Of course.'

'How come?'

'Because she's a friend, a family friend.' He smiled, benign. '*Notre petite.* The little Gabrielle who so enchanted us. My other son, especially.'

'Not Marc?'

'*Pas du tout.*' A wistful smile. 'Benoît.'

'They were . . .?'

'*Très proches.*' He nodded. 'In love. Always. Gabrielle *et* Benoît. *Presque mariés.*'

'When?'

'Many years ago.' He shaded his eyes with his hand, looking for his other son. '*Benoît . . . quand est-il mort?*'

'*Il y a quinze ans, papa.*'

Benoît died fifteen years ago. He'd been engaged to Gabrielle. Faraday didn't know what to say. He felt like a trespasser.

'I'm sorry,' he managed at last. 'I shouldn't be here.'

'You are welcome. Please . . .' Stern waved a frail hand at the plate of madeleines and insisted Faraday help himself. 'You've seen the little one? The little girl?'

'Of course.'

'And how is she?'

'Tiny. *Un petit bout de chou.*' A scrap of a child. Faraday managed a smile. His French was coming back.

'We were pleased to help.' The old man nodded. 'For me it was an honour.'

'Help?' Faraday was lost again.

'Of course. With the money. Gabrielle phoned me from Egypt. You were there. You were there with her in the hospital.' He touched his own head, a gesture of sympathy, then reached forward and patted Faraday on the knee. 'She worries about you . . . *notre petite*.'

'She does?'

'Very much. You know that I'm Jewish? Did she tell you that?'

'No. She told me nothing. Nothing about Benoît. Nothing about you.'

'*Vraiment?*' He smiled. He seemed to approve. Life today, he said, was full of confessions. People wanted to share all of themselves. It had become a kind of disease. Here in France. Maybe in England too. But Gabrielle, it seemed, had resisted the infection. 'Good,' he said. 'Very good.'

'So she phoned you from Egypt . . .?'

'*Oui.* She wanted money for the little one. I knew about these children. I knew about Gaza. It was everywhere, on the television, in the papers. *Atroce, n'est-ce pas?*'

Faraday could only agree. Grotesque. Horrible. Atrocious. He'd seen the results himself. It seemed, in some unfathomable way, to have changed his life. But why would someone Jewish offer that kind of money?

'You want the truth? I was ashamed. I'm still ashamed. I'm not a Zionist. I have no wish to live in Israel, *Monsieur*. But these are my people, these are Jews, and what they are doing is wrong. So . . .' he leaned forward again '. . . I was so happy to help.

I've had a good life, a lucky life. After my wife died, Marc looks after me. Family is important. You think so too?'

'Yes.' Faraday felt himself nodding. 'Of course.'

'And so now the little girl. Leila. She's coming to you? She's going to be part of your family?'

Faraday left the question unanswered. He wanted to know more about Benoît.

'He was in the army ... my son. He was a paratrooper. *Quel gars*!' What a lad.

Gabrielle, he said, had met him on holiday in Sharm-el-Sheikh. In those days the resort had barely existed. Benoît loved scuba diving. Gabrielle was trying to learn.

'*Et voilà.* He was always generous, Benoît, but that year he came back with a special present.'

'Gabrielle?'

'*Oui.* Our little enchantress. You say this in English . . . no?'

'Yes.' Faraday nodded. A weaver of spells. The perfect description.

'And then they live together for a while, fall in love properly. My son, he wants to get married.'

'And Gabrielle?'

'Not so keen. But she loved him. I know she loved him. Why? Because she told me so. Here, in this room. She called me *papa.* I love this word.'

Faraday said nothing. After Benoît, he thought, a grumpy English *flic* must have been a sore disappointment.

'So what happened to your son?'

'He died. He was in a helicopter in Corsica. With the army. The helicopter crashed. *Quelle horreur*.' He winced, then looked away.

The memory appeared to drive the air out of

him. He seemed to physically deflate. His other son fetched a box of Kleenex and put it on his lap. Faraday, watching the old man plucking for a tissue, sensed that this was something that probably happened often.

He reached for another madeleine, wondering how far to take this conversation. He'd come to bury a relationship that had mattered more to him than anything else in the world. That single act, he'd told himself, would leave him with a kind of peace. Now, thanks to his own preconceptions, he was more troubled than ever. He'd spent thirty years in the Job learning why you never assumed anything before testing it first. If only he'd paid more attention.

From somewhere deep in the apartment came the sound of a buzzer. Marc left the room. Faraday heard a brief murmur of conversation. The old man was looking at his watch. Time to go, Faraday thought.

He got to his feet and extended a hand. The old man peered up at him, shaking his head.

'*Pas encore*,' he said softly. Not yet.

Confused, Faraday wondered whether to sit down again. Then he recognised the metallic crash of the lift door in the shared hallway, followed by more conversation. Marc was already out there, already waiting, the sentry at the gate. Faraday was looking at the flowers on the balcony, the line of terracotta pots, the carefully tended stands of geraniums, marvelling at their resilience. In the depths of winter, he thought, a blaze of colour and light.

'*Chéri?*' The voice was soft. He hesitated, then glanced round. The black beret. The hoop earrings.

And a huge bunch of lilies from the florist on the corner.

Gabrielle.

*   *   *

Winter was back at Blake House when Jimmy Suttle arrived. He'd spent most of the day at the QA, keeping Marie company while she waited for Bazza to regain consciousness. She sat beside the bed, stroking his hand, whispering in his ear, telling him about Ezzie, about the kids, about how they wanted him home, back safe, and when he finally stirred she nuzzled his bristly face with her cheek and told him she loved him. The news opened Bazza's eyes. He seemed to recognise Marie. He even managed the beginnings of a wink for Winter. But then the darkness overwhelmed him and he drifted away again.

Winter waited for Suttle to come up in the lift. Marie wanted no one to know about what had happened to Mackenzie. It was, she said, a family affair. No publicity. No agonising to friends. No thunder from the Pompey tom-toms. Just a discreet silence.

Suttle looked knackered. He turned down the offer of a drink and produced an A4 envelope from under his anorak. It had started to rain again, he said. With a bit of luck he might make it home by nine.

'So what's this?' Winter was looking at the envelope.

'Little present.'

'Who from?'

'All of us.'

'Including Willard?'

'Yes.'

Winter nodded, intrigued, then opened the envelope. Inside were five sheets of A4 paper, single-spaced typing. He glanced at the top page. It seemed to be an intel report. He'd seen hundreds of these things on Major Crime jobs.

'So who's Martin Skelley?' he said.

'He's a face from Liverpool. He's made a bob or two from the laughing powder and set himself up in a distribution business. It's all in there. Help yourself.'

Winter nodded, his eyes returning to the report.

'But what the fuck's any of this got to do with me?'

Suttle was already on the way to the door. He paused, looked round.

'He's got your toot, mate.' He offered a tired grin. 'Your boss might want to get it back.'

Afterwards

Bazza Mackenzie made a full recovery. The original stroke diagnosis was abandoned in favour of something the neurological consultant termed a 'minor cerebral event', a description that Mackenzie viewed as a borderline insult. Nonetheless, he agreed to take things easy for a while and reluctantly consented to leave the day-to-day management of his affairs to Winter and Marie.

On the Sunday Winter swapped the black bin liner containing Johnny Holman's kit for 350,000 euros. He drove Lou Sadler back to Blake House and wouldn't let her leave until he'd counted the lot. Once he'd finished, he gave her a lift to the hovercraft terminal and planted a peck on her cheek before she stepped out of the car. She lingered for a moment or two, amused by this small gesture of affection, and offered to send Monique Duvall over for a freebie, but Winter wasn't having it. He'd seen what freebies had done to Johnny Holman. Thank you, but no.

Two days later, with minimal information from Bazza, he drove to Gatwick airport and met three successive flights from Malaga, standing in the arrivals hall with a large oblong of cardboard on which he'd inked the word mackenzie. Nobody showed up.

Operation *Gosling,* meanwhile, slowly ground to a halt. The Coroner recorded a verdict of unlawful killing with respect to the four bodies recovered from the remains of Monkswell Farm. Forensic examination of the Freezee delivery van produced nothing of evidential value, and exhaustive enquiries in the vicinity of Skelley's lakeside home failed to unearth any trace of a body. Both Suttle and Parsons remained convinced that Holman had been driven north and dumped in Derwent Water, probably in the middle of the night, but supposition never cut much ice with the CPS lawyers responsible for taking prosecutions to court. In the absence of either Maarika Oobik or the Polish driver, both of whom had vanished, *Gosling* was effectively treading water. After a couple of months bail conditions were dropped as far as Lou Sadler and Max Oobik were concerned. His passport restored, Oobik left the country within days.

Sixty-four kilos of cocaine had also disappeared. His health improving by the day, Mackenzie maintained a lively interest in getting a fairer settlement for his nest egg. When Winter denied having the least idea where the toot might have ended up, he refused to believe him. Three hundred and fifty grand, he repeated, was a stitch-up. Winter, still sitting on the contents of Suttle's intel report, still biding his time, could only agree.

Then one night, when he judged Bazza's mood to be near-perfect, Winter raised a name that he thought might conceivably be of interest. Mackenzie had never heard of Martin Skelley, but ignorance was never something that cramped his style. By now he'd dumped his mayoral ambitions and decided to stand as an independent candidate for one of the city's two parliamentary constituencies. The general election was barely months away. In dire need of campaigning funds, he told Winter they needed to sort the fucker out.

'Fucker?' Winter enquired.
'Skelley,' Mackenzie confirmed.

* * *

From Paris, Faraday and Gabrielle returned to the Bargemaster's House. On his GP's recommendation, Faraday signed himself up for a three-month intensive counselling course. This did little for his peace of mind but ticked the boxes necessary if he was ever to seriously contemplate a return to work.

The sessions with the young therapist developed into a bit of a game, and Faraday kept himself amused by making most of his past life up. The only episodes for which he had the remotest affection were the early years with J-J and more recently his relationship with Gabrielle.

Days when he could talk about her became the high spots of an increasingly bleak existence. He described their life together in great detail and with enormous pride. He understood the size and shape of the mountain they'd climbed together, and he had genuine respect for the decision she'd finally taken once Leila's treatment was complete. To accompany the child back to Gaza and to try and make some kind of life for themselves was an act—in Faraday's view—of great courage. One day he'd like to think that the Bargemaster's House would draw her back, but as the months went by after her departure for the Middle East he had to accept that this possibility was becoming more and more remote. By June her occasional letters had ceased altogether. Nor did she ever use the phone.

When his doctor, increasingly alarmed, suggested

stronger medication, Faraday declined. He also refused to accept that he might be suffering from clinical depression. Everything, he insisted, would pass. And then, fingers crossed, he'd be back to work.

In midsummer he attended the party Lizzie and Suttle threw to celebrate the birth of their daughter. There he met a colleague of Lizzie's, a recently divorced journalist from the *News*. Her name was Gill. They had a brief affair which Faraday brought to an end within a week.

Days later a letter arrived from the Personnel Department offering Faraday the post of Theme Champions' Coordinator on the Safer Portsmouth Partnership. The department's head was keen on the challenge this new departure represented and was confident that Faraday's wealth of experience would be viewed as a huge asset by the partnership's various stakeholders. She also pointed out that the hours would be both civilised and predictable, unlike the ceaseless demands of Major Crime.

That evening Faraday typed a letter to his son, J-J. Faraday said he was glad about some things, sad about others, but on the whole he thought they'd made a great team. The Bargemaster's House was his for keeps. Take care, son. God bless. He addressed the letter and put it on the small table in the hall. Then he lay on the sofa as the light drained from the harbour, listening to Mahler's Ninth Symphony.

At dawn, hours later, Faraday climbed the stairs. It was a flawless August morning, high tide, barely a feather of wind on the harbour. He stood at the bedroom window, staring out over the water, letting the rich spill of sunshine bathe his face. After a while he began to swallow the thirty Co-Proxamol tablets he'd bought the previous day, sluicing them down with generous gulps of the Côtes-du-Rhône he'd put aside for Gabrielle's return.

Seconds before he lost consciousness he thought he heard the distant call of a solitary curlew but—deep within himself—he knew he couldn't be sure.

Acknowledgements

My thanks to the following for their time and advice: Marie-Caroline Aubert, John Ashworth, Jos Axon, Dorothy Bone, Janet Bowen, Chloe Bowler, Debbie Cook, Nigel Crockford, Diana Franklin, David Grundy, Andy Harrington, John Holman, Jack Hurley, Cheryl Jewitt, Hamish Laing, Martin Law, Mark Leonard, Heidi Lewis, Terry Lowe, Tina Lowe, Shelly Malan, Peter Mawhood, Clare Sharp, Danielle Stoakes, Eunan Tiernan, Adge Tilke, Serge Vidal, Ian Watt, Alyson West, and Charles Wylie.

This book came from a journey Lin and I made through Syria, Jordan and Sinai which happened to coincide with the Israeli attack on Gaza between December 2008 and January 2009. After the first sentence, given the circumstances, the story wrote itself. Anyone interested in what happened in Gaza, and in the wider background, might turn to *Gaza: Au Coeur de la Tragedie* by Yves Bonnet and Albert Farhat, and to *Witness in Palestine* by the indefatigable Anna Baltzer.

A special thank you to my editor, Simon Spanton, and to my wife, Lin. No one could ask for a better travelling companion.